Walter Winward was born in Yorkshire but spent most of his formative years in Liverpool. He has rarely, as he puts it, 'worked for wages', choosing instead to travel wherever his nose led him and do whatever turned up. He has lived in the States, North Africa, France, Malta, Turkey, the Middle East, Mexico and Sweden, and has had a variety of occupations from Royal Marine Commando to professional gambler. In between times, as well as writing for the stage and films he has completed ten books, seeing one of them, *The Conscripts*, top of the bestseller lists.

'One of the more original tales of espionage…tautly and credibly written' *The Irish Press*

'A thrilling spy story set in the chill climate of the 1980's… the action races to an electric climax as peace in Europe hangs by a slender thread' *Fife Free Press*

'Intriguing'
The Yorkshire Post

Also by Walter Winward

THE CANARIS FRAGMENTS
THE BALL BEARING RUN
SEVEN MINUTES PAST MIDNIGHT
HAMMERSTRIKE

and published by Corgi Books

Walter Winward

Cougar

CORGI BOOKS

COUGAR

A CORGI BOOK 0 552 125148

Originally published in Great Britain by
Hamish Hamilton Limited, under the title
THE LAST AND GREATEST ART

PRINTING HISTORY

Hamish Hamilton edition published 1983
Corgi edition published 1985
Corgi Canada edition August 1985

This book is set in 10/11 pt Plantin

Corgi Books are published by Transworld Publishers Ltd., Century House,
61–63 Uxbridge Road, Ealing, London W5 5SA, in Australia by Transworld
Publishers (Aust.) Pty. Ltd., 26 Harley Crescent, Condell Park, NSW 2200,
and in New Zealand by Transworld Publishers (N.Z.) Ltd., Cnr. Moselle
and Waipareira Avenues, Henderson, Auckland.

Printed and bound in Canada
Cover printed in U.S.A.

For Sara and Charlie, with very much love

Saddle me White Surrey, Richard's himself again

EBERSWALDE

The temperature had dropped five degrees in as many minutes. Huge black clouds lumbered across the sky before a biting wind, while underfoot the morning snowfall was four inches deep and already starting to freeze. Somewhere in the distance a hunting rifle cracked. Neither man paid the sound more than peripheral attention. They had both heard enough gunshots in their lives to recognize by instinct that they were not the hunter's quarry. In any case, the half-dozen plainclothesmen hovering discreetly out of earshot by the two cars parked at the edge of the forest were there to ensure that the meeting was not interrupted or the safety of the principals jeopardized.

The taller of the two men was also the older by several decades, though the wrinkles on his forehead and around his eyes were not merely due to advancing years. Like the rest of his face, the lines told of a lifetime in the open air, squinting through binoculars against the sun, watching for that sudden telltale movement that could be the probing snout of an enemy tank, whether in war games or, as it had been forty years earlier, against the real thing. His was the tough, determined countenance of the natural predator, and in spite of his age his body was lean and hard. He seemed unaware of the cold.

In complete contrast his companion felt sure he was going to freeze to death given another thirty minutes in the open. Although he wore a heavy fur-lined coat, boots, huge mittens and a fur hat with ear flaps, he stamped his feet continuously and clapped his hands in an effort to keep the circulation flowing. Beneath the hat were the features of a man in his early forties, features that showed, perhaps, too many years of good living. He was carrying twenty pounds excess weight and developing a double chin that was going to be murder to lose if he ever became vain enough to bother.

In Moscow he would have been categorized as a minor functionary with an unimportant ministry; in France the proprietor of a semi-successful bistro. In England he would be typecast as a suburban husband who wears funny hats at Christmas and chases the typists, while Middle America would think of him as a good joe who could hold his liquor and who probably had an inexhaustible fund of dirty stories. His was that sort of face although he was none of those things.

He was, he knew, unattractive to all but the most undesirable of women, a state of affairs that didn't bother him. He was neither physically repulsive nor asexual, just less interested in human relationships requiring emotional commitment than in ideas. He treated women at their face value, which is the last thing any of them want. Paradoxically, he got on with aggressive feminists much better than with their opposites. Feminists understood that he didn't give a damn about women one way or the other, an attitude they could accept.

People who did not know him well considered him to be self-indulgently enigmatic at best and a time-server at worst, assessments he did nothing to discourage, caring little for subjective opinions made in ignorance. Had he been asked to list his own major qualities he would have put them in no particular order, as shrewd, decisive and calculating, characteristics he would need in abundance during the weeks ahead.

'So, the time is coming.' Speaking in German, the older man's words were a statement, not a question.

'It's coming.' His companion answered in the same language. 'We may not be right on schedule,' he added after a moment's hesitation.

'Why not? You have a problem?'

'Not a problem, quite the reverse. The computer threw up some interesting data which we might be able to use to our advantage. We're working on it.'

'What sort of data?'

'I don't think I can tell you the details. It's probably better if you don't know.'

'I should be the judge of that. I hope you people are not playing some devious game outside the original scenario.'

'We're not.'

'I don't like improvisation.'

'There won't be any. The computer data may not be relevant or we may not be able to use it. If we can you'll hear about it sooner or later. If not, I'd be burdening you with unnecessary information. You already have enough to worry about.'

'Like the timetable,' said the older man sourly.

'Like the timetable,' soothed the younger man. 'Believe me, we won't allow this new data to interfere with that in any way. If there is a delay it will be at the front end of the operation. I doubt you will even be aware of it. We're only telling you out of courtesy.'

'You're beginning to use the first person plural with greater regularity. *We* won't allow this new data to interfere and *we* are only telling you out of courtesy. A psychoanalyst might judge that to be an unconscious wish to share responsibility should anything go wrong.'

'Nothing will go wrong.'

The older man grunted. 'I don't know whether I find such faith touching or naïve. I made a few jottings several weeks ago concerning how many ways everything *could* go wrong. I gave up when I reached fifty.'

The younger man nodded silently. At least fifty, he thought. He was dying for a cigarette but unwilling to remove his mittens. He had, in any case, resolved to cut down, get somewhere below his normal two packs a day. 'That cough is positively sepulchral,' the doctor had said at his latest medical. He had been impressed by the physician's use of the adjective.

'Will we be meeting again?' asked the older man.

'Before the event, almost certainly. Afterwards, who knows?'

'Who indeed. At least you're making the assumption that there will be an afterwards, which is reassuring. Or is it a computer prediction?'

'A bit of both.'

The older man glanced up at the sky. He had a long drive ahead, as did his companion, whom he wasn't sure he trusted. For that matter, he wasn't sure he trusted any of them, yet he had no alternative, as they didn't. He wondered if the world had always been like this, a handful of men deciding the fate of the remainder. He concluded it had.

'I shouldn't worry about it if I were you.'

Startled, he realized that he had allowed his mind to wander and that his companion had read his thoughts.

'Worry about what?'

'The future. The past is more honest.'

'I regret I do not understand that.'

'The future is an untapped barrel of deceit and strife, uncertainty culminating in defeat, death. Where we use electronics to predict it, remove some of the fear, the ancients used the phases of the moon or the entrails of animals. The past cannot be altered or manipulated conveniently to produce a desired result.'

'And the future can be?'

'Isn't that what we're doing?'

The older man felt the cold of the day for the first time. 'You,' he said, 'will go far.'

'You,' said the young man deferentially, 'have already been there.'

With the first flakes of a fresh snowstorm already falling, they walked slowly back towards the cars. Halfway there the older man said: 'You know, you're not how I imagined you would be when I first read your dossier.'

'Nor are you, sir.'

'You misunderstand me. I didn't expect a philosopher. I suppose that's the Irish in you.'

'Irish?'

'Your name. Cassidy. That's Irish, isn't it?'

'Two or three generations ago, perhaps. I'm an American now.'

MANHATTAN (i)

Alison yelled through to the shower that he was wanted on the phone. He told her to take a message. A few moments later she shouted that the caller was his garage. The repairs to the Mustang would cost four hundred dollars plus parts. Were they to go ahead? If so, could they please have confirmation in writing? A cheque for two hundred dollars as a deposit would also be appreciated as this was not an insurance claim. Jesus, he thought.

'Say I'll get back to them in a day or two.'

Not for the first time Nick Tasker wondered why he bothered living in Manhattan, especially in the Village, where apartment rents had skyrocketed since the trendies moved in. And rent apart, everything was so damned expensive. Body repair shops had for years padded the bills on insurance claims, which in turn had forced insurance companies to raise premiums. The cost of a pair of theatre tickets followed by a decent dinner was enough to give a man heart failure. Nor could you walk anywhere any more without checking that your life insurance was fully paid up and your karate instructor hadn't graduated by mail. Go home, something urged him. Go somewhere safe, sound and peaceful, if a cocktail containing those three ingredients still existed on a planet rapidly going to hell. Why stay in the Big A? Because, as Mallory or someone said about Everest, it's there.

He towelled himself dry, and slipped on the Japanese robe Alison had bought him a few days after the start of their affair, three months ago. She was in the kitchen, watching the six o'clock news on the portable. His drink was already prepared: J & B just covering two cubes of ice, water on the side.

'Have we still got a world?' he asked, nodding in the direction of the television.

She lowered the sound. 'If you can call it a world. The State Department doesn't seem to like something the Chinese are doing, the Chinese are upset with the Russians, and the Russians are having one of their periodic attacks of paranoia. Everyone who disagrees with them is a fascist or an imperialist. Nothing is getting in or out of Kennedy, Newark or La Guardia because of the snow, though the weatherman expects that situation to ease when a warm front or a hot front or an all-quiet-on-the-western-front moves in from somewhere, presumably if it can get a flight. The Mayor is attending a charity banquet this evening in aid of Third World poverty or some such. Judging by the guest list, the cost per head would doubtless solve the problem overnight. The President is expected to make an important speech on the economy in the next day or so, hopefully not needing his toes as well as his fingers to count on. Reports that the First Lady fell and broke her hair are being vigorously denied by the White House. End of bulletin on this merry March evening.'

Alison Cameron smiled the smile that had made her internationally famous as a photographer's model and was considered by Madison Avenue to guarantee the success of any product her manager advised her to endorse. She was, by the most exacting standards, extraordinarily beautiful, with a classic heart-shaped face that was crowned by a luxuriant mop of chestnut hair many of her competitors swore was dyed but wasn't. At five feet seven inches tall and one hundred and twenty-five pounds she had publicly confessed in a magazine article that she thought herself too short and too heavy to model furs. 'My tits are too big. Besides, fur looks better on the original owner.' She was twenty-eight years old and reckoned she had another two or three years at the top before being forced to retire. 'Then I can eat and drink what the hell I like without worrying that every little calorie that goes in is going to pop out somewhere.'

After ninety days or so of bliss without wedlock, Nick

could still not believe his luck. He was seven years older than Alison, five inches taller and maybe forty pounds heavier. And about three hundred thousand a year poorer. His annual income as a freelance journalist plus the occasional royalty cheque from two not very successful non-fiction works wouldn't have kept her in shoes. He was not really given to self-doubt but after their first week together he had asked her, during the small hours with perhaps too much whisky inside him, what she saw in him. She could have taken her pick from Albuquerque to Zalma, Missouri.

'I like you,' she had said. 'This is probably not the great love of either of our lives, but you're handsome and sexy and going just a teeny bit grey. You're not the least bit stuffy or intense for a writer. You can crusade without becoming tedious and it might surprise you to learn that even a muddle-headed wanton such as yours truly has read some of your pieces. I like what you say and the way you say it. I also like the fact that anyone born English is crazy enough to try and make it over here, especially in your particular rat race.'

They had met at one of the publishing bashes Nick sometimes received invitations for. In this case the book being launched was on the subject of a new diet which, if the publisher's handout was to be believed, was guaranteed to make every twelve-stone matron a veritable sylph in six weeks. As a you-too-can-look-like-this gimmick, some bright spark in publicity had come up with the idea of inviting famous models to the opening, and Nick had gone along because it had been a slow month for money and publishing parties usually went overboard serving drinks, whether the book was about a diet or not. He was not disappointed. The waiters served champagne exclusively, which, according to the book's blurb, was an acceptable part of the regimen. A joke going the rounds said that after buying champagne there wouldn't be enough money left for food, which was a sure way to lose weight.

Somewhere during the course of the evening he had seen this ravishing redhead making desperate signals to him from across the room. She was surrounded by tall, bronzed men, and at first he had glanced over his shoulder, wondering who she was beckoning. She had raised her green eyes towards heaven: No, I mean you, you dummy. An hour later they were drinking rough red wine and eating bowls of pasta in an Italian place.

His English background had come up immediately, though he hardly ever thought of himself as English any longer. He had lived in Manhattan for seven years and considered himself a New Yorker in all but dress and speech, which remained determinedly Anglo-Saxon.

They didn't sleep together on the first or second nights. They did on the third. Alison kept on her own apartment because that was the way she wanted it. When she was in town, however, she spent much of her time with him in the Village. Marriage was never mentioned; she had tried it once in Decatur, Illinois, when she was nineteen. It hadn't worked out.

'What about the Mustang?' Alison asked, sipping her customary early evening glass of white wine.

'What about it?'

'Can you afford to have the work done?'

'I can afford it. I'm not sure I'll bother. I ask myself, why do I need a car in Manhattan? A red Mustang, for Christ's sake. I'm asking for someone to rip me off.'

'The police got it back quickly enough.'

'I'd have preferred them not to.' Nick shook a cigarette from a packet on the side. 'I cut the insurance cover. I'm no longer insured for accidental damage to the vehicle, only for theft or if the bloody thing catches fire. I could make out some kind of case, I'm told, for damage occasioned through theft, but the company might fight the claim. I could wind up paying more in lawyer's fees than the repair bill.'

'How will you get about if you sell?'

Nick exhaled a perfect smoke-ring.

'Dear Alison,' he grinned, 'I don't suppose anyone in your income bracket has ever heard of the IRT, much less travelled on it.'

'Don't you believe it,' snorted Alison. 'When I first came in from the sticks with my hair in braids, the subway was my second home on days like today. I used to ride up and down for hours just to keep warm. What no one had told me back home was that beauty contest winners looking for the big breaks were a dime a dozen in New York, or that the Y was full of bull dykes looking for innocent country girls to prey on. Not that I knew that a dyke was anything other than a Dutch sea wall.'

'Now that I don't believe.'

'What, that I was innocent or that bull dykes didn't take a shine to me?'

'That that copper head of yours was ever in braids.'

'I'll show you a photograph one day. When I married the late and unlamented ex, I looked like an auditionee for *Oklahoma*. The group picture – in full colour too, by all that's holy – gave the impression that all the guests had rented their costumes from the wardrobe of an early Doris Day movie. Things don't change much in Illinois, as my old grandpappy would have said.'

The telephone rang again.

'Your turn,' said Alison.

When Nick returned he was frowning.

'Don't tell me,' said Alison. 'The garage wants an answer right now or the car goes to the breakers.'

Nick shook his head. 'No, it wasn't the garage. It was . . . I don't know who the hell it was.'

'Huh? You'd better start watering your drinks.'

'I'm being serious. I don't know who the caller was. He didn't identify himself. I picked up the receiver and a man's voice told me to steer clear of some town in South Dakota. I didn't catch the name.'

'Just that?'

'No. He added that if I didn't do as I was told I might meet with an accident. Then he hung up.'

Nick held out his glass. Alison added fresh ice and refilled it.

'A practical joker maybe,' she said. 'Or the caller got the wrong number.'

'No. He knew my name.'

Alison handed him his glass. 'So what are you writing about or researching in South Dakota that could be upsetting somebody?'

'Nothing. I'm still working on the neo-Nazi series, how groups of Nazis or something very similar are starting to come out of the woodwork in greater numbers in this country as well as in Germany and the rest of Europe. But I've only published one article and that had nothing to do with South Dakota. Bloody strange.'

'Worry you?'

'Not really.'

'Maybe you should tell the police anyway.'

'What can I tell them? That someone I don't know is threatening me regarding a town I've never visited? Besides, I can't go running to the police every time some crank warns me off. People in my business have to expect threats once in a while. It goes with the territory. There's always someone who doesn't like what I've written about them.'

Alison remembered the first article she had read by Nick Tasker, long before she met him; an exposé of the Ku Klux Klan's activities in Alabama. Nick had written about and named half a dozen minor political figures who were closet members. One politician, who had aspirations to higher, national office, had publicly stated that Nick was in for a rough ride if he ever set foot in Alabama again. On another occasion he had revealed that an international chemical corporation with mining interests in the south-west was hiring wetbacks at five dollars a day to work under the most hazardous conditions in several of its mines. Some of the Mexicans had been killed in rockfalls; the remainder were too frightened to say anything for fear their unofficial status would be discovered. The company had eventually proved that top management had known nothing of local arrangements, that the hiring and firing at that level was done by two men, who had been dismissed. The rumour was that they had been paid substantial sums to take the rap, though this, of course, could never be legally established. Nevertheless, Nick told Alison later, he had almost been killed twice in the immediate weeks after the article appeared. The first time was a hit-and-run set-up, a car which barely missed him and didn't stop. The second time, in response to a telephone call, he arranged to meet an anonymous informant who said he had fresh intelligence on the Mexicans, intelligence that would nail the chemical corporation once and for all. The informant didn't make the midnight street-corner rendezvous; a couple of thugs did. If Nick hadn't sensed danger and raced for his car as the thugs approached, he doubted he would have lived to tell the tale.

He had nothing, naturally, to connect the chemical corporation with either incident, insufficient evidence to swear out a complaint. Hit-and-run accidents were common enough in New York, and had the street-corner attack succeeded, the police would have put it down as a mugging that had gone wrong.

Nick's reputation in his profession was, generally speaking, high. Most of his fellow journalists recognized and admired the doggedness with which he followed a story through to the end; only a handful called him the Cracked Crusader and Batnick. To the others he was a welcome thorn in the side of big companies which abused the law or cheated the public, and the terror of the KKK and other illiberal organizations. Once or twice there had been surreptitious attempts to have him deported as an undesirable alien, but on those occasions the fourth estate closed ranks and asked, in print, what crime Nick Tasker had committed to warrant banishment. His work permit was always renewed on demand.

'They've got the wrong boy is all I can think,' he said to Alison. 'I'm not the only Tasker in the phone book. They're mixing me up with someone else.'

'They?'

'I'm assuming it wasn't a crank call from a loner. Anyway, the man said something about *we'll* see you meet with an accident. It's a mistake, that's all.'

'If you say so.' Alison looked doubtful.

'I do say so. If he'd warned me off something I was working on or had worked on, I'd think differently. As it is, I'm not letting one guy with a broken accent give me sleepless nights.'

'What sort of broken accent?'

'Didn't I mention that? He sounded as though he hadn't long been off the boat from Italy or Sicily.' Alison's eyes widened in alarm. 'Look, I know what you're thinking,' added Nick hurriedly, 'but you're wrong.'

'I hope to hell I am.' Alison simulated a shudder. 'If you're

11

mixed up in mob activities I wouldn't take odds on your chances of reaching thirty-six, and I'm speaking from experience. There are Italian and Sicilian connections in the modelling business, behind the scenes stuff. There's gossip that they have money in some of the agencies, which strikes me as a reasonable supposition when you consider the commission agents take from their top earners. I've never had dealings with them myself but I know girls who have, who've been asked to model clothes at private showings for special customers who turned out to be very swarthy gentlemen and their lady friends. The way they operate, they make your Klan and chemical acquaintances look like escapees from Doctor Zeuss.'

'You don't have to tell me. I read the newspapers as well as write for them. Anyway, not every American who talks with an Italian accent is a criminal.' Nick shrugged. 'I've always kept well away from that sort of crime.'

'Truly?'

'Truly. I'd tell you otherwise. I've never had any dealings with the mob and I haven't been in South Dakota since I don't know when. Honest Injun. They've got the wrong Tasker. Let's forget it.'

While Alison showered Nick stood in the dark by the living-room window, sipping his whisky and staring out at the snow and the almost deserted streets. Getting a taxi tonight was going to be difficult, and briefly he was tempted to call the people who were giving the drinks party and tell them that neither he or Alison could make it. He resisted the temptation, knowing how he would feel if he were the host and the phone suddenly started ringing with fictitious tales of sudden head colds. Besides, Alison enjoyed going out.

He liked the view from his fifth-floor window and often stood there with the lights out and the curtains unpulled, watching the street below. That corner of the living-room was his work area, containing a desk, files, typewriter, and the various other trade tools of the working journalist. On his desk at present were several folders of notes for his series on the apparent resurgence of neo-Nazism, together with the near-complete second article. Years ago he had carried work-in-progress around with him, mindful of the fear that plagued every writer, that of the theft or destruction of irreplaceable material. He gave up this surrender to neurosis two-thirds of the way through the second draft of his first book, when he found himself turning up for lunch and evening drinks clutching two briefcases and a bulging Jiffy bag. If the book went to a third draft he'd need a suitcase.

He heard Alison call from the shower. 'Come and scrub my back.'

He went to her and slipped out of his robe.

'We'll be late,' he said, stepping in beside her.

She kissed him. 'So we'll be late.'

MANHATTAN (ii)

By nine o'clock Nick had had three generous whiskies, a couple of sandwiches and something that tasted like chicken in a vol-au-vent, two minor disagreements with some diehard Republicans on the present administration's foreign policy (which Nick suggested was a hybrid born of wishful thinking out of panic), and a mild flirtation with an attractive public relations lady who insisted that her job was honourable. 'My function is to sell my clients, no matter what *they're* selling or how bad it is. After all, even a murderer is entitled to a defence. Whether his lawyer believes him innocent or guilty doesn't enter into it.'

He had lost sight of Alison half an hour ago, inevitable, he thought ruefully, at such a gathering. She had donned her favourite party-going outfit of a knee-length black cocktail dress, black stockings and four-inch heels. Even if every man present had not recognized her instantly from her photographs, Nick had no doubt that she soon would have been the centre of attention, outshining, as she did, every other woman in the room but doing it with such natural style that she made few female enemies. Although in many respects she was the least self-centred woman he had ever met, the professional in her knew how to dress to kill. From past experience he knew he was unlikely to see her again for more than a few minutes at a time before they left.

Their host was a glossy magazine tycoon, Vincent Kaplan, a 52-year-old divorcé with an unquenchable appetite for 19-year-old girls, the latest of whom could be heard telling anyone within earshot how Vinny (Nick winced) planned to run a series of features around her in one of his publications, the object being to put her into films. If Nick was any judge, the girl wouldn't be around long enough to rate more than a couple of lines and maybe a twenty-second TV walk-on. She was pretty enough with a figure that doubtless did wonders for Kaplan's considerable libido, but none of his playmates ever lasted long. In spite of his wealth and the East Side penthouse overlooking the river, Vincent Kaplan wanted something none of his girls could give him: he wanted to be twenty-five again with everything ahead of him.

'Mr Tasker?'

The man who addressed him was around thirty-five, with thinning hair and horn-rimmed spectacles. He was wearing a well-cut dark suit and seemed somehow out of place beside the other male guests, most of whom were attired less formally. Government type was Nick's immediate impression.

'Yes, I'm Tasker.'

'Frank Stone. I saw you were in need of a refill and took the liberty of bringing one over.'

Nick accepted the proffered glass, placing his empty one on the tray of a passing waiter.

'Thanks. Have we met?'

'No. I heard your name mentioned and asked someone to point you out. I'm a fan of yours, you might say. I read your recent article on the new Nazis. Impressive.'

'Thank you. I'm always pleased to meet a fan. In my case they're spread pretty thin on the ground. Are you in the publishing business, Mr Stone?'

'Frank, please.' Nick shook the extended hand. 'No, I'm in industrial security, anti-bugging devices and so on. Most of our clients are in the commercial sector, though in the past year we've done one or two jobs for the government.'

Which explained the suit, thought Nick. Anyone who had regular dealings with Washington tended to dress conservatively.

'I wasn't aware the government did much outside contracting. I thought they had their own specialists.'

'Mostly they do. However, my company is the market leader in several areas. For example, we've developed . . .'

15

He stopped and clicked his tongue. 'But I think it might be unwise to discuss such matters with a journalist of your reputation.'

'Pity,' said Nick. 'For a moment there I thought I might get something more out of this get-together than a sore head.'

'Not a chance, I'm afraid. Anyway, I didn't know government security was your field.'

'It isn't, except journalists are like cows. We devour everything in sight and regurgitate it when necessary. I haven't anything planned when I finish my present series. A few thousand words on how Washington protects us or, alternatively, prevents us finding out what the politicians are up to would have been ideal.'

'You'd have wound up disappointed.' Stone smiled. 'For the most part, there's nothing very sinister in government or industrial security. People with long-range directional microphones pointed at the windows of foreign embassies mainly exist in thriller writers' imaginations. It happens, of course; I'm not trying to give the impression it doesn't or that ways have not been devised to counter eavesdroppers. Largely, however, security devices are designed to deter stenographers from walking off with a year's supply of stationery or paper-clips.'

'You're being too modest.'

'Perhaps a little modest but no more than a little.' Stone finished his drink and put the glass on the table behind him. 'My life is mostly routine, I'm sorry to say. Well-paid routine, admittedly, though one day is pretty much like the next. Unlike yours, I would imagine.'

If only you knew, thought Nick, peering over Stone's head to see how Alison was making out. She was holding court in a group that contained Vincent Kaplan and saying something that made Kaplan laugh. She caught Nick's eye and gave him a broad wink.

'It's not as glamorous as the general public seems to believe,' said Nick, wondering how soon he and Alison could make their excuses and leave. The snow was still falling last time he looked, and cabs would be harder to find after ten o'clock than they had been at eight. He didn't fancy walking forty blocks in this weather. He was sure Alison wouldn't be overjoyed with the notion either. 'Either on the journalist side or the book-writing side. It's mainly hard work, laborious research, and having a lot of doors slammed in your face. The image of the hard-bitten reporter in a battered trilby and trenchcoat, drinking bourbon from the pint flask in his pocket, went out years ago, if such a man ever existed outside Hollywood. Also, no one shouts "hold the front page" any longer. I'm not sure they ever did. Whether you're a staff journalist or a freelance, the public only sees your byline or your face on the TV screen, which is really the last act and, I suppose, has its glamour. To have got that far, however, has meant a lot of nights like tonight waiting in a doorway or sitting around bars, which I can assure you is far from glamorous.'

'Still,' said Stone, beckoning a waiter with a full tray, 'you must have had some excitement researching your latest project.' They each took a fresh glass. 'I can't remember all the details but I seem to recall you writing that one of the neo-Nazi organizations you contacted wasn't anxious to give you details of its membership; that several of the organization's heavies told you, more or less, to get out of town or else. You didn't say where the town was, I noticed.'

'No, I'm saving specific details for maybe the fourth or fifth article. In the first three or four I'm just trying to give the general background of what I see as a new threat to the western world.'

Stone raised his eyebrows. 'You'd put it as strongly as that?'

Nick nodded. 'I would. Like you, I don't want to give away too many trade secrets until I'm ready, but I have friends, Jewish friends, in various parts of the country who say they see happening here what happened in Germany in the Thirties.' Nick juggled a cigarette out of his packet and lit it. 'These friends of mine, many of whom have personal experience of Nazi Germany, are convinced that anti-Semitism is on the increase in the United States. They can quote hundreds of cases – and I do mean hundreds – where synagogues have been vandalized, Jewish businessmen harassed and in some cases attacked, Jewish centres of

17

leisure fire-bombed or otherwise destroyed. As in Nazi Germany, they tell me, very little of what happens appears in the national newspapers or on television. And this is what concerns them. The German Jews didn't believe that anything bad could happen to them, that attacks on them and their businesses were isolated incidents without central direction. And we all know what happened in Germany.

'My friends see parallels here. Nothing tragic may happen for a few years, perhaps a decade, they accept. But sooner or later, maybe in a time of economic crisis, the country will need a scapegoat. The Jews are frightened – no, terrified – that they'll be the scapegoats again, with ordinary citizens, men and women who today would be horrified and indignant if it were suggested that they held Nazi sympathies, joining the marches and waving the flags, turning a blind eye while their neighbours are led off to concentration camps. You think it couldn't happen? So did the German Jews.'

'It still sounds incredible.'

'I accept that. But is it any more incredible than the recent attempts to rehabilitate Hitler? After all that man was responsible for, wouldn't you consider it almost impossible for any right-thinking person to view him as anything other than consummate evil? But no. There have been a number of works in the last ten years suggesting that Hitler was maligned, that he had nothing to do with, or any knowledge of, the extermination programme. Furthermore, these same writers argue, what about the United States' own record during the war, the arrest and internment of Japanese Americans after Pearl Harbor? They also point out that my own country, England, invented the concentration camp during the Boer War. And if the SS committed crimes, they contend, what about the crimes we never hear about perpetrated by the American OSS and the British SOE?

'My Jewish friends also suspect – and I have to make it clear to you that it's no more than a suspicion – that the government or the government's security services covertly encourage the new Nazis, recognizing that one day such organizations may have their uses. There is also some evidence that a number of senior officers in the FBI and the

CIA furnish the neo-Nazis with money from government slush funds.'

Nick realized that he had emptied his glass without noticing that he was drinking, and that he was talking far too much.

'Sorry to bend your ear like that,' he told Stone. 'I don't usually lecture fellow guests at parties.'

'Please,' said Stone. 'I find it fascinating if bizarre. Also disturbing if what you wrote is true, that there are dozens of Nazi cells all over the country, each one preparing for *Der Tag*.'

'Hundreds,' said Nick. 'Hundreds, not dozens. Virtually every State has a parent organization controlling a number of branches. Not only in Dixie either, which is where one would expect to find it. New England has its share, as does Iowa, Illinois, Indiana, Texas.'

'South Dakota?' asked Stone, so quietly that, for a moment, Nick thought he had misheard.

'I beg your pardon?'

'South Dakota. I was wondering about South Dakota.'

'Why?' Nick's knuckles whitened around his empty glass. 'Why is South Dakota so significant?' He took a step closer to Stone, whose eyes narrowed in alarm. 'Do you come from South Dakota?'

'No, of course not. I'm from . . . What does it matter where I'm from? And what's wrong with you? Are you drunk or something?'

'I'm not drunk or something and I want to know why you asked me about South Dakota.' Nick's voice had risen a couple of octaves. He leaned forward and grabbed Stone by the lapel. 'I asked you a question, you son of a bitch. I'd like an answer. Why did you ask about South Dakota?'

A dozen pairs of eyes were on Nick as Stone tried to loosen the grip on his lapel. Nick refused to let go. Although part of him was horrified, he found himself shaking Stone and shouting.

'Why did you want to know about South Dakota? *Why?*'

Nick knew he had had one or two drinks too many for rational conversation, but his vision was unimpaired. Out of the corner of his eye he saw more people heading towards the commotion, among them Alison, Vincent Kaplan and a pair of Kaplan's manservants. Alison reached him first.

'Nick! What's the matter? Let him go, for God's sake, Nick! Let him go!'

'You'd be wise to do as the young lady says,' drawled Kaplan, spreading his arms to indicate to his manservants that no strong-arm tactics were necessary for the moment. 'Take it easy, Nick. If you've got a beef with this guy, discuss it elsewhere. Don't break up my party.'

Nick released his grip on Stone's lapel. Stone backed off, losing himself in the crowd. Nick heard him say as he disappeared, 'I don't know what came over him. One minute we were having a friendly discussion, the next he grabbed me and started behaving like a lunatic. He must be drunk.'

'Are you drunk, Nick?' asked Kaplan, motioning his servants to get the party going again. Within a few seconds Nick, Kaplan and Alison were alone in a corner. 'Been over-indulging at the hospitality trays, huh?' The magazine publisher tried to make light of the incident.

'No,' said Nick, shaking his head. People were still staring at him. 'No. I've had a few but nowhere near enough to make me aggressive. It was something he said that I obviously misinterpreted. I'm sorry, Vincent. I didn't mean to ruin the party.'

Kaplan clapped him on the shoulder. 'Don't worry about it. It would take more than a minor argument to ruin one of my parties. But easy on the whisky, son, okay?'

'Easy is right,' said Alison, her face a dark cloud. 'Easy meaning enough.'

'You don't have to leave,' protested Kaplan.

'We do,' said Alison, who was wise enough to realize that their host would not be sorry to see the back of them. 'It's getting late and we'll have trouble finding a cab anyway.'

'My chauffeur can drive you home.'

'Bless you, Vincent, but no.' She pecked him on the cheek. 'A few lungfuls of fresh air will do this boy of mine the world of good.'

'If you're sure.'

'I'm sure.'

'I should apologize,' muttered Nick. 'Apologize to Stone.'

20

'You'll do no such thing, not tonight,' retorted Alison. 'He might want to take a swing at you this time. I'll get his address from Vincent tomorrow. You can give him a call.'

'I don't think I know him,' said Kaplan. 'He must have come with someone. Still, I'll find out who he is and let you know.'

In the elevator Nick explained to Alison what had happened.

'And when he mentioned South Dakota I saw red,' he concluded. 'It's all a bit vague now, except I swear to God he did it intentionally, to goad me into doing something stupid. As I did,' he finished lamely.

Alison's concern showed in her eyes.

'You're working too hard. It was a coincidence, that's all. Christ, you can't go around punching everyone who mentions South Dakota or you're going to wind up paying assault damages for the rest of your days. There can't possibly be a connection between your voice on the phone and Stone.'

'Maybe you're right.' Nick tried a feeble grin. 'Of course you're right.' But he wasn't sure.

The doorman of Kaplan's building reckoned that finding a cab on a night such as tonight would be almost impossible.

'I tried phoning one for another resident fifteen minutes ago. I got no reply from any of the numbers. They've all gone home. Your best bet is to walk and hope to pick up a cruiser.'

Alison flashed him her most winning smile.

'I can't walk in these shoes. Besides, you've got a huge umbrella and we haven't. There must be three inches of snow out there and it's still falling.' She produced two ten-dollar bills as if by magic. 'Would you mind doing it for us?'

'I'm not supposed to leave my post,' grumbled the doorman.

'Please,' said Alison.

The doorman hummed and hahed and mumbled under his breath before agreeing.

'Awright, Miss Cameron. For you I'll do it.' He pushed her hand aside. 'But I don't want a tip. Just slip me a signed photograph next time you're passing. Make it to Harry and Martha. Harry is me. Martha's my wife. And don't let

21

anyone in until I get back. I'll pull the door locked. You open it by pressing this button here.' He showed her where it was under his desk.

'You're an angel,' said Alison.

'I'm a sucker for a pretty face, is all. I'm fifty-eight years old. You'd think I'd've learned by now.'

He selected one of several umbrellas from a stand in the corner and squared his cap before going out through the glass doors. They saw him peer up and down and shake his head. Then he disappeared.

'Fame,' muttered Nick.

'Don't knock it, buster.'

Harry was back in five minutes. Behind him they saw the outline of a Checker cab.

'There's hardly anything on the damned streets at all,' he said after Alison had let him in. 'Excuse my mouth, Miss Cameron. I was lucky with that one. I found him parked round the corner by the phone booth, waiting while one of his passengers made a call. They're going downtown. I said you were a famous model in a hurry to get to an assignment and they said you could share.'

'Thanks, Harry.'

'Don't forget that photograph now.'

'Where are you folks going?' asked one of the men in the back after Alison and Nick climbed aboard and closed the door.

'The Village.'

'East?'

'Greenwich. And I'd like to thank you for sharing with us,' said Nick. 'We'll pay for the fare for all of us, naturally.'

'Wouldn't hear of it. Me and my associate are going in that direction. You're not taking us out of our way.'

The cab moved off slowly, the driver following the tyre tracks made by other vehicles, windscreen wipers hissing noisily. Nick took a closer look at the two Samaritans. The man who had done all the talking up to now was a thick-set individual in his forties. His companion was thinner and younger. Both men wore dark suits, overcoats and hats, and occupied the rear seat facing forward. Alison and Nick sat opposite them on the jump seats. The thin man was taking more than a passing interest in Alison's legs, while she stared out of the window, pretending not to notice.

Crossing East 34th Nick turned his head to give the driver precise directions. The thick-set man anticipated him.

'He knows,' he said laconically.

'Knows what?' asked Nick, puzzled.

'Where you're going.'

'I might as well give him the exact address.'

'He knows that too, Mr Tasker,' said the thin man. The accent was less stage Italian than on the phone, but there was no doubt it was the same voice.

Nick had difficulty finding his own. Eventually he managed, 'Look, what the hell *is* all this?' That he was right about Stone Nick was now certain; inexplicable events were tumbling far too fast after one another to be called coincidence. Stone and these men were somehow connected, and Harry the doorman had not found a cab parked round the corner by accident. The occupants, including the driver, had been waiting for him and Alison to leave the party. 'How do you know who I am?'

'We know a lot more than that about you, Mr Tasker,' said the thick-set man.

Nick glanced across at Alison, who looked bewildered but not frightened. Nick wasn't so sure she shouldn't be scared rigid. He tried to judge the speed of the cab and calculate whether he could jump out while it was moving without suffering serious injury. He concluded he could; their speed was under 20 mph and the snow would help break his fall. But Alison wouldn't make it, not dressed as she was and without warning.

'You're upsetting a lot of people, Mr Tasker,' went on the thick-set man. 'Upsetting them considerably.' His tone was soft and polite, apologetic, which emboldened Alison.

'Look, mister,' she said, 'I don't know who you are or what you want. I do know that kidnapping's a federal offence which can put you in jail until you're too old to care. So stop the cab right now. We'll walk the rest of the way.'

'You'd be well advised to keep out of this, Miss Cameron. Your boyfriend's in trouble. Don't make it worse than it is.'

'And don't threaten me,' snorted Alison haughtily. 'If you

23

know my name too, you'll know who I am and that I have some powerful friends in this town.'

The thick-set man sighed wearily. He motioned to his companion, who produced a heavy automatic pistol from his overcoat pocket. Holding the gun in one hand he leaned forward and slid the other underneath Alison's coat and dress. Reaching for the top of her thigh, he took an inch of soft flesh between forefinger and thumb, and pinched hard. 'Stockings,' he said. 'Nice.' Alison's sudden scream was a mixture of shock and pain.

Nick threw himself across the cab at the thin man, who, anticipating the move, parried it easily with his left arm while simultaneously bringing the gun barrel down across Nick's face, breaking the skin. Nick grunted in agony, his senses reeling. The thick-set man got hold of him by the shoulders of his topcoat and hurled him against the driver's partition.

'For Chrissake,' snarled the driver over his shoulder.

'You,' said the thick-set man to Alison, 'shut up. And you,' he added to Nick, 'put something to your face and listen.'

Nick fumbled in his pocket for a handkerchief. He could feel the blood running into his mouth. Alison cowered in the corner, terrified now.

'Can I get up?' mumbled Nick.

He was lying in a heap on the floor of the cab. When he had launched his attack the jump seat had sprung back into the partition.

'Yes. But behave if you want to save yourself and Miss Cameron further trouble.'

Nick lowered the jump seat and sat on it, holding his face. 'You've got the wrong Mr Tasker . . .'

'Don't you ever learn?' The thick-set man raised his voice for the first time. 'You're here to listen, that's all.'

'I'm listening.'

'Good. I'll make it brief. Some friends of ours are annoyed at the enquiries you've been making east of Rapid City, South Dakota. You know where I mean, on US 14 between Philip and Midland.'

'I don't even know where Philip is,' said Nick. 'Or

Midland, I've never . . .'

The thick-set man groaned aloud. 'For God's sake, don't you know what *listen* means? You won't be told, will you? You have to make it tough on yourself. Make the son of a bitch listen,' he said to his companion.

Nick shielded his face to ward off a second blow, which never came. Instead, the thin man stretched out an arm and tore open Alison's coat from top to bottom, afterwards ripping her dress from her shoulders to her waist. He silenced her screams by back-handing her across the mouth, then broke the front fastening of her flimsy black brassière with his left-hand. He placed the muzzle of the automatic against her left breast, pressed hard and twisted the gun viciously, leaving a circular weal which burned. Fearful of screaming, Alison nevertheless whimpered like a kicked puppy, believing she was going to be shot.

'Now are you willing to listen in silence?' the thick-set man demanded of Nick. 'Any further unsolicited comments will mean Miss Cameron really getting worked over.'

Nick nodded, not trusting himself to say even Yes.

'Right. I'll continue. You are, as I was saying a moment ago, to discontinue your researches between Philip and Midland. Furthermore, from now on the whole of US 14 between Quinn and Pierre is out of bounds to you. Go anywhere else and do anything else, but leave that stretch of real estate out. Have you got that? Tell me if you understand.'

'I understand,' said Nick dully, not understanding at all.

'I hope you mean what you're saying because if you don't, we'll be back. And next time we'll be a little rougher.' He peered out of the cab. 'Where the hell are we?'

'Fourteenth and Third.'

'Okay, dump 'em.'

Nick and Alison found themselves on the snow-covered sidewalk near an all-night diner, which had remained open despite the weather. Leaving Alison sheltering in a doorway, Nick went into the diner to call the police.

Thirty-five minutes later Frank Stone placed a long-distance telephone call, using a credit card, from a booth in the

Hilton.

'It went fine,' he said. 'Tasker reacted exactly as you predicted. It was a good idea to steal and wreck his car. It compelled him to use other forms of transportation, which made him vulnerable.' In answer to a question he added: 'No, I've sent them on their way. They'll be out of town in a couple of days. In the meantime, they'll lie low. The cab'll be returned to our own stable by a different crew. If Tasker spotted the number or the driver's name, it won't mean anything as the vehicle doesn't legitimately exist.'

Stone listened for a few moments before saying: 'Well, we're still weathered in here. Maybe tomorrow. I had thought of staying at the Hilton but I guess the budget doesn't run to that. No, it was a joke. No, I'll make sure Tasker doesn't see me around. Kaplan was no problem. By the time he came to look for me I'd gone. Yes, I agree. We're off and running.'

Stone hung up. He looked around the opulence of the Hilton. The hell with it, he thought.

At the other end of the line, Cassidy held the receiver in his hand for a long time before cradling it. Providing Tasker reacted in accordance with the computer's prognosis, the first stage was going well.

'I swear to God,' Nick said, 'that I know nothing about Philip, Midland, or US 14. I don't know what they were talking about.'

The time was approaching 1 a.m. The police patrol car had driven them home and taken statements in which Alison and Nick had revealed everything that had happened since the mysterious phone call earlier in the evening. The police had concluded that it was a case of mistaken identity. They had promised to try and trace the cab and the assailants, but without a number or the driver's ID it would be difficult. Nor could Vincent Kaplan help on the subject of Frank Stone. A call to the magazine publisher disclosed that Stone had left the penthouse shortly after the argument, before Kaplan could talk to him. None of the other guests admitted bringing him. The odds were on Stone being a gatecrasher, a not unusual phenomenon.

Wearing a bathrobe, Alison was on her third brandy,

Nick his second. Before leaving, the police had asked if either needed hospital treatment; both had declined. After he had bathed his face and applied antiseptic, Nick had observed that the wound was superficial. Alison was more shocked than physically hurt, although the mark left by the gun muzzle would, she surmised, keep her out of low-neck gowns for a while. She was also angry, now that the nightmare was over and the brandy having a therapeutic effect, at being man-handled in such a way and having a perfectly good coat and one of her favourite dresses ruined.

'Well, they weren't the mob anyway,' she said, 'for which I suppose we should be thankful. For a while back there I envisaged us taking a midnight stroll in the Hudson wearing concrete boots, which would have done nothing for my image, not to mention the blood pressure of the high-class cordwainer whose products I endorse.'

Nick smiled, wincing a little as the skin around his wound tautened. Alison Cameron was one hell of a woman. Ninety-nine out of a hundred of her sex would be under sedation after such an experience.

'No, they weren't mob,' he agreed, 'but they've got something to hide up around Midland.'

She sensed the curiosity in his voice. 'I hope that statement doesn't mean what I suspect it does.'

'That I might take a little trip to South Dakota? It's a thought.'

'It's a death wish. Are you crazy? Look in the mirror again. Look what they did to you when you didn't know anything. They'll have your balls if you start nosing around, and I wouldn't like you to lose that part of your anatomy. A busted face I can live with; a eunuch I can't.'

'It's too good a lead to let go,' insisted Nick. 'Mostly a journalist has to find his own stories. I've been handed one on a plate.'

'Where your head'll be joining it before the month's over. Stick to your Nazis; they're safer.'

'It's my Nazis I am sticking to.' Now that he had had time to reflect, Nick was convinced that the evening's happenings were somehow tied in to his current project, albeit in a way he didn't understand. 'Listen, you know and I know that

I've been nowhere near US 14. The police assumed it was a case of mistaken identity because my evidence pointed them in that direction, and it's what I've also been assuming up to now. But what if we're all wrong? The guys in the cab seemed to believe they had the right man and they knew your name too. Let's go along with that theory for a second, that the Nick Tasker they wanted is this Nick Tasker but that they believe I'm enquiring into something I'm not, some area or group I haven't touched. Okay, now all I'm working on at present is the neo-Nazis. It should therefore follow that tonight's incident is connected with that.'

'There's an awful lot of ifs in that theory.'

'Nevertheless, I can't pass it up.'

Alison peered at him over the rim of her glass. 'So we leave snowy Manhattan and spend a few days in even snowier South Dakota?'

'Not we, me.'

'Why?'

'Because I don't know what I'm looking for and I may have to go into some peculiar places to find out. I probably won't learn anything. In the attempt, however, I'll be asking a lot of questions, which is certain to get around. After that it could get dangerous. He travels fastest et cetera.'

'Why can't you sell insurance or work in a bank?' asked Alison, feigning petulance while accepting the logic of Nick's argument. 'When will you leave?'

'As soon as the weather clears and there's a flight. I doubt I'll be away more than three or four days.'

'That's three or four days too long. Sorry, I'm being womanly pathetic or pathetically female, whichever way you like your adverbs fried. But *be careful*,' she emphasized.

'Extreme caution will be my watchword.'

'Huh,' said Alison.

SOUTH DAKOTA (i)

Nick arrived by air in Rapid City two days later. The announcement from the flight deck as the plane taxied was a weather forecast of snow and then more snow, with temperatures close to freezing during the day and below at night.

At the Avis desk he asked for something not too big. The girl offered him a tan Chrysler with only six thousand miles on the clock after scrutinizing his American Express card suspiciously and making a phone call to confirm the card was valid. They didn't see many men with English accents in Rapid City.

The car came equipped with tourist maps, which Nick studied carefully before deciding that his best bet was to take Interstate 90 east to the US 14 turn-off for Pierre, the state capital (pronounced 'Peer', he recalled). The thick-set spokesman in the New York cab had warned him off the whole of US 14 between Quinn and Pierre, particularly around the towns of Philip and Midland. From Rapid City to the US 14 spur, he calculated, was something like sixty miles, with a further one hundred and ten to Pierre. The one-way trip shouldn't take him more than three hours, depending on road conditions.

Driving east, with the Black Hills behind, the Badlands on his right and Mount Rushmore over his right shoulder, he realized he had no idea what he was looking for. The most he could do to begin with was study the lie of the land, allow his journalist's instincts to guide him. He trusted those instincts implicitly; they rarely let him down. Today he would motor as far as the outskirts of Pierre before turning round and finding a motel for the night, preferably between Philip and Midland, where he would ask a few questions.

South Dakota was accustomed to inclement weather and the road surface was clear of snow, the snow ploughs having done their job earlier in the day, pushing the previous night's fall to the side of the highway. Once on US 14 he found he could cruise easily at sixty except where temporary road signs warned him to slow. The standard of driving out here, he thought, was far superior to that found in Manhattan, apart from one mad bastard in a blue Ford, a simulated fox's brush flying from the radio aerial, who stuck on his tail for a couple of minutes west of Midland before pulling out and roaring away. Nick shook his fist impotently at the solitary occupant, a man huddled deep in a tartan windcheater and wearing a red hunting cap.

By 4 p.m. Nick had taken a distant look at the Missouri River, on which Pierre stood, and was travelling west again, watching a watery sun sink over the Black Hills. It would be dark in under an hour, by which time he expected to have found somewhere to stay for the night. He was tired after the flight and his hours on the road, and he was anticipating eagerly a hot shower, a stiff drink and a good dinner. Later he would telephone Alison, who had said she would curl up with a book in his apartment rather than go back to her own.

He was midway between Pierre and Midland before he saw the car tailing him, its headlights dipped. It came no closer and dropped no further behind than seventy or eighty yards. When he accelerated, the car behind did also; when he reduced speed, so did the other vehicle.

Not especially worried at first, Nick went over the possibilities in his head. Number one, it was unlikely that anyone knew he was arriving in Rapid City today or any other day. Number two, why would anyone follow him? And number three, if anyone *was* following him and he was not imagining things, were they connected with the Manhattan threat? He found it hard to believe that the men in the New York cab would monitor his every move.

Where US 14 made a virtual ninety-degree turn south for Midland, Nick decided to put his shadow to the test. He decelerated gradually; the speedometer needle crept backwards a mile or two at a time. When it reached forty-five, Nick suddenly stamped on the accelerator, drew clear of the following car, changed lanes and signalled left. Allowing the signal a few seconds to register with the driver behind, Nick chose his moment, flashed a sudden right, and pulled across the front of a large truck and trailer, just as a sign indicated a right-hand slip road. He had no thoughts of taking the slip road; he simply wanted to see what the driver behind would do next.

The truck's horn blared angrily. A moment later the pursuing car drew alongside the Chrysler. Nick saw that it was a blue Ford with a fox's brush flying from the radio aerial. The driver was wearing a tartan windcheater and a red hunting cap pulled low over his eyes, effectively disguising his features. Right, you bastard, thought Nick, I've seen you before. He pushed the accelerator pedal to the floor, wishing briefly that he had not asked the Avis girl for a small car.

The Ford responded, keeping level in the adjacent lane. The truck and trailer fell behind as the Chrysler and the Ford raced away into the gathering dusk, leaving Nick in no doubt that someone had kept track of him in Manhattan and somehow knew he had booked through to Rapid City. What was unclear, for the moment, was the Ford driver's intentions. They did not remain obscure for long.

Using its superior speed, the Ford pulled ahead fractionally, until its rear axle was level with the Chrysler's front wheels. Then the driver fish-tailed, flicking the steering wheel quickly right and left and sideswiping the Chrysler, trying to force it off the road. Metal scraped against metal with a banshee howl while Nick fought to keep the Chrysler on an even keel. The Ford driver was evidently an expert, keeping his rear fender well clear of the Chrysler's front one to avoid accidental locking.

Half a dozen times Nick was hit. On each occasion he was pushed nearer the edge of the highway and possible oblivion. The Ford had the centre of the road, and the advantage. Nick could only counter by trying to correct and straighten up whenever he was struck. When he tried to brake, to put the Ford ahead, the other driver anticipated the move and braked also. What the Avis girl was going to think of him,

Nick thought with bitter humour, didn't bear contemplating.

Then the Ford was gone. The driver accelerated two or three miles an hour and brought his back axle abreast of the Chrysler's hood before braking hard and fast while spinning the steering wheel to the left, thus going into a momentary rear-wheel skid and pushing the Chrysler right off the road and on to the hard shoulder, where loose snow quickly arrested Nick's forward momentum and enabled him to bring the car to a halt without it rolling over. It didn't occur to him that had the red-capped driver truly wanted to kill him, he could have made a much better job of it.

For a minute or more Nick sat stock still, shocked, breathing heavily. The truck and trailer he had offended earlier roared by but didn't stop, its driver tooting shave-and-a-haircut-two-bits. Thanks a lot, thought Nick.

After a while he felt calm enough to get out – using the passenger door, since the Ford had buckled the lock on the driver's side. He was surprised to find that the damage to the Chrysler was no more than superficial. The bodywork along the entire offside was going to need major surgery and the front fender and grille were dented and scratched, but when he opened the hood he detected nothing amiss underneath. The radiator was in one piece, meaning that the cooling system was intact. He could make it to the nearest motel, which if he remembered correctly, was only a few miles up ahead.

As he climbed behind the steering wheel a battered VW filled with teenagers pulled up alongside and asked if he needed help. He thanked them and said no, he thought he could make it. He didn't want company for the moment; he wanted time alone, to think. If the Chrysler gave out on him between here and the motel or refused to start at all, he could easily hitch a lift.

To his relief, the plugs sparked first time. He tested the headlights; no problem there either. Maybe he should give up driving altogether, he thought as he reversed on to the highway. First the Mustang and now this. Somebody was really trying to tell him something.

But what, he wondered as he fumbled in his pocket for a

cigarette. Okay, to keep clear of Philip, Midland and US 14; that much he knew already. But keep clear why and of what? None of it made any sense that he could see, yet there had to be a connection between the incident in the New York cab and this last attempt to run him off the road. It was unthinkable that the two occurrences were unrelated.

Fifteen minutes later the motel beckoned through the gloom and the first flakes of a light snowfall. A flashing neon sign read Vacancies. He limped the Chrysler on to the forecourt, parked it, and was reminding himself that one of his first jobs would be to call Avis when he saw the blue Ford in one of the bays. He couldn't believe his eyes. Surely it wasn't the same vehicle? But when he walked over to examine it he saw that it was, unmistakably. The fox's brush was hanging from the radio aerial and the nearside wing was dented and scratched. Right, you bastard, he thought with vicious satisfaction while making a mental note of the registration number, let's find out what this is all about.

The desk clerk confirmed that he had a vacant cabin for an overnight stay, adding, in answer to Nick's next question, that it wasn't motel policy to give out the names of other guests. He would not even check the register to see if the number of the Ford was listed against a resident. But Nick had spent a working lifetime dealing with uncooperative minions.

'I was involved in a minor collision with a blue Ford a few miles back,' he said politely. 'He damn near killed me and didn't stop. I got his number, however, which is the same number as the blue Ford parked outside. Now I don't want to cause you any trouble, but the people I hired my car from are not going to be very happy at the state it's in. I'm not very happy myself, for that matter.'

The desk clerk shrugged disinterestedly. 'I'm sorry. I've got my orders.'

'Don't be sorry,' said Nick. 'You've done nothing wrong. The driver of the Ford has. I appreciate your position, but if you won't help me it'll have to be the police. I doubt they'll be as courteous as I am or, if you've anyone occupying a cabin who shouldn't be there – someone and his secretary for example – that you'll be very popular when a patrol car pulls

33

up.' Nick smiled. 'Let's try again, shall we? As far as I could judge, the driver of the Ford was about my size, wearing a tartan jacket and a red hunting cap. You may remember him checking in or asking for his key.'

The desk clerk accepted defeat. The management would not appreciate the police on the premises.

'What did you say the number was?'

Nick gave it. The clerk checked his list.

'There's no one staying here driving a car with that number,' he said after a moment. 'Maybe he called in for a drink or something to eat. The bar's one way, the dining-room the other. Follow the signs.'

'Thanks,' said Nick. 'I'll fetch my bag and register later.'

He tried the dining-room first, which was almost empty this early in the evening. The bar had a dozen customers, all male, all taking advantage of the cut-price happy hour tariff. Not one wore a tartan jacket.

Outside the bar, Nick was on the point of returning to the desk to enquire whether there was anywhere else in the motel a non-guest might be when he caught sight of a man leaving the cloakroom adjacent to the lobby and hurrying for the exit. He was bareheaded and even without the windcheater Nick would have recognized him.

'*Stone!*' he yelled.

Startled, Stone whipped round. He identified the source of the shout before breaking into a trot, running for the forecourt. Nick raced after him.

'Say, you can't . . .' the desk clerk started in protest.

The snow was falling thickly now, the storm the weather forecasters had promised. Stone sprinted for the blue Ford, which he'd parked nose out, ready for a quick getaway. He had a thirty- or forty-yard lead, which had narrowed to twenty yards by the time he flung open the driver's door, evidently unlocked, and threw himself inside. A moment later the engine stuttered into life and the headlights came on. Which was when Nick slipped on the snow and fell. Before he could get to his feet Stone had engaged forward gear and, tyres screeching, roared off down an avenue of stationary cars. The last Nick saw of his lights he was heading east on US 14.

A pair of strong hands helped him up. They belonged to a man wearing a battered leather flying jacket over a pair of dark-blue overalls who had just descended from the cab of a Chevy pick-up.

'Crazy bastard'll get himself killed, driving like that in weather like this.'

'I hope not,' growled Nick without thinking. 'I'm saving that pleasure for myself.' He dusted the snow from his trousers. 'Thanks.'

'Don't mention it. What happened?'

'He ran me off the road a few miles back and didn't stop. I thought I'd lost him until I saw his car here.'

'Did you get the licence number?'

'I got that, all right.'

'State plates?'

'Yes.'

'Then your worries are over. The cops will have his address in an hour.'

Nick was far from sure he wanted the police on the scene. That they could trace Stone he had no doubt, but bringing in officialdom was normally a certain way to ruin a good story. He was here to ask questions, find out why he was being threatened. Since he had Stone's number he would go about tracing him in his own time, using his own methods. The police could wait. Nevertheless, he said he would give them a call from the motel as soon as he had registered and unpacked.

'You're staying here, then?'

'That's the general idea, though the way I charged through the lobby a few minutes ago they'll probably ask me to move on.'

'No, they're okay. I call in regularly when I'm in the area. They regard all overseas visitors as people from another planet. I don't mean to be nosy, but that is an English accent, isn't it?'

'It is,' admitted Nick.

'You're a long way from home.'

'Not really. Manhattan's home these days.'

'See what I mean? People from another planet.' The man grinned. 'Cliff Tyson,' he said.

Nick shook hands and gave his own name.

'Maybe we can have a drink when you're unpacked,' suggested Tyson. 'I was in England for a couple of years in the Seventies. London and East Anglia mostly, though I got around. Air Force,' he added by way of explanation, 'until I reached the conclusion that Uncle Sam was never going to make me a rich man. I've got my own electrical goods business now. It's a good living and I don't have to salute the customers.'

'Around here?' asked Nick.

'Midland.'

Perfect, thought Nick; a tradesman with local knowledge. Where better to begin asking questions?

'I'll see you in the bar in fifteen minutes.'

The desk clerk pulled a long face when Nick reappeared carrying his suitcase, and pushed across the register without comment. Five minutes later Nick was calling Alison in New York. The line, however, was busy. After several attempts he gave up. He would try her again in an hour.

Tyson was sitting at the bar, waiting for him. Now that they were inside in better light Nick could see that he was a man in his middle forties with thinning fair hair. He looked very fit.

'J & B and ice, water on the side,' Nick told the barman.

'Get through to the cops?' asked Tyson.

'Not yet,' answered Nick. Nor had he called Avis, who would want to know whether he had made an official report of the accident, as the hire terms stipulated. 'To tell you the truth, I'm not sure I'm going to, not for the moment, at least.'

'Oh?' Tyson's expression was one of surprise.

Nick opted to come more or less clean with Tyson. The ex-air force man would be unlikely to answer questions from a total stranger unless he knew why they were being posed. Without going into elaborate detail, Nick explained that he was a journalist investigating a story and that his earlier brush with the driver of the blue Ford was not the first.

'I met him in New York a couple of days ago, shortly before three men abducted me and the girl I was with and made some threats.'

36

'What kind of threats?' Tyson appeared fascinated.

'They weren't specific. However, I was left in no doubt that something unpleasant would happen unless I steered clear of US 14 around Midland and Philip.'

'What were you investigating, the last time you were here?'

'This is where it all becomes bizarre. I haven't been here before. At first I thought they'd got the wrong man, or the right man but the wrong story. I was still fifty per cent inclined to believe that until Stone ran me off the road.'

'Stone's the guy in the Ford?'

'Right – although I didn't know he was the driver when he sideswiped me.'

Tyson signalled for another drink. Nick insisted on paying. Tyson nodded his thanks before saying. 'Okay, so why are you telling me all this?'

'Because you might be able to help, being a local man. As I just explained, this is my first time in the area. I don't know what I'm looking for or why I'm being warned off.'

Tyson frowned. 'You said you were on a story.'

'That's true. To the best of my knowledge, however, it doesn't concern South Dakota.'

Nick could see that Tyson was perplexed. You and me both, he thought. He debated how much he should tell Tyson about his current series of articles, concluding that it would have to be everything. He could hardly solicit assistance otherwise.

'You're in the wrong neck of the woods,' said Tyson eventually. 'If there are any crypto-Nazis between here and Sioux Falls I've never heard of them. We've got our share of right-wingers, sure, John Birchers and Daughters of the American Revolution, but no one who wouldn't willingly have put a bullet through Hitler's skull if he hadn't done it himself forty years ago. For that matter, I wouldn't pursue that line of enquiry too openly. There are guys around here who fought against Germany in World War Two. They wouldn't take too kindly to accusations of being closet Hitler-lovers.'

Nick inclined his head, as if accepting the advice. But he'd heard similar sentiments before, in small towns that turned

37

out to be little Munichs once the topsoil was removed.

'I'm not saying that any veterans are involved,' he said, 'or that the new Nazis parade up and down Main Street wearing swastika armbands and singing the Horst Wessel. Some of the groups I've investigated are no more than ten or twenty strong, and remain in the woodwork, listening to tapes of Hitler's speeches. Misfits, most of them, living in a dreamworld. Never heard a shot fired in anger. Some groups are larger and less reluctant to hide their politics, blaming the Jews – Negroes and other ethnic minorities too, but mainly the Jews – for everything from hard-core pornography to water pollution, and citing the nineteen eighty-two destruction of Beirut as an example of Jewish intransigence and lack of concern about anything that stands in the way of international Zionism. I mean no offence to you or the majority of other people in South Dakota, but my problem is this: if Stone and his henchmen are not Nazis, then who the hell are they and why the threats?'

'Sorry I can't help,' said Tyson, somewhat gruffly, Nick thought.

'Don't worry about it. In my business you get accustomed to dead ends. I'll keep asking around until I come across someone who might have seen something strange.'

Tyson had his glass to his lips. He put it back on the bar without drinking. 'In what way strange?'

Nick sensed a subtle change of attitude.

'I'm not sure. Anything out of the ordinary, anything that puzzled the person who saw it or heard it.'

'Well now . . .' Tyson produced an ancient pipe from the top pocket of his overalls, filled it with tobacco from an oilskin pouch, and struck a match. 'Well now,' he repeated.

'Well now what?' said Nick.

Tyson made sure his pipe was well and truly alight before answering. 'It may have nothing to do with what you're looking for, but I do some hunting up in the hills.' He thumbed vaguely over his shoulder. 'Nothing big, you understand, and with the weather like this nothing much at all. But I like to get away from the store whenever I can. It can be tough going, what with the snow and all, though that doesn't bother me. A man learns a lot about himself up there on his own.'

'Go on,' encouraged Nick. 'You saw something up in the hills.'

'Maybe.'

'Maybe?'

Tyson hesitated. 'I'd like to think about it.'

Nick thought he was angling for a fee. He offered to pay for Tyson's time, if Tyson would explain what he had seen and Nick considered it worthwhile availing himself of Tyson's services as a guide for a return visit.

'Keep your money,' said Tyson, not unpleasantly. 'That's not why I want to think about it. Give me twenty-four hours.'

'It'll be pitch dark this time tomorrow,' Nick pointed out. 'If you've got something to show me that I feel I might want to see, we'll have to meet earlier.'

'Fair enough, make it midday. I'll collect you out front. Buy yourself some cold-weather clothes if you didn't bring any. Boots, trousers, a good thick jacket.' Abruptly, Tyson finished his drink in a single swallow. 'I have to be going.'

'Until tomorrow, then,' said Nick, and thought very little more of it throughout dinner. Over the years, he had learned not to get too enthusiastic about what others thought was important. Tyson might turn out to have something or nothing, with the odds on nothing.

Later, before telephoning Alison, he called the Avis depot in Rapid City. The answering machine, as he had hoped, informed him that the premises were closed for the night and asked if he would care to leave a message at the tone. He elected not to. Time enough to explain how one of their precious Chryslers had come to be wrecked and why he hadn't contacted the police.

Alison answered on the second ring. 'How's the wandering boy? And where?'

Nick gave her the name of the motel in case she needed to reach him. 'I'll be here for at least one more night, probably two.'

'Don't tell me, the girl on the desk is a nineteen-year-old blonde who has a thing about Englishmen.'

'The girl on the desk is a man, and he isn't too happy with

me.' Nick explained about his run-in with the Ford, and later seeing Stone. He also told Alison about Tyson. 'Maybe it's a lead.'

'It's more likely to be trouble. Not Tyson or whatever his name is, but Stone. He's not going to go away, Nick, and that's your second warning.' Nick heard the anxiety in her voice.

'Don't worry, I'll watch my back.'

'And front and both sides, if you don't mind. Call me tomorrow?'

'Of course. And you can expect to see me a day or two afterwards, weather permitting. What's it like?'

'The snow's eased, but it's damned cold. I'm scrunched up in front of the fire with a book and a very large brandy, and I'm still freezing. Another hour of this and I'm heading for bed with my hot-water bottle or my vibrator. What the hell, I'll make it the water bottle. I can wait for the real thing.'

'Set that to music and you can sell it to Coco-Cola.'

'Take care,' said Alison, signing off.

'You too.'

SOUTH DAKOTA (ii)

Nick was awake at eight and breakfasted by nine. He postponed calling Avis until the evening and chose not to risk the Chrysler for his shopping expedition to Philip. Instead, he telephoned for a cab, asking the driver to wait while he kitted himself out with a pair of sturdy walking boots, cord trousers and a quilted parka. For good measure he added two thick sweaters and a leather cap with earflaps, charging all his purchases to his American Express card, and reminding himself that this trip had better pay off, otherwise Amex was going to have to wait for its money.

Tyson was as good as his word, arriving with the pick-up in front of the motel at five minutes to noon, where Nick was waiting for him, dressed to go. It was bitterly cold and the sky hung heavy with menacing black clouds, though so far today there had been no sign of snow. Tyson's 'twenty-four hours to think it over' seemed to have been resolved positively. At least, the previous evening's hesitancy was no longer evident.

'You're going to think this weird,' said Tyson, when they were heading west on US 14, 'but in a few minutes I intend asking you to blindfold yourself. There's a scarf on the dash. We've got a long ride, two and a half or three hours, and you might find it uncomfortable. But that's the condition. What I'm going to show you may have nothing to do with what you're looking for. If it isn't, that'll be the end of it. If it is, I don't want you writing about how you found it and incriminating me.'

'Incriminating?'

'All right, involving me.'

41

'I wouldn't anyway, not without your permission. The only rule professional journalists pay much attention to is the one about not revealing our sources.'

'Maybe. I prefer not to take that kind of chance, however. Okay?'

'Anything you say.'

'Right. Blindfold up now, then.'

Nick tied the scarf around his eyes, not attempting to cheat by leaving a gap at the bottom, which Tyson would not have been slow to spot. Although mystified by the request and half inclined to think that Tyson was melodramatizing, he experienced a flutter of excitement in the pit of his stomach. Maybe Tyson *did* have something to show him.

After a few miles of trying to gauge which way they were travelling and on what sort of roads by listening to the traffic sounds, he gave up and dozed off, sleeping fitfully until a sudden lurch almost pitched him into the windshield.

'Sorry about that,' said Tyson. 'We just left the last of the regular roads.'

Nick judged they were on some kind of rough track by the manner in which the pick-up was bouncing around.

'Are we nearly there?'

'Not far now. Then we walk.'

'What time is it?'

'Coming up to three.'

'Do I still have to wear this thing?'

'Only for a few more minutes. If you stretch forward you'll find a brandy flask under the dash. Help yourself.'

Nick did so, gratefully. He had lost some body heat while sleeping. Apart from that the outside temperature had dropped. He wished he had remembered to include gloves on his shopping list.

Ten minutes passed before Tyson brought the pick-up to a grinding halt, switched off the engine and applied the handbrake.

'You can look now.'

Nick unfastened the blindfold and blinked. Thick snow lay everywhere. They were in a wood or a forest, trees anyway at the foot of some high ground. There was nothing else, or anyone else, in sight. Nor was there any sign of a path

42

except the track they were on. This too, however, petered out a little way ahead.

Tyson slung a pair of binoculars around his neck. 'It'll be dark in an hour, less for us due to the trees. We'd better get going.'

'How will we find our way back in the dark?'

'We'll have these.' Tyson produced two powerful flashlights, one of which he handed to Nick. 'In any case, I know these hills.'

Which he obviously did, Nick thought several minutes later, for Tyson had unhesitatingly cut a path through the foot-deep snow, eighteen inches in places, until he reached a flowing stream, which was invisible from the pick-up. Its course was evidently their route upwards. Where water flowed, snow wouldn't collect.

The stream at this time of year was no more than a meandering trickle, with a depth of six inches. It would be a different matter when the spring thaw arrived. Then it would become a torrent.

For the first few hundred yards Nick attempted to emulate Tyson's example of stepping from rock to rock, keeping his feet dry. After a couple of falls which soaked his trousers, he abandoned the idea. Better wet feet than a sprained ankle.

After half an hour, always climbing, Tyson stopped. He waited for Nick to catch up.

'Brother, are you out of condition!'

'Manhattan living,' wheezed Nick, listening to his pounding heart and vowing to give up cigarettes and whisky, and join a squash club. He looked about him. They were still well below the timber-line and it was getting darker by the second. 'Are we there?'

'Not yet. Another ten minutes. I'll go slower from here on because I don't want to lose you. Nor do I want you to use your flashlight.'

'Who the hell's going to see it up here except maybe a deer or a bear?'

'Wait and see. Stick close.'

With Tyson never drawing further ahead than half a dozen paces, they followed the stream for another four hundred yards, climbing, in the process, one hundred and fifty feet. Nick plodded forward with his eyes firmly fixed on Tyson's waist. He was therefore only half aware that the ground was levelling off when he heard Tyson whistle softly. Looking up, he saw they were approaching a kind of plateau, from the far side of which, through the conifers and in what could only be a valley, light shone, artificial light. The closer they got, the stronger the light became, although it was impossible to identify the source because of the trees. Nick's immediate assumption was that they were nearing a village or hamlet. Not possible, his more rational self countered. Who'd be crazy enough to build up here? A lumber camp, perhaps?

He was considering all the possibilities when he collided with Tyson, who had stopped suddenly and was standing, legs apart, in the middle of the stream, which now broke right, snaking across the plateau between the trees. Recovering his balance, the ex-air force man gestured up front. Nick narrowed his eyes, squinting through the timber. The artificial light was being reflected off something metallic a hundred yards away. It took him a moment to work out that he was looking at a barbed-wire fence, eight or ten feet high, following the contours of the ground and extending in both directions for as far as his eye could see. At intervals large notices were attached to wooden stakes punched into the earth.

'Try these.' Tyson handed Nick the binoculars.

Nick adjusted the focus screw and trained the glasses on one of the notice-boards. The stencilled words leapt out at him.

> YOU ARE APPROACHING US GOVERNMENT PROPERTY. UNAUTHORIZED PERSONS ARE NOT PERMITTED TO PROCEED BEYOND THIS POINT. VIOLATORS ARE LIABLE TO BE SHOT ON SIGHT.

'Now perhaps you understand why I made you wear the blindfold,' said Tyson. 'I came across it by accident a few days ago. From what I can gather it's a military installation. With a difference. It wasn't here a month ago.'

'What kind of military installation?'

'You'll be able to see for yourself in a minute. The stream runs very close to the perimeter wire, just through there.'

'What about guards or dogs?'

'Not this side of the wire. We should be okay but keep your voice down.'

Baffled and intrigued, Nick followed Tyson and the stream, the light from the valley growing brighter and brighter the further they went and the closer they got to the barbed-wire fence. Finally Tyson halted and held up his hand. They were fifty feet from the fence and, apparently, that was as close as the stream came. Tantalizingly, the base of the fence was on slightly higher ground and the source of the light invisible from where they stood.

'This is as far as the stream takes us,' said Tyson. 'You'll have to wade through the snow. Keep your head down and take the glasses. I'll wait here.'

The packed snow came up to Nick's knees as he stumbled towards the fence. When he reached it and peered down into the valley, he grunted with astonishment, scarcely able to believe the evidence of his own eyes.

The floor of the valley was, he estimated, five hundred feet below his position. The light illuminating the area came from six watchtowers, the like of which he had seen a thousand times in old newsreels and motion pictures about World War II. Four of the towers stood at each corner of a barbed-wire compound, which was a rough rectangle measuring six or seven hundred yards by one hundred. The remaining two watchtowers were in the centre of each of the longer sides. The searchlights within the towers played slowly backwards and forwards, up and down.

At intervals throughout the compound were wooden huts, twenty in all. Milling around the huts, pacing up and down to keep warm, were men, women and, it seemed, children – all of them dressed in striped two-piece prison garb identical to that worn by the inmates of concentration camps in the Third Reich. On every garment was sewn a yellow Star of David. At the far end of the compound was a more substantial building, square in shape and dominated by two massive chimneys. To his horror Nick recognized it as a crematorium.

Walking among the prisoners (for what else could they be, Nick asked himself) were uniformed armed guards, each with a huge dog on a long chain. One of the dogs, apparently at the instigation of its handler, made a sudden dart for a group of prisoners, barking and snarling, fangs bared, held in check only by the chain around its throat. The sound of the guards' laughter drifted up to Nick, as did the terrified screams of the prisoners. Though not permitting the dog to attack, the guard nevertheless raised the billy-club he carried and lashed out at the defenceless group, cracking the nearest prisoner across the neck and shoulders and not stopping until the man sank to his knees.

Nick focused the binoculars on the guard, determined to commit his face to memory. He saw the brutal countenance of a man in his late twenties, scarred across his right cheek; a face straight out of Auschwitz or Dachau. For that matter, the entire incredible scene, though being enacted in present-day South Dakota, was right out of a Nazi extermination camp. Except for the guards' uniforms. They were not SS and neither were they American. He had seen something similar somewhere, but where? Then he had it. They were Russian uniforms. The guards were all wearing the uniform of the Red Army!

Completely engrossed by a sight totally beyond his comprehension, Nick failed to hear a branch snap some distance behind him. Nor, until it was repeated, did he hear a familiar voice call, very softly, 'Mr Tasker.'

He whipped round. Tyson was still standing where Nick had left him, and close by, cradling a rifle in his arms and leaning against a tree, was Frank Stone.

Nick understood in an instant that Stone and Tyson were far from strangers to one another; also, for some unknown reason, that they and others had conspired to lead him here, lead him by the nose.

'I don't understand,' he said slowly, aware that silhouetted against the camp lights he made a perfect target.

'You will, Tasker,' said Stone. 'You will.'

Stone was going to kill him. Nick didn't understand that either, but why else the rifle? For some reason best known to

Stone and Tyson, they were going to shoot him.

Except they were not if he could help it. Away from the lights of the camp the blackness was absolute. There, among the trees, he would be safe. Although he still had the flashlight, he doubted he could find his way down again, not unless he used the stream as a guide and that, of course, was what they would expect him to do if he managed to escape. He would have to spend the rest of the night in the hills, risk dying of exposure. But that gave him a chance of surviving. Stone, presumably, was offering none.

He struggled through the knee-deep snow towards Stone and Tyson, the latter now brandishing an automatic pistol. They let him come while backing off and keeping him covered. When he felt the stream lapping at his ankles, he knew he had to make a break for it immediately.

'I'm waiting for an explanation,' he said, and hurled the binoculars at them.

Keeping low and weaving, he stumbled downstream, falling every three or four strides. He thought he heard Tyson shout 'Don't shoot him!' and Stone responded 'I'll have to!' – and then the sudden crack of the rifle coincided with an unbearable pain in his chest and the warm, salty taste of blood in his mouth. Christ, he thought, pitching forward and striking his head against a boulder. Christ.

Then he was dead.

Three hours later Stone made a long-distance telephone call from a roadside booth. At the other end of the connection, Cassidy listened with growing annoyance to Stone's explanation of how Nick Tasker had died. That had not been part of the scenario.

He gave Stone precise instructions regarding the disposal of Nick's body, which was covered with a tarpaulin in Tyson's pick-up.

'Then clean out his room. Get someone to pay his bill. Leave no loose ends. Don't use Tyson,' Cassidy ordered. 'I need him there. Make other arrangements. I trust you can do that without fouling up.'

After cradling the handset Cassidy poured himself a drink and looked longingly at his open cigarette-box before irritably snapping the lid shut. He was already close to his self-imposed limit for the day, which was far from over yet.

Drink in hand, he opened the file on his desk and made marginal notes against several paragraphs. The names Coughlin and Garfield caught his eye, and he thought long and hard about those two individuals way into the small hours.

LONDON (i)

The overhead neon lighting flickered and died, throwing the small office into darkness. Susie, the junior of the two typists, said, 'Shit' in a loud voice as she hit several wrong keys on her electric IBM. Right at the end of the damned letter too! The Tipp-ex correcting strip would take care of the top copy but not the three carbons, two of which had to go out as ordinary mail. Well, she wasn't going to retype the whole thing at this time of the evening. She would finish off, remove the sheets, and amend the copies in ink if she could not realign them in her machine. Mr O'Brien could like it or lump it. This wouldn't happen if he would invest in a Xerox, but he was too mean for that.

While all this was going through her mind she had reached for a wooden pointer on the window ledge, stood on her chair, and, stretching, tapped the malfunctioning light. The actions were reflex, something she had evidently done on many occasions. After a moment the light came on again, and stayed on.

She remained on the chair until she was sure the office was not about to be plunged into darkness for a second time. She also remained there because she knew how attractive she looked from that angle, her short skirt revealing long, shapely legs. Her face was no more than average, she would be the first to admit, but her figure was excellent. Not that the other two occupants of the office were likely to notice. The senior typist was a dried-up old stick in her fifties, a spinster who had probably never had a man or wanted one. She gave Susie all the boring jobs such as making the tea, opening the morning mail, filing and fetching stamps from the post office. Susie retaliated by calling her 'Maud' instead of 'Miss Chambers', something she knew infuriated the older woman. Susie didn't care. At nineteen she cared for little other than hedonism, a word she would not have recognized.

As for Mr Dunbar, he was a real puzzle. His voice was that of an educated man, far too educated, she would have thought, to be employed as office manager by a middle-sized firm of Paddington builders. Office manager! That was a laugh. With only two typists to oversee he was no more than a glorified clerk, really, though to do him justice he never called himself office manager; only Mr O'Brien did that, to make the firm seem grander than it was. 'I'll get my office manager on to that.' 'You'd better talk to my office manager for the details.' Poor Mr Dunbar.

Susie was never quite sure why she thought of him as 'poor Mr Dunbar', but she did. He seemed so out of place here and had done for the eighteen months or so he had been employed by O'Brien, arriving just three months after she had joined the firm right out of secretarial school. She had told her mother about him, and her mother had offered the opinion that he was a gentleman fallen on hard times. Susie supposed that was true, though he never spoke about his past, about what he had done before he came to work for O'Brien, or received personal telephone calls. She suspected he had once been in the army – an officer, of course. Something about his manner suggested that. She had learned that he was forty when, on opening the mail one morning, she had seen a communication from the National Insurance people which gave his date of birth.

When any of her girl friends asked her about her job, for whom she worked, she invariably described Mr Dunbar as craggily handsome in a slightly rumpled, gone-to-seed way. (She had seen a hero similarly characterized in a magazine story, and had liked the description. It also suited Mr Dunbar.) His hair was dark, neither long nor short, with a few wisps of grey. She knew he was just under six feet tall because she was five feet eight in her high heels and still only came up to the bridge of his nose. He was broad across the shoulders without being too muscular, and slightly underweight. She guessed he didn't eat very much – no wife to look after him, she was certain. He did, however, drink. Each lunchtime he returned with the smell of whisky on his breath. He was nowhere near what she would call a drunk, but she supposed he spent his lunch hours in one of the pubs around Paddington Station, eating a pie and drinking a couple of whiskies. She had made it perfectly clear (she thought) that she would not refuse if he ever asked her to join him one midday or evening. He never did. Which was a shame since he was certainly good-looking enough to make any girl proud to be seen with him. What was more, she thought she could do something for him, make him happier. Not sex, though she doubted she'd say no if he propositioned her. In fact – something she would not admit to a living soul – she sometimes fantasized about him, imagined caressing him and calling him 'Alex, darling'. She guessed a lot of girls her age felt the same about their bosses, even though, strictly speaking, Mr O'Brien was her boss and not Mr Dunbar. For Mr O'Brien she would not so much as lift a finger, the fat, beer-swilling pig! Mr O'Brien had tried to paw her, put his hand up her skirt, at the Christmas drinks session – it couldn't be called a party – last year. He was making a thorough nuisance of himself until Mr Dunbar had sidled up to him and whispered something in his ear. After that, O'Brien hadn't bothered her again, though she had seen he was furious with Mr Dunbar. He hadn't done anything about it, however.

'Can't you ask Mr O'Brien to get us a new light or have this one fixed?' she said, still on the chair.

Alex Dunbar glanced up from his desk and smiled to himself when he saw Susie showing off her legs. 'I'll mention it again. Thanks for fixing it, Susie. You're the only one who knows the trick.'

Susie tossed her blonde curls and stepped to the floor, overhearing Maud mutter something about it not being the only trick she knew. She decided to ignore the old cow. It would be undignified to do otherwise.

Ten minutes later, with the letter in her typewriter corrected and placed in Mr O'Brien's tray, she collected her coat and umbrella from the rack, picked up the evening mail, and said good night. Maud ignored her, but Mr Dunbar gave her a slight nod and bade her good night also. She wished she were going out with him this evening instead of dull old Derek, who worked at Barclays. It would be the usual routine, a couple of rum and Cokes in the Green Man, the cinema or a disco, then back to Derek's place. Perhaps she wouldn't go to bed with him tonight.

At a quarter to six Alex glanced over his shoulder at Maud, who was adding up columns of figures with a pocket calculator.

'Finish off,' he said. 'We might as well get an early night.'

Although office hours were nine to five-thirty, both he and Maud regularly worked longer. Alex knew that Maud did so because she had nowhere to go apart from the Belsize Park double bed-sitter, her unmarried sister and a dreary evening in front of the television.

'Won't Mr O'Brien be coming back?'

'No. He's gone to Ealing to price a conversion. He'll probably go straight home from there. If not, he's got his own key.'

Maud packed away her things, donned her coat and a plastic hood over her hair, and made for the door.

'It's turning to sleet,' she said, peering out.

'It probably won't last.'

'You said that last night, and it did.'

'Well, we're all fallible and March can't last for ever. G'night, Maud.'

Alex timed his own departure for five to six. He had figured out long ago that it took him anywhere between four minutes twenty seconds and five minutes to walk to his usual pub, depending upon traffic. London opening hours were five-thirty to eleven, but he never liked to get there too early. In the first place, the frantic drinkers from the surrounding offices were always waiting outside at 5.29 and it was 5.45 before the first rush cleared. In the second place, his money wouldn't last if he got in too early.

The barman knew him by sight if not name.

'Evening, sir. Nasty weather. Usual?'

Alex nodded, and the usual appeared: a large whisky and water, no ice. Once served, he made his way to a corner table, where he took out his copy of *The Times* from a cheap briefcase. He had completed the crossword at lunchtime, read most of the newspaper, for that matter, but it was a kind of protection, *The Times*. He could prop it up against an ashtray, open at any page, and no one would take any further notice of him.

At the adjacent table bar one, a quartet of people – two men, two girls, all in their twenties – were discussing an advertising campaign. It was that sort of area. One of the girls, a dark-haired beauty who was well aware of her looks, had taken exception to something one of the men had said. 'I know your attitude, John. If women didn't have tits they'd be hunted.'

'And rightly so,' retorted the John in question, a beefy fair-haired individual with a petulant expression. 'Anyway, I've seen you batting your eyelashes and wiggling your hips to get an account. There's not much of the feminist about you, Liz, when the bottom line is a quarter of a million billing.'

Alex turned to the overseas news section, his eyes flicking across the page rapidly, interested particularly in stories filed from cities he knew. He found he was still able to read between the lines, judge what was really happening from just a few paragraphs. Occasionally he even recognized names from the past, names that were attached to embassy titles the holders did not actually warrant.

He sipped the second whisky slowly, making it last. The budget would only run to one more before he would be compelled to leave. He sometimes thought he was a fool to himself, spending as much at pub prices as would buy him half a bottle to drink at home. Then again, going home wasn't much fun.

While walking to the bar for his third drink, he accidentally bumped into the fair-haired John coming the other way. The collision was not Alex's fault. John was attempting to carry two foaming pints, two gins and two tonics in hands that were not designed for such a feat. He was also looking over his shoulder to see if he'd picked up all his change. Some of the beer spilled down his suit and he dropped one of the gins and a full tonic.

'For Christ's sake.'

'You weren't looking where you were going,' said Alex mildly.

'Don't give me that. You could see I had my hands full.' John went across to his own table, deposited the remains of the order and returned to retrieve the empty gin glass and tonic bottle from the floor. He tapped Alex, who was in the process of being served his third drink, on the shoulder. 'You know the rules. You knock something over, you replace it.'

'And so I would had it been my fault.' Alex paid for his drink and added water. 'Excuse me, you're in my way.'

John refused to budge. The man whose path he was blocking was his own height but fifteen years older and twenty pounds lighter. No problem. In his rugger-playing days he'd been considered a tough loose forward.

'I'll let you through when you've bought another gin and tonic,' he said. 'I'll forget about the mess you made of my trousers.'

'You're making a mistake,' murmured Alex. Out of the corner of his eye he observed that John's three companions were following the dialogue with keen interest, though the dark-haired beauty, Liz, seemed concerned and about to get to her feet.

'Really?' sneered John. 'We'll see about that.'

He planted both hands in the centre of Alex's chest as Alex tried to push past. Unhurriedly, Alex turned and put his drink on the bar. The pub was fairly crowded and no one was paying them any attention. Even the barman, who had heard the beginning of the argument, had been called away to serve another customer.

Alex was anxious to avoid trouble. The pub was convenient for his evening drinks and he wanted to continue using it, sitting quietly at his usual table. He did not want to draw attention to himself.

'I'm asking you nicely,' he said. 'Take your hands off me and let me through, and we'll forget all about it.'

'And I'm asking you just as nicely to pay for the drink you spilled.' John emphasized his request by pushing Alex, who reached up quickly and grabbed both the younger man's wrists, just as the dark-haired Liz loomed up.

Using his thumbs against the base of John's little fingers, Alex forced his wrists outwards and down, pressing against the joints. John had to bend his knees or suffer two broken hands. His cheeks reddened and his jaw dropped at the sudden, excruciating pain. He tried not to groan but couldn't help himself.

'You're hurting him, for God's sake,' said Liz.

Alex turned to her. The look in his eyes frightened her for a reason she was never able later to understand.

'I don't want to,' said Alex. 'Tell him to sit down and behave and I'll let him go.'

By this time John was almost on his knees and the rest of the pub was beginning to take notice.

'Do it, John, please,' urged Liz.

John nodded his acquiescence. There were tears forming, part pain, part humiliation. Alex let him go. He staggered off to his table, massaging his wrists. The pub went back to its own business.

'That was unnecessary,' said Liz.

'Agreed,' he said, surprising her.

'He's a fool and a loud mouth, but you could have broken something.'

'Someone will, one day, unless he learns to curb that temper. He might not be so lucky with the next man he offends.'

'Meaning that you're some kind of ultra-tough, macho saint, and that we should all be grateful to you, is that it?'

Alex gazed directly into her eyes, holding them locked to his. She tried to look away and found she couldn't.

'Meaning that it's not very bright to argue with strangers.'

Liz returned to her group, her expression one of puzzlement. She felt as if she had been hypnotized, though she knew that was not the case. Chastized too, verbally put firmly in her place without the man once raising his voice. She didn't like it; it made her feel uncomfortable. She was accustomed to controlling the men she met.

Alex swallowed the whole of his drink while standing at the bar, annoyed with himself for permitting a stupid hothead playing to the gallery to ruin his third whisky, which would normally have lasted another ten minutes. At one time he would have been able to avoid situations like that instinctively. He supposed he was out of practice.

He collected his briefcase and newspaper from where he had left them and walked towards the street door. John said, without much confidence, 'I'll remember you.'

'I hope you do,' said Alex sincerely. 'I really hope you do.'

Outside, the sleet turned to icy rain as Alex hurried home, a basement flat in one of the streets off the Bayswater Road, opposite Hyde Park and half a mile from Marble Arch. He paid thirty-five pounds a week for the privilege of living in central London, his accommodation consisting of a large bed-sitter, kitchen, bathroom and separate lavatory. The five-storey Georgian house of which the flat formed the base was occupied on a long lease from the Church Commissioners by a merchant banker, his wife and teenage daughters. Alex had lived there for eighteen months. He hardly ever saw his landlord except on rent days.

The first thing Alex noticed as he descended the ten steps to his front door was a chink of light shining through a vee in the drawn curtains; the next that the door itself was ajar. A dozen possibilities flashed through his mind, including the obvious one of burglars or his landlord's wife nosing around. What he did not expect to see was his former head of section standing with his back to the gas fire and drinking a cup of tea.

'Ah, you're here,' said Calderwood. 'I hope you don't mind, I let myself in rather than bother the good people above. You really should invest in a new lock. A child could open that one. I also made myself a cup of Earl Grey. A mug, I should say. Don't you run to cups and saucers? Personally I prefer Lapsang Souchong, but that of course would be quite unacceptable from a mug. You're looking thinner. Do come in and shut the door, my dear fellow.'

'Make yourself at home,' said Alex.

'I see you're still interested in Napoleon,' said Calderwood, inclining his head in the direction of two open volumes on Alex's small desk. 'Personally, I always thought General Foy was too kind to him in *Histoire de la Guerre de la Péninsule*, whereas Heilmann was absolutely honest in *Der Krieg in Deutschland und Frankreich*.'

'That was von Plotho,' said Alex.

'I beg your pardon?'

'Von Plotho wrote *Der Krieg in Deutschland und Frankreich*. The only work I know by Heilmann relating to the period is *Feldmarschall Fürst Wrede*.'

'Really? Ah well, military history was always your speciality, not mine.'

'What are you doing here?' asked Alex, removing his raincoat and hanging it on the rack.

'Passing, just passing. Well no, that's not strictly speaking true. Do you have anything to drink in the house, by the way? I looked earlier but could only find a third of a bottle of Johnny Walker. I didn't like to help myself as it seemed to be all you had. Water will do if the establishment doesn't run to soda. About half and half.'

Alex went out to the kitchen, where he poured an inch of whisky into each of two glasses, adding water from the tap. He didn't bother to ask himself the purpose of Calderwood's visit. Calderwood would tell him in his own good time.

Alex returned with the drinks. 'Sorry the glasses aren't crystal.'

The irony was lost on Calderwood. 'Not to worry, old chap. Cheers.'

He hadn't changed much in eighteen months, thought Alex. Perhaps a few more worry lines and a little more grey in the hair, but otherwise he was the same tall, thin, straight-backed patrician Alex remembered, a perfect facsimile of the archetypal upper-class Englishman as depicted by foreign cartoonists. From his beautifully groomed moustache down to the tips of his polished (but not too highly; that would be vulgar) shoes, it was hard to imagine him doing anything at weekends other than striding across rugged moorland with a stout blackthorn stick and a couple of muddy dogs yapping at his heels. He had an in-built disdain, which he did little to conceal, for anyone not of his background and social habits, which embraced just about everyone. He possessed positively no sense of humour, and his one saving grace was a keen mind – carefully hidden because being too clever was also vulgar. He had an absolute belief that the English were the only nation capable of governing themselves and others, and, some of his underlings said of him, had been seen to suffer physical pain when the passing of the British Empire was referred to. During World War II he had served with military intelligence, and afterwards, during the worst of the Cold War, with untrumpeted distinction in the field and behind a desk. When the SIS moved to Century House in Westminster Bridge Road in the late Sixties, Calderwood was given control of the Berlin desk. He was the man who originated the stratagem that all MI6's mail be addressed to a non-existent Mr G. H. Merrick at the Foreign Office, or PO Box 850. Alex had known him a long time, and admired him but didn't like him. He suspected Calderwood felt the same about him.

'I hear you're still drinking and getting into arguments with young men in public houses,' said Calderwood.

Alex wasn't surprised that Calderwood knew of the earlier incident. It was a ten-minute walk from the pub to his flat. Any of the other customers could have been one of Calderwood's men and phoned ahead to let Calderwood know that Alex was on his way.

'I'm not a drunk,' said Alex.

'I didn't say you were. I'm sure that's long past. Nevertheless, moderation in all things is my motto.'

'I gave up drinking completely once.'

'You did?'

'Yes,' said Alex slowly. 'It was the worst afternoon of my life.'

Calderwood looked at him blankly before understanding dawned. 'Oh, I see. It's a joke. Very good.' He was still standing in front of the gas fire, warming his backside. Or maybe, thought Alex, he thinks he might catch something if he sits down. In Calderwood's world, the basement was where the servants lived or unwanted furniture was stored. 'How's the job?'

'You know where I work?'

'Of course. We like to keep in touch with our old boys.'

'The job's fine. It's mechanical, doesn't tax me, and

provides me with just enough money to eat and drink and keep this place on.'

'Excellent. I'm delighted to hear it.'

Now apparently warm and unafraid of bugs in the upholstery, Calderwood left the fire and sat at the desk, placing his drink on a closed copy of General Rapp's *Mémoires Écrites Par Lui-Même*.

'If you don't mind,' said Alex.

'What? Oh yes.' Calderwood scoured the desk for a drinks coaster and, finding none, cradled his whisky. 'You were saying?'

'I wasn't saying anything. You, I believe, were about to tell me what you're doing here.'

'Was I? I don't recall that, but perhaps you're right. I mean, perhaps you're right in asking me to state my business. After all, I did break into your flat, didn't I? I suppose you'd be quite entitled to call the police and have me arrested.'

'Upon the which you'd show them that pass you carry and I'd doubtless be the one spending the evening behind bars.'

'Yes, there is that.' Calderwood looked pleased with himself. 'Upon the which, did you say? Such a fine turn of phrase you have, Alex. I always did like that about you. Upon the which. Almost Shakespearean.' He finished his drink and sat tapping his glass. Alex decided he was not going to refill it. 'I suppose I'm here on an errand of mercy, actually. Perhaps not mercy, but something akin. You have a brother, do you not?'

Alex started involuntarily. That was the last thing he had expected. He hadn't thought consciously about Nick for years.

'Yes, I have a brother. What about him?'

'I'm sorry to tell you he's dead. I'm equally sorry that I have to be the bearer of the bad tidings. In the Middle Ages you could have had me executed, assuming you were in a position of power, of course. The name he was using, as I understand it, was Tasker. He was living in New York and had been for some years, though he retained his British passport. The Americans contacted the Foreign Office as a matter of routine, enquiring about next of kin. The FO processed the matter in the usual way and, to cut a long story short, the papers landed on my desk when it was realized that Nick Tasker was Alex Dunbar's brother. I decided to see you in person, as I am one of the few people who know where you live. Also, the FO was more than a little concerned that someone in my section had a brother they knew nothing about. I must confess to a moment's apprehension myself. I checked your file. You mention a brother, naturally. What you did not mention is that he lived in the States and used the name Tasker. Your mother's maiden name, I believe.'

Alex examined himself for feelings and found no more than vague sadness; the sharp dagger of grief he had experienced on Melanie's death had emptied his emotional account. He hadn't seen Nick since the middle Seventies, almost ten years. They had been close as boys but had gradually drifted apart, Alex to the army and all that followed, Nick into journalism. Looking back, it was hard to believe they had shared the same parents. Alex was more like his father, another army man who had served with the Special Operations Executive during the war. Nick resembled his mother in character and looks. He had disapproved of Alex's connections with the security services, though never knowing precisely what his elder brother did. He had never seen eye to eye with his father, who had wanted him to join Alex in the army, which Nick had steadfastly refused to do, arguing, with some justification, that he would have made a lousy soldier.

There had been both major and minor disagreements between the two brothers though never a titanic row after which they had sworn not to see each other again. Rather, a gradual erosion of filial affection had taken place, with Nick going one way and Alex another. After their parents died, they had drifted apart completely.

'Yes, Tasker was our mother's maiden name,' said Alex. 'He used it professionally.'

'Why?' asked Calderwood. Sharply.

'I've really no idea.'

'Come, you must have some. Could it be that he disapproved of the way you earned your living?'

'I work for a builder's.'

'Don't be obtuse,' said Calderwood irritably. 'I mean before that.' He examined his empty glass, concluded it was to remain empty, and placed it on the desk, away from the books. As though regretting his display of irascibility, a luxury he rarely indulged in with subordinates past or present, he added, 'I mean, did your brother consider your previous occupation alien to his own beliefs? I'm not asking out of mere curiosity.'

'I suppose so,' answered Alex. 'Obviously I couldn't talk much about my job, but Nick knew what I did and didn't like it. Not just the cloak-and-dagger stuff. He couldn't see why I had joined the army at all.'

'He was a pacifist, then? Or a Communist?'

Alex resisted the urge to laugh. The idea of Nick being a Communist was risible. He had enjoyed his creature comforts as much as anyone, and more than most.

'No, he wasn't a Communist. Or even a pacifist the way you would use the word. His opposition to the army was more a manifestation of the pressures he grew up with than anything else. He was expected to join the army and didn't want to. He couldn't understand why I had.'

'I see,' said Calderwood thoughtfully.

Alex decided he needed another drink, which he could hardly have without offering Calderwood one. He brought in the remains of the Johnny Walker from the kitchen and a small jug of water.

'Help yourself,' he said, adding: 'You haven't yet told me the circumstances of Nick's death, how or where.'

'No, I haven't.' Calderwood watered his drink. 'The fact is, it wasn't an accident or natural causes. He was found shot outside Denver, Colorado. Two days ago.'

Alex was shocked. 'A mugging?'

'No. That's what makes the whole business so peculiar, vis-à-vis you, I mean. My information is that the weapon which killed him was a rifle. I haven't visited the United States for some years, but the last I heard the muggers were not using rifles. Odd, don't you think?' Before Alex could answer he went on: 'Do you know what he was working on, what he was currently writing about?'

'Of course I don't,' said Alex. 'How could I? I read one of

61

his books several years ago and saw a syndicated article he'd written on the Ku Klux Klan a while back. That's all. If you've done your homework you'll know we didn't keep in touch. Why, do you know what he was working on?'

'I do. I made it my business to find out as soon as I learned he was your brother. He'd published one long article on the rise of neo-Nazism in the States, and there were four or five more in the pipeline. I believe at least one of them attempted to establish a connection between American Nazis and the European variety, especially the clandestine German kind. Now I find that somewhat alarming. A journalist writing about German Nazis has a brother who was once an exceptional operative in Berlin. Then the journalist is found dead, killed by a rifle bullet. My sixth sense prickles, Alex, it positively prickles.'

Alex snorted with disbelief. 'You're trying to create a conspiracy where none can possibly exist. I haven't been in the business for almost two years, and I wasn't operational for two years before that. Whoever shot Nick for whatever reason can have nothing to do with me.'

'Perhaps,' mused Calderwood. 'Then again, perhaps not. Look, are you doing anything for the next couple of hours?'

'No,' said Alex cautiously.

'Splendid. I passed what looked like a decent Italian restaurant on the way down. Perhaps you'd allow me to buy you dinner.'

'I wouldn't have thought you and Italian dinners mixed. Especially not at this hour.' The time was barely seven o'clock.

'Ordinarily you'd be right on both counts. However, tonight I intend to make an exception.'

'Why?' asked Alex, knowing he was going to accept the invitation. His fridge contained only cheese and eggs, and there was precious little more in his larder than baked beans and soups. Besides, the whisky bottle was empty.

'No particular reason,' said Calderwood, 'apart from a natural anxiety to set my mind at rest concerning any possible connection between your brother's unfortunate death and your time in Berlin. I'm also instructed to tell you the date and place of his funeral, and who to contact regarding his estate. He wasn't a rich man, I gather, but there's a lease on an apartment to be considered as well as his personal possessions. My information is that he wasn't married, which makes you his sole heir if he died intestate.'

'You seem to have found out an awful lot in forty-eight hours.'

'In much less than that, old chap, much less. But just think of it as part of my job.'

LONDON (ii)

An hour and a half later, over the remains of a bottle of Lachryma Christi, Calderwood said, 'I always thought the department treated you rather shabbily in view of your record in Germany. And Ireland, of course. You were very good in Ireland.'

'Nobody was good in Ireland. We wouldn't still be there otherwise.'

'Government policy, old chap.' The restaurant had filled up since eight o'clock and Calderwood was keeping his voice down. 'We could have wiped out the Provisional IRA ten years ago, but it's useful training for the troops for when the street violence really hits this country.'

'The new dark age?'

'Precisely. You know it's coming as well as I do. Anyway, you were good. Just thought I'd mention it in case no one did at the time. I tried to keep you behind that desk, of course, arguing that every man's years in the field are limited but that you could still do a first-class administration job or perhaps pass on your operational experience to the younger chaps at Fort Monkton or Borough High Street. I'm afraid I was overruled, even though everyone was most sympathetic. Nonetheless, revoking your pension was, in my view, most uncharitable.'

'I don't want to talk about it,' said Alex.

It still hurt, even after four years, remembering how Melanie's body had been discovered in a back alley in the Berlin suburb of Zehlendorf. She had been raped before her attackers had killed her.

He hadn't wanted her in Berlin at all. Even Calderwood,

64

he recalled, had advised against it. But she was a private citizen, stubborn and strong-willed, and had insisted. 'I've been a service wife for six years and I've only spent one anniversary with my husband. This year I'm going to make it two.' They found her corpse the day before the anniversary; they never found her killers. She was only going out, she told Alex, for a couple of hours' sightseeing; she had never visited Berlin before.

At first he had suspected the East Germans or the KGB of paying off old scores, yet there was never any proof to link either to the murder. Nevertheless, for three days after her death Alex waged a personal vendetta against everyone he knew who had connections with the East, even to the extent of compromising his own cover and jeopardizing carefully built-up networks. While he didn't actually kill anyone, he handed out severe beatings to several men before his own people caught up with him and flew him home under sedation.

After a long period of sick leave, they put him behind a desk and tolerated his bouts of drunkenness and absenteeism for almost two years before taking disciplinary action prior to showing him the door and rescinding his pension rights. He had become a liability and the Firm had no further use for him.

For the next six weeks he spent his life in pubs. At closing time or when he was barred as a troublemaker, he moved on to drinking clubs. He was dimly aware that he was being tailed day and night for fear, now that he had lost his anchor, he would try to return to Berlin and take up where he had left off in the search for his wife's killers. Although security officers at all the major airports and seaports had his name, photograph and passport number on their stop list, his former masters were well aware that he was a trained operative able to use his initiative. They didn't trust him not to take a day-trip to France and try to reach Berlin overland. It would not have been the first occasion he had crossed East Germany undetected.

When his money began to run out and he was on the point of being evicted from his digs for non-payment of rent, he knew he had to get a job. His only qualifications were fluent

German, adequate French, and almost twenty years in the services, his postings during the majority of which he could not itemize on a curriculum vitae. The Firm had an entire department which specialized in finding positions for ex-officers who could not reveal too much of their background, but it refused to help. Furthermore, jobs he applied for independently suddenly proved to be filled at the interview. The solution, he knew, was to quit drinking heavily and let it be known that he was no longer interested in making trouble. When he reduced his daily consumption to just a few drinks and stayed at home evenings, the next job he applied for, with O'Brien, he obtained. He never found out whether someone had had a quiet word with O'Brien; nor did he care.

During his first week at the office, an anonymous voice on the telephone suggested that it might be a good idea if he moved house, switch to a neighbourhood where no one knew him, start again. If he agreed and cared to present himself at a certain address in Bayswater, he would find there was a flat to let at a not unreasonable rent. Whether the merchant banker upstairs had any connections with the Firm, he never ascertained. Alex suspected he did. The Firm had contacts in all kinds of places.

From time to time during his initial months with O'Brien, he was conscious of still being under surveillance. But shortly before Christmas the same year his shadows disappeared, presumably satisfied that his drinking was under control and that he no longer represented a security threat. Until this evening, he had never met anyone from the Firm since his dismissal.

'Yes, most uncharitable, that business about your pension,' Calderwood repeated. 'Especially as the Treasury, because we don't officially exist, has yet to find a way to tax it. A few extra thousands a year without levy is a godsend in these days of rampant inflation. Makes all the difference between living comfortably and simply existing.' He paused to be sure he had Alex's undivided attention. 'It's not out of the question that yours could be reinstated.'

Alex began to get an inkling of why Calderwood was treating him to dinner. He surmised his answer would be negative, whatever the question, but as Calderwood was footing the bill he elected to hear him out. He was still relatively young with not much future ahead of him. He could certainly find a use for those extra thousands, providing there were not too many strings attached.

'How?' he asked.

Calderwood grunted with satisfaction at crossing the first hurdle without argument. 'Not here,' he said. 'Too many ears. We'll go to my club.'

He settled the bill – in cash, Alex observed – and added a miserly tip. Once outside they walked down to the Bayswater Road, where they were fortunate to find a vacant taxi almost immediately. 'Piccadilly,' Calderwood told the driver, saying no more until he and Alex were ensconced behind two stiff brandies in the club's smoking-room.

'As I said earlier,' Calderwood opened, 'when I made the connection between Nick Tasker and Alex Dunbar, I was less than happy. No, please bear with me,' he hurried on, as Alex shook his head. 'There's more to this than meets the immediate eye, as you will soon learn.'

He steepled his fingers while arranging his thoughts.

'Item: Nick Tasker was investigating neo-Nazism in the States and Europe, particularly Germany. Item: you were once active in Germany in general and Berlin in particular. Item: Tasker is shot dead by a rifleman. Item: our American friends in the intelligence community have been making their presence felt much more than usual in Berlin in recent months, contacting – though infiltrating is probably the *mot juste* – underground right-wing groups which, if some of them no longer call themselves Nazis, undoubtedly espouse the same odious political doctrines as Hitler. Item: via a Berlin source I am not at liberty to divulge we have come across the code word Cougar on half a dozen occasions since the Americans stepped up their Berlin activity. At least, we assume it to be a code word, although we don't know what it means. Item: the Americans are up to something in Berlin which they're calling Cougar and which probably involves neo-Nazi groups. Item: your brother may have stumbled across what it is, by accident or design, during his investigations. Conclusion: which was why he was killed.'

'By the Americans, the Company?' said Alex incredulously.

'Or by the neo-Nazis they're interested in. Yes.'

'Christ, that's a leap in the dark. It wouldn't stand up in court.'

'Perhaps not.' Calderwood smiled thinly. 'Anyway there's more.'

'Before you go on,' interrupted Alex, 'why don't you simply ask the Americans what Cougar is? Or don't we co-operate any longer?'

'Not as much as we might. Since Blunt was unearthed as the fourth man and the newspapers have speculated on a fifth and sixth, the Americans have become a little wary about sharing intelligence. They've never really forgiven us for Philby. Besides, Cougar could be a maverick operation not sanctioned by the Director. We'd really like some hard facts before demanding an explanation, otherwise they'll tell us to go to blazes and mind our own business or, much more seriously, request details of *our* current independent undertakings, which could be embarrassing.'

Alex nodded. Nothing much had changed, it appeared, in two years. 'You said there was more.'

'There is. The department has had men in New York and elsewhere working round the clock on this for the last twenty-four hours.

'Your brother was found with a full set of documents in his wallet – which seems to rule out robbery even if being killed with a rifle doesn't. The Denver police informed the New York police, who set the appropriate wheels in motion on discovering your brother was British. When the Foreign Office dumped the whole lot in my lap and we had confirmed the relationship between the pair of you, I had a man visit your brother's New York address, purporting to be from our embassy. He found a girl there, a Miss Alison Cameron. She's some sort of famous model, I believe, though I confess I have very little interest in such matters. She had paid for, or was in the course of paying for, your brother's body to be flown to New York for burial, which makes her rather more than a casual friend. She was also in a state of great distress and bewilderment, telling my man that she couldn't understand how your brother could have been found in Denver when he had telephoned her the night before his body was discovered from somewhere in South Dakota. I forget where offhand. He had flown to South Dakota, she said, on a story concerned with the series on neo-Nazism he was writing. He had told her on the telephone that he intended staying in South Dakota for a few more days. He had even given her the address and phone number of his motel in case she needed to reach him. He would not have left for Denver, she insisted, without telling her. Her conclusion, one I share, was that he had been killed somewhere near 'where he was staying and his body transported to Denver to throw the police and any other investigative agencies off the scent.'

Calderwood fumbled in a pocket for his pipe, which he proceeded to fill from a well-worn tobacco pouch. He struck a match but blew it out immediately.

'Now I don't know how you read all that,' he said. 'To me there's more here than an ordinary killing. A normal killer would not take the trouble to transport his victim's body several hundred miles across various state boundaries with all the risks inherent in such an operation. A normal killer would either panic and run like hell or dispose of the body on the spot. Tasker's murder bears all the signs of being planned and executed by an organization as opposed to an individual. An organization, moreover, with large resources. I'm sorry, I didn't mean to make it all sound so brutal and clinical. I keep forgetting he was your brother.'

Alex acknowledged the apology with a faint shrug. After so many years' estrangement he too found it difficult to absorb that the subject under discussion was his own flesh and blood. He was also disinclined to accept Calderwood's interpretation of events. That something out of the ordinary had led to Nick's death seemed beyond question, but it did not, on the data to hand, amount to a conspiracy.

'By a large organization you're presumably referring to the Company, the CIA,' he said, making it a statement.

'I am.' Calderwood nodded his head vigorously. 'I know they're not supposed to operate domestically, but there again neither are we and we do – if we can manage it without our opposite numbers in Curzon Street finding out. It has to be the CIA or someone they're protecting. There's no other link between your brother, neo-Nazis, Berlin and the mysterious Cougar.'

'You're jumping to conclusions again. Nick's death might not be connected in any way. In fact, the evidence you've presented points strongly in the opposite direction. The CIA wouldn't have left documents on a body. They wouldn't have left a body at all. If Nick was killed because he was making a nuisance of himself, he would have quietly disappeared or his death made to look like an accident.'

Calderwood tutted impatiently. 'They're not infallible, Alex. God knows, none of us is. We've all made mistakes. However, if I were to consider offering a prize for general incompetence the CIA would be a front-runner. Their top people in planning are splendid; their field operatives little more than plainclothes policemen.'

'Talking of which,' said Alex, 'has this Miss Cameron told the police of her suspicions?'

'She has, is my information. She also wanted to bring in the FBI. I'm not familiar with American law, but as I understand it a murder which involves the crossing of state boundaries is a federal offence. The police were not inclined to take her seriously, certainly not to the extent of calling in the FBI. She talked quite freely to my man, believing that the embassy might bring some pressure to bear on the local and federal authorities. Both the Denver and New York police naturally accept that a murder has taken place. Neither force concedes that his death had anything to do with the story he was working on. How can they, without concrete proof? Dozens of murders occur daily in the United States. The police have learned to live with the fact that a great majority of them will never be solved.'

'How do they explain his body turning up in Denver?'

'They can't. They are, however, unwilling to admit that he was spirited there after being killed elsewhere. My man spoke to them also. They checked with his South Dakota motel. The management says his bags were removed and his room vacated some time during the evening of the day following his call to Miss Cameron. An envelope paying for his accommodation, in cash, was left at the desk. No one saw by whom. A call was made to the people he hired his car from, telling them where it could be collected, which was near the bus station in somewhere called Sioux Falls. He'd signed a credit card slip for the hire apparently, so that would automatically be paid by the credit card company. There was some mention of damage to the car. The police see no mystery other than the identity of his murderer. He checked out of his motel, paid his bill and drove to the bus station. As far as the police are concerned he left South Dakota under his own steam, whether by bus or a prearranged lift they have no way of telling.'

'But you don't believe all that?'

'I do not. For example, why did he settle his motel account in cash yet pay for his car hire with a credit card? Why did no one see him leave? It smells, Alex. I'm more of a mind to believe Miss Cameron's story, which dovetails neatly with my own theory concerning CIA involvement. I'll accept the police version only if they provide incontrovertible proof.'

'What do you want of me?' asked Alex, although he thought he already knew the answer to that.

'Ah,' said Calderwood, peering at him slyly over the rim of his brandy snifter. 'Do I have to spell it out for you? Yes, perhaps I should. We – I – would like you to fly to New York within forty-eight hours. The funeral, I am informed, is to take place two days from today. I'm sure you'd like to be there – not only to pay your last respects but to tidy up your brother's estate. While in New York I would ask you to question Miss Cameron in greater detail, get her to tell you the whole story as she sees it. Then go through your brother's papers, his notes. Make a list of the names he mentions, the places he visited in the course of writing his series on neo-Nazism. You know the routine. If you deem it necessary go to South Dakota, to where he stayed. Hunt around, ask questions. Who did he talk to and when. Who did he meet. You've done it a thousand times in the past.'

'And who'll be paying for all this?'

'We would, the department. You'd be taken back on strength on a temporary basis, perhaps permanently if you so desired and everything went according to plan. You were

71

a damned good man, Alex, one of the best we ever had. You suffered a fearful loss and naturally went to pieces. We couldn't do other than get rid of you.' Calderwood smiled reassuringly. 'But that's in the past.'

'Why me?' asked Alex. 'Never mind how good I was, I was fired. Doubtless there's an entry on my file that says I'm unreliable. I've been out of the field for four years and out of the business entirely for two. I'm rusty, out of touch. I'd ask the wrong questions. If the CIA are involved I'd be blown in five minutes. I wouldn't even see them coming.'

Calderwood did not agree. 'You underestimate yourself, Alex. I'll guarantee you'll be your old self twenty minutes after you're back in harness.'

'That's not a guarantee you'd find a bank accepting as collateral. You must have a dozen men who could do the job better, including the phoney embassy man who has already established himself with Miss Cameron. He has the added advantage of being on the spot.'

'If I did have a dozen men who could do what I require, I'd use one of them.' Calderwood put a match to his pipe. When it was going he continued, 'You're tailor-made for what I need. You're the dead man's brother. You can ask questions without anyone suspecting you're interested for reasons other than family ones.'

Perhaps, thought Alex. However.

'What if it doesn't end in New York or South Dakota?' he wanted to know. 'What if there *is* something in this theory of yours that connects Nick to Cougar and Berlin? What if the answers you're looking for can be found only in Berlin? The last I heard, I was *persona non grata* in the city.'

'Only because you'd embarked upon a one-man war that was threatening to destroy in a week networks and agents it had taken us years to establish. If the answers lie in Berlin, that's where you'll go.' Calderwood leaned forward confidentially. 'Its perfect for you, Alex. Berlin was your beat. You had a feel for the city and the undercurrents of our interests there which was uncanny. You were as much at home in Berlin as you are in London.'

Calderwood could see he was not getting through.

'Look,' he said, 'if you no longer want to work for us on a

72

permanent basis, treat this as a temporary assignment. When it's over or you reach a dead end, you're a free man again, if that's what you elect to be. Consider it from this angle – the government will be paying you to find out who killed your brother. The moment you agree to rejoin us you will be granted full privileges and pay at your former rank. Also, at the end of the day I shall make it my personal business to see your pension is restored with absolutely no conditions attached. Go to America for us, Alex. Follow this through. We need you. Anyone else will be second best.'

'You seem to forget I have a job. I can't just fly off to New York at the drop of a hat.'

'Temporary leave of absence can be arranged,' promised Calderwood mysteriously, leaving Alex in no doubt that the Firm had somehow influenced O'Brien into taking him on in the first place. 'If you want it, your job will be waiting for you when you're finished, mark my words.'

Alex had marked them well for the past three hours. In the last analysis, however, he was not at all sure he wanted to rejoin the department, for a one-off assignment or otherwise. While he would be the first to admit that he had behaved in an extraordinarily irresponsible manner for the two years following Melanie's death, the Firm, although quite entitled to dispense with his services, had, in his view, overstepped its authority by rescinding his pension. Unfortunately in such cases, the injured parties had no right of appeal. Nor could they publicize their grievances by talking to the newspapers, whose editors had a long list of standing instructions when it came to security matters. The department needed him now and was apparently willing to make amends. The question was, did he need the department?

He could, he supposed, fake accepting Calderwood's offer and use department funds to go to New York and attend Nick's funeral. Then, after a few days, he would fly back and inform Calderwood that there was nothing to be learned. The trouble with that was that Calderwood wouldn't believe him, would see straight through the stratagem. And as Alex knew from past experience, Calderwood could make a lot of trouble when offended.

Nor was he sure he wanted to be at the graveside. The dead were dead. Paying one's last respects, as Calderwood put it, to a brother he hadn't seen for a decade amounted to hypocrisy. Any tidying up of Nick's estate could be accomplished by mail or be left to Miss Cameron, who, if Calderwood's account of her distress was accurate, was entitled to whatever Nick had owned, whether or not he had made a will.

About the only advantage in Calderwood's offer was the chance to return to Berlin. Melanie's killers' trail would now be very cold indeed, but during the last four years, especially when he was feeling particularly bitter, he had comforted himself with the thought that one day he would track down and eliminate the men who had taken her life and destroyed his.

'I'd like to think about it for a while,' he said.

'By all means. Overnight?'

'I was thinking more in terms of a week.'

Calderwood frowned. That did not suit him at all.

'The funeral's the day after tomorrow,' he said. 'Surely you want to be there? Miss Cameron is bound to be, but after that who knows? After that she may go away.'

'Nevertheless, I want a week.'

Over a second brandy, Calderwood marshalled impressive arguments against such a lengthy delay. To no avail. Alex stubbornly refused to be railroaded into a hasty decision.

'Very well,' said Calderwood eventually, emptying his glass and tapping the tobacco from his pipe, 'a week it is.' He was clearly annoyed. 'I'm still at the same number if you change your mind in the meantime.'

Alex was faintly surprised that Calderwood had given in so easily, without more of a fight or even tacit threats. His ex-chief's determination always to have his own way was legendary.

LONDON (iii)

When Alex returned to work from lunch the following day, O'Brien called him into his office, which was separated by a partition from the general office. The beefy Irishman did not invite him to sit down.

'There was a mistake on the Black Bull Hotel estimate,' he said gruffly, pushing a document across the desk. 'You left out a whole page of figures, eight hundred pounds' worth. Now they want me to keep to the figures we quoted or we lose the business. So what have you got to say about that?'

Alex examined the estimate. He remembered checking it after Susie had typed it a week earlier. There had been nothing wrong then.

He flicked to the back page. Where the bottom line, when it had left his hands, had clearly indicated a carry-forward figure with the word 'sub-total', now 'sub-total' had been amended to 'total' and two thick lines drawn underneath.

'They're trying to pull a fast one,' he said. 'Look, you can see where they've changed it. They've removed the last page.'

'Think again, Dunbar,' said O'Brien nastily. He tossed over the office copy, which was also missing the last page. Again, however, 'sub-total' had been changed to 'total'.

'I don't understand,' said Alex, genuinely puzzled. 'Someone's doctored both copies.'

'Doctored my arse! And I understand only too bloody well! You came in pissed one afternoon. Instead of doing the job I pay you to do you let a wrong estimate go out, costing me eight hundred quid or a lost job. You probably had your hand up the skirt of that stupid young tart Susie who typed

75

this.'

'Now wait a minute,' said Alex.

'Don't wait a minute me!' roared O'Brien. 'Are you trying to tell me you don't have a few drinks every lunchtime? Christ, the office reeks of whisky after two o'clock.'

'What I drink and when I drink has nothing to do with you.'

'It does when mistakes like this happen. Anyway, it's the last time. You're fired. You can clear out right away. We'll send you what we owe you.'

'You can't do that,' said Alex, dismayed.

'I can and I have. Collect your things and get out. If you're still on the premises in ten minutes I'll call the police and have you prosecuted for trespass.'

Alex suddenly saw daylight. That O'Brien was enjoying himself enormously, never having forgotten the Christmas incident when Alex had told him to leave Susie alone, was neither here nor there. O'Brien was not firing him out of malice or because of an obviously falsified document. O'Brien had been got at. Calderwood had not given up so easily after all.

'Don't ever let me see you on a street corner late at night,' said Alex quietly.

Maud and Susie had overheard most of the row through the thin partitioning, and Susie her own name mentioned.

'What did I do wrong, Mr Dunbar?' she asked anxiously, watching with growing disbelief as Alex packed his things into his briefcase. Surely the fat slob hadn't sacked Mr Dunbar?

'Nothing Susie. Nothing at all. It's high time I moved on anyway.'

Alex collected his coat from the rack by the door. Susie, he noticed, seemed about to burst into tears, and even Maud's eyes looked a little moist.

'Take care of yourself,' he said to the girl. 'You too, Maud.'

Outside he made for the Great Western Hotel, where he knew he would find a telephone that had not been vandalized. He announced his name to the operator and asked to be put through to Calderwood, who was evidently waiting for his call.

'You bastard,' said Alex.

Calderwood took the execration in his stride. 'I need you with me, Alex,' he said, not troubling to insult Alex's intelligence by feigning innocence. 'A week's too long.'

'I don't have to rejoin you. I can find myself another job.'

'I wouldn't count on it. Remember the bother you had last time? It could happen again. Besides, before you turn me down there's something you should see. I would have shown it to you last night, but I didn't want to open up old wounds. It concerns Melanie's death. Shall we say the bar of the Grosvenor Hotel, Victoria, at six thirty? It shouldn't be too crowded at that hour.'

A little before six Calderwood kept an appointment with O'Brien under the clock at Victoria Station. The Irishman had met Calderwood, whose real name and occupation he did not know, on only two previous occasions, and he freely admitted to himself that the man scared him stiff.

'You did well,' said Calderwood in normal conversational tones, secure in the knowledge that the homegoing commuters were more interested in their trains than in eavesdropping. 'I'll pass it on to those concerned.'

'And I'll hear no more from the Inland Revenue?'

'Probably not.'

'Only probably? I'd like a letter or something from them telling me I'm off the hook.'

'I'm sure you would. I'd like a few hundred acres in Norfolk and twin silver-mounted Holland and Hollands, but life, regrettably, does not consist of a series of agreeable gifts commensurate to services rendered. We can't always have what we want. No, I don't think our tax-collecting friends are likely to write you a formal letter of exoneration, although I don't suppose you'll hear from them again providing you behave and don't in future fail to enter cash payments as accountable receipts.'

'I won't.'

'I'm delighted to hear it. It's been estimated that undeclared income – or the black economy as the Treasury likes to call it – costs the country two thousand million pounds a year in lost revenue. Honesty is always the best

77

policy, I've found. Tell the truth and shame the devil my mother used to say. Where is it you catch your train for? Sevenoaks, I think you said. I know it well. Good yeoman stock down there, backbone of England. Well, I won't keep you.'

O'Brien hesitated. 'Is our business finished – you, me, Dunbar?'

'I expect so. However, one never knows, does one? I'll be in touch if I need you again.'

O'Brien watched him march smartly off, shoulders back, chin up, in the direction of the station entrance to the Grosvenor. He came to the same conclusion Alex Dunbar had a few hours earlier. Bastard.

Alex was a few minutes late owing to the heavy traffic at that time of the evening. Calderwood was at the corner table, on his second gin and tonic. There were only half a dozen other customers in the large bar.

'I ought to punch your head,' said Alex, sitting down.

'I'd feel the same in your position. I bought you a whisky, by the way. I'm afraid the ice has melted. Believe me, I didn't want to involve you with O'Brien in what must have been a distasteful charade. You left me no alternative, however. How did he go about it?' Alex told him. Calderwood snorted with disgust. 'The man has no finesse. He really will have to try harder in future or pay the penalty.'

'What have you got on him?'

'A little cooking of the books. We began liaising with the Inland Revenue about the time you left us, I think. Amazing what they turn up for us and how anxious the transgressors are to atone for their venality, do the department a small favour here and there rather than face a hefty fine or even a prison sentence. The tax boys took some convincing at first that they should co-operate, but they were leaned on from a great height and eventually agreed to give it a try. After all, we all work for the same political masters, do we not?'

'Don't include me in that,' said Alex. 'I can still tell you to go to hell if I don't like what I hear, take my own chances.'

'Of course you can,' soothed Calderwood. 'Somehow, however, I don't think you will.'

78

From his briefcase he extracted a thin file in a manila folder, which he passed across the table. The typewritten legend on the outside gave Alex a terrible jolt. It read: *Subject – Melanie Dunbar (deceased)*.

The contents of the folder comprised two documents. The first, a summary of the investigation into Melanie's murder, signed by a high-ranking West Berlin police officer from the political liaison division, and dated a week after her body was found. It was written in German with an English translation alongside. The second document was draft notes for an internal memorandum compiled by the CIA Berlin station chief for the Deputy Director of Operations, Langley. Placing the folder on the table because his hands were shaking, Alex began with the police version of events, reading it in the original German.

According to the porter who ordered her a taxi, Melanie Dunbar left the Basel Hotel on the Kurfürstendamm some time between 12.20 and 12.30 on the afternoon of her disappearance. Since Mrs Dunbar was a striking-looking brunette, aged thirty-two but seeming younger, Detective Schneider had no difficulty tracing the taxi driver, who took her to the Tiergarten Zoological Gardens, dropping her at the main entrance before one p.m.

Schneider made exhaustive enquiries at the Zoo, eventually finding an employee, Hans-Willi Leibnitz, who thought he recognized a photograph of Mrs Dunbar. Leibnitz further thought he had seen Mrs Dunbar talking to two men in the vicinity of the lion enclosure. Leibnitz could not say whether or not the men were German, but they must have spoken good English because, as I understand it, Mrs Dunbar had no foreign languages. Regrettably, at the time of writing the two men have not been traced. Nor did Schneider find any evidence to suggest that Mrs Dunbar took a taxi *from* the Zoo. The implication, therefore, is that she chose to walk or was offered a ride.

A report from another division reached Schneider's desk on the 25th. An eyewitness had made a statement to the effect that a woman answering Mrs Dunbar's description was seen entering the Grünewald accompanied by two men around three p.m. the day she disappeared. The local division had naturally made enquiries in the area of the forest because it is so close to Zehlendorf, where the body was found. The eyewitness, Frau Lotte Dreyer, claimed that the woman she had seen appeared to be drunk. It should be noted that this particular section of the Grünewald is a notorious lovers' rendezvous.

The above information all came to my attention on the 26th, when, after making several telephone calls, I immediately took Detective Schneider off the case upon confirming that Mrs Dunbar was the wife of Alex Dunbar, who is known to this office. There could be political overtones to the murder, although I must emphasize that, at present, there is no evidence to support such a contention.

To conclude, I suggest we allow the matter to lie fallow for a week. If at the end of that period there is no indication that this is other than an ordinary killing, I further suggest that Detective Schneider be allowed to continue his investigations.

The police summary, a photocopy, ended there, with no indication whether and in what manner Detective Schneider had proceeded. He had, in any event, been unsuccessful.

Alex turned to the draft notes compiled by the CIA station chief. From the style and content it was obvious that they had been dictated and that what Alex was reading was a verbatim transcript. It also became apparent that the draft notes had remained exactly that; that no formal report was ever submitted to Langley. The transcript was dated the day after Melanie was found.

We have a domestic problem here concerning field agents Coughlin and Garfield, who've got themselves into something of a jam. They picked up an Englishwoman at the Zoo on the 22nd. Melanie Dunbar, who I've since learned from a contact at police headquarters is the wife of Alex Dunbar, who works for Six. After a few drinks Coughlin suggested to Mrs Dunbar, a stranger to Berlin, that he and Garfield show her some of the sights. She agreed, commenting to Garfield that she was bored. She made no mention of her husband's occupation.

They had drinks in several more bars, drove to the Grünewald for a walk, then, around five p.m., all headed for Coughlin's apartment, where Mrs Dunbar consented to have sex with both operatives. According to Garfield's testimony Mrs Dunbar then said she felt ill, nauseous. She went to the bathroom, where they heard her vomiting. Coughlin wanted to get her back on the streets right away, but she passed out on the bed. The two men opted to let her sleep it off, and went out for something to eat. When they got back at seven Mrs Dunbar was dead. She had apparently choked on her own vomit.

Coughlin and Garfield panicked. They waited until dark, took Mrs Dunbar down to the car, and drove her over to Zehlendorf, where they disarranged her clothes before leaving her in an alley, making it look as if she was a rape victim. Doubtless the post-mortem will determine the precise manner of her death, though there will be nothing to indicate that she did not die in the alley after a sexual assault.

Coughlin and Garfield then went home and slept on it until today, when they concluded they'd better come clean with me in case they had been seen. I've put them on the first plane to Washington, carrying classified material which had to be returned to Langley anyway. If I elect to make this report formal, I suggest (a) that no disciplinary action be taken against either man, whose stories I accept; (b) that they be given every lousy job under the sun for as long as possible. Either way, they are to be relocated in another sphere of operations.

The draft notes finished there, though there was an addendum written by hand and dated ten days later, and a signature. The addendum said: *Leave it off the record. Better that way. Police are getting nowhere.* The signature was Lionel M. Cassidy.

'I'm sorry,' said Calderwood, when Alex closed the folder. 'I rather hoped you'd never have to see that.'

Alex got to his feet slowly, his face ashen. He hurried towards the men's room where he locked himself in a cubicle. He felt better after being sick. While rinsing his mouth at one of the wash basins, under the contemptuous gaze of the cloakroom attendant, he attempted to compose himself. On the way back to the table he stopped at the bar and ordered another gin for Calderwood and a brandy for himself.

'How long have you known?' he asked, his voice steady.

'Several weeks. That file was just part of a consignment pilfered from the CIA Berlin station offices by a malcontent German who used to be on their payroll but who is now on ours. His name wouldn't mean anything to you. He delivered the entire package as evidence of good faith, having had an argument over money with the current station chief.'

'Current?'

'Cassidy's appointment was only temporary four or so years ago, around your time actually. Did you ever meet up with him?'

'No,' said Alex dully.

'I didn't think so. He was sent in as a trouble-shooter when many of the Company's networks on the other side of the Wall were falling apart. A nasty piece of work, I assure you. I crossed swords with him on more than one occasion. You are fortunate not to have become involved with him. You might not be here now if you had. In order to salvage the Agency's operations in East Berlin, he deliberately exposed some of my people over there. They were executed, of course. He had the names of virtually everyone who worked for me, yours included no doubt. Naturally I could never prove anything against him. He was far too cunning for that. Yes, a very malignant individual. I'd give a lot to square the account.'

'Then do it,' said Alex.

'I beg your pardon?'

'Do it, God damn it! There's signed proof in that folder that Cassidy covered up a murder.'

'It doesn't say murder,' murmured Calderwood.

'You mean you accept what Cassidy has written?'

'I have no reason to doubt the authenticity of the document.'

Alex looked at his former section head with growing hatred. 'You bastard. You knew Melanie.'

'I did.'

'Yet you believe she was a drunken whore.'

'No.'

'Then what? If you accept that fiction you accept that she spent her last afternoon in bed with Coughlin and Garfield.'

'I only said I have no reason to doubt the authenticity of the document. I didn't say I believed the content.'

'I don't follow you.'

'Then let me make myself clear. I find it very strange that that folder, especially insofar as it indicts those two agents in particular, should turn up on my desk when it did.'

'I'm still not with you.'

'Bear with me, and let me ask you a question. Are we agreed that only Coughlin and Garfield know what really happened on that dreadful day in Berlin?' Alex nodded. 'Cassidy could have been deceived, though the man is only odious, not a fool. Nonetheless, Coughlin and Garfield could have lied to save their own necks.'

'Not could have, did.'

'Very well, did. Therefore only Coughlin and Garfield can undo the lie. To do that we need them in person. Cassidy alone is no use, though I shall put out feelers to ascertain his present whereabouts. Coughlin and Garfield are a different problem. We don't know what they look like or where they are.'

'We don't even know whether they're alive or dead, or, if alive, whether they're still with the Agency or not.'

'Oh, I think we know that,' said Calderwood. 'However,

before you ask me to elaborate, another question. Earlier I said I was sorry I had to show the report to you. You haven't asked me why I did, why I reopened an old wound.'

Alex realized he hadn't, having been totally preoccupied with the contents of the folder. 'But you're going to tell me.'

'In a moment. May I take it you would go to considerable lengths to trace Coughlin and Garfield and, if you found them, would shortly thereafter kill them? If so, that would disturb me. The department never kills in anger, Alex, you know that. Only as an expedient.'

Alex smiled grimly. 'You may take it that when I kill them I shall not be angry. That would be an unnecessary waste of emotion. Besides, they have some questions to answer.'

'I'm glad to hear it and, that being the case, we may be able to help one another.'

'Get to the point.'

'You still haven't seen it, have you? You still don't understand why I think your brother's death somehow involves you. Consider the names, Alex, Coughlin and Garfield. An acronym of the first three letters of each spells Cougar. Now, may I see about a new passport for you?'

MANHATTAN

Hatless in spite of the bitter wind blowing in from the river and the occasional flurry of snowflakes, Alex watched the coffin being lowered into the grave, finding it hard to accept that his brother's body lay inside. Throughout the short service and eulogy he had searched his innermost depths for some emotion, without success. They were not burying Nick; they were burying a stranger.

He had flown into JFK late the previous evening, to be met at the immigration barrier by Calderwood's man on the spot, Dunean Hamilton, who had put him up for the night in the apartment the Firm kept in Manhattan for visitors. Hamilton was an ex-Royal Marines captain, a robust twenty-eight-year-old who looked as though he could take care of himself. This was his first overseas posting with the department. After expressing his formal regrets at Nick's death, Hamilton said that his instructions from London were to return to Washington as soon as Alex had finished with his services. Alex had told him to stick around until after the funeral, and to stop calling Alex 'sir'. Their ranks were not that disparate and, besides, it made Alex feel old.

They stood well apart from the other mourners. Alex was surprised at how many there were, upwards of a hundred, including, because of the circumstances of Nick's death, two or three obvious plainclothes policemen. He recognized Alison Cameron from Hamilton's description. She was leaning on the arm of a burly man in his fifties.

'Who's that with her?'

'Vincent Kaplan. He owns a couple of dozen very profitable magazines, ranging from the softcore girly type to one or two highbrows. His interests are mostly in this country, though he has several minor publishing ventures going in the Far East, notably in Japan and Hong Kong. His main hobby is teenage girls – all over the age of consent, I hasten to add.'

Alex was impressed. 'Do you carry a lot of information like that around in your head?'

'I wish I could say I do; I can't. I asked one of the embassy researchers to compile a list of everyone your brother had written for in the last three years. Kaplan was one of them, though not recently. It appears to be over, incidentally.'

Most of the mourners were returning to their cars. A few seemed inclined to linger and offer their condolences to Alison Cameron until they were waved away by Kaplan.

'You know where my brother lived, don't you?' asked Alex.

'Yes. I interviewed Miss Cameron there.'

'Okay. Pick up my bags and deliver them to that address. If Miss Cameron doesn't object I'll use it as my New York base.'

'Right. Then do I go back to Washington?'

'We'll see. I haven't been in the States for some years. I don't know anywhere outside New York and DC, and those not very well. I may need a guide who's accustomed to driving on the right. I'll think about it.'

'Fine.' Hamilton held out his hand. 'In case you don't need me, it's been a pleasure meeting you, sir. I'm only sorry it had to be under these circumstances.'

'Thanks.'

Alex caught up with Alison and Kaplan as the pair were about to enter the leading car in the cortege. 'Miss Cameron?'

Alison turned, startled to hear an English accent. Even though her eyes were red from crying Alex could see that, beneath the black veil covering her face, she was an exquisite beauty.

'Beat it,' said Kaplan brusquely.

Alex did not take offence. 'I'm Nick's brother, Miss Cameron. I flew in last night.'

'Brother? Nick never told me he had a brother.'

'We haven't seen each other for a long time. May I talk to you? It's important.'

'Let's see some ID, mister,' said Kaplan, far from convinced that Alex was other than a reporter with a fresh approach or someone else from the embassy.

'I'm afraid that wouldn't help as everything I carry is in the name of Alex Dunbar. Dunbar was Nick's real surname; Tasker was our mother's maiden name. Look, he had a jagged scar about three inches long on the inside of his left forearm. He cut it on broken glass when he was ten. He also had an appendectomy scar,' Alex added, conscious that the observation could be regarded as inept if Nick and Alison Cameron had not been sleeping together. To hell with it; this was no time for social niceties.

'Yes, all that's true,' agreed Alison. 'I remember asking him about the scar on his arm. And I think I've also seen the name Dunbar on some old correspondence.'

'I really do need to talk to you,' said Alex, 'and perhaps go through Nick's private papers. I thought we might go to his apartment. I understand you're not satisfied with the official version of his death. I'd like to know why in detail.'

Alison glanced anxiously at Kaplan, who seemed satisfied that Alex was who he claimed to be.

'My car and chauffeur are at the end of this line of vehicles,' said Kaplan. 'He'll drive you wherever you want to go. I'll make your excuses to the others,' he reassured Alison. 'Call me if you need anything.'

'Bless you, Vincent.'

Alison remained silent, kept her face averted and a handkerchief to her mouth throughout the drive down to the Village, not speaking until they were inside Nick's apartment, which she entered with her own key.

'The drinks are over by the desk,' she said. 'If you'll excuse me for a moment, I'd like a brandy. Help yourself to anything you want.' She paused. 'I think I've got that wrong somehow. After all, this is all yours now.'

When she returned she had taken off her veil and hat, and applied a little make-up. Alex handed her the brandy.

'Before we begin,' he said, 'may I say that this is not all mine, as you put it a moment ago. I'm not here as a potential beneficiary. You're welcome to take anything you want. Live here, for that matter. The only snag there is that I need somewhere to stay while I'm in New York. I hope you don't mind if it's here.'

'Of course not. I have my own apartment, in any case. And thank you for the offer about Nick's things. I'll sort out what I'd like to take in a day or two. I don't expect it'll be much. I'm sure you understand that it would be too painful to have too many of Nick's personal belongings around. For the same reason, I couldn't live here any longer. I made up my mind I'd only stay until after the funeral.' She hesitated, unsure of how, or whether, to continue. Finally she said, 'People have told me I'll get over it, forget. Do you think they're right?'

'That depends on how close you were.'

'Close enough. It wasn't an earth-shaking love affair on either side, which somehow makes it worse. I feel I've lost a very dear friend – no, something more than a friend – and my emotions don't really know how to cope.'

'Talking sometimes helps.'

'Oh, I'll talk all right.' Alison leaned forward in her armchair to emphasize the point. 'I'll talk to anyone who can find the bastards who shot him. Ask me what you like, but before you do would you indulge me for a while? Would you tell me a little about yourself and your relationship with Nick? It's something of a shock, discovering he had a brother. You don't look very much alike.'

'What would you like to hear?'

'Anything – childhood, parents, schooldays. Anything at all.'

Alex spent twenty minutes telling her where he and Nick had grown up, their parents, the house they had lived in, resorting to fiction when the facts did not quite suit the occasion. He said little about how he and Nick had gradually gone their separate ways, judging that she would be less than forthcoming if she suspected that the two brothers had never had much in common after adolescence. Nor did he tell her his real reasons for being in America. He simply said that the Washington embassy had contacted the Foreign Office in London as a matter of routine a couple of days ago. In turn he had been informed of Nick's death and the fact that she, Alison, was unconvinced that Nick had travelled to Denver willingly.

Twice she left the room for a few minutes at a time, returning dabbing her eyes. He knew the tears would vanish before long. He had been through the same thing himself.

'Thank you,' she said eventually. 'Now please ask your questions.'

'Just tell me anything that comes into your head.'

While she talked she paced the room, explaining that it helped her to think. She told him everything from the beginning, concluding with Tyson's name.

'He was a man Nick met in the motel bar. Nick had an appointment with him the following day. He owns an electrical goods store or some such in the area. Although he seems to have been the last person to see Nick alive, the New York police told me he was interviewed and cleared of complicity. He said he dropped Nick off at the motel around six in the evening and that was the last he saw of him. But it's all lies, Mr Dunbar!' she blurted out. 'I don't know how Tyson is involved if at all. I do know Nick would never have gone to Denver without phoning me. He just wouldn't have. And why did no one see him check out or pay his room account? It's all connected somehow with the series he was writing on the Nazis, except I don't know how. But he wasn't killed by a mugger or a crazy. Nor was he killed in Denver.'

'Can I see his notes for the series,' asked Alex, 'his research material and anything else connected? I'd like to go through all his papers later, but for the moment we might find some answers there.'

'They're in the second and third drawers down, right-hand side, of his desk.' Alison was still on her feet, staring out of the window at the traffic below. 'It's not locked. They're usually left on top. I put them out of sight yesterday.'

Alex walked over to the desk and opened the second and third drawers. Both were empty apart from a few paper-clips and rubber bands.

'There's nothing here.'

'There must be.' She joined him at the desk. 'I don't understand. I put them there myself.'

She rummaged through the other drawers. Nothing resembling Nick's research files was in any of them.

'Is anything else missing?' asked Alex, suspecting that the answer would be negative. Whoever had burgled the apartment had only wanted Nick's notes.

'I can't say offhand.' Bewildered, Alison looked around. 'Everything seems to be here. I'd have to take a thorough inventory to be sure. Are you trying to tell me Nick's files have been stolen?'

'Probably during the funeral.'

'But who would do such a thing?'

'That's something we'll have to find out. It would appear to confirm, however, that Nick's murder is somehow connected with his work.'

'Then we must inform the police.' Alison reached for the telephone. 'They'll have to listen to me now.'

'No, don't do that.' Alex took the receiver from her hand and replaced it on the cradle.

'Why ever not?'

The doorbell rescued Alex. Duncan Hamilton, with Alex's bags, stood outside.

'Will you be needing me any more, sir, or should I return to Washington?'

'I'll be needing you. Go back to the apartment and wait for my call.'

Alex shut the door and picked up his bags. He turned to find Alison standing behind him.

'That was the young man from the embassy, wasn't it?'

There was no point in denying it. 'It was.'

'He called you sir.'

Damn Hamilton, thought Alex angrily. 'He was just being polite.'

'I don't think so. In fact, I'm beginning to think you're not Nick's brother at all. Anyone half acquainted with him would know about his scars, and you could have invented the stories about your childhood. Who are you really, Mr Dunbar, and why won't you let me call the police?'

Alex improvised as he went along, after reiterating firmly

enough to convince Alison that he *was* Nick's brother.

'In the first place Hamilton calls me sir because I work for the government – as he does, except I'm of a higher grade. I'm nothing very spectacular, just a pen-pusher, a glorified clerk. To put it another way, Hamilton cleans the ink wells that I dip my pen in.'

'If you work for the British government you'll have a diplomatic passport,' said Alison sharply.

'That doesn't necessarily follow, though in my case it happens to be true.'

Alex produced from an inside pocket the diplomatic passport that all SIS officers on foreign assignments carried. Alison examined it carefully before handing it back, grudgingly impressed.

'In the second place,' said Alex, 'you may call the police if you wish and report the break-in. Personally I'm against it. The police haven't been very interested in your theories up to now, and the theft of a few papers will hardly change their attitude. Bringing them in could also make things awkward for me. If they get the idea I'm meddling in a murder case they may try to get my credentials revoked. I've travelled three thousand miles to find out what happened to Nick, mainly because I heard that you don't think it was a simple case of murder. All right, I'm inclined to agree with you. The least you can do in return is give me a few days.'

Alison studied him in silence, not sure whether to trust him. Nevertheless, he was right about police lack of interest. Perhaps the police themselves were somehow involved.

'All right,' she said finally, 'where do you propose to start?'

Alex heaved a quiet sigh of relief. 'Here, with Nick's desk, though I don't hold out much hope of finding anything. After that, I'll want to see Mr Kaplan. Perhaps he can tell me something more about the man who caused the trouble at the party. What was his name, Stone?'

'Yes, Stone. I doubt Vincent will be able to help, however. He'd never met Stone before and hasn't seen him since.'

'Well, we'll see. If he can't I'll go to the motel where Nick met Tyson, perhaps have a word with Tyson. If that proves fruitless I'm out of ideas.'

Well, not quite, thought Alex, though he couldn't tell Alison Cameron that if he drew a blank in South Dakota his next stop would be Washington, where he would look up an old friend or maybe two, ask them what they knew of two men called Coughlin and Garfield.

'Can I do anything?' asked Alison.

'You can call Kaplan and tell him I'd like to see him – this evening if he's free. Then you can write down everything you've just told me about Stone, Tyson, the motel. After that,' Alex concluded, 'you'd do well to take a sedative and get some sleep. You've had a tough day. Stay here if you want to. I'll try not to make a noise.'

'No, I'll go home,' Alison made a valiant attempt to overcome her sorrow with bitter humour. 'And I'll get falling-down drunk within easy reach of something soft. I'll call Vincent from the bedroom. He'd kindly loaned me the use of his apartment for a few final drinks with some of Nick's closest friends. I'll probably burst into tears if anyone offers condolence.'

'You needn't be embarrassed on my account.'

While Alison placed her call Alex went through Nick's desk with a toothcomb, finding nothing to explain how his dead brother's work tied in with Coughlin and Garfield. Whoever had stolen his files had made a thoroughly professional job of it. Alison returned as he was finishing. In one hand she held a single sheet of paper; in the other her hat and veil.

'Vincent will see you at eight o'clock. I've written down everything I can think of including his address and phone number. Mine too in case you want to reach me. I won't be there from the day after tomorrow, however.'

'You're going away?'

'Yes. My manager has brought forward some overseas modelling assignments. He seems to think it will be better if I work. I guess he's right. I'll be abroad for about three weeks, but please get in touch if you learn anything. Vincent will know where I am.'

'Do you need a taxi?'

'No. Vincent's sending his car. It should have arrived by the time I get downstairs. I've left a duplicate key on the bedroom dressing-table. If I may, I'll hold on to my own for the time being.'

'Of course.' Alex showed her to the door. 'It'll pass, you know,' he said.

'You seem very sure.'

'I am.' He looked into her deep, troubled eyes. 'Believe me, I am.'

After she had gone he poured himself a J & B, the only whisky he could find. He left it standing on the desk, untouched, while he telephoned Hamilton.

'I've warned you once and now I'm warning you again,' said Alex. 'Don't call me sir in public or in private. Not ever. You landed me with a hell of a lot of explaining to do to Miss Cameron. If you must call me something call me Alex or Dunbar, I don't give a damn which. Have you got that?'

'Yes – Alex,' confirmed Hamilton, chastened.

'Good. I don't expect to have to repeat that injunction. If I do have occasion to you'll be back with the Royal Marines as Plymouth catering officer before you can blink.'

'Understood.'

'Okay, so now we've cleared the air I want you to do a few things for me. First, go to an outside phone and call Calderwood in London. Tell him I'm busy but that I'm going to require your services as my right hand until further notice. Ask him to square it with your section chief in Washington. Second, find out the times of planes tomorrow afternoon to South Dakota's major airport and ring them through to this number. More than likely I won't be here, but there's some kind of answering machine at this end that'll take your message if I can discover how the devil to operate it. Next, ascertain the time of planes to the same destination tonight and get on one. When you arrive, check up on the address of a man named Tyson, who has an electrical goods business in or near a town called Midland. Do nothing else. We'll both be talking to Mr Tyson soon. Last, meet me at the airport with a car on the first plane landing after, say, seven p.m. Have you got all that?'

'Yes, sir. I mean, yes, Alex. What about accommodation?'

'Good point.' Alex referred to Alison's list and gave

Hamilton the name of the motel Nick had stayed at. 'Separate rooms or cabins or whatever the Americans call them, if you don't mind. I like my solitude. If the desk clerk wants to know how long we'll be in residence, keep it open-ended. Two nights at least, however. We'll pay Tyson a visit first a.m. the day after tomorrow.'

'Right.'

'Is there anything you want to ask me?'

'Only if I'm to be told what the assignment is.'

'I'll have to clear that with Calderwood. At the moment this is on a need-to-know basis. Without intending to pun, if I need you longer than a few days, you'll get to know. Anything else?'

'No.'

'I haven't given you the telephone number here. How the blazes can you call me if you don't know the number?'

'I already have it. I took a note of it when I first saw Miss Cameron.'

'When you *first* saw Miss Cameron you took down a telephone number? You need your eyes tested. But okay, I stand corrected.' Alex was about to hang up when he remembered a question he had forgotten to put to Hamilton the previous evening. 'Tell me,' he asked, 'before you joined the department, where was your last active-service posting?'

Hamilton hesitated before saying, 'I don't believe I'm at liberty to divulge that information.'

'Don't be ridiculous. I only have to ask Calderwood to find out.'

'Then I'd rather you did that.'

Alex replaced the receiver. He was still suffering slightly from jet-lag, having arisen that morning at what was, in United Kingdom time, three a.m. Otherwise he felt alert and vital, in better shape than he had for years. He picked up the glass of whisky and contemplated the contents briefly before pouring them back into the bottle. He was not, he told himself, making a grandiose gesture or forswearing hard liquor. For the moment, however, he did not need a drink.

His sense of euphoria would have diminished considerably had he known that his entire conversation with Hamilton had been recorded and was even now being transcribed.

Bathed, shaved and changed, Alex was shown into the penthouse apartment's huge drawing-room by an unsmiling servant as the grandfather clock in the passage chimed eight. A pretty brunette with a quite staggering figure was sitting on a high stool at the corner bar, stirring a cocktail with a swizzle-stick. She was, Alex estimated, no more than nineteen.

'Hi,' she said.

'Good evening,' responded Alex.

A second later Kaplan entered, wearing a beautifully tailored dinner jacket and a scarlet cummerbund to conceal an incipient paunch. 'Out,' he ordered the girl.

'Aw,' she pouted.

'Out,' repeated Kaplan. She went, swaying seductively all the way to the door.

'Why do I bother, is a question I often ask myself,' said Kaplan, watching her performance over the top of his gold-rimmed spectacles.

'And what's the answer?'

'I'm still trying to find out. All I know is that when I was in my forties I went for women in their twenties. Now I'm in my fifties it's teenagers. They've got a cell waiting for me somewhere if I ever make seventy.'

Alex was fractionally taller and a dozen years younger than the publisher, but Kaplan looked as though he could give any man not a professional athlete a run for his money either in a boxing ring or on a tennis court.

'Can I fix you a drink?' asked Kaplan.

'A beer will do fine.'

'One beer coming up, as well as an apology for being a bit short with you this morning.' Kaplan deftly uncapped a bottle and poured the beer into a frosted glass. 'I didn't know then you were Nick's brother. You have my sympathy there. I knew him well, and liked him. We all did.'

'Not everyone,' Alex reminded him.

'Huh? No, not everyone. I'd give a lot to get my hands on the sons of bitches who shot him, for Alison's sake as much as anything.'

Alex accepted the beer with a nod of thanks. 'Will she be all right by herself tonight?'

Kaplan shrugged. 'Who can tell? I wanted her to sleep here overnight. She wouldn't have it. Nor would she let me get someone to sit with her. She's not the suicidal type, if that's what you mean. She'll get drunk, I guess, and cry a lot. It's better she gets it out of her system. You know she's going away in a couple of days?'

'She told me.'

'I arranged it, as a matter of fact,' said Kaplan, with no trace of self-importance. 'Through her manager, I mean. I've been wanting her to inject a little class into one of my magazines for some months now, and this seemed as good a time as any. It's not a philanthropic gesture, by the way,' he added. 'Purely business. She gets herself photographed wearing jewellery or perfume or whatever it is for the client and they take space in my magazine in a three-way deal. Everybody wins. Three weeks in the Far East will do her the world of good. The Japs and the Hong Kong Chinese will love her.'

Alex suspected that Kaplan was a little in love with her himself.

'Now about Stone,' said Kaplan, taking a cigar from the humidor on the bar and clipping the end with a silver cutter. 'I told Alison on the phone that I wouldn't be able to give you any more information than I've already given the cops, but she asked me to see you anyway. The fact remains, however, that I haven't seen Stone since the night of the party. I still don't know how the hell he got in. None of my other guests would admit bringing him. Then again, I didn't know half of them myself. It's like that in my business. My office sends out a few dozen invitations, some of which end up in the hands of freeloaders. The publishing racket is one long round of drinks parties. Even in Manhattan people get sick of them and pass their invitations on to someone else. Something like that must have happened here. That's all I can tell you.'

Alex was not too disappointed. He had half expected as much.

'And no one saw him leave? The doorman, for example.

No one called him a cab?'

'Not that anyone can recollect. It was a pretty lousy night, three or four inches of snow with more coming down. A bunch of people worried about getting home left soon after Nick and Alison. Stone must have gone out with that crowd. You've got a tough job ahead of you.'

'Tough job?'

'According to Alison you've formed yourself into a one-man posse to try to find out who shot your brother.'

'Not exactly,' said Alex. He did not want that kind of gossip making the rounds of publishing circles or anywhere else. 'I flew over for the funeral. Miss Cameron seems unhappy with the police version of events. I plan to do some digging to see what turns up, though I don't suppose I'll succeed where the police have failed. If that proves to be the case, I'll tidy up the loose ends of Nick's estate and go home. I can't take indefinite leave of absence from my job on what could turn out to be a wild-goose chase.'

'Ah yes, you're with a British government department, aren't you?' murmured Kaplan. 'Alison mentioned that also. Some sort of desk job, she said.' The publisher's eyes narrowed shrewdly. 'Funny, I can't picture you behind a desk.'

Alex drained his glass. 'Well, it takes all sorts.'

'Yes, I guess it does. Another beer?'

'No, thanks. I won't keep you any longer. I appreciate you giving me your time.'

'Think nothing of it. I'm sorry I wasn't any help.'

Kaplan accompanied Alex to the elevator.

'You might like to know,' he said, 'that I've put the word out among certain people for information about Stone, offered a substantial sum as bait. If anything comes of it, I'll be in touch. Alison said you're staying at Nick's place.' Alex confirmed that he was. 'Fine. As I said, I liked Nick a lot and I'm very fond of Alison. If there's anything I can do, any time, you just have to name it. I've got connections in a few odd places.'

'I'll bear that in mind,' said Alex.

An hour later, in Midland, South Dakota, Cliff Tyson had

the first of two long-distance telephone conversations with Frank Stone.

'You'll be receiving a couple of English visitors the day after tomorrow,' said Stone. 'My instructions are that you show them whatever they want to see. After all, we've nothing to hide, have we? Not now.'

'And then I can get back to being a storekeeper again, right? I tell you, my wife's starting to suspect I've got a girl on the side, the peculiar hours I've been keeping lately.'

'Now, now, Cliff,' chided Stone. 'You're being well paid.'

'So you say.'

'You should have stayed with the Company. The Company protects its own.'

'It didn't do much for me after the Bay of Pigs.'

'Before my time, Cliff, but I understand a lot of guys took a fall around then. You were young, you could have made a comeback. Opting out and joining the air force isn't the brightest thing I ever heard of anybody doing. Anyway, look after your visitors. And stay close to the phone tonight. I'll be talking to you again later.'

'And telling me what's going on?'

'Not your concern, Cliff. Just do your own small part. There'll be an envelope in the mail in a few days and that's the last you'll hear from us.'

'I hope so.'

'You can bank on it. Oh, and remember the rules. You never say anything to anyone about all this, not now or ever.'

'What the hell could I tell them?'

'That's the spirit, Cliff.'

SOUTH DAKOTA

Snow had fallen every day, sometimes twice or more a day, since Tyson had driven Nick Tasker to the clearing where he now brought the pick-up to a halt and switched off the ignition. In places the drifts were four feet deep. The snow would not affect their ability to climb, of course, as he intended taking the same route he had with Tasker a week earlier. But cutting a path from the pick-up to the stream was going to be hard work, especially for the Englishmen. He had loaned them waterproof trousers and heavy jackets, and they had bought calf-length boots from the camping store. Nevertheless, they looked what they were, city types.

The hell with them. All he was concerned about was obeying orders and taking them up to the plateau. After that, he couldn't give a good goddam if they both had coronaries. Or if he never heard another word from Stone and that bastard Cassidy. He didn't care what spooky game they were playing. He had learned a long time ago, with the Company as well as the air force, that the way to get on in this world was not to ask too many questions.

'From here we climb,' he said. 'Across there and up there, using the stream.' He pointed.

Alex wondered aloud what the devil had brought Nick out here.

'He didn't say.' Tyson pulled on a hunting cap and slung his binoculars around his neck. 'He hired me as driver because I know the countryside, and here's where I drove him.'

'*Don't make it too easy for them,*' Stone had advised during the second phone call. '*You met Tasker in the motel bar, where*

*he gave you fifty bucks to show him what he wanted to see. His
damaged car works in our favour here. He didn't want to risk it on
a long journey. Nor did he want to go back to Avis and get
involved in a hassle. Be awkward. You're a busy man; you've
got a business to run. You can't take time off. Make 'em pay,
they'll expect that.'*

Tyson had, demanding a further fifty dollars and gas
money. 'What about the police?' he had asked Stone. 'If the
Limeys check with the cops they'll find I gave them a
different story, that I didn't take Tasker anywhere near the
site. Maybe that was a mistake.'

*'Don't be a damned fool. Cassidy would have had both our
heads if you'd taken the flatfoots within ten miles of the site.
Anyway, they won't check with the cops. Believe me, these guys
won't go anywhere near the cops.'*

'No, sir,' lied Tyson to Alex. 'He didn't say a word. He
was a bit weird, if you want my opinion.'

'I don't,' said Alex.

He didn't like or trust Tyson. Earlier that morning when
they had walked into his store, it was almost as though he was
expecting them. Nor had he questioned, when Alex had
introduced himself as Nick's brother, the different
surnames.

Although it was broad daylight, even Tyson found the
climb tough, much tougher than last time. Following the
course of the stream, it took them fifty minutes to reach the
plateau where Nick had first seen the barbed-wire fence and
the notices prohibiting unauthorized persons proceeding
further.

Not that the fence or the warnings were there any longer.
The daily snowfalls had naturally covered the footprints of
the men who had removed them, but even so Tyson had to
admire the manner in which everything had been so
efficiently dismantled. Even though this region was virtually
deserted throughout the winter months, the logistical side of
the operation must have caused a few headaches,
particularly as it had been essential not to attract too much
attention. Though Cassidy had been clever there. Stone had
hinted that the operation's cover was that of making a film; if
anyone asked, the comings and goings were those of the film

crew on location.

Breathing heavily, Alex caught up with Tyson. Hamilton was some fifty yards further behind, labouring in spite of his comparative youth and vowing to abjure the embassy cocktail circuit. A year earlier, serving with the Royal Marines, he would have been able to run up the hill in full fighting order and put ten shots in a two-inch group from two hundred yards.

'Why have we stopped?' asked Alex.

'Because we're here,' replied Tyson. 'You paid me to show you where I brought Tasker. This is it. Just over that crest up ahead is a valley. That's what Tasker wanted to see.'

Tyson led the way through the knee-high drifts to where, seven days ago, Nick had peered through the barbed-wire into the valley below. Now, however, the valley was empty. There were some signs of recent activity, both vehicular and pedestrian, but no people, no buildings. The site had been cleared the day after Nick was killed. *Hot dog*, thought Tyson.

'So?' said Alex.

'So this is it,' said Tyson. 'I don't want to speak ill of the dead but I told you before, your brother was weird.'

Alex let the comment pass. 'And everything was like this last time?'

'Exactly.'

'Nothing down there that isn't there now?'

'Nothing. Christ, this is the middle of nowhere. You won't see a human being apart from the occasional hunter in these parts from November through mid-April. Okay, I know,' said Tyson before Alex could interrupt, 'there's obviously been some traffic through the valley not long ago, but not when we were here. Maybe that's what your brother came for. He was some kind of journalist, wasn't he? I don't know. He didn't confide in me.' *Play it dumb*, Stone had said. 'Like I told you, I was just the driver. If he wanted to pay me fifty bucks for a few hours' work, that was fine by me.'

'You should take it up on a full-time basis,' said Alex caustically. 'You're into a lucrative business. A few more like us and you can start thinking about an early retirement.

101

Let me borrow the glasses.'

Scowling, Tyson passed them across. Alex adjusted the focus screw and swept the valley. If it had snowed daily for the past week, as Tyson said it had, then judging by the residual depth of the furrows, the vehicles that made them had been very large and heavy and probably tracked. He made a mental note to call the meteorological office to check how many inches had fallen in the last ten days. With that information to hand, together with the depth of snow in a particular furrow, simple arithmetic would tell him when the vehicles were here. The same calculation would also reveal whether Tyson was a liar.

At the far end of the valley was what appeared to be a gorge. Whatever lay beyond was out of sight because of the height of the surrounding hills, but presumably that was how the vehicles came in and went out.

Tyson confirmed that the gorge led to a rough dirt road which wound through wooded country until it reached a minor highway about a mile further on. A few years ago the route was used by lumbermen; now, however, this region was part of a conservation zone where woodcutting had been proscribed by statute until the end of the century.

Hamilton grunted with disgust.

'What's the matter with you?' asked Alex.

'Now he tells us there's a road,' said the ex-Marine. 'After climbing for an hour we find there's another way in.'

'You asked me to show you where I took Tasker,' growled Tyson aggressively. 'Well, mister, I just did. Anyhow, my pick-up wouldn't have made it through the gorge. The lumber road is more or less impassable in this sort of weather.'

'Not to everyone, evidently,' said Alex. 'In any case, I'd like to take a closer look.'

'Down there?' Tyson shook his head. 'Count me out. Fifty bucks didn't buy you an alpine guide.'

Alex studied the terrain. Where they were standing was roughly five hundred feet above the floor of the valley, and the angle of the slope was far from acute. It shouldn't be too difficult. The trail they blazed during the descent would help them on the return trip.

'Game?' he asked Hamilton.

'Do I have a choice?'

'Of course you do. You can go voluntarily or you can be ordered to go.'

'I'll volunteer.'

'Good man.'

'How long do you expect to be?' asked Tyson.

'As long as it takes.' It suited Alex that Tyson showed no interest in accompanying them. 'Just make sure you're here when we get back. If we didn't pay for an alpine guide, we paid for a round trip.'

'We've only got about three hours' daylight left,' protested Tyson. 'The temperature'll start falling in an hour and if it snows while you're down there you'll be in big trouble.'

Alex glanced up at the clouds. He doubted it would snow before dark.

'You're a pessimist, you know that?' he said to Tyson. 'If people like you had been around in seventeen seventy-six, you'd still be a colony paying taxes to the Crown.'

Tyson grimaced. He would have traded a week's profits for a chance to knock some of the arrogance out of this Britisher, but he held his annoyance in check, suspecting that Dunbar was deliberately trying to provoke him.

The descent proved easier than Alex had imagined. Beneath the powdery surface of the morning's fall, the snow was packed hard. Even though he and Hamilton slipped several times and travelled a few yards on their backsides, they were in the valley in fifteen minutes. Through the binoculars Tyson followed their every move.

'What are we looking for?' asked Hamilton, brushing snow from his waterproof over-trousers.

'I'm not sure. Anything that might tell us who was here and when, and on that subject get yourself a stick and measure the depth of snow in one of those furrows. Scrape away the stuff until you reach caterpillar tracks. Other than that, just keep your eyes open.'

'Right.'

Accepting that whatever he might find would be at least five or six inches beneath the surface snow, Alex crisscrossed the valley in the furrows, keeping his eyes peeled and, every so often, kicking away the top layers of snow. After half an hour he had unearthed several empty vegetable cans of recent origin and a half-gallon plastic canister that had once held water. A few dozen yards away Hamilton was having no greater success.

Alex was on the point of conceding that they would find nothing in the valley to explain why Nick had been killed, when Hamilton hailed him. 'Over here.'

Alex joined him. 'What is it?'

Hamilton pointed with a forefinger. Driven into the ground at the end of one of the furrows was a wooden stake, painted red. It had not been observable despite its colour through the binoculars because it was considerably shorter than the sides of the furrow. It was, however, obviously a marker of some sort.

'Let's see what's underneath.'

Within a couple of minutes Alex was holding a round leather case six inches in diameter. It was fastened with a zip and contained what seemed to be a camera lens. Although Alex was no photography expert he would have laid odds that the lens came from a movie camera. In a side compartment was a strip of film about three feet long. Holding it up to the light proved unrewarding; the images were too small.

'Interesting,' said Alex. 'The question is, was the marker left by the owner to remind him where he had buried the case, or was it left for us?'

'What do you mean by that?' asked Hamilton curiously.

'I don't know. Call it a gut feeling.'

An extended search of the same area produced no further finds, and after twenty more minutes Alex opted to call it a day.

'Did you get the measurements I asked you to take?' Hamilton confirmed that he had. 'Fine,' said Alex. 'Don't say anything to Tyson about the lens or the strip of film.'

Retracing their steps to where they had left Tyson turned out to be substantially more exhausting than descending, and dusk was closing in before they gained the top of the hill. Even so, Alex insisted on a five-minute rest before returning 'to the pick-up. Surprisingly, Tyson raised no objections.

'Did you have any luck?' he asked chattily.

'Luck?' queried Alex. 'What sort of luck?'

'Any sort. Did you find anything? I thought I saw you pick something up.'

'Some tin cans, an old water container. They could have been there for years.' To change the subject Alex said, 'Do you know the location of the nearest meteorological office?'

'No. There's probably one in Rapid City or Sioux Falls. Or you could try the weather section of the TV station. The number's in the book. Do you want to know what the weather's going to be like tomorrow? If so, I can tell you.'

'No,' said Alex. 'I want to know what it was like last week.'

In the pick-up on the road back, Tyson, in answer to Alex, reaffirmed that he had dropped Nick at the motel around six in the evening the night he disappeared. 'I didn't see him again.'

'But you know his hire car was found at the bus station and his body in Denver.'

'So the cops told me.' Tyson bit his tongue. He wanted to keep any mention of the cops out of the conversation, whatever Stone thought.

'And that no one saw him check out of the motel even though his account was paid for in cash?'

'I heard something of the kind.' Tyson took his eyes off the road for a moment and tossed a glance across to Alex. 'Look, I know I was the last one around these parts to see him alive, but if you think I had anything to do with his death, you're crazy. Somebody saw him after me, and that was the guy who pulled the trigger.'

'Nobody's accusing you of anything.'

'They'd better not be.'

After he had dropped his passengers at the motel, Tyson drove to a roadside booth and put in a call to Stone at the number Stone had given him.

'How did it go?' asked Stone.

Tyson told him, adding that he thought Dunbar had picked up something on the site. 'He denied it, but I was watching the pair of them through the glasses the whole time. I know he found something.'

Stone seemed unworried. 'There was nothing there that's going to help them. You saw for yourself, we disinfected the entire site.'

'Disinfected,' said Tyson. 'Christ, that's a word I haven't heard for years. Anyway, there's something else I think you ought to know.'

He explained about Alex wanting the location of the nearest meteorological department. This time Stone sounded disturbed. 'Did you ask him why he needed it?'

'I did. I thought he might be planning another trip out there tomorrow. He told me it was last week's weather he was interested in.'

At the other end of the line, Stone understood immediately why Dunbar wanted that information. And once he had it he would be back to see Tyson.

'Where are you calling from?' he asked.

'A public booth.'

'Okay. Go home and stay there. I'll catch you later.'

In his motel room, Alex allowed the scalding needle-spray shower to restore some life to his aching muscles. Afterwards he towelled himself vigorously dry. The clothes he had borrowed from Tyson lay in a heap on the floor; he would return them, as promised, the following day, when he might also have a more solemn reason for calling on their guide.

Once dressed he asked the operator to connect him to Hamilton's room, telling the younger man to meet him in the bar in ten minutes. The time had come to do something about Hamilton, either release him to return to his normal duties or petition Calderwood to have him seconded for the duration. Alex rather suspected it would be the latter, which would necessitate requesting permission from Calderwood to explain the assignment. Hamilton had displayed remarkable patience up to now in not posing unanswerable questions, but he could hardly be expected to operate efficiently if kept in the dark.

In the bar, they ordered beers and found themselves a quiet corner.

'How would you like to work with me on a permanent basis?' asked Alex.

Hamilton's eyes shone. 'I'd like that a lot.'

'Can the embassy spare you?'

'I'll say they can!' Hamilton snorted with irritation. 'I don't do anything except sort through foreign signal traffic and occasionally follow someone.'

'That's par for the course first time out. Did you expect Moscow or Berlin? You wouldn't last a day. If you were lucky you'd be sent home with your cover blown. If you were unlucky you'd be picked out of the river.'

'I didn't spend my military service as a wages clerk,' said Hamilton indignantly.

'Where did you spend it?' asked Alex. 'All right, we've been through that before, and you don't have to answer. Calderwood will tell me when I phone him. I hope he's not going to give me bad news. You took a hell of a long time climbing that hill earlier.'

'I'm a bit out of condition.'

'You're a *lot* out of condition. Do something about it. This business may not be resolved in the United States where we're among friends, more or less. If we get into trouble I'd like to think you can look after yourself.'

'Get into trouble with who?'

'Later.' Alex took a sip of his beer. 'Tell me,' he went on, 'what do you know about me. You just agreed to work with me, but you don't know a damned thing about me. At least, I assume you don't.'

'I know a little.' Hamilton took a cigarette from his pack, thought about his lungs, and replaced it, pushing the pack out of reach. 'At Fort Monkton you were held up by the instructors as a glittering example.'

'They mentioned me by name?'

Fort Monkton, a Napoleonic fortress opposite Portsmouth Harbour, was the department's principal training establishment for sabotage and demolition, used not only by SIS personnel but by friendly foreign intelligence services also. Kim Philby had attended a course there in 1951.

'No, not by name,' said Hamilton, 'but the instructors were fond of telling a story about one man they had on a training course who, during an exercise, successfully beat the TV security system and wired up, with live charges, the officer's mess before making a call from an outside phone to the guardroom. The caller said that anyone trying to get in or out of the mess before the charges were automatically neutralized at three a.m. would find himself in a thousand pieces across half of Hampshire. The instructors never told us who the saboteur was. Those of us who kept our ears to the ground, however, heard Alex Dunbar mentioned more than once.'

Alex remembered the occasion well. It had happened many years ago. He'd arranged a date with an admiral's daughter before the announcement was made cancelling all shore leave. The exercise was not due to begin until nine p.m., but the girl could not get away from home before ten and would have to be back by two. Thus while everyone else was dining, he set his charges. He was back in the fort by two thirty and in bed by two forty-five, having learned from the guard commander that the exercise had been called off. One or two people had never forgiven him.

'You'll probably find similar stories about Menzies or Oldfield,' said Alex.

'Probably,' agreed Hamilton.

'And I wouldn't believe all I hear, if I were you.'

'I try not to.'

'Excellent. Anyway, is that all you know about me?'

'Yes.'

'And you still want to work with me?'

'It's better than sorting signals.'

Alex managed a smile. 'Let's hope you think so a week from now. Anyway, we've yet to clear it with Calderwood. Washington's our next stop, where I imagine I could get a coded message to London and a reply within a few hours. Nevertheless, I need to talk to Calderwood tonight – about other matters as well as about you. What do you know about GCHQ, Cheltenham?'

'Only that it's the government's communications centre, and that the US National Security Agency has use of the facilities there.'

'It used to be able to monitor inward and outward cables, among other things. Can it do the same with telephone calls that are not dialled directly, that go through the operator?'

'I don't know. I imagine so. If it can't, the Americans at this end probably can. Don't *you* know?' asked Hamilton, puzzled.

'Let's just say I've been out of the active side of the business for a year or two,' answered Alex casually. 'I'm not conversant with the latest electronic wizardry.'

Alex signalled for two more beers, which were brought over by a pretty blonde wearing a miniskirt over fishnet tights. Alex paid and told her to keep the change. Hamilton's eyes followed the girl back to her position at the end of the bar.

'I hope I'm not going to have trouble with you,' Alex said.

'Not after today's exertions, you're not. Besides, I have a regular girl in Washington.'

'*Regular?* You're starting to talk like an American. The English word is "steady".'

'All right, I have a *steady* girl in Washington. Is that against the rules?'

'Not if it doesn't affect your efficiency, which I'm about to test. Do you understand why I asked you to take that furrow measurement this afternoon?'

'Of course.'

'Good. Then while I'm calling London, you get on to the local weather people or the TV station and establish *precisely* the number of inches of snow they've had in the last ten days. By the time I finish my call I expect you to be able to tell me when the last of the vehicles left the valley. Use your room phone. I don't mind the switchboard overhearing your enquiry. I'll use one of the public phones in the lobby. If I can't do anything about the NSA listening in, at least I can prevent the motel operator knowing all our business and spreading it around. I've a feeling the desk clerk we spoke to last night doesn't much like the English.'

'I'm Scottish,' said Hamilton.

'If you don't tell anyone, I won't.'

Together with a new passport, currency and credit cards, Calderwood had issued Alex with a telephone charge card. The international operator advised that there would be a few minutes' delay in contacting London, and that she would call him back on the number he had given. While waiting,

Alex stretched his legs in the lobby and examined the paperbacks. There were entire displays of the latest Ludlum and Deighton, as well as a revolving rack of a book entitled *The Canaris Fragments*, which Alex had read in the English edition and had found impressive in its delineation of Germany in the immediate post-war period.

When the telephone rang, Alex had to wait several minutes before Calderwood came on the line.

'Where are you?' asked Calderwood.

Alex told him. 'I suppose we can assume this is not a secure line.'

'That would be advisable.'

'In which case I shall have to be cryptic. We've made some progress today, the details of which I'll put in the bag or telex when I get to Washington, which is our next port of call.'

'Ours?'

'Yes. I'd appreciate keeping my present companion for the foreseeable future, unless you can think of a reason why he may be unsuitable.'

'I can think of none.'

'Is it possible to give me a brief rundown on his recent background? I'd like to be sure I'm making the right decision.'

'I'm certain you are.' There was a long pause. 'This is difficult,' went on Calderwood eventually, 'but prior to his present posting he was cloak-and-daggering in Ulster on temporary attachment to the SAS.'

'I'll settle for that,' said Alex. 'May I take it that I'm accredited to whoever wields the power in DC?'

'You may take it to be thus, although I feel it might be wiser to let as few people as possible know you're in Washington. Our resident there is a man called Egerton. He would not have been my personal choice. He can be an awkward customer. Use him only if you have to. Otherwise, use your companion as liaison officer. He'll see you get anything you need. Egerton will be instructed to co-operate, but I would prefer him not to know of your existence. These are murky waters, Alex. The fewer involved, the better.'

'I'll have to brief my companion on the assignment. He'll be ineffective otherwise. Perhaps not everything, just as much as I deem necessary.'

'Whatever your judgement tells you to do. He has the clearance. Do you want your back covered?'

'I don't think so. It may become complicated if I'm never quite sure who the unfriendlies are.'

'As you wish. I'll hear from you, then?'

'Shortly.'

The line was disconnected. In London, Calderwood wondered if Alex had been serious in not wanting his back covered or whether he had been unwilling to specify his requirements over an insecure line. 'Back covering' was SIS terminology for the infiltration of a covert operative whose function was to protect his principal without the principal knowing who his cover was. Some officers liked it, some did not. Calderwood decided to take no chances. He had excellent connections in Washington.

Alex returned to the bar. Duncan Hamilton was already there, chatting to the blonde cocktail waitress, who went back to her post when Alex reached the table.

'I thought you were tired.'

'I am. I was asking her if she remembered your brother. No luck, I'm afraid. She wasn't on duty the night he was here.'

'It was good thinking anyway.' Alex nodded his approval. 'I should have thought of it myself. You're in, by the way. Official from Calderwood. No more monitoring foreign signal traffic. I'll brief you later. In the meantime, what happened with the weather bureau?'

Hamilton had the figures in his pocket diary.

'From the measurements I took, give or take an error of ten per cent, the vehicle tracks were made the day after your brother was killed. Certainly not before. Do you want to know how I arrive at that conclusion?'

'No. I take it you're numerate, which means Tyson was lying.'

'Not necessarily,' said Hamilton. 'You're making the assumption that there was something in the valley when Tyson and your brother were there, and that the vehicles arrived to take that something away.'

'You don't agree?'

111

'I agree that's the most probable interpretation of the available data. There could be others.'

'Such as a circus arriving in town, pulling in and pulling out in one day? Come on. Nick didn't fly fifteen hundred miles to look at a deserted canyon. There was something there, which Tyson saw too. What's more, he's going to tell us what it was. He said he lived above the store, didn't he? We'll take back the clothes we borrowed, that'll give us an excuse.'

'Now? Don't we get to eat?'

Alex checked his wristwatch; the time was approaching eight p.m. and neither of them had tasted food since breakfast.

'All right, dinner first, business later. Though if you're going to work for me,' he added lightly, 'you've got to get accustomed to skipping meals.'

An hour and a half later, on the road to Midland, Alex explained how he proposed tackling Tyson. Over dinner he had briefed Hamilton as far as he thought necessary, telling him how Calderwood suspected that Nick's interest in neo-Nazis was somehow connected with an operation, code named Cougar, that the CIA were running. Cougar, he added, was an acronym of the first three letters of Coughlin and Garfield, two known CIA field officers. He said nothing about his personal interest in the pair.

'If Tyson's with his wife or friends, that's no use,' said Alex. 'We've got to get him alone, away from the store. Then we lean on him. We don't say we *believe* he was lying this afternoon; we say we *know* he was. After that, we play it by ear.'

'What if he refuses to co-operate? We're the foreigners here, not Tyson. If he tells us to go to hell there's not a lot we can do about it.'

'He'll co-operate,' said Alex soberly. 'One way or another he'll talk.'

But as they neared Tyson's store some sixth sense told Alex that he was wrong, that in all likelihood Tyson would not be saying anything to anyone ever again. The flashing lights of the two police patrol cars were visible three hundred yards away, and Alex did not have to be told that they were pulled up outside Tyson's.

'Drive right past and park.'

Hamilton did so. Alex got out and walked back.

'What happened?' he asked one of the many bystanders, adopting a passable American accent.

'Some kinda robbery,' answered a burly man. 'I heard one of the cops say Tyson must have surprised someone burgling the store. The bastards shot him clean through the head. Jesus, Cliff Tyson. It's hard to believe.'

'He's dead?' Alex injected some compassion into his voice.

'As mutton. The paramedics took him away twenty minutes ago. His wife too. They missed her but she's hysterical. Poor son of a bitch.'

'They catch the guys?'

'No. They'll be in Nebraska by now.'

'It didn't just happen, then?'

'No. Around nine fifteen someone said.'

Alex walked back to the car.

'They've killed Tyson.'

Hamilton was shocked. 'Who are they?'

'Someone who didn't want us talking to him again, someone he must have told we were enquiring about weather reports. He died at nine fifteen or thereabouts,' added Alex significantly.

Hamilton understood. 'While we were eating.'

'Yes, while we were eating.'

'It was necessary,' Cassidy had said when Stone called him with the news. 'I know you must have found it distasteful, but it was necessary.'

From his position at the window of the bar Stone could see the lights of the police cars. He reflected on Cassidy's words, thinking that he hadn't found it distasteful at all.

ARLINGTON (i)

After an hour's delay changing planes in Chicago, Alex and Duncan Hamilton arrived at Washington National shortly before four p.m. Eastern Standard Time the day following the Tyson killing. Hamilton lived on the same side of the Potomac as the airport, in Arlington. On the flight down he had confessed that he did not live alone, that the one-bedroom apartment was shared with his 'steady'. He hoped that did not constitute a security breach.

'What does she do?' Alex had asked.

'She's a teacher.'

'Does she know what you do?'

'She thinks I'm a diplomatic courier.'

'Has she been vetted?'

'I did it myself.'

'I'll wager that was a revelation. As an insight into yourself, I mean.'

'It was. I felt like some seedy divorce detective.'

Alex had elected to take Calderwood's advice and steer clear of the embassy and the resident-in-chief, Egerton. He would therefore not be able to take advantage of the various accommodation facilities the embassy provided for visitors. Hamilton offered to put him up if he didn't mind a tight squeeze and the couch. Alex didn't think much of the idea.

'Your girl might object. How long have you been away?'

'A week.'

'Then she'll certainly object. Take me to a small hotel somewhere near you. I'll want a private bathroom and so on, but nothing too fancy.'

Hamilton found Alex an hotel near the Virginia Square

Orange Line Metro station, explaining that he lived less than three blocks away. After registering and depositing his bags, Alex bought Hamilton a beer in a nearby bar.

'It's too late to do anything this evening,' he said, 'but tomorrow, you've got a busy day.' He produced the leather case containing the camera lens and strip of film, and passed it over. 'For God's sake don't lose it. In the morning, take the lens and the film to whoever you can trust to keep his mouth shut in the photographic surveillance section, without Egerton knowing.'

'There's a good chap there, Bob Hazeldene. He develops everyone's holiday pictures as a sideline,' said Hamilton, as though that put Hazeldene's reliability beyond question.

'Then ask Hazeldene to identify the camera this lens comes from and to reproduce the film ten times or so and splice each section together. I think it's called a loop. I want thirty feet that I can repeat over and over again through a projector.'

'He'll see what's on the film,' Hamilton pointed out.

'That can't be avoided. In any case, we don't know if there's anything of value to be seen yet.' Alex was silent for a moment. 'You say you can trust Hazeldene?'

'Yes. He's no friend of Egerton, if that's what you mean.'

'That's not entirely what I meant, but it helps. I'd like to meet him. Bring him to the hotel as soon as the loop is ready. We'll need portable projection equipment also.'

'Right. Do you want me to call you first or just turn up?'

'You'd better call me. I won't be going far if I go anywhere, but call me to be on the safe side.'

'Will do. Anything else?'

Alex contemplated his beer. As Calderwood had said on the telephone, they were entering murky waters. One man – above all others – could help to clear them, if he was still around, still active.

'Yes. I used to know a Company man by the name of George Andrus. The last I heard he was in Washington. I'd like you to trace him, nothing more. No approaches. I just want to know if he's still alive and where he lives.'

'And this is not official, I take it.'

'Dammit, of course it's not official,' snapped Alex.

115

'Didn't I make myself clear yesterday evening? You work for me now, not Egerton or anyone else. If there's any trouble I'll sort it out or, through me, Calderwood will.'

Hamilton's cheeks reddened. 'Got it,' he said, tight-lipped. He added, 'I did understand that, you know.'

Alex regretted raising his voice. 'I'm certain you did.'

But Hamilton had not finished. 'No, I'm not quite sure you are. As I said in the motel, I've heard the name Alex Dunbar before, albeit only in Fort Monkton. A week ago I was filing signals and once in a while shadowing a known Soviet agent. It was boring. I didn't like it. It wasn't what I was used to – elsewhere. I know what happens in the intelligence game. It's similar to what happened in the RAF – and I assume the Luftwaffe – in the last war. My father was a Spitfire pilot. He used to tell me that during the Battle of Britain a pilot either made a kill on his first two or three sorties, or never. It depended upon his own ability and who helped him, gave him advice. It's the same in this business. I could have been filing signals for another two years before being posted elsewhere. I was lucky. Because of your own bereavement and by accident, I was the man who met you at Kennedy. We got along, if you don't mind me saying so. However, you could have ditched me when you talked to Mr Calderwood. You didn't. You wanted me on your team. I appreciate that. If I ask questions it's only because I want to learn, not because I don't know who I work for. End of statement.'

'I'm glad your time in Ireland taught you to speak out.'

'You know about that?'

'Of course. I may be forty years of age and going slightly grey; I'm not entirely senile. Nor do I take someone on without finding out a little about him. My survival might depend on that other person. Now, back to George Andrus.'

Hamilton had the grace to accept the rebuke. 'I'm sorry. That monologue must have sounded terribly pompous.'

'Forget it. Do what I ask about Andrus and tell me tomorrow. As for tonight, you'd better get home to that girl of yours.'

'Are you sure you won't come with me, have something to eat with us if nothing else?'

116

'For Christ's sake,' said Alex irritably, 'don't patronize me. You're not old enough.'

Towards ten o'clock, however, after eating an excellent Italian dinner, Alex mildly regretted not taking Hamilton up on his offer. For the first time in years he envied the comfort and relaxation another was doubtlessly presently enjoying. Not the sex; that was secondary. What he really envied in Duncan Hamilton and his girl was the impenetrable armour with which lovers surrounded themselves, the exclusivity of mutual fondness. She would tell him about her day at school and ask him about his trip. He would have to be evasive of necessity, but they would be close.

Pathetic, he told himself as he undressed. Absolutely pathetic. Melanie was dead, and that was that. His function was to find and destroy her killers and vindicate her reputation, albeit that the calumnies levelled against her were known to only a few. He was not really concerned with Cougar or Calderwood's interest in it. But if Cougar led to Coughlin and Garfield, then, momentarily, the objectives of Calderwood and Alex Dunbar were identical.

Before showering he checked the phone book for the name of George Andrus. There were several and he decided to leave it to Hamilton.

Late the following afternoon Hamilton called him.

'You are not going to believe this,' were his opening words.

Alex heard the excitement in his voice.

'I'm old enough to believe anything apart from Santa Claus and the hereafter. Don't say anything over the phone.'

'We'll be with you in an hour. That is, I'll be accompanied by our resident photography expert.'

Bob Hazeldene turned out to be a tall, skinny individual in his middle thirties. His thinning gingery hair was uncombed and his raincoat could have done with an excursion to the cleaners. Alex knew the type well; there was one in every embassy and they lived in a world of their own, never happier than when they were elbow-deep in undeveloped film or figuring out a new method for photographing a target undetected.

'Pleased to meet you, Mr Dunbar.'

Alex's hand came away from the shake smelling of some kind of chemical.

Hazeldene's projection equipment was in a small container the size of a tool-box; the screen, folded up like a roller-blind, and the tripod legs it stood on were in a canvas case. While Hamilton set up the screen, Hazeldene unpacked the projector, talking continuously. His enthusiasm for his subject knew no limitations.

'You wanted to know about the lens. It comes from a 16mm movie camera of not very good quality manufactured in the Soviet Union before 1939. Not much before, however. I'd never actually seen or held one until today. I had to go to my reference books, but I can give you the technical reasons for my opinion if you'd care to hear them.'

'They wouldn't mean anything to me,' said Alex. 'Go on.'

'I doubt whether the camera this lens was attached to was ever used by a professional motion picture maker. The standard gauge for pros is 35mm and has been since Edison invented his Kinetograph before the turn of the century. However, sixteen mill. was used widely for wartime newsreels. That's all I can tell you about the lens apart from the fact that it's scratched. That may not be important in itself, but if it's any help to you the lens was on the camera that took the film you asked Duncan to give me. That film, by the way, has a soundtrack band with no sound on it. Presumably it was shot without a mike. I made a loop of thirty-six feet, since sixteen-mill. is shot at thirty-six feet a minute. Your original footage lasts approximately five seconds. The film's in black and white and of poor quality. The subject matter is unmistakable. Ready, Duncan?'

'Ready.'

While talking Hazeldene had done complicated things with spools and plugged in the projector to the table lamp socket. 'We'd better have the lights off,' he suggested. 'As I say, the quality's poor.'

Poor, perhaps, but not so poor as to make the scene that unrolled time and time again unrecognizable. Shot from a distance, every five seconds the same group of people appeared on the screen: five adults, men and women, and a child, all dressed in the garb of concentration camp inmates.

118

On each uniform was the Star of David. The child backed away in terror as a huge dog held by a guard lunged forward, snarling. Grotesquely because of the loop, the child's terrified reactions and the expressions of horror on the adults' faces were reproduced a dozen times a minute, making it appear as if they were being tormented in perpetuity. Behind them was part of what appeared to be a hut, and in the distance, though it was difficult to tell because of the scratch on the lens, a watchtower.

'Can you freeze any of that?' asked Alex.

'No,' answered Hazeldene. 'That's layman's language. What looks like a freeze on screen is simply the same frame printed repeatedly, which I couldn't do here without mutilating the strip. However, I anticipated you might require something like that and made a couple of stills from one of the end shots. They're not very good,' he apologized, 'and I couldn't make them any larger than ten by eight without ruining the focus completely. But I think they're good enough for you to be able to see something very unusual.'

Hazeldene switched off the projector and turned on the lights. He handed over the two stills.

'Tell me what I'm supposed to be looking for,' said Alex. 'I'm no use at guessing games.'

'The guard's uniform,' said Hazeldene. 'I didn't spot it at first, either, but I've had the advantage of viewing the loop for much more than a couple of minutes. Photographers have retentive memories for visual subjects and something about the tunic bothered me. Anyway, I looked up the whole thing in another reference book. The strip you gave me, I think you'll agree, *seems* to have been part of a film shot in a Nazi concentration camp. Everything about the people in it and the background is reminiscent of photographs and newsreels we've all seen. The guard has his left profile to us in the still. If he were a Nazi camp guard he would be wearing SS runes and a sleeve eagle. That man is not. He's wearing the uniform and insignia of a World War II Russian corporal. The Russian word for him is *Mladshiy Serzhant*, junior sergeant.'

'So he's an SS guard who happens to have acquired a

119

Russian corporal's tunic,' said Alex. 'Or he's a Russian POW who sold out to the Nazis to save his own skin. That wasn't unusual.' He was convinced by neither argument, however. What would three feet of film apparently shot in a concentration camp be doing lying under a red marker in South Dakota?

'No,' said Hazeldene triumphantly. 'No, he's not an SS guard wearing a Russian uniform, and nor is he a World War II Russian corporal. For that matter, he's no one who was alive during the last war. He's about twenty-five, would you say? Thirty at the most. Okay, so while the lens is from a camera that antedates 1939, the film isn't! Again I can give you technical details if you want them, but the date of manufacture of that strip of film is very recent. So is the developing process. No one but an expert, if you'll excuse my immodesty, would be able to tell, however. It's a very clever fake. If you were to ask me for my opinion, Mr Dunbar, I'd say that someone has done everything in his power to convince the untutored viewer that what he's witnessing is a film shot forty years ago.'

'Maybe,' murmured Alex.

'There's no maybe about it,' said Hazeldene a trifle offended.

Alex said he had not meant to cast doubt on Hazeldene's professional opinion. 'On the other hand, you made the assumption a minute ago that the location was a *Nazi* concentration camp. There's no evidence to suggest that. What if it was a Russian camp? They did and do have them, you know.'

'The same logic applies,' said Hazeldene. 'Whether it's a Russian camp or a Nazi camp, it isn't one that existed during the war, no matter how clever the cameraman has tried to be.'

'Run the film again.'

While the three men watched the child repeatedly cower away from the snarling dog, Alex asked Hazeldene if the photographer would care to hazard a guess regarding where the film was shot, though he thought he knew the answer to that question – a valley in South Dakota which Nick had stumbled upon or been led to, and which had killed him.

Two days ago it had killed Tyson because Tyson would have been in a position to reveal that the deep furrows in the snow had been made by the vehicles which took away the buildings that had comprised the camp, and perhaps also the inmates.

'Not a chance,' said Hazeldene. 'Judging by the shadows there's a lot of overhead artificial lighting around. I wouldn't be able to tell you the latitude even if I knew the time of day.'

Announcing that he'd seen enough, Alex asked Hazeldene to switch off the projector and turn on the lights. He thanked the photographer warmly. 'I'd like to hold on to your equipment for a day or so.'

'By all means. It's my own personal stuff.'

'And I'd be obliged if you'd say nothing to anyone about all this. Especially Egerton.'

'You can count on it. Nice to have met you, Mr Dunbar. See you soon, Duncan.'

'So,' said Alex when he and Hamilton were alone, 'what do you make of it all?'

'I haven't the faintest idea. You?'

'Not a clue. Did you manage to trace George Andrus?'

'I did. I spent all morning on it, much to Egerton's chagrin. He's received word from London that I'm on a special assignment, and doesn't much like it. He knows nothing of you, of course.'

'Andrus,' Alex prompted him. Hamilton referred to his diary.

'He's not with the Company any longer, and hasn't been for several years. My information is that he was invalided out, though I don't have details. He's now the proprietor, shareholder and just about everything else of a one-man-band public relations outfit over in Crystal City, which is this side of the river between the Pentagon and the airport. He's rarely in a hurry to go home. Most evenings until around nine he can be found in Amelia's, a very fancy bar-cum-restaurant in the Crystal City Underground complex. It numbers a few members of Congress among its regulars. Mr Andrus sometimes goes there to eat, sometimes to have a few drinks.' Hamilton shut his diary. 'That's it.'

'That's a lot of information for a morning's work,' said Alex admiringly. And then suspiciously: 'You didn't go to

Langley for any of this?'

'Of course not. I may have been filing signals for the last few months, but I've managed to build up a small list of contacts.'

'That's why you're here,' said Alex. 'That's why you're in Washington and not Berlin or Moscow for your first posting. You'll meet one or two people here who'll be useful to you throughout the remainder of your career.'

'Were you ever posted here?'

'Not the way you mean. It was different in my day.' Alex consulted his wristwatch; it was not yet seven. 'Right, I'll be getting over to Amelia's.'

'I'd like to call home first.'

'You're not coming.' Hamilton's face fell. 'You're a glutton for punishment, you know that?' said Alex. 'Here am I giving you yet another night off and you want to work. No, this is going to be a meeting between old friends. George might be reluctant to open up in front of a stranger.'

'He might not be willing to open up at all.'

'Meaning?'

'I mentioned that sometimes he doesn't eat; he just drinks. I got the impression from my contact that he drinks rather a lot.'

'Quite a few people have been that route,' said Alex quietly. 'George Andrus is an old man. As a younger man, very young, he was with the OSS during the war. He's seen more and done more than either of us can ever hope to, never mind Ireland. The IRA are a bunch of amateurs compared to some of the people George has come up against. If he wants a drink, he's earned one.'

'It was a comment, not a criticism,' said Hamilton defensively, wondering if the day would ever come when he could open his mouth without offending Alex Dunbar.

'I should hope it was.'

'I didn't mean to infer he was a drunk, just that sometimes he has more than he can carry.'

'We all have days like that. How do I get to Crystal City?'

'You take the Orange Line to Rosslyn and change there to the Blue Line.'

'I'll take a cab,' said Alex.

ARLINGTON (ii)

He found George Andrus sitting at the oak bar, drinking red wine and contemplating one of the replicas of World War I aircraft suspended from the ceiling. If this was one of his 'off' days, it wasn't showing. Nor did he seem other than prosperous. His dark-blue suit was beautifully tailored, his shoes (the neglect of which, as Alex knew from personal experience, being the first sign that someone had lost interest in his appearance) highly polished. He was engaged in animated conversation with two men who were also drinking red wine; they were apparently discussing the aircraft above their heads.

Although Alex hadn't seen him since Berlin, he recognized him instantly. He would be sixty-two or -three now, and the years had not been unkind to him. He was shorter than Alex, slim and distinguished-looking, with a shock of carefully groomed white hair. If his public relations outfit was a one-man band, the music evidently pleased the listeners.

Alex ambled up to the bar. 'I think you'll find it's a Sopwith Camel.'

'No, it isn't.' Andrus turned towards him. 'It's a . . .' His eyes widened in astonishment. '*Alex? Alex Dunbar?*'

'The very same, George. How are you?'

'*Alex!*' whooped Andrus. 'How am *I*? Never mind me, how the hell are *you*? What are you doing here? Are you in town for long? How the hell *are* you? This is an old friend of mine from England,' he said to his companions. 'I haven't seen him for years. Alex Dunbar.'

Alex promptly forgot the other men's names. 'I hate to

123

interrupt,' he said to Andrus, 'but I wonder if we could have a few words in private.'

'A few? Have a hundred. A million. Listen, what can I buy you to drink? The wine's good and the tap beer's great.'

Alex settled for a beer. Once served, he and Andrus retreated for what passed as a quiet corner in Amelia's. After a few minutes' small talk Andrus said, 'I heard about Melanie. It shocked the hell out of me.'

'Yes, I forgot. You met her, of course.'

'In London six or seven years ago. We lunched at some French place in Soho. Jesus, Alex, I meant to write but you know how it is. What can a man say when something like that happens? And I had my own troubles round the same time.'

'Serious?'

'Serious enough for me to be given my marching orders. I was long past the age for active duty anyway, but I was hoping to stay on, even if it was only a desk. The thought of retirement scared me stiff.'

'What happened? I heard you were no longer with – your former employers.'

'But presumably you are?'

'Sort of,' said Alex cautiously.

'Then I'd better be careful what I say,' smiled Andrus. 'Ah, what the hell. It's all blood under the bridge now. Remember I was deputy chief of the Berlin station?' Alex nodded. 'Well, we were losing a few too many agents. Nothing sinister, just something that happens from time to time. Natural attrition was always part of the game and we expected losses. However, these were too heavy for Langley, who flew in a troubleshooter, a punk by the name of Cassidy, a real whizzkid. I don't know what kind of fitness report on me he sent back home, but the vibrations were suddenly very hostile.' He tapped his glass. 'I was already drinking more than was good for me and Cassidy's presence made it worse. Anyway, Langley sent for me and told me that was it. Goodbye. Time to fold my tent and softly steal away. They gave me that desk for a while, then showed me the door. It wasn't so hard. I still had a few friends in senior posts from the old OSS days. I got my gratuity and pension and some help in setting up a public relations outfit, which is what I do now. I don't really have to look for clients. One way or another Langley points some good accounts in my direction. I live well. I never married, you'll recall, so every cent I make stays with me. Mind you, I'd have given a lot to have had Cassidy's ears and balls as trophies. He became head of station for a while later, I think. Got rid of me and my chief and stepped in. One of these low-profile types. Hardly anyone ever saw him, but you knew he was there.'

Andrus shrugged his elegantly tailored shoulders and lifted his glass. 'Here's to the old days, except I don't suppose that's much of a toast as you're still in harness.'

'I only said sort of.'

'Yes, I noticed. Funny, I'd heard you were out completely.'

'Who told you that?'

'Christ, I can't remember. Scuttlebutt. You know how it is with the old Berlin hands. Anyway, the rumour was obviously wrong.' Andrus wrinkled his forehead. 'You haven't said what you're doing in Washington, or is it indiscreet to ask?'

'I came to see you.'

'Me? Then this isn't a chance meeting? No, how could it be.' Andrus pursed his lips. 'Okay, what can I do for you?'

'I need some information.'

'Use channels. Last I heard, we were still on the same side.'

'Can't do. I need a favour on the old-boy network without anyone knowing who the old boy is.'

'I'm not sure my connections are that good any more.' Andrus brought out a slim, leather-bound notebook and uncapped a gold pen.

'Two Agency names,' said Alex, 'Coughlin and Garfield. They were in the field in Berlin when you were there.'

'During my time? I don't think so. What about them?'

'Anything about them. Who are they, what are they, where are they. Anything you can dig up.'

'I'll do what I can. Are they active?'

'I believe so.'

'Then that could bring some of the Langley heavies knocking at my door.'

'Not if you're careful. I really need this information, George.'

'I'm sure you do. What the hell,' said Andrus jokingly, 'nobody lives for ever. How long have I got?'

'The sooner the better.'

'Which means yesterday. All right, anything else?'

'If you can spare the time there's a film I'd like you to look at.'

An hour later Alex switched off the projector and turned on the lights.

'I don't get it,' said Andrus.

'Nor do I,' said Alex. 'I don't know whether what you've just seen is in any way connected with Coughlin and Garfield. I suspect it may be. Something the matter?' Andrus was staring at the now blank screen.

'I'm not sure. Maybe it's my memory playing tricks. On the other hand, something about that strip of film strikes a chord – and I don't mean the obvious one. That or something very like it reminds me of an operation the OSS mounted or considered mounting late on in the last war.'

'Do you want to tell me about it over dinner? My treat.'

'No. If you want this information in a hurry I'd better start digging now. Tonight. Let's meet for lunch tomorrow. I can give you a progress report. I'll call you around eleven.'

It was eleven forty-five before the phone rang, by which time Alex was getting anxious.

'Don't mention me by name,' said Andrus hurriedly. 'This is shittier than I thought. I'd feel happier if we met in the open. Do you know the John F Kennedy site in Arlington National Cemetery?'

'I can find it.'

'It's no distance at all from the Visitors' Center. You can either walk or take one of the concessionaire buses. I'll meet you there in half an hour.'

Alex was a few minutes late. It took him several more to pick out Andrus among the sightseers surrounding President Kennedy's grave.

They walked south along Roosevelt Drive.

'I'll begin with the film,' said Andrus. 'I told you last night it seemed familiar. Now I know why. Bear with me until I've finished.'

Andrus pulled at his woollen gloves. A watery sun shone through broken cloud over the Pentagon, but otherwise it was a cold, early-spring day.

'Prior to Hitler's Ardennes push in December 1944,' Andrus began, 'many of the Allied brass were predicting that the war would be over by Christmas or soon afterwards. When the Nazi offensive narrowly failed, the same senior officers realized that there was a hell of a lot of hard and bitter fighting ahead. The Wehrmacht still had four to five million men under arms, including crack Waffen SS troops. Germany was far from beaten. On the other hand, large numbers of Allied soldiers, particularly GIs, were demoralized. Unlike the European and British armies, they were thousands of miles from home. They'd believed they'd be back with their families before the end of the year, but here they were, in the middle of freezing winter, still fighting a determined enemy, one who'd come within an ace of wiping them out in the Battle of the Bulge. If the Wehrmacht could counter-attack like that when all previous indications were that it was falling apart, what were the German commanders going to do next? It was a long way to Berlin and a lot of men were going to die.'

Andrus neatly sidestepped a couple of children who were racing up Roosevelt Drive, laughing and shouting. Their furious parents – the facially-scarred husband a veteran of a more recent war – yelled at them to conduct themselves with more dignity.

'The Allied psychological warfare team came up with a few ideas to keep the troops happy, boost morale. Mostly these were nothing more than regular food parcels and mail, and live entertainment well to the rear of the front lines. Divisional brothels were also seriously considered before getting the thumbs down, and not for the obvious reason that the GIs' mothers, wives and sweethearts would pillory any administration that contemplated such a move. No, divisional brothels were proscribed because, in the psychologists' opinion, a sexually contented soldier wouldn't fight as hard as one who was frustrated. It makes a kind of crazy sense when you think about it. Anyway, that was one idea that didn't get off the drawing-board, but another, even more outrageous, did. It was the brainchild of someone high up in the OSS. You can probably guess his name if you put your mind to it.'

Alex thought he could: Allen Dulles.

They walked on in silence while Andrus marshalled his thoughts.

'The British and American governments,' he continued, 'had known about such places as Auschwitz, Treblinka, Bergen-Belsen and so forth for some time, and also, to a certain extent, what was going on there. Much of what they knew came from Jewish sources, although our respective governments, to what should be their eternal shame, were unwilling to accept the whole truth. Perhaps their inaction can be justified up to a point because they lacked hard intelligence. All they had were rumours – rumours that mass exterminations were taking place. These were largely disbelieved, however, because it was impossible for civilized people to accept that any nation would systematically set out to destroy a particular ethnic group. We – that is, the Americans – admitted that in wartime many Jews, gypsies, Slavs and so on would have to be incarcerated as potential enemies of the state, as had happened to US-Japanese citizens after Pearl Harbor. Doubtless some of the people imprisoned by the Nazis would die through disease or of malnutrition. Their corpses would be burned for hygienic reasons, cremated, which explained the occasional eyewitness and photographic evidence we were getting from Europe. Rumours that something much more sinister was taking place were therefore largely dismissed by intelligence, although our psychological warfare people, supported by the OSS, considered that some capital could be made of the camps. What the Allied soldier in general and the GI in particular needed was a shot in the arm, an injection of fighting spirit. Which is where we come to the devious bit.

'In a remote part of Montana, under conditions of absolute secrecy, a phoney camp was built. Watchtowers were constructed, barbed-wire fences, rows of huts for prisoner accommodation – and crematoria, complete with chimneys. The whole number. And if it all sounds macabre and disgusting, Alex, you have to remember we were fighting a war we were not yet sure we could win.

'The object was to dress long-serving inmates of US military prisons in concentration camp uniform, others as SS guards. A complete scenario was written to show quote an average day unquote in a *Vernichtungslager*, an extermination camp. It would be photographed on movie film of inferior quality with hand-held cameras, as though it had been done clandestinely in a genuine camp, and smuggled out. Fake beatings would be shown, dummies on gallows, dogs. Mock executions would be filmed and queues of people seen heading for the quote showers unquote. Later those same people – now replaced by dummies – would be filmed being loaded into the crematoria ovens. Still photos would also be taken.

'Women prisoners as well as men could easily be found, though the absence of children was held to be a drawback until someone suggested using small women dressed up as kids.

'When the film was completed and the stills taken, the end product would serve two useful purposes. The movie would be screened to Allied troops in Europe, to show them the kind of bestiality they were fighting; and hundreds of thousands of the stills would be dropped over German towns and cities during regular bombing raids, revealing to the German people what was being done in their name. Goebbels could rave until he was blue in the face that it was all vicious Allied propaganda. That wouldn't convince our troops. Nor would it convince more than a handful of Germans because – and this is where it worked beautifully for us – although *we* didn't believe the stories of mass murder, we wanted the German people to believe them. Ironic, no? Anyway, alongside conventional methods of waging war, the pictures would help sap the morale of the Third Reich while simultaneously boosting ours. Keep going left,' said Andrus. 'We'll go down Porter and along Eisenhower back to the Visitors' Center.

'Because it was such a complex operation it took several

months to set up and shoot. By the time the film and the stills were ready, Allied troops were across the Rhine, in Germany, seeing at first hand the real horrors the psychological warfare unit had tried to create fictionally. The project was shelved, copies of the film and accompanying documentation buried in a vault and forgotten about.' Andrus paused. 'Until recently, that is. I can't give you an exact date because I don't have one. In the last weeks, however, three copies of the film and OSS documents detailing the whole plan have disappeared. So too have agents Coughlin and Garfield. Shall we get some lunch?'

They each ordered hot pastrami on rye and coffee in a stand-up sandwich bar which was packed with the lunchtime crowd. There was no danger of their conversation being overheard.

'Langley is going quietly bananas,' said Andrus, 'the more so because no one can figure out what Coughlin and Garfield are up to. They just upped and vanished. There's a theory going the rounds that some time soon there'll be a blackmail letter in the post.'

'I'm not sure I understand,' said Alex.

'Then try this for size. When the war ended the Allies took possession of tens of tons of Nazi documents. In not one of them is there a *single* mention of genocide as an instrument of policy. Even at the Wannsee Conference, which took place in January 1942, chaired by Heydrich, only the term 'final solution' was used, which many of those present genuinely – and I do mean *genuinely* – thought entailed deportation to the newly acquired territories to the east. At this time the Wehrmacht was virtually unstoppable, so the whole idea made sense. Only Eichmann of those who survived professed to know what 'final solution' actually meant. He said, during his trial by the Israelis, that Heydrich had told him bluntly something to the effect that the Führer had ordered the physical extermination of the Jews. But no record of that conversation exists.'

Andrus took a bite of his sandwich and chewed on it for several seconds before continuing.

'At Nuremberg all the defendants from Goering downwards denied any knowledge of extermination camps.

Even when the defendants were shown films taken by the advancing Allied armies, they said that such camps as existed must have been few and staffed by a handful of madmen. The Führer had never decreed genocide. Any evidence to the contrary had been *faked by the Allies to blacken the defendants and obtain convictions.*'

Alex began to see daylight. 'Which to some extent was the truth.'

'Right. Now perhaps you can see why Langley is tearing his hair out. Many Germans in all age groups don't believe or don't want to believe that Hitler advocated genocide. Both the Nazis of the old school and those of the younger generation prefer to believe that much of the photographic evidence was planted by the Allies, faked. I've even heard it suggested that if it's possible to fake a moonshot, as happened in that movie *Capricorn One*, how much easier would it be to construct phoney camps? And that suggestion is correct, of course. It *was* done, and now Coughlin and Garfield are walking around with the physical proof, which, if it ever became public knowledge, would be embarrassing to say the least, and possibly a great deal more than that.'

'How so?' asked Alex.

'In the first place, Germany's extremists would claim that if one film could be faked, why not many more than one? They'd have a field day, contending that everything that happened to Germany in the immediate postwar period, the dividing of the country into east and west and the isolation of the natural capital, Berlin, only took place because the world was horrified at what had occurred in the camps.

'Then there's another argument that the right-wing could put forward: that Israel would not exist were it not for six million dead. Think about that, Alex, because there's some logic in it. Israel came into being on a wave of world sympathy. Many well-informed people doubt it would have been created were it not for the terrible sufferings the Jews had undergone at the hands of the Nazis. But what if someone produced testimony that at least part of the historical record is spurious? The right-wingers would go to town, and I mean right-wingers all over the planet, your own National Front as much as anyone. It doesn't bear thinking what the PLO propaganda machine would make of it. Since Beirut and the massacres at the Chatila and Sabra refugee camps, Israel has had a terrible press. The PLO would say that the illegal Israeli occupation of Palestine began as a Jewish plot, that the Jews themselves knew that nothing like six million were killed in the holocaust. Don't look so incredulous, Alex. A big lie is better than a small lie, that's basic.'

Andrus finished his coffee, his throat very dry.

'There's one last item that's worrying Langley. Since Schmidt was deposed as chancellor of the Federal Republic and the conservatives installed, there have already been one or two comments about a new, greater German nationalism. No one's being specific at present, but it's a fact of life that a large proportion of the conservatives do not accept as permanent the existence of two Germanies, which, they argue, were created unjustly. I might add that many East Germans would not be unhappy if they were back in the fold. All right, that's doubtless impossible politically, but Coughlin and Garfield could cause a hell of a lot of trouble at street level if they released the film and supporting documents to television. They're walking around with a fused bomb. What they plan to do with it no one yet knows, but Langley is concerned enough to have put out an open contract on the pair of them. Terminate with extreme prejudice on sight.'

'Is there any word regarding their present whereabouts?' Alex asked casually.

'Not much. I might hear something later today or early tomorrow. One theory is that they're still in this country, but a little bird told me that the Company is pulling out all the stops in Bangkok, Hong Kong and Tokyo. However, no one's really got a clue where they are. I suppose logic would dictate that they head for Germany if they plan to do something dramatic with what they've stolen. Alternatively, they could just as easily sit tight in a Japanese hotel and try to make a deal from there, whether it involves blackmailing Langley or trying to make a sale to an interested party such as the PLO or the German neo-Nazis. Of course, I'm assuming that the object is blackmail or a sale. It could be any of a dozen other things. And what we don't know is how they're connected with that piece of film you showed me last night. You never told me where you obtained that, incidentally.'

'No, I didn't,' said Alex, thereby closing the subject.

Nor did he understand the connection himself, though the OSS wartime scenario and the images on the strip were too closely linked to be coincidence. It therefore followed that the OSS film interlocked with Cougar and, in some obscure manner, with Nick, except that how that could be defeated him. At the back of his mind he sensed conspiracy, that he was being manipulated. But that was simply a sixth-sense reaction he could not substantiate.

He became aware that Andrus was talking to him.

'Sorry, I was miles away.'

'I said be careful,' repeated Andrus. 'I don't know what's going on and, frankly, I'd rather not know. Still, don't get out of your depth.'

They left the sandwich bar at a few minutes before three p.m. Andrus flagged down a cab and asked if he could drop Alex anywhere. Alex shook his head; he had plenty of time to kill. He would use it to walk leisurely back to his hotel, get some exercise and think over what he had learned.

'You'll keep in touch?' he said to Andrus. 'I'll be here for a day or two more yet.'

'I'll do what I can.'

When Andrus returned to his office his secretary, who doubled as receptionist, informed him that two men were waiting for him in the anteroom.

'They said you were expecting them but there's no entry in the appointments book.' Her tone implied rebuke. Bosses were not supposed to do anything without informing their secretaries.

'It was something I arranged last night. Sorry, Marjorie, I forgot to mention it. Look, why don't you take the rest of the afternoon off. I'll be engaged for a couple of hours and I won't want to see anyone else. Hook up the answering machine so I won't be disturbed.'

'Well, if you're sure,' said Marjorie doubtfully, thinking that Mr Andrus had not been himself all day, cancelling the morning appointments just like that and spending at least a couple of hours on his private line, to which she had no listening access.

'I'm sure. See you tomorrow.'

Cassidy was sitting in an armchair, flicking through a magazine. Stone was over by the window, looking bored.

'You'd better come through here,' said Andrus, unlocking the door to his private office. 'If you want something to drink it's in the cabinet.'

Cassidy declined with an impatient wave of his hand. Stone helped himself to a small straight gin, into which he popped a stuffed olive.

Andrus sat behind his desk, feeling more secure at having a barrier between himself and the Company men. Not that they'd threatened him physically when they called on him in the small hours, but there were worse things than physical violence that could happen to a man of his age.

'Nice little place you have here,' said Cassidy chattily, toying with an unlighted cigarette. 'Very nice indeed. You must be pulling in a lot more money than you were in the old days.'

'I make out,' said Andrus sullenly.

'Oh, we know that, George, we know you make out. In fact, I can tell you down to the last dollar how much you turned over last year. Mind you, you wouldn't be doing so well if the Company didn't push the business your way. For that matter, you wouldn't be doing anything at all. The Company keeps you afloat. In return we expect reciprocal loyalty. It was hardly the act of a good citizen to make surreptitious enquiries about a couple of active field men on behalf of a foreign government.'

'I made those enquiries on behalf of an old friend.'

'Of course you did. Nevertheless, that old friend works for British intelligence. You should either have said you couldn't help or reported the matter direct to Langley. You're out of the business, George. It was most unwise to meddle.'

'I didn't know,' said Andrus.

'Didn't know what?' queried Cassidy pleasantly. 'That any, repeat *any*, enquiries regarding Coughlin and Garfield would reach my ears within the hour? Of course you didn't.

How could you possibly know that? But it's a sign of old age when you can't think at least one jump ahead. That's why we had to bounce you from Berlin. You were getting sloppy. All those agents being blown. Dear me.'

'All right,' said Andrus bitterly, 'you've made your point.'

'I hope I have. I sincerely hope I have. Pour George a drink, Frank.'

'I don't want a drink.'

'You'll have one anyway,' said Cassidy, an edge to his voice. 'Frank would like another and I know he dislikes drinking alone. I'd join you if I didn't have to watch my weight. Give him a brandy, Frank.'

In spite of himself, Andrus drank half the brandy in one gulp. He wasn't surprised to find his hands shaking.

'That's better,' said Cassidy. 'It wouldn't seem right if an old acquaintance couldn't have a drink when he so obviously needs one. I almost said "old friend", but that wouldn't be accurate, would it? You and Dunbar are what I would term "old friends". I suspected he'd contact someone he knew from Berlin when he reached Washington, but I was quite surprised to find it was you. There again, I suppose *you* were surprised to find me standing on your doorstep a few hours ago. It's a funny thing about our business; you keep on bumping into the same old faces.'

'I don't have to take all this, you know,' said Andrus, emboldened by the brandy. 'You're on private property. All I have to do is pick up the phone and call the cops. The CIA isn't allowed by statute to operate domestically. Nor can it threaten private citizens. The last I heard, they hadn't changed the rules.'

'Quite right, George, they haven't. However, calling the cops would be most unwise. Wheels within wheels, you understand. Even if some over-zealous rookie risked his badge by arresting us, he'd be out on his ass within a week – and would find it most difficult obtaining other employment. As for yourself, you'd find the IRS examining your books with a magnifying glass. You'd also find yourself running out of clients very rapidly. And at your age, George, do you really want that?'

'Be careful of the time,' said Stone.

'I'm watching it,' Cassidy acknowledged. 'Okay,' he went on, addressing Andrus, 'we've had our little chat, which I trust will not be misinterpreted. Now you can tell me how your conversation with Dunbar went, if you told him everything you were supposed to.'

Fifteen minutes later Cassidy grunted with satisfaction.

'And he's asked you to keep in touch?' Andrus nodded. 'Then you'd better do just that. I'll tell you what to say. In the interim, I think it's time he ran into a little trouble. He's way ahead of schedule and we can't have that. How many men have you got tailing him?' Cassidy asked Stone.

'Three. Plus the mobile.'

'Can you reach them?'

Stone held up an electronic bleeper. 'I gave them George's number here.'

'Then wait by the reception phone, speak to them from there when they call in. I want to have a private word with George, make sure he understands what he's got to do next.'

ARLINGTON (iii)

Alex became aware that he was being followed and had identified two of his shadows as he approached Virginia Square from the east, along Pershing Drive. One of the men, wearing a fawn trenchcoat and a cream leather fedora, was on the other side of the drive, keeping abreast. The second, in a bright-blue windcheater, scruffy jeans and sneakers, all inconsistent with his well-groomed hair and clean-cut features, was forty yards ahead of Alex, on the same side. Unless there were two other men dressed identically making for Virginia Square, he had seen this pair earlier in Arlington Boulevard. And where there were two there would be a third, because three was the classic number in a surveillance team.

To test his suspicions Alex slowed to a snail's pace. The man in the trenchcoat didn't hesitate. He crossed the road in front of Alex, slapping a rolled newspaper against his thigh as he did so. On cue, the shadow in the windcheater ran through the traffic to the far side of Pershing Drive. The change of position was all very cleverly and efficiently accomplished, with the minimum of fuss.

Alex glanced over his shoulder to see if he recognized anyone behind. He did not. Nonetheless he was puzzled. His shadows must have picked him up at the sandwich bar, which meant they'd seen him with George Andrus and also tailed him from his hotel to Arlington Cemetery. If they knew where he was staying, though how they did was a mystery, why follow him back – unless this wasn't surveillance but something more sinister? The opposition had wiped out Tyson without so much as blinking. Maybe he was next on the hit list.

In 7th Street he stopped a passer-by for directions, a genuine request as he was lost. He was advised to continue along 7th to Irving, where he should turn left for a block until he came to 6th. Four blocks further on was Lincoln, where a right would lead him to Virginia Square.

While absorbing this information Alex kept one eye on his chaperons. Rather than dawdle they should have changed places a second time. They hadn't. Windcheater was pretending to tie his shoelace while Trenchcoat was faking having trouble lighting a cigarette. Alex could not help thinking that they were making themselves very obvious. He was shortly to find out why.

Midway between 7th and 6th, while waiting for a break in the traffic to cross Irving and with a stream of fast-moving vehicles only feet away, he was jostled from behind, thrown off balance. A woman screamed. A man's voice bellowed a warning. Then he was falling under the wheels of a black sedan, cursing with what he was sure was his final breath his own stupidity. His shadows had wanted to be seen. While his attention was on them and how to lose them, it was the function of the team's third member to make him the latest addition to the Arlington road-casualty figures.

Those thoughts occupied a thousandth of a second. In the next thousandth Alex heard the shriek of brakes and felt someone grab at the tied belt of his raincoat, yanking him backwards. He cracked his head as he hit the sidewalk. The oncoming sedan missed him by inches.

When he next focused he was sitting with his legs outstretched, his back against a wall. A dozen faces were peering down at him. One voice said, 'He's all right,' – another, 'He can thank the young lady for that. He was damned lucky.'

Several pairs of hands helped him to his feet. He leaned against the wall, touching his head where it had struck the kerb. It was already starting to ache like hell but the skin was unbroken. And other than that he was unhurt. He'd live.

'Thanks,' he said to no one in particular.

'British,' someone muttered in a tone that implied: what else could you expect from a country that drives on the wrong side of the road?

Gradually the crowd dispersed – with the exception of one woman whose face was partly hidden by a headscarf. Alex checked the street. His chaperons had vanished.

'Are you okay?' enquired the woman.

'Fine, thank you. Was it you who grabbed my belt?'

'Yes. I was right behind you, saw you stumble, and reached out instinctively.'

'You were *right* behind me?'

'Yes. You'll have to be more careful if you want to survive the States. We're an aggressive lot. If we want to cross a road we make a bee-line for the other side. Anyone in the way gets trampled. Still, I apologize on behalf of my fellow citizens. The Atlantic alliance is in a bad enough shape as it is. We can ill afford decimating vacationers. Do you need a doctor?'

Alex said he didn't, wondering if this woman was the third member of the surveillance team. He hadn't been looking for a female. Perhaps the team's instructions had only been to frighten him. Or, better still, effect the introduction that had just taken place. Very well, he'd play along.

'I could use a brandy, though. Perhaps you'd join me, Miss er . . .'

She hesitated fractionally, he thought. 'Deuntzer. Karen Deuntzer. And no brandy, thanks all the same. I made it a rule years ago not to drink before seven.'

Alex gave his own name. 'A cup of coffee then,' he suggested. She was obviously anxious to get away, which didn't fit his theory at all.

He shammed a dizzy spell, clutching her arm for support.

'Look, you really should see a doctor.'

'No, I'll be okay. Is there somewhere close by we can get a cup of coffee?'

'There's a place up the street I sometimes use on my way home. It doesn't serve alcohol. If you want that brandy there's a bar along the block.'

'No, coffee will do me fine.'

Once served, Karen Deuntzer took off her headscarf and shook her ash-blonde hair. She was thirty or so, Alex estimated, five feet four and slim. Apart from her hair, her best features were her large pale-blue eyes and a generous mouth. She wore a gold ring on her right hand, in the manner of divorcees. Unless the ring was a prop, which he was beginning to doubt. She looked more like a schoolteacher than anything else.

'Sorry about almost passing out on you back there,' he said, 'and thanks again.' He raised his coffee cup in a toast. 'I'm also sorry the whole incident did not take place at seven fifteen. Then I could have treated you to something stronger.'

'Not really. At seven fifteen I shall be asking my young son what he did with himself today.'

'You have a son?'

'You sound surprised. Yes, I have an eight-year-old. When he's not at school he and a dozen others in my neighbourhood are looked after by professional minders, towards whose salaries all the working mothers make a contribution. Some of the mothers are widows, some divorced, and two, like myself, never bothered to marry. If it's not a perfect system, it does give all the mothers an opportunity to follow their careers, in my case with a law firm. There, does that satisfy your curiosity?' Karen Deuntzer smiled pleasantly.

Alex kicked himself. If she was not an experienced liar, he'd had Karen Deuntzer figured all wrong. 'And you save lives as a hobby.'

'I'd hate to try and make a living out of it. You're my first this year.'

Fifteen minutes later they went their separate ways, Karen declining Alex's offer of a shared taxi since she lived within a few blocks.

At the hotel, Alex asked for his key. The desk clerk frowned. 'But you've already checked out, Mr Dunbar.'

'I have? Why would I be asking for my key if I'd checked out?'

'There must be some mistake. Your two friends came along earlier, said you were delayed, and settled your account.'

'What two friends?'

'I'd never seen them before. One was a man about your build wearing a light-coloured overcoat and a leather fedora. The other had on a blue windcheater. I wouldn't have let

140

them pay or enter your room if they'd wanted to take your bags, but they didn't.'

'They paid in cash, no doubt.'

'Yes, in cash. I accompanied them upstairs, where they packed your bags and said you would be collecting them later. They're in my office.'

'When was all this?'

'Half an hour ago. There's nothing wrong, is there?'

There was no point in making a scene. It had been a smooth, professional operation carried out while he was having coffee.

'No, there's nothing wrong. They made a mistake, that's all. It's tomorrow I'm leaving, not today. You haven't let my room?'

'No, sir.'

'Then I'd be obliged if you'd re-register me and have my luggage sent up. A film projector and a screen were among it.'

'They're with your bags, Mr Dunbar.'

And so they were. The loop of film, the camera lens and the still photographs, however, had all vanished. So much for Karen Deuntzer working for a law firm. He was losing his touch.

Still, he was puzzled. Why had Karen Deuntzer and the phoney life-saving act been needed? They had known where he was staying, known also that he had spent the afternoon with George Andrus. They could have stolen the loop, lens and stills much earlier.

Alex scanned the local phone book for Karen Deuntzer's name. He didn't find it. While at the phone he called Duncan Hamilton's home number. A woman's voice said that she was expecting him shortly. Alex left a message for Hamilton to meet him at the hotel as soon as possible.

Next he dialled George Andrus' office, being answered by a machine. Alex hung up and phoned Amelia's, asking the operator to have Andrus paged. When the former CIA man came on the line, his voice was thick with drink.

'There's been a slight change of plan,' said Alex. 'I have to fly out tomorrow. You said at lunch that you might have something else for me tonight?'

'Maybe I do.'

'What does that mean?'

'It means I don't want to talk about it over the phone. How about coming down here?'

Alex wasn't keen. 'Somewhere quieter,' he suggested. 'What about your office?'

Andrus gave him the address.

'I'll be with you in three-quarters of an hour.' Alex thought for a moment. If Andrus was on a bender, in forty-five minutes he could be incapable of coherent conversation. 'Give me a clue, George,' he coaxed. 'Be as cryptic as you like.'

Alex heard the clink of a glass. Andrus had evidently taken his drink to the phone. Jesus.

'George?'

'Right, I'm with you. It's big Alex, big and weird. The two men we were discussing this afternoon are definitely no longer in this country. Word is they're heading for the rising sun the long way round. The Company computer has been working overtime in conjunction with the airlines. My information is that they left several days ago for the Middle East. After a few false trails were eliminated, the smart money remains on Bangkok, Hong Kong and Tokyo.'

'Go on,' encouraged Alex.

'That's more or less it,' slurred Andrus, 'except that neither you nor the Company are the only ones in the hunt. A couple of other big organizations have got to hear about the merchandise and are anxious to make a bid. Foreign organizations. Are you with me?'

Alex said he was. 'Okay, George, no more over the phone. You can give me the details later. And take it easy on the sauce, hey?'

Alex disconnected. At the other end of the line Andrus replaced his own receiver and grinned drunkenly at the man waiting to use the phone; a man who, when he had walked into Amelia's earlier, had deposited in the cloakroom a fawn trenchcoat and a cream leather fedora.

When Hamilton arrived Alex explained about the theft of the loop, lens and stills. Not that it mattered too much, he added, except for the identity of the thieves. Bob Hazeldene

142

had presumably told them everything that was to be learned about the origin of the strip and the lens.

'I'll tell you the rest on the plane.'

'We're going somewhere?'

'That we are. London to begin with. I'm sorry to drag you away from your girl after you've only just got back, but you'd better inform her you'll be away for some time.'

'When do we leave?'

'First available flight tomorrow. In the meantime, we're going to see George Andrus. After that, I want you to go to the embassy and use their facilities to contact Calderwood. Don't log the call. Tell Calderwood I'd appreciate a meeting as soon as possible, away from home office. Tell him also we'll be needing lots of currency, US dollars. That'll make him sick.'

Hamilton's eyes shone with excitement.

'By the way,' said Alex, 'you don't carry a gun over here, do you?'

'No. Do I need one? I can arrange to draw one from the armoury.'

'Probably not tonight. However, make a mental note to ask Calderwood for the facility. Even though we'll be travelling on diplomatic passports, I'm out of touch with the way airlines run their security these days. If we're not allowed to carry arms on board, we'll need them made available at each port of call. Okay, let's go and see Andrus.'

Alex sensed there was something wrong as they approached the outside door, which was ajar. Lights were blazing in the reception area, the anteroom and Andrus' private office. The American was slumped across his desk, a bottle of brandy and a half-full glass near his right hand. A few feet away, ground into the carpet, was a pair of broken spectacles.

Andrus wasn't drunk; he was dead. An autopsy would doubtless show that he'd died of a heart attack brought on by an excess of alcohol. The pathologist would be making a mistake, said Alex. Somewhere on Andrus' body there would be a tiny puncture made by a hypodermic containing a massive shot of digitalis or some similar drug.

'How can you be sure it wasn't a coronary?' asked

143

Hamilton.

'Because I don't believe in coincidence. George Andrus was making enquiries on my behalf. Three-quarters of an hour ago he was as healthy as you or I. I was with him last night and part of today. I never saw him wearing glasses. Presumably he only did for reading and writing. He must have lost them in a struggle. His killer or killers then trod on them on the way out, either accidentally or deliberately as an act of contempt. They're too far away from where he's sitting for him to have dropped them and crushed them himself.'

Gently, Alex raised Andrus' right arm.

'See this sheet of paper? He'd started to write something.' Alex squinted. 'Three words. *Brief summary of* . . . He was making notes when they killed him.'

In the street Hamilton said, 'Has it occurred to you that an awful lot of people are being killed but that we're being left severely alone? Your brother; Tyson; Andrus.'

'It has,' said Alex. 'Almost as though they're saving us, or at least me, for something, wouldn't you say?'

Calderwood's town residence was a two-bedroom bachelor apartment overlooking Regent's Park. For a song, he had bought the long lease as an investment in the middle Seventies when the previous occupant, a Hungarian working for the KGB, had become careless with his dead-letter drops and thus ceased to have any further interest in the flat owing to being tried *in camera* for espionage and sentenced to thirty years in a maximum security gaol. Unfortunately for the Hungarian he was not of sufficient rank or importance for anyone on his side to consider an exchange. Thus he would doubtless live out the remainder of his life behind bars, though in this, as far as captured agents were concerned, he would not be alone. At any one time, HM prisons contained thirty or so men and women like the Hungarian, who were always tried *in camera*, whose names never made the newspapers, and who became, to all intents and purposes, non-persons.

Internal security and the arrest of spies on Crown soil were the exclusive province of the Colleagues, as MI6 called MI5. Accordingly, any perquisites such as long leases at give-away prices were generally carved up among themselves. But Calderwood, through a Berlin double agent, had been instrumental in tipping off MI5 about the Hungarian, and as a result was offered the lease by a grateful department head, whose own would have rolled had the Magyar remained in business for much longer. Calderwood had no qualms about accepting. It was not, in any case, he considered privately and ungratefully, that much of a reward. The address was the wrong side of the Bayswater

Road by a country mile, and unfashionable by several postal districts. His immediate neighbours, whose means of earning their crusts were on his desk within a week, comprised, in part, an advertising whizzkid, a property developer, a restaurateur, and a record company executive. All very rich in their own right, no doubt, but he would have wagered a largish sum that not one of them would have been able to select a decent claret without reference to the label and one of those funny little paperback books such people carried as a vade-mecum. It was *that* sort of area.

He installed Alex and Hamilton in the apartment, explained, in the manner of a primary school teacher to a remedial class of five-year-olds, how the washing machine and dishwasher worked, and issued orders that Alex was not to leave, not even to stretch his legs, until he had written a full and comprehensive account of everything that had transpired since Nick Tasker's funeral. Hamilton could run errands and act as general factotum while Alex completed his labours. During the twenty-four hours this took, allowing for fatigue due to jet lag and some sleep, Calderwood stayed at his club, being no believer in sharing accommodation with his underlings, albeit that the apartment was his.

When Alex, writing in longhand, finally finished the narrative that was a quarter the length of the average book, he put the sheets of paper in a large OHMS envelope and handed the package to Hamilton with instructions to deliver it to Calderwood wherever Calderwood was and not to wake him when he returned, unless the big news was the Second Coming. 'On second thoughts not even for that. I guess I'll hear about it.'

After Hamilton left, while it was still daylight outside, Alex tumbled into bed, fully clothed. When he was roughly shaken awake some hours later, it was dark. He heard heavy rain pounding against the windows. Although the snow had vanished during his absence in the States, the English winter was far from over yet.

'What is it, for Christ's sake?' he mumbled. 'I told you to let me sleep.'

'Calderwood's in the sitting-room,' said Hamilton. 'He wants to go over the report with you.'

146

'Christ, can't it wait? What time is it?'

'Coming up to nine.'

'Give me fifteen minutes for a shower, shave and a change of clothes.'

'Calderwood said now. I quote: Kindly wake Mr Dunbar and tell him I'd like his company immediately.'

'Go back and tell him that Mr Dunbar presents his compliments but needs a quarter of an hour. If he doesn't like it, he can lump it. I quote.'

Alex felt better when he walked into the sitting-room. Calderwood was in the armchair nearest the gas fire, one hand stretched out absently, warming it. There was a gin and tonic at his elbow and the report on his knees. Hamilton was perched uncertainly on the edge of a high-backed chair. Evidently annoyed at being kept waiting, Calderwood did not look up when the door opened; Alex crossed over to the drinks table and poured himself a stiff gin, adding ice from the bucket and a little tonic.

Alex took a second armchair away from the gas fire. The central heating, part of the services the block's owners provided, was going full blast, and the room was unbearably hot.

Calderwood placed the report on the floor. He took a notebook and gold pencil from his pocket.

'So what does it all mean?' he asked Alex.

'I haven't the slightest idea.'

'But you do assume a connection between the film strip you found – and lost – in South Dakota and the film and documents Coughlin and Garfield have apparently absconded with?'

'The similarities make that almost certain.'

'Except the original OSS film showed fake camps staffed by equally spurious SS guards, while the South Dakota strip depicted a similar scene but with Soviet guards.'

'Again faked,' Alex reminded him.

'Of course again faked,' said Calderwood irritably. 'I have read the report, difficult though it was at times to decipher your handwriting.' Calderwood tapped his pencil on the notepad. 'My problem is this. As I explained to you ten days ago, we've known about something called Cougar, the

147

apparent infiltration of German neo-Nazi groups by CIA operatives, for several months, but according to this account it's only recently that Coughlin and Garfield disappeared. Therefore, is Cougar a Company operation that has now gone wrong, or are Coughlin and Garfield part of an ongoing plot, their apparent disappearance being part of it?'

Alex glanced at Hamilton before answering, wondering just how far Calderwood wanted the younger man involved with the finer details. Calderwood gave Alex a brief nod. Evidently Hamilton was not to be kept in the dark.

'My information from George Andrus,' said Alex, 'was that Langley is tearing his hair out.'

'That doesn't mean anything,' intoned Calderwood loftily. 'Andrus was out of the business. Whatever he told you could have been deliberately fed to him.'

'But if they were using him,' argued Alex, 'why kill him?'

'You're assuming it was a Company termination.'

'I'd stake my life on it.'

'In that case the Company had finished with him or, more likely, thought he might tell you more than he should for old times' sake.'

'That's how I read it,' admitted Alex.

'And takes us no further forward,' said Calderwood. 'Are we being used, I wonder?' he asked of no one in particular. 'Are our moves part of the calculations?'

Hamilton cleared his throat.

'Yes?' enquired Calderwood, who disliked his thought processes being interrupted.

'Why not simply ask the Company?' said Hamilton, bravely if naïvely. 'Show everything we have to Langley and ask them what the devil's going on.'

'And do you think they'd tell us? I've already been over that strategy with Mr Dunbar. They would deny that Cougar existed and tell us to mind our own business. I do not have to remind you that recent events at Cheltenham have not made our American cousins very happy with our level of security. In any event, I'd rather like to resolve the puzzle ourselves. Who knows, there could be something in it for us. Unless of course Mr Dunbar feels that the spadework he's done – and excellent spadework it is, Alex – is enough and that the rest can be turned over to our Far East operatives.'

'Just try it,' muttered Alex.

'I beg your pardon?'

'I said I'd prefer to see it through.'

'Yes, of course.' Calderwood examined his fingernails. 'I wonder if you would permit me to tell Hamilton something of your personal involvement in all this? There may come a time in the next few weeks when you are compelled to act outside the book of rules. It might help Hamilton if he understood why.'

'Go ahead. I need some fresh air anyway.'

'You may take my umbrella,' said Calderwood magnanimously, 'it's a filthy night out.'

Being unfamiliar with the area, Alex spent ten minutes looking for a pub, where he drank two pints of inferior beer. Not until he left did he realize that he hadn't been tempted to order a whisky or retreat to a corner and hide behind a copy of *The Times*.

When Alex returned to the apartment it was apparent from Hamilton's expression that he now knew the circumstances of Melanie's death.

'Ah,' said Calderwood unnecessarily, 'you're back. Hamilton, you may pour each of us a drink. And do, for heaven's sake, take one yourself. The restocking will come out of department funds since this is strictly speaking a briefing.'

Calderwood took his pipe from his jacket pocket and began to fill it. Then he abandoned the whole exercise, placing the pipe and pouch on the side table.

'Let me tell you about a little theory I've concocted,' he said, gazing at the ceiling. 'I have had the advantage, don't forget, of coming to all this afresh, and am perhaps more able to discern the wood from the trees as it were. What I am about to say may be very wide of the mark. At least I hope it is. Until we find Coughlin and Garfield, however, it's the only theory that fits the known facts.'

He toyed with the pipe, occasionally using it to underline an argument.

'Let us ignore the wartime OSS film and supporting documents for the present. Their disappearance along with

149

Coughlin and Garfield came from Andrus who, I think it would be prudent to assume, was fed that information by someone at Langley, possibly Cassidy, whose name keeps cropping up with monotonous regularity. I don't believe the OSS film is relevant to Cougar. I do believe that the one shot in South Dakota – of which there must be a good deal more than the strip you found – is. Coughlin and Garfield may well have absconded with that. However, that's by the by for the moment. What we have to ask ourselves is why it was made in the first place.

'Consider this, the impact that such a film, purporting to be genuine, would have if released to the German media – a film showing a wartime extermination camp staffed by Soviets. Can you imagine the reaction? The neo-Nazis would claim what thousands of others have asserted since the end of the war: that although some extermination camps run by the SS undoubtedly existed, the majority of the Third Reich's leaders knew nothing about them, that genocide was never official policy; that many of the photographs we've all seen were faked to ensure that the defendants at the first Nuremberg trial were convicted and executed. It would be alleged that it was the Soviets, no friends of the Jews then as now, who were responsible for the greater proportion of six million deaths. Handled cleverly, it could even be suggested, as Andrus said, that the Israelis knew from the start that the Nazis had not committed all the atrocities they were accused of, but that it was in Israeli interests to promulgate the great lie.'

'That's crazy,' scorned Alex. 'No one would believe it.'

'You think not?' Calderwood managed a trace of a smile. 'Who would have believed that Kim Philby, who came within a hair's-breadth of heading our service, was actually working for the Russians until he defected? Nearer in time, who among the general public knows that the IRA is funded largely by international left-wing terrorism and that the last thing the Provisionals care about are Roman Catholics and Protestants? Or that, in Great Britain, companies with such innocent-sounding names as Technical and Optical Equipment and United Machinery Organization Plant Hire are actually Soviet multinationals trading here quite legally?

People believe what it suits them to believe. However, let us develop the scenario a little further.

'Berlin is not the most stable of cities at the best of times. It's a fuse waiting for a maniac with a lighted match, which the South Dakota film may be. I would wager considerable sums that twenty-four hours after its appearance there would be anti-Russian demonstrations, possibly riots, on the Berlin streets – led by the neo-Nazis, of course, and orchestrated by the CIA. Ordinary Germans would not be slow to climb on the bandwagon. And why not? For a generation the ordinary German has been reviled for what certain of his fellow countrymen did to the Jews. If the Russians claimed the film to be Western propaganda, who would believe them with their record of anti-Semitism? They would be compelled to take action, especially if the Berlin unrest found an echo in West German cities and, perhaps, in East German border towns, many of whose inhabitants still consider themselves to be part of a greater Germany rather than a Soviet satellite and would like nothing more than to shuck off the Soviet yoke. No, please allow me to finish,' said Calderwood mildly when Alex tried to interrupt.

'Now what, you might ask, would the NATO forces be doing if the Soviets elected to encircle Berlin or move half a dozen armoured divisions closer to the East-West border? NATO ground commanders would take counter-measures, naturally. However, their front-line troops are little more than death-or-glory battalions. They could be overrun by Soviet armour in twenty-four hours. For that matter, it has been calculated that the Russians would control the whole of West Germany within seventy-two hours – unless tactical nuclear weapons were used. Look.'

Calderwood tore a page from his notebook and made a rough sketch.

'That's Berlin. Just south of there is Zossen, where the C-in-C Soviet Forces Germany has his HQ. He has twenty divisions under his command, of which nine are tank divisions. He could cut through the NATO defences like a knife through butter.'

'All because of a bloody film that's faked anyway,' said

Alex. 'That's insane.'

'Not at all,' retorted Calderwood. 'I'm not giving anything away when I tell you that certain senior American military and political figures are convinced that one day in the not too distant future NATO will have to face the Soviets. What they fear most is that the time will not be of their choosing, every commander's nightmare. The wargamers have predicted that the conflict will be bitter, brutal, bloody and short, with many millions dead. They have further prognosticated that, providing it is kept localized – and by that I mean European – it will not mean the end of the world, at least not the American world. As civilization will therefore continue, in whatever form, all US political leaders since Nixon have stipulated that the US must never be seen to have made the first move. Politicians are peculiar animals. Once they have attained their earthly goals their only concern is their place in the history books. It is for this reason, much though the hawks in the Pentagon have argued in favour of a pre-emptive first strike, that the doves have always won the day. But if the Soviets made the first move, if they were seen to adopt a belligerent posture and appeared ready to back up their threats with force or arms, then the Americans would have a golden opportunity to fight a tactical nuclear war three thousand miles from American soil.

'This is not science fiction, gentlemen. Some of us in the intelligence community have documentary proof that the Pentagon hawks wish to test the calibre of their machines and men before internal conflict, urban riots brought on by mass unemployment and the gradual erosion of the dollar's purchasing power, makes the arms race impossible to win. During the Falklands War I had it said to me in all sincerity by a senior US officer that he envied the United Kingdom's opportunity to test troops and hardware under battle conditions.'

Calderwood drained his glass and handed it to Hamilton for a refill.

'You're oversimplifying, with due respect,' said Alex. 'Okay, your theory makes some kind of sense. God knows, anyone who's studied history is aware that wars can start for reasons less significant than a reel of film. I can accept your interpretation of Cougar and also that German anger would be huge if it were thought that the Soviets were responsible for many of the crimes historically attributed to the Third Reich. I cannot accept that the Russians would do other than laugh their heads off, deride the whole exercise for what it is, a CIA plot to discredit them and their wartime leaders. They would demand a copy of the film. Their technicians would quickly come to the same conclusion as Bob Hazeldene, that the entire footage is an elaborate fake.'

'Not,' said Calderwood slowly, 'if they too are looking for an excuse to fire the opening shots of World War III.'

'You can't be serious!'

'Why ever not?' Calderwood was genuinely surprised. 'There are hawks in the Kremlin too, hawks who argue that if some sort of limited conflict between east and west is inevitable, now is as good a time as any. The Soviets have tens of thousands of men under arms in Afghanistan, men and *matériel* that cannot be deployed elsewhere in a hurry without creating a huge vacuum. They have advisers in Poland, a country that still makes the Kremlin nervous, as Czechoslovakia and Hungary did a generation ago. The present US administration is committed to spending more and more on arms. In a recent report to Congress Caspar Weinberger pledged the greatest peacetime arms package in history – almost *850 billion* pounds over the next five years. Former Secretary of State Haig at the time of his resignation was petitioning the President to ditch the 1975 Helsinki agreement and detente with it. The Soviets know this.

'The US is wooing Red China,' he went on. 'At a recent opening of the Peking Trade Fair, Assistant Secretary for Trade Administration, Lawrence Brady, said that America was now prepared to sell to China equipment that was twice as advanced as goods previously cleared for export – *or even more sophisticated material*. He did not define what he meant by the latter, but it's no secret that the US Defence Department would consider a contract to equip the Chinese Armed Forces a tactical triumph, in time leading to closer links, including agreements to share military intelligence

153

and even co-operate against threats to China's borders, where it has been estimated that a million Soviet troops are deployed. And big as the Soviet Union is, it hasn't unlimited manpower. You're a student of Napoleon, Alex, although it's basic military tactics from company commander level upwards: concentration of forces wins battles. If I am anywhere near correct in my interpretation of Cougar, the Soviet Union might decide to play the CIA at their own game and sham feeling threatened by a resurgence of neo-Nazism in order to justify taking what would otherwise be regarded as dangerously provocative steps. Of course I could be wrong. Much depends on whether Coughlin and Garfield have genuinely disappeared – with the South Dakota film, not the wartime OSS version – or whether they're being controlled by Langley in the second phase of an extremely complicated plot. I don't know the answer to that. I do know that we have six weeks to find some kind of answer, because in six weeks the Russians begin their annual spring manoeuvres, which are always a headache for NATO. One day, the theory goes, the Russians will let their tanks roll on, straight across the North German Plain.'

The gas fire spluttered and hissed, the only sound in the sitting-room for several minutes. Eventually Alex asked, 'Isn't this something you should put before the Director without delay?'

'Telling him what? All I have here is hypothesis. If I make it official the Director will be compelled to inform the Joint Intelligence Committee, which automatically means involving the PM. I would rather keep the Director *and* the politicians out of it until we have some hard facts, which only Coughlin and Garfield can supply.'

Calderwood saw that Alex was frowning.

'Is something bothering you?'

'Quite a few somethings. Mostly, however, that I can't shake the feeling I'm being used. Not the department, me personally.'

'You're becoming paranoid.' Calderwood got to his feet, pocketing his pipe and pouch. 'You'll remain here for the next two days while I contact our residents in Bangkok, Hong Kong and Tokyo, ask them to make some preliminary

154

enquiries. It will also take me forty-eight hours to justify to the department's paymaster your exorbitant demand for US dollars.'

'Credit card transactions wind up in computers and can easily be checked,' said Alex. 'We may not want our movements logged.'

Calderwood made for the front door.

'By the way,' he said over his shoulder, 'in accordance with standard procedure you'll each be required to make out wills before you leave. I'll have the necessary blanks ready for you the day after tomorrow. Do make your instructions unequivocal and tie up any loose ends before you board the aircraft. Good night, gentlemen.'

Hamilton waited until he heard the front door close. 'Cheerful soul, isn't he?'

'You've seen him on one of his better days.'

Hamilton brought his drink closer to the fire, sitting in the armchair vacated by Calderwood.

'Do you think he's right?' he asked after a moment. 'That a reel of faked film could plunge Europe into a nuclear war?'

'Probably,' said Alex. 'Do you remember how the last war started? I don't mean Hitler invading Poland and being given an ultimatum by Chamberlain, but the justification the Nazis used for their invasion?'

'Not clearly.'

'The plan was Heydrich's, calling for a Polish attack on a radio station at Gleiwitz. The "Poles" were actually members of the SS Security Service. After shouting anti-German slogans down the microphones, they retreated, leaving behind a number of bodies in German uniforms to prove that a fight had taken place. The corpses, of course, had been selected beforehand from concentration camps – "canned goods", Heydrich code-named them. The operation was under the command of an SS officer, Alfred Naujocks, who can justifiably be said to have begun World War II. Yes, I believe that something as trivial as a reel of faked film could incinerate Europe. It all depends upon how much the potential belligerents want to fight. If we believe Calderwood there are people in both camps who are itching to pull the trigger. Anyway, to hell with it for one night.

Let's have another shot of Calderwood's liquor and turn in. My body may be in London but my head's in Washington.'

While Hamilton was pouring, the telephone rang. It was Calderwood, calling from a pay phone.

'I've had second thoughts about you remaining there for two days, Alex. On reflection I've decided that you and Hamilton could use some mild exercise and time on a firing range. I think it would be wiser if I kept you away from Fort Monkton to discourage the inquisitive. I'll therefore arrange for you to travel to Somerset, to a house we keep for very special personnel near the village of Dulverton. You may find some SAS down there. You will have nothing to do with them and nor will you discuss your assignment with anyone. In particular you will not leave the grounds. There's a rather splendid pub called The Anchor several miles away in Exbridge. You will not patronize it. You're in Somerset for two days' target practice and fresh air. Since a driver will be calling for you at six tomorrow morning, I'd advise that the drink you've undoubtedly just poured be your last. Pleasant dreams.'

'Bastard,' said Alex.

BANGKOK (i)

Dressed for a wintry London, Alex and Hamilton stepped from the KLM 747 at Bangkok to be hit by a solid wall of heat, the outside temperature being in the low nineties. But it was the humidity that pole-axed them, and they were both sweating copiously by the time they reached the arrivals building, where a tall sun-tanned young man kitted out in a lightweight suit quickly recognized them and detached himself from the remainder of the crowd waiting to meet the aeroplane. He introduced himself as John Herrick and ushered them through the diplomatic gate with minimal formality, joking with the immigration officer in fluent Thai.

'*S'bai dee roo?*' he said, after shaking hands. 'That means how are you and is about as much Thai as you'll need apart from *nee tawrai* and *pom rak kun*, which means "how much" and "I love you" respectively. How was the flight?'

'Long,' said Alex.

They had taken off from Heathrow at nine a.m. the previous morning, changed planes at Amsterdam and refuelled at Dubai at some unearthly hour. Flying time from Heathrow was thirteen hours, but as Bangkok was seven hours ahead of GMT, they had effectively been on the go for almost a day. It was now late afternoon in the Thai capital and Alex, unable to sleep on the plane, felt ten years older than he had in Calderwood's London apartment. The mild exercise promised in Somerset had also been anything but undemanding, involving early-morning runs, long hours in the gym and on the assault course, and refamiliarization classes in basic field craft and safety techniques. His shooting had improved, as had Hamilton's; that aside, he felt as though he needed six months' convalescence in the South Seas.

They had 'escaped' from the Dulverton house once, the second evening, accompanied by two SAS captains who were being prepared for something sinister about which they would obviously say nothing. Alex had termed the break-out an initiative test, which had got no further than the Anchor pub to which Calderwood had granted his seal of approval. There they had drunk five pints of beer apiece and passed a pleasant couple of hours, masquerading as tourists, chatting to the landlord, who had flown in Liberators during the war. They had only left when a casual snippet of conversation revealed that the man drinking whisky at the far end of the bar was a writer of thrillers. The last thing the four of them needed was for someone with a professional eye to ask himself what a quartet of very fit strangers was doing on vacation at that time of the year.

The memory of those pints made Alex's mouth water as Herrick directed them to an unmarked car and muttered something in rapid Thai to the driver.

Alex and Hamilton sat in the back, Herrick next to the driver. 'You'll find a couple of packages under the seat,' said Herrick. They each pocketed a standard SIS-issue Browning and a box of shells.

As the car made its way from the airport to the centre of Bangkok, the driver beating a regular tattoo on the horn, Alex asked if it was always as hot as this.

'Not always,' said Herrick, who appeared unaffected by the temperature. 'You've come at the start of the summer, which lasts until June. After that is the rainy season, from July to October. That's when you really get the humidity. Even the old hands feel it then. I've booked you into the Montien, by the way, on Suriwong Road. Pretty fancy, but the telex from London said you were to have the best or something approximating to it. There's a snake farm right across the street, though I'm told they don't get out very often.' He chuckled at his own wit.

The question of accommodation had been discussed with Calderwood before they left London. The Firm was usually notoriously unwilling to sanction anything other than the meanest hotel, but Alex had argued that Coughlin and Garfield, if they were in Bangkok at all, would put up where the Europeans stayed, attempt to lose themselves among the tourists. Calderwood had agreed. Within reason, the budget had no limits.

'Just as long as it's air-conditioned,' said Hamilton, staring out of the window at the incredible beauty of the Thai women.

'He's young,' said Alex.

'He's about twice the age of some of the girls he's looking at, who are considered well over the hill by the time they're in their early twenties.' Herrick pointed to one riding pillion on a motor scooter. 'Prostitute,' he said laconically. 'The guy doing the steering is her pimp – or rather he works for the organization which handles the girls. You won't find very many freelance hookers in Bangkok; they're all controlled by organized crime, towards which the authorities turn a blind eye. You don't often see the girls during the daylight hours, but after dark they hit the streets like moths. You only have to stand in front of your hotel and there'll be a dozen motorized girls at your beck and call within thirty seconds. If you're tempted, be careful. Most of them are clean enough and honest enough, though prices start at around one hundred US dollars. The only caveat is, take them into your hotel, don't go with them no matter what they promise you or whatever discounts they offer. In your hotel you're pretty safe; they won't go for your wallet or credit cards while you're still trying to stop your heart pounding. If they do – that is if you're tempted to try the local flesh – get on the phone down to reception immediately. Most of the big hotels have security guards dressed in what look like paramilitary uniforms and carrying nightsticks you could fell an elephant with. The hotels will tell you that the guards are there for your own protection, to thwart the bandits who occasionally think it would be a clever idea to dash into a hotel lobby with guns and rip off the first bunch of tourists they see. I'm not joking. It does happen. The guards are there partly to prevent that and partly to stop an ambitious hooker making a run for it with your American

Express card, which some of the pricier girls will accept in lieu of cash, incidentally. If you can get to the room phone before the girl gets to the lobby, that's the end of the girl. The guards don't mess around with those nightsticks. If she makes the street, you've had it. As you can see for yourself,' he grinned, 'they all look alike. Clones.'

'I wouldn't find it hard to get used to,' murmured Hamilton.

'Well, I'll have to see if I can fix you up before you leave,' said Herrick, 'maybe take you to a club where you can pick your own by numbers. A militant feminist would have apoplexy here. Thailand is very much a male-dominated society. Not far now,' he added, as the car passed a huge Buddha, with which Bangkok seemed replete; those and temples. 'How are you off for local currency?'

'Nil,' said Alex. 'We're carrying dollars.'

'Change a few at the hotel,' advised Herrick. 'US dollars are precious out here. If you hand over a ten-dollar bill for a two-dollar purchase you're unlikely to get the correct change, even though the Thais are mostly very honest. However, they're renowned for not suffering fools gladly, and anyone waving ten dollars, which is about the average weekly wage for a cab driver or a teacher, does, in their opinion, deserve all he gets. Here we are.'

The air-conditioned interior of the Montien was a welcome relief after the heat and humidity of the street. Herrick, taking their passports, said he would see to the checking-in procedure while they set up the beers. 'The lobby bar's the best place at this time of day. It's just along there. You can't miss it.'

In tall frosted glasses the beers were being placed on the table by a waiter (not one of the two leggy Thai waitresses, Hamilton was disappointed to note) when Herrick appeared and gave them each a key and returned their passports.

'Your bags are on the way up. I did a deal with the management, who know me quite well and who were most impressed by your diplomatic passports. Two rooms for little more than the price of one. Both doubles – in case a combination of Thai heat and Thai beauty overcomes one or both of you. You can sign the registration cards later. You'll find a stocked refrigerator in each room. Cheers,' he said, raising his glass.

'How much do you know?' asked Alex after a moment.

'Very little.' Herrick held up his hands, palms outwards. 'And that's the way I'd like it to stay. In fact, that's the way I'm told from London it *is* to stay. You're looking for two Americans, Coughlin and Garfield, who may be making surreptitious noises, possibly via the Bangkok underworld, that they have something to sell. They may be in Bangkok, they may not. They may not be travelling under their own names. They might also have been and gone. You don't have photos or any other descriptions. They're Company men, and the Company is not very happy with them. That's all.'

'*Are* they here or *have* they been through?'

Herrick shrugged. 'I'd say not. That is, I'd say they're not here now and, if they were here, they acted as tourists and did nothing out of the ordinary. I've made several enquiries, but of necessity I've had to be vague and keep a low profile. You have to understand the way it works in Bangkok, for the intelligence residents, that is, whichever country employs them. Our main contacts for something like this would be the Bangkok underworld, which, believe me, is very powerful and ruthless. Apart from the girls and the massage parlours, the underworld chiefs and sub-chiefs have eyes and ears everywhere – hotels, bars, restaurants. You name it. If ever I want to know something that can't be obtained in any other way, I go to my own particular contact – you may meet him later tonight or tomorrow if he agrees – and hand him my problem. I have a fairly substantial slush fund for that sort of transaction. In this case, on hearing from London, I asked him if he could find out anything about two Americans not acting the way tourists normally act. He put out his feelers – bellboys, waiters, bartenders, hookers. And nothing. A big zero. If Coughlin and Garfield are here they're keeping very quiet, which doesn't seem to fit in at all with someone who has something to sell.'

'Maybe Bangkok's just a staging post,' suggested Hamilton, 'a stopover en route to . . .' Alex held up a cautionary finger. 'Elsewhere.'

'Maybe,' agreed Herrick. 'However, I wouldn't lay a lot of

161

money on it, because my contact came back to me with one very curious item. I wasn't the only one asking questions about Coughlin and Garfield, not by a country mile. In Bangkok your Americans are very much on the wanted list.'

'Did he identify the other interested parties?' asked Alex.

'No, not enough information. The Company, obviously, but that's as far as it goes for now.'

Herrick broke off as the waiter, noticing their empty glasses, came over and asked politely if they required further service. Alex ordered three more beers. Herrick waited until they were on the table and Alex had signed the room chit before continuing.

'There's more, however. My contact tells me that enquiries are not only being made about two Americans. Enquiries are also being made about two Englishmen who have an interest in the Americans. A largish sum of money is on offer for information regarding the two Englishmen, which we have to assume are you and Hamilton, whose presence in Bangkok, by now, will be fairly common knowledge among the interested parties. Now all of this was very puzzling to my contact, as it is to me although I know better than to ask questions. But here we have a situation, as the French would say. Two Americans are being sought by fellow Americans, two Englishmen and others. In turn, the two Englishmen are being hunted by either the Americans or the others. Yet the Englishmen arrived in Bangkok only an hour ago. You can see why my contact is confused.'

'He's not the only one,' said Alex. 'I think we'd better meet this contact of yours.'

'When? He is not, shall we say, always available.'

'The sooner the better. If Coughlin and Garfield are not here, there are only two, perhaps, three, other places they can be. If they're not in Bangkok, we're catching the next plane out.' He saw Hamilton's look of bleak disappointment. 'All right, I'm catching the next plane out. I'd hate to deprive you of maybe the one chance you'll ever have of sampling Thai ladies. We should split up anyway. If Herrick's contact has nothing to offer for now, you can stick around and catch me up in a couple of days.'

'I'll make the call,' said Herrick. He was back within five

minutes. 'He'll see you tonight, late, around midnight. I'll pick you up here earlier and show you some of the sights. Oh, a word of advice. Don't expect it to get any cooler or less humid after dark. It won't. If I were you I'd slip out and buy some lightweight shirts and trousers. Alternatively, there are a couple of good shops right here in the hotel, on the lower level. They'll be able to fix you up.'

After making their purchases Hamilton and Alex took the elevator up to their rooms, which were opposite one another. Alex planned to get a few hours' sleep. Hamilton said he intended taking a shower and changing his clothes, then seeing the sights. He left Alex in no doubt what sights he expected to see.

Alone, Alex stripped down to his underwear and examined the contents of the fridge. He elected to have a third beer. The effect of the long flight and the temperature outside had left him almost totally dehydrated.

He had just uncapped the beer when there was a short rap on his bedroom door. Hamilton, he thought, slipping the catch.

The door was only a few inches ajar when a foot on the other side thudded into it, flinging it fully open and in the process knocking Alex to the bedroom floor. A moment later a man was standing over him, one foot planted on Alex's chest, which would have been a foolish move on the part of the assailant, rendering him vulnerable to a swift counter-attack, had it not been for the automatic pistol the newcomer was pointing directly at Alex's head. Behind him a second man glanced up and down the hotel corridor before closing the door and locking it. Without a word this individual went directly to the bathroom and turned on the shower. Anyone now knocking on the door would hear the water running and assume Alex was washing away some of the day's grime. This pair, was Alex's fleeting thought, were evidently professionals.

BANGKOK (ii)

'You may get up now, Mr Dunbar,' said the gunman in English with a trace of an accent.

Not Americans, then, thought Alex, struggling to his feet and rubbing his elbow where it had caught the wall. Nor Russians, either, if he were any judge. He'd had enough dealings with the KGB during his Berlin days to know the type. These two had spent their lives in the sun, in the open air, in a healthy climate. The gunman was tall and blond, his companion shorter with coal-black hair. Both were muscular, bronzed and European in features. Neither had yet reached the age of thirty.

'No tricks, please.'

Alex sat on the edge of the bed. Near-naked as he was, he felt helpless. The gunman's warning was unnecessary. Until he'd had time to collect his wits he was not about to tackle an armed man; two armed men, for that matter, as it was highly likely that the dark-haired man was also carrying a weapon somewhere beneath his lightweight jacket.

'What the hell is all this?' asked Alex eventually. 'Robbery? If so you're out of luck. My credit cards, cash and passport are in the hotel safe.'

'I don't think so, Mr Dunbar,' said the blond, not unpleasantly. 'You came in on the afternoon KLM flight via Amsterdam and Dubai, being picked up by John Herrick who brought you and your companion, Duncan Hamilton, directly to the hotel, where the three of you had several beers in the lobby. Herrick made a telephone call, spoke to you briefly, and left. You and Hamilton came straight up to your rooms. You didn't once go near the desk. Herrick arranged the formalities. In any case, we're not here to rob you. Had we wished to do so we'd have been gone by now, and you would be unconscious.'

'Then if you're not thieves, what?' Alex had one eye on the beer bottle near his left foot, wondering if he could reach it and somehow use it as a weapon before the gunman fired. *If*, of course, the gunman would risk a shot, which Alex doubted. On the other hand, there were other ways of dying apart from a gunshot wound, and either of the two intruders appeared capable of knowing most of them. Alex concluded that he would get nowhere near the beer bottle before one of his attackers got to him. 'If you're not thieves, you've obviously broken into the wrong room. I'm a businessman passing through.'

'Selling what, Mr Dunbar? Toys? Ladies' lingerie? Whatever it is the competition must be tough. From where I'm standing I can see a scar across your right shoulder that can only have been made by a bullet, and one on your right rib cage which I would judge was inflicted by a knife. Really, Mr Dunbar, grant us a little intelligence. You're Alex Dunbar. You travel on a diplomatic passport and you were met at the airport by a man who is known to be the SIS resident in these parts. You are also employed by SIS or MI6 or the Firm, or whatever you choose to call it. You are here looking for two Americans, whose execution has been ordered by the CIA because of films they're carrying. Your job is to find the Americans before the CIA does. Why, we're not sure. This should be a domestic matter between the Company and two renegade former employees.'

'Really?'

'Yes, really. However, we're not interested in harming you. We too are interested in those films, which could cause endless trouble for many innocent people if made public. People who have already suffered enough many years ago when the scenes depicted were real and not make-believe.'

Mossad, thought Alex, suddenly understanding; the Israeli intelligence arm comparable to the British SIS and the American CIA. It all fitted. The bronzed, good-looking youngsters were Jews fearful that a Nazi resurgence could only harm their beleaguered country if the films fell into the wrong hands.

Alex had worked with Mossad agents in the past, in Berlin and elsewhere, and knew them to be totally ruthless. They had no friends except members of their own service. Their only creed was Israel's survival. They would not hesitate to kill him if, by doing so, the State of Israel was secure for even one more hour.

Alternatively, why should they kill him? Hadn't Herrick said that enquiries were being made and money changing hands not only to establish the whereabouts of Coughlin and Garfield but also those of two Englishmen? It was possible, indeed highly likely, that some of the enquiries were Mossad's. How the Israelis knew as much as these two seemed to and how they knew he and Hamilton were coming to Bangkok long before they arrived would have to wait until another day. For the moment, the two Mossad agents were looking for information, not blood.

'Mossad,' he said simply.

The blond gunman shrugged non-committally. 'It's of little importance that you know. We want Coughlin and Garfield before anyone else gets to them. We also need what they're carrying and presumably trying to sell. If all else fails, we shall become bidders. However, we require more than the destruction of the material. For example, before Coughlin and Garfield absconded, what did the CIA intend doing with a film showing a World War II Soviet guard ill-treating Jewish concentration camp inmates?'

'Surely that should be obvious,' said Alex. 'Since Brezhnev's death and Andropov's succession, things have not been travelling as smoothly as they should in the Kremlin. There were many in the Politburo who opposed Andropov; they still do. A power struggle was and is taking place.'

Alex improvised as he went along.

'The CIA know this. Perhaps they intended taking advantage of it and causing an international incident in, say, Berlin, by releasing the films to neo-Nazi groups and encouraging them to street violence. Moscow would be forced to respond. The Americans would then be able to see

166

who held the real power and to what lengths he would go to retain it.'

'What's British intelligence's interest in all this?' asked the dark-haired Israeli, speaking for the first time. 'Why is London so concerned about a few reels of film that it sends two agents halfway across the world to track them down?'

'Britain is in NATO's front line,' said Alex. 'In some respects Britain *is* NATO's front line. What happens in Germany one day affects Britain the next.'

'But why send you?' persisted the questioner. 'We know something about you, Mr Dunbar. You're on our files. Your speciality is Germany, Berlin in particular, not the Far East. Your man Herrick has forgotten more about Bangkok than you will ever learn. So why you?'

Alex could see no objection to telling the truth; Mossad probably knew it anyway.

'Coughlin and Garfield killed my wife in Berlin four years ago,' he said quietly. 'I didn't learn their names until recently. My interest in this is mostly personal.'

'Ah,' said the blond Israeli. 'And you in turn will dispose of them when you find them?'

'Yes.'

'Before or after you've ascertained their mission?'

'What mission?'

'Don't treat us as fools, Mr Dunbar. Mossad is far from convinced that the two Americans are running without Langley sanction. We have no reason to believe it's all a double bluff, that Coughlin and Garfield, far from being actively hunted by the CIA, were given orders to run but keep out of sight for a few more weeks yet.'

'With what object?'

'To release the films in Berlin ten days or so before the Warsaw Pact spring manoeuvres, foment discontent, anti-Soviet feeling, among the German neo-Nazis. Provoke a crisis. Ten days would barely give the diplomats time to resolve it. The Russian tanks would roll and keep on rolling. The Soviets would accuse the Americans and the Bonn government of trying to promote a counter-revolution in their client state of the German Democratic Republic, where Mossad knows for certain there are many old Nazis and even more younger people who despise the Soviet system, who long for a United Germany. While the tanks rolled across the North German plain the Soviets would propagandize that all they're doing is protecting their East German comrades from western subversion. Their cause would be backed by thousands of left-wing politicians and trade unionists throughout Europe, especially in your own country, Mr Dunbar, where men we could both name, household figures, have been preparing all their lives for such a day. In short, there would be war. You see, Mr Dunbar, we agree in essence about CIA involvement. Where we disagree is in their use of Coughlin and Garfield.'

While keeping his weapon trained on Alex, the blond gunman opened the fridge with his free hand and tossed two bottles of beer to his companion, who caught them deftly, uncapped each, and handed one back.

'You in the west,' the Israeli went on, 'have not fought a war for forty years. I don't count Korea, Malaya, Vietnam, the Falklands, the various police actions against the Mau Mau or EOKA. They involved no London Blitzes or Pearl Harbors. Bloody though they were, they happened thousands of miles away. You have concluded that there can never be another war where the home country is as much under attack as the soldier with his rifle. We Israelis see matters differently. We've all lived in the front line since 1948. When determined men want war, there will be war.'

For several seconds the only sound in the room was that of the shower, still going full blast.

'So there could be war in Europe,' said Alex. 'I'm not saying for a moment that I accept your hypothesis of collusion between Coughlin, Garfield and Langley, but if I did, where does Mossad come in?'

'At two points.' The blond gunman took a long swig of his beer and wiped his mouth with the back of his hand. 'First, any attempt to revive Nazism will always be ruthlessly crushed by us. Second, Israel relies on the United States and, to a lesser degree, France for supplies of vital war *matériel*. If both those countries were otherwise engaged or, worse, both lost so much military equipment in even a limited war that their factories would need to work flat out for the next five years to make up the domestic shortfall, who would supply Israel? No one. Our enemies would seize the opportunity to destroy us once and for all. We need help, Mr Dunbar, specifically, your help. Will you give it?'

For the moment Alex did not answer. To begin with he did not much care for being asked for assistance while the suppliant had a pistol pointed at his chest, though there was more to it than that. Where, for example, had Mossad obtained its knowledge of the filmed events in South Dakota, and were the PLO in Bangkok? Where Mossad was to be found the Palestinians were usually not far behind.

'You don't need my help,' he said. 'Even if you did, I'm unlikely to give it under duress.'

The gunman glanced at his compatriot, who spread his hands in a Gallic gesture of please yourself. After a moment's hesitation, the pistol disappeared into a concealed shoulder holster.

'You might as well turn off the shower as well,' said Alex amiably. 'I hear they have a summer water shortage in Bangkok.'

When that was done, the blond Israeli said, 'Perhaps you'll explain why we don't need your help – because, believe me, I think we do. Whether Coughlin and Garfield are colluding with Langley or not, Tel Aviv has ordered the destruction of the films. They would cause only trouble for Jews in general and Israel in particular.'

'You mean there might be some truth in the suggestion that the Soviets did have extermination camps for Jews?'

The two Israelis exchanged glances.

'Yes,' said the blond. 'We have some evidence that the glorious Red Army' – he spat out the words – 'had several camps for East European and Russian Jews, who were killed under orders from political commissars. The numbers, however, were few. Whatever the Nazis say, six million Jews died in Hitler's camps. Nevertheless, by skilful propaganda our enemies could increase the Russian deaths dramatically, thus confirming the views held by Hitler's apologists. Now, will you help us – by joining forces with us? We'll achieve more by working together than separately or against each other, especially as it's towards the same end.'

169

'I'd like to help myself to one of those beers that are going on my room tab.'

The dark-haired Israeli uncapped a bottle and passed it over warily. Alex drank greedily.

'In the first place,' he said, his thirst quenched, 'I don't think I can. I have no more idea than you where Coughlin and Garfield are. If I did, I'd have to keep it to myself, otherwise my masters would begin to ask where my loyalties lay, which, in our business, can prove fatal.

'In the second place, I repeat that you don't need me. If you're right about collusion, a single phone call from your Foreign Minister to his counterpart in Washington will resolve the whole problem.'

The dark-haired Israeli smiled grimly. 'That would be like a pygmy asking a giant to kindly get off his foot – or else.'

'Then your government goes public,' said Alex, knowing it could not.

'Impossible. All we have up to now is conjecture, no proof. Without hard evidence, a country the size of Israel cannot make public accusations against one of its best friends without inviting severe repercussions. We have our orders. Coughlin and Garfield are to be found, interrogated and destroyed, together with the material they carry.'

Alex was not surprised by the answer. Politicians rarely wanted to upset delicate applecarts by awkward questions to their opposite numbers in other countries. Which was why governments paid people like the Mossad duo – and himself and Hamilton, for that matter – handsomely to do their dirty work for them.

The Israelis spent the next few minutes in rapid, fierce and whispered conversation, conducted entirely in Yiddish, which Alex did not understand. Even so, it wasn't difficult to figure out that they were discussing his fate, having concluded that he could not or would not tell them anything. The blond agent seemed to be arguing in favour of leaving it at that; his companion evidently disagreed in the manner that left little room for doubt what his solution to the problem was.

Alex weighed the odds. Reasonably fit as he was after Dulverton, and naturally strong, he realized he could not hope to come out the winner in a brawl with two men who were both ten years younger and in the peak of physical condition. Nor could he reach the 9mm Browning that was now in his jacket pocket, the jacket itself being across a chair on the far side of the bedroom. With surprise on his side he might just have got there in time and turned the tables on the Israelis except for one small item: the box of shells lay unopened in the other pocket.

Nevertheless, he was not going to place his faith in the superior debating skills of the blond Israeli and had already made up his mind to make a try for the empty gun and hope to bluff it out when there was a knock on the door. A moment later Hamilton's voice called, 'Alex? It's me. Open up.'

The blond agent swiftly motioned to Alex to silence and whispered, 'Is that your partner?'

'Yes. He knows I'm in here. We'd arranged to have a drink in my room and discuss our next move as soon as we'd both showered and changed,' Alex lied.

'Tell him to go away.' Both Israelis had drawn their weapons. 'Tell him that you've only just got out of the shower, that you'll meet him in the bar for that drink.'

Alex had no intention of opening the door anyway and wouldn't have done even if the Israelis had demanded it. He didn't want Hamilton walking into the trap he himself was already in, especially as Hamilton was the key to getting rid of the Israelis without, hopefully, any bloodshed. It all depended upon Hamilton remembering one of the tricks they'd both been reacquainted with in Dulverton.

'Tell him you'll meet him downstairs. Now!' Alex felt a pistol against his ribs. 'And no signals or you're both dead men.'

'I'm only just out of the shower,' called Alex. 'Make that drink in the lobby bar. I'll have my usual vodka and tonic, easy on the tonic.'

'What?' Hamilton was clearly mystified. 'Let me in, I'll wait for you while you dress.'

'For Christ's sake, you Irish idiot, I'm dripping all over the carpet. Give me ten minutes and I'll join you.'

'Okay. Whatever you say.'

The dark-haired Israeli put his ear to the door. 'I think

171

he's gone.'

'Am I going to see him in ten minutes?' asked Alex. 'Or do you have other plans for me?'

'We were discussing that a moment ago,' answered the blond agent, 'as you doubtless gathered. Do you understand Yiddish?'

'No. But it wouldn't take a linguist to deduce what the conversation was about. You're for calling it a day and cutting your losses. Your bloodthirsty companion is for cutting something in the region of my jugular.'

'He's not really bloodthirsty. Before joining us he was considered a first-class tank commander and before that a potentially brilliant agronomist.'

'I'm not in the least interested in his curriculum vitae. I'm more interested in who was winning the argument. The last I heard, Mossad did not go in for killing agents of friendly powers.'

'Nor does it now. The problem is, we want Coughlin and Garfield ourselves. We do not want competition. You are competition. It would solve a lot of problems if you'd consider returning to London and confessing failure.'

'Not for me,' said Alex. Where the hell was Hamilton? Surely to God he hadn't swallowed that malarkey about a vodka and tonic, anathema to a whisky drinker? 'You know my personal reasons for wanting Coughlin and Garfield. They haven't changed.'

'Then I'm afraid we've reached an impasse.'

Believing that Hamilton had blown it, Alex was about to adopt his original plan of making a dive for the empty Browning when there was a rattle of a key in the bedroom door, the sound of a high-pitched male voice saying '*Kop kun*' – thank you – and then Hamilton was in the doorway, sizing up the situation in a flash and pointing, before they could raise their own guns, a very obviously loaded automatic at the startled Mossad agents.

Kicking the door shut with his heel he asked, 'How was my accent?'

'Atrocious.' Alex relieved the Israelis of their weapons. 'Anyway, what kept you?'

Hamilton was indignant. 'It took me two minutes to find a

172

floor waiter and bribe him – you owe me thirty American dollars – to give me his pass key, and another minute to establish the Thai words for "thank you". Then thirty seconds to load this. I estimate I've been away less than five minutes since you called me an Irish idiot. Okay?'

'Okay,' smiled Alex.

'Who're these people?'

'Mossad.' Alex explained briefly what had transpired. 'They were trying to make up their minds whether or not to kill me.'

'What was the verdict?'

'I doubt we'll ever know.'

'It was still being discussed,' said the blond Israeli. 'I think I was winning.'

'I'm delighted to hear it,' said Alex. 'There was a moment a while ago when I thought you weren't.'

'What do we do with them?' asked Hamilton, his Browning never wavering for an instant. Nor, from the look in his eye, would he have hesitated to use it if necessary.

Alex's response to the question surprised the Israelis; he returned their pistols to them, still loaded. 'We let them go. We're on the same side, although one of them, at least, has yet to learn that.'

The blond agent holstered his sidearm, angrily snapping his fingers at his companion who was slower in doing so and calling him a few choice names in Yiddish for good measure.

'Thank you, Mr Dunbar,' he said courteously. 'We could hardly have envisaged such generosity.'

'As I said,' said Alex, 'We're on the same side. Apart from that, if we killed you I'd have to spend the rest of my life looking over my shoulder to see if the man, or woman, behind me was a Mossad agent out to level the score. I prefer not to live like that.'

The Israelis made for the door.

'One more thing,' said Alex. 'For reasons I've already explained, I hope I catch up with Coughlin and Garfield before you do. But if you get to them first, remember what they did to my wife. Your service can reach my service via the usual channels with the result. *L'chaim.*'

'*L'chaim*, Mr Dunbar.'

'Now you son of a bitch,' said Alex, 'let's hear why you were knocking on my door when the last thing you told me was that you were going to see the sights.'

'Penury,' answered Hamilton without a trace of embarrassment. 'I remembered Herrick saying that the minimum fee for one of the girls was around a hundred dollars, and I had slightly less than that in my pocket. As you're the paymaster on this trip I was coming to you for a sub. I didn't think Calderwood would take kindly to receiving a credit card voucher made out to Madame Chung's Massage Emporium or some such, and I reckoned if I went down-market to the fifty-dollar bracket, I might end up with more than I bargained for, the sort of thing that requires a few litres of penicillin to clear up.'

Alex's mouth had dropped open in astonishment.

'You mean I possibly owe my life to the fact that you couldn't keep your libido under control for a few hours?'

'You owe me more than that.'

'How come?'

'Thirty dollars for the pass key and a course in basic Thai.'

Herrick picked them up in the Montein lobby at nine p.m. Although Alex and Hamilton were now more suitably attired for the climate, the heat outside the hotel, even at that hour, took their breath away.

A different car, somewhat more luxurious, with a different driver stood at the roadside. Herrick explained that he had four drivers on his team, whom he used in rotation. Tonight's change of vehicle was just basic security, in case anyone had followed them from the airport earlier in the day. Alex told the resident about his confrontation with the Mossad agents.

'What did they look like?' asked Herrick, his hand on the car door.

Alex described them in detail.

'Then that perhaps explains something,' said Herrick, 'though it poses more questions than it resolves. I called in at police headquarters on my way over here. I try to get in at least two or three times a week, make "contributions" to the police fund and smile a lot. The police know or suspect what I do, of course, as they know about the other countries' residents. It pays to keep in with them. They can make life bloody difficult if they take a dislike to your face.'

A beautiful girl, her silk dress split to the top of her thigh, roared up on the pillion of a motorcycle. Herrick said something to the rider in Thai, who promptly turned his machine and went off hunting custom elsewhere.

'I told them you were French,' said Herrick. 'Around these parts the French are known to be very tight-fisted.'

'You were at police headquarters,' Alex reminded him.

175

'Yes. I was passing the time of day and generally trying to find out whether anything was happening in Bangkok that might interest us, when I was handed a report by the man I usually see. I say he handed it to me. What he actually did was give an academy award performance about opening it and leaving it on his desk while he went out of the room. I didn't have to be told twice what was expected of me. I flicked through the report. It concerned several murders that had occurred just an hour and a half earlier on the other side of the Phra Bridge. Four people in all. From the descriptions you just gave me two of the corpses were your Israelis. The other two were Middle Eastern types. They were officially described as Arabs in the report, but that description covers a multitude of sins in Bangkok. Anyway, let's assume they were Arabs. All four men had been shot at close range, presumably with silenced pistols as nowhere in the report did anyone say anything about hearing shots. There were no papers or other means of identification on any of the bodies.'

'The PLO and Mossad getting to grips, do you think?' said Alex.

'The police haven't drawn that conclusion and probably won't. They have enough crime of their own to contend with without importing any and turning the streets of Bangkok into an Israeli/Arab battleground. However, a PLO/Mossad confrontation would appear to be what we're supposed to think. Then again, I've never yet heard of four people in a close-range shoot-out all dying within feet of one another. Somebody usually survives, the quickest on the trigger.'

'Still, it's not impossible.'

'No, it's not impossible. But I haven't finished yet. There was a witness – not to the shootings, but someone who saw a car being driven off at high speed just after he came across the bodies. The witness was bright enough to take down the car number, which my policeman friend had kindly encircled in red ink. It's the number of a vehicle from the CIA resident's pool. Just as he knows my numbers by heart, I know his. So the question is, gentlemen, why is the Company knocking off the PLO and Mossad opposition but apparently leaving you alone?'

'I don't follow,' said Hamilton.

'I do,' said Alex. 'If Mossad can get to me it wouldn't be difficult for Company operatives to do so either – if the name of the game is no-holds-barred. I see what Herrick's driving at. It would appear that the Company is protecting us from the unwelcome attentions of other intelligence services.'

'But why?' asked Hamilton.

'I'll tell you when I know,' said Alex. 'What will the police do?' he asked Herrick.

'Not much. The Company resident has the same arrangement with the police as I do. It may cost the US Treasury a little extra in the envelope next week, but it will be forgotten. The Company man will merely say that the eyewitness misread the licence number of the car. As I told you earlier, the dollar is a mighty powerful bargaining counter in these parts. Anyhow, let's get on our way. Are you two carrying?'

Alex and Hamilton said they were. Herrick had not supplied them with shoulder holsters and both men were using the classic alternative, their Brownings stuck into the rear waistband of their trousers and covered by their lightweight jackets.

'This seems to be something of a violent city,' said Alex lightly.

'It can be,' agreed Herrick. 'However, the only reason I ask is that the man we're going to see has an aversion to guns – other people's. In the nether regions he occupies they tend to go off rather unexpectedly and he has made it a lifetime rule not to be at the other end if the unexpected happens. You'll be asked to give them up before you see him. You'll be perfectly safe and you'll get them back when you leave.'

'Who is this man?' asked Hamilton, when they were in the car and under way.

'I told you this afternoon,' said Herrick. 'An underworld contact of mine, quite a powerful figure. He has an unpronounceable name for *farangs* – that's us, white people – and he's known everywhere as Mr Harry. Don't ask me why. He's been called that for as long as anyone can remember. He speaks excellent English, though don't be offended if he and I drop into Thai once in a while. It's not

177

meant to be an insult; it's just that he may want to say something to me that has nothing to do with our business but which may be important for him to learn. If I give the right answers, he helps us out. Quid pro quo.'

Herrick was again in the passenger seat next to the driver, with whom he exchanged a few words.

Herrick said, 'He's reminded me that we're running early and asked if you wanted to see something of the city. I told him that I didn't think Hamilton, at least, was interested in temples and Thai artefacts.'

'You make me sound no more than a horny philistine,' said Hamilton with mock indignation.

'The *mot juste*,' smiled Alex. 'Prove he's not,' he added to Herrick. 'Stuff some culture down the little blighter's craw.'

'Okay, but I'll keep it short and sweet because I'm on Hamilton's side. That temple over on the left there, the Wat Trimit, contains the Golden Buddha, which is ten feet high and cast in five and a half tons of solid gold. Last I saw, gold was around four hundred dollars an ounce, so you'd be looking at around eighty million dollars' worth of graven image. Might be a bit tough smuggling through Heathrow, though.'

A little later Herrick pointed out the Wat Sutat, which was two perpendicular poles seventy or eighty feet high topped off by a crossbeam. The structure resembled a giant swing minus the ropes and seat, which was what Herrick confirmed it was, or used to be.

'Interesting story there,' he said. 'For several hundred years until 1932, the Thais held an annual contest between three teams of four men. Each team took a turn. While one of the men stood on the seat of the swing, the other three pushed him to gain momentum, the way children do in amusement parks. Eventually he would be level with the crossbeam, which as you can see is damned high and must have taken a lot of nerve. The trick was to go completely over the top with your swing ropes taut, at which point you'd be one hundred and fifty feet from the ground and travelling like a bullet. On the way down the other side you were expected to catch a fat purse full of gold from an adjacent bamboo pole. With your teeth. If you caught it your team kept it and were probably set up for life. If you missed it the next team had a crack. Some legends have it that the top of the bamboo pole was sharpened to a point. If you made the slightest error you were impaled. I guess you also lost the match. End of cultural guided tour. We're almost there.'

Without any prompting from Herrick the driver made a left turn and then another. Now they were travelling through unlit back streets, a far cry from the brightly illuminated main roads of central Bangkok.

Alex checked his wristwatch. It was only nine thirty. 'Your driver's right about us running early,' he said. 'I thought the meeting was for midnight.'

'So it is,' confirmed Herrick, 'but I did promise Hamilton some entertainment. Who knows how long you'll remain in Bangkok? Mr Harry has his offices above a club. His club, in fact. You might find what goes on inside enlightening.'

Unbidden, the driver brought the car to a halt outside what would have seemed, in western terms, to be a three-storey warehouse. The only indication that it might be anything else was a neon sign above a heavy door that read, in English, DRAGON CLUB. Underneath were several words in Thai which presumably said the same thing.

'A couple of pieces of advice before we go in,' said Herrick. 'First, we'll park our guns as soon as we enter. That will make everyone feel a lot happier. We want to make a good impression, and handing them over at the door will reach Mr Harry's ears within fifteen seconds. It will show we trust his employees and therefore him. Trust is a big thing with Thais, even among those who give orders for throats to be cut the way the rest of us ask for a pint of beer.

'Secondly, and most important, etiquette. Very vital. My contact is always Mr Harry, never plain Harry. Next, Thais consider the head the most important part of the body, the feet the least. So don't point your feet directly at Mr Harry when you're sitting opposite him. He'll assume you don't think he's important and be mortally offended. Penultimately, don't ever touch any Thai and especially not Mr Harry on the head. That's even worse than pointing your feet at him. I know we in the west sometimes cuff people playfully around the ear or ruffle their hair, but if you do that to a Thai, even though you're a *farang*, blood will be spilled. Lastly, the Thais are a small people physically. Mr Harry is about average, say five feet four. They don't like people towering over them and it's not polite, as it would be in England, to get up if your host has occasion to leave the room. Stay put. For that matter, grab a seat as soon as you enter his office and sit there. He won't rise to greet you, nor will he offer to shake hands. I know it all sounds a little eccentric, but that's how it is.'

Herrick said something to the driver, who promptly folded his arms, put his head on his chest, and closed his eyes. He appeared to be asleep even before they were out of the car.

'What happens to him for the next three hours?' asked Hamilton out of curiosity.

'Three hours nothing. He'll stay there until morning if necessary.'

'Until morning?' Alex raised his eyebrows. 'How long is this meeting going to take? We've only got one question: does Mr Harry know where Coughlin and Garfield are?'

Herrick grinned. 'I know, I know. In London or Washington that question could be answered with a simple yes or no. Out here it's different. There are formalities, customs. Mr Harry may choose to answer directly, whether negatively or positively, right away. It depends how he's feeling and what else he has on tonight. The Thais have a word for it – several: *Mai pen rai*. Roughly translated it means "that's the way it goes". They're not in a whole hell of a rush to do anything. One of the first things that was pointed out to me when I arrived is that the dogs don't even chase the cats.'

Herrick rapped on the heavy door with his knuckles. After several seconds a judas-hole, about shoulder height for the average westerner, was slid to one side. A pair of expressionless almond eyes belonging to a Thai man of indeterminate years scrutinized the visitors. Evidently Herrick was recognized or expected, for the door was immediately opened to admit the newcomers, who found themselves in a small anteroom, ten feet by ten, which served as a cloakroom. On the right-hand side were numerous pegs for hats and coats. Most were not in use. Only tourists, with their innate mistrust of foreign weather, would be carrying a light evening coat during a Bangkok summer, and no Thai wore a hat after sunset. At the opposite end of the anteroom to the front door was a second door. Beyond this, music could be heard, western music, disco style.

The Thai bowed deeply from the waist and said 'good evening' in accented English. Herrick parroted the greeting, also in English, before switching to Thai and rattling off half a dozen sentences.

'The hardware, please,' said Herrick.

Alex and Hamilton passed over their Brownings, both loaded. The boxes of ammunition were in the Montien's safety-deposit vault, in a brown-paper parcel to deter the curious. Alex noted that Herrick took his own firearm from a custom built shoulder holster and that the gun was not a standard-issue Browning but a Walther PPK.

Herrick said, 'I saw too many James Bond films as a youngster. Besides, the Browning has a tendency to jam when you can least afford it.'

'Not if you grease the shell-casings with Brylcream.'

'Fort Monkton?' asked Herrick.

'Berlin,' said Alex.

A wall of noise assailed their eardrums as Herrick led the way through the second door, which brought them into a semi-darkened auditorium that held around thirty average-size tables, most of them occupied (by male Thais and *farangs* in roughly equal proportions) and set back in rows from a raised stage no larger than the anteroom. Multi-coloured stroboscopic lights shone through the glass floor of the stage, on which a deliciously proportioned Thai girl was dancing topless to the frenetic taped disco music. The girl's loins were covered with a fringed white miniskirt, under which she wore nothing. The overall effect was more erotic than had she been totally naked. On her feet she wore high-heeled golden sandals tied with crisscross thongs to mid-calf.

Near the rear and to one side of the auditorium was a long bar, a large notice in Thai and English above it stating that table service only was available. Seated on high stools at either end of the bar, obviously separate groups although the reasons for the division would not become apparent until later, were a dozen or so Thai girls, the group on the left marginally outnumbering that on the right. They all wore off-the-shoulder silk dresses in a variety of brilliant colours, each dress having the customary thigh-length split up one side. The girls' exquisite features, enhanced by the subtle use of cosmetics, were picked out by several spotlights shining from the roof, and their skin tones varied in hue between dark brown and pale gold. On each girl's stool was a large plastic disc giving a number. There were no prizes for guessing their occupations.

'We'll get a table in a minute,' yelled Herrick above the din. He jerked his head in the direction of the stage. 'This one's about to go into her finale.'

As the pace of the music increased the disco dancer went into a series of pirouettes, each one quicker than the last, each keeping her fringed miniskirt spinning level with her hips and revealing a wedge of carefully groomed pubic hair. When the beat reached such a tempo that it seemed impossible she could turn any faster, she managed, by some trick of dexterity, to unfasten the skirt and send it flying, because of her momentum, into the audience, where there was an immediate scramble for the trophy. Herrick explained that whoever wound up with the skirt got to spend thirty private minutes with the dancer for a quarter of her usual fee.

When the music stopped she stood quite still, breasts heaving, body glistening with sweat, facing forward, smiling at the rapturous applause. Then the strobe lights beneath the dance floor were extinguished. When the house lights came up a few seconds later the girl had gone. There were no encores. A Thai club like any other club could only serve drinks and make money when the customers' minds were not preoccupied.

A waitress in a cheongsam led them to a vacant table three rows from the front. Perhaps the club's air-conditioning plant was not functioning efficiently or perhaps the combined unsatisfied lust of a hundred men had raised the temperature ten degrees, because the atmosphere was stifling. After consulting Alex and Hamilton, Herrick ordered rum-and-Cokes in tall glasses all round.

When the drinks arrived Hamilton nodded in the direction of the bar girls on their numbered stools.

'How does that work?' he asked Herrick.

'You pick a number, tell the waitress which one you've chosen – you're not allowed to approach them directly – and she'll send your number over to your table, or alternatively, get the girl to meet you by that door across there. Either way, you work out your own deal.' Herrick pointed a finger at the ceiling. 'If you want to go the whole hog there are rooms up there to accommodate you. You can choose two numbers or even more if you're up to it and can afford it. If you just want the girl to sit at your table and buy her a drink – and you'd be surprised how many men do – then that's okay too. It'll cost you, however. They don't drink anything other than Coke on duty and wouldn't dream of charging you for fizzy water and calling it champagne. But even a Coke will set you back ten dollars. Whoever said talk was cheap hadn't spent much time in Bangkok. Do you see anything that takes your fancy?'

Hamilton squinted. 'I wouldn't say no to any of them, though if my life depended on it I'd take number four in the left-hand group.'

Herrick grinned. 'Remind me to have a word with your insurance broker. Or your optician. Number four in the left-hand group – in fact, everyone in the left-hand group – might give you thirty minutes to remember, though if "she" did you're a security risk. The left-hand group aren't women at all. They're men, transvestite prostitutes.'

Even Alex, who thought he'd seen it all in Berlin, was astonished.

'You're kidding,' said Hamilton.

'You're welcome to prove me wrong, my treat. Bangkok is renowned for its glamorous drag queens, and they're highly respected members of an honourable profession, not freaks. They're particularly popular with the French and the Germans. Highly paid too. They remove all unwanted body hair with depilatory cream, grow their tresses like a girl and have them styled regularly, become experts in make-up.

Some of them undergo surgery to increase the size of their breasts. There's only one item they can't do anything about outside a trip to Switzerland, but you can find that out for yourself, if you wish.'

'No thanks,' said Hamilton. 'I'll pass.'

Herrick nodded. 'Wise decision, because in a few more minutes the floorshow restarts. If they're keeping to the usual running order you'll shortly see a couple of the most gorgeous girls you've ever set eyes on. They're twins, and they do a double act that would raise Lazarus.'

'You've got company,' said Alex.

Herrick turned his head. Behind him stood a middle-aged Thai in a white suit. He inclined his head politely and whispered a few words in Herrick's ear. After acknowledging Herrick's response with what was evidently an apology for coming to their table uninvited, he left them.

'I'm afraid you're going to miss the twins,' said Herrick. 'That was one of Mr Harry's minions. Apparently the great man is ahead of schedule this evening and has some personal business to attend to later, which doubtless means that someone will be found face down in the Chaophya river tomorrow morning. He'd like to see us right away.'

BANGKOK (iv)

As Herrick had predicted, Mr Harry did not rise to greet them when they were ushered into his office by a Thai guard who scanned their bodies with a practised eye for concealed weapons. Apparently satisfied, he allowed them to pass.

There were no formal introductions. In Bangkok anyone admitted to Mr Harry's presence would be expected to know who he was, and he would not have allowed them anywhere near him unless he knew who they were.

Herrick gestured Alex and Hamilton to two of the three chairs which were already in position in front of Mr Harry's desk and angled in such a way that no visitor's feet would be pointing directly at Mr Harry. After bowing slightly, Herrick took the third chair and said something in Thai. From his tone and Mr Harry's reaction, Herrick's words were evidently ones of gratitude for Mr Harry's courtesy in seeing them. Alex thanked his lucky stars he'd never had the misfortune to be posted out here. Perhaps one could get used to the heat, but the beautiful girls were no compensation for the ever present need to be polite to the point of obsequiousness.

Mr Harry clapped his hands softly. 'Tea,' mimed Herrick, making a pouring motion beneath the cover of the desk.

While waiting for the tea to arrive, Alex took the opportunity to study Mr Harry. His age was incalculable, somewhere under fifty would have been Alex's guess. His eyes were hard, vicious even, those of someone who knew precisely what he wanted and didn't much care how he got it. He was inclined to plumpness, though there were indications that at one time he had been extremely fit and strong. For a Thai he was broad across the shoulders, and his hands looked as if they had once done honest, or perhaps dishonest, toil. Not recently, however. His nails were beautifully manicured, and on his left pinky he wore a thick gold ring with a huge diamond in the centre, his only concession to ostentation apart from a gold wristwatch. Indeed, he appeared less affluent than the middle-aged Thai who had approached their table earlier. While his suit was of good quality material, the cut could have been better, and his office was little more than the desk he sat behind, the chairs in front of it, and several filing cabinets. The windows overlooking the street were heavily curtained, no doubt, thought Alex, to avoid giving a sniper an easy shot.

When the tea arrived in a silver pot on a silver tray upon which stood the most delicate porcelain teacups and saucers together with a dozen slices of thinly cut lemon in a silver dish, Alex surreptitiously glanced at his own wristwatch. Less than a conversationist minute had elapsed since Mr Harry clapped his hands, yet he proceeded to pour immediately. Alex doubted that the Thai gangster had ever seen a teabag and would much less serve them to guests, but decent tea required six minutes to infuse, being stirred in the pot after three. He was startled when Mr Harry apparently read his thoughts.

'Fortnum and Masons's Royal Blend, Mr Dunbar,' he said in almost flawless English. 'When I sent my associate to your table I judged it would take him two minutes to reach you and a further sixty seconds to explain to Mr Herrick that I wanted to see you immediately. Allowing you one minute to finish your drinks and two more for you to get up here, I instructed that freshly boiled water be poured on to the tea leaves five and one half minutes ago.' He said a few words to the guard who had carried in the tray, who bowed and left the room. 'It should now be perfect. Near the lemon dish you will find tongs to transfer the lemon to your cup. There was really no need to consult your wristwatch.'

Alex apologized in English, thinking – Christ, it's catching, and wondering at the power of a man who could gauge his visitors' movements and intentions to within seconds.

'Please do not apologize,' said Mr Harry, though obviously pleased that Alex had. 'It was good to know that there are certain *farangs* who understand the art of tea-making. Others I have entertained in this office have searched the tray in vain for milk and sugar.' He seemed scandalized. 'One even had the temerity to ask if he could have whisky instead of tea. As if men can discuss matters of import with liquor fogging their brains! I did not do business with that man.'

Frankly, Alex preferred Earl Grey to Royal Blend. This cup, however, was different to anything he had ever tasted, the perfect refreshing drink for a hot night. He sought the words to express his appreciation, eventually, if inadequately, coming up from the dim recesses of his memory with: 'It is good to take tea and comfortable advice.'

Again Mr Harry surprised him. 'I believe Keats meant something entirely different with those lines, Mr Dunbar, but I appreciate the sentiment I know you intended. It is also a most appropriate comment, for now the tea has been served must come the advice, which I regret will not be what you hoped for. Coughlin and Garfield are not in Bangkok. Nor, to the best of my knowledge, have they ever been. Many men have enquired of their whereabouts, of course, but they are not here. Some who made enquiries are now dead.' He turned his gaze on Herrick. 'I heard about your visit to police headquarters earlier, and the report you were allowed to see. I must confess this entire affair puzzles me. Here we have several groups of foreign agents seeking two men who are not in Bangkok. It's very strange. This is not to say, naturally, that Coughlin and Garfield will not appear tomorrow or the following day, but if I were you, Mr Dunbar, I would continue your quest elsewhere.'

Christ, thought Alex, he could have sent one of his minions to tell us that or picked up the phone. Then he realized that that would not be how Mr Harry worked. A request made by a friend, Herrick, on a personal basis – albeit that the friendship had as its lynchpin money or the exchange of information – had to be answered on a personal basis. Like the tea and the elaborate use of the prefix 'Mr',

187

that was only polite.

'Is it possible to pose a question or two?' asked Alex, now finding it second nature to fall into this ultra-formal way of speaking.

'Of course.'

Alex chose his words carefully. 'I mean no disrespect, Mr Harry, but isn't it possible that Coughlin and Garfield are in Bangkok without your knowledge? None of us knows what either looks like. We are handicapped because we lack photographs. Hundreds of Americans must fly in to Bangkok every day, some with package tours, some independently.' Observing Herrick's look of warning, Alex applied a little balm. 'I'm sure a man in your position will have many contacts at the airport and elsewhere, but is it not *just* conceivable that two men whose faces we would not recognize if we were standing next to them could be in Bangkok without your knowledge? Again, I mean no disrespect.'

'I realize that, Mr Dunbar,' said the Thai to Herrick's obvious relief, 'and your supposition would have merit were it not for one glaring omission. The American CIA, who have their own contacts with men such as myself as Mr Herrick has with me, are also looking for Coughlin and Garfield. They have not, I am reliably informed, found them, although the CIA, surely, would have photographs. Take my word for it, Mr Dunbar. Coughlin and Garfield are not and never have been in Bangkok.'

Which seemed to be that, thought Alex. He turned to Herrick.

'Perhaps you would be good enough to thank Mr Harry in your own way for his courtesy and assure him that should we ever be in a position to do him a service, it will be willingly undertaken.'

Although Mr Harry naturally understood every word it appeared appropriate to Alex that the closing remarks should be made in the host's own language. Maybe he could get used to all this diplomatic stuff, Alex thought cynically.

Herrick gabbled away in Thai for several minutes, with Mr Harry nodding periodically. Once there was the faintest glimmer of what could have been a smile.

Finally Herrick pushed back his chair and got to his feet. 'Out,' he said laconically.

Again there were no handshakes or other familiar gestures of departure.

In the passage outside the office they were met by the same guard who had admitted them. He had their sidearms in his hands.

'Mr Harry wants us to use the back stairs out,' said Herrick. 'I didn't ask why.'

Halfway down the first flight Alex had an idea. The guard was leading the way, followed by Hamilton. Alex pulled Herrick to one side and whispered rapidly in his ear.

'I'll do it by phone,' said Herrick. 'If I walked back into Mr Harry's office now without a formal invitation, I'd be dead before I turned the door handle.'

The driver of their car was surprised to see them back so soon.

'Where to now?' asked Herrick.

'Back to the Montien,' answered Alex. 'We'll discuss our next move over a long beer.'

'Amen to that,' said Hamilton. 'What the hell was that stuff he gave us to drink anyway?'

'Bloody philistine,' muttered Alex.

'My next port of call,' he said half an hour later, when all three of them had polished off one beer and signalled for refills, 'is Hong Kong.' He saw Hamilton stare at him. 'Yes, I know,' he added, 'I wasn't going to make that public even to Herrick unless it was necessary. Now I think it is. You see,' he said to Hamilton, 'you're not coming with me, not for now. I'm pretty certain Mr Harry's right and that Coughlin and Garfield are not here or have ever been. He did point out, however, that they could arrive tomorrow or the next day, which would make us look pretty sick if we were both in Hong Kong. So you stay here for two more days. Keep in touch with Herrick as well as doing whatever else you've got in mind. If nothing's happened in two days, join me in HK.'

'Where?'

'Any suggestions?' Alex asked Herrick. 'I don't know Hong Kong.'

'Aren't you being met?'

'Not on this occasion. Hong Kong's home ground for us, don't forget, not like Bangkok. I've got a couple of phone numbers I'll get around to using sooner or later, though this whole business is starting to look like hunting a needle in a haystack,' With the haystack not necessarily being in the Far East, he added to himself. The more he thought about it, the more he was convinced he was being given the runaround. However, for the moment he had to follow orders. 'What about a hotel?' he asked Herrick.

'The Hong Kong itself,' said the Bangkok resident without hesitation. 'It's of the same standard as this, and has the added advantage of being vast. It contains literally hundreds of shops and restaurants. It's a good place to get lost in if need be, to lose anyone who might be shadowing you.'

'Can you book me in for tomorrow?'

'Consider it done. I'll also arrange your flight. There's a Thai Airways departure at nine a.m. I'll check seating availability and let you know. I'll also pick you up out front around seven a.m. The traffic gets pretty congested in the morning and all my drivers know the short cuts. Don't forget to leave your Browning with Hamilton. Even with a diplomatic passport the security check at the airport can be tough.'

At nine twenty the next morning, while the Thai Airways airbus was over the Gulf of Siam and Alex was being treated to the delights of Thai hospitality – namely, on the house, as much champagne and orange juice as he could drink with his breakfast, followed by, for passengers whose stomachs were accustomed to such things, tumblers full of Rémy Martin, again free – Duncan Hamilton received a visitor to his bedroom. Still in his robe, he opened the door to be greeted with a smile by what had to be the most beautiful Thai girl imaginable. She handed him a note in Alex's handwriting. It read: 'Courtesy of the pick of Mr Harry's private stable, this one's on Herrick and me.'

BERLIN

Twenty-four hours later and eight thousand miles west of Bangkok, shortly after two a.m. on a bitterly cold night, a meeting took place in a side street of the Moabit district of West Berlin. It had been arranged in a great hurry at Cassidy's request, and the American's elderly companion was less than happy that a certain amount of security had had to be sacrificed for speed. The older man had an electronic device in his overcoat pocket. This emitted an ultra-high frequency bleep, inaudible to human ears, to distort reception on either directional microphones or hidden recording machines, but it was more to punish Cassidy, whom he recalled from the Eberswalde meeting hated the cold more than most, that he, the older man, insisted upon walking as they talked. The cars in which they had arrived in Moabit were left standing idle a few dozen yards from one another, the occupants of each watching anxiously for any sign of treachery. Other guards, representatives of both sides, kept more or less level with their principals on the far side of the street. Still others had raced ahead and concealed themselves in doorways or positioned themselves on street corners. Although it was late, Berliners were renowned night-birds and many were only now making their way home. To suspicious minds, any one of them need not be what he seemed.

'Well?' asked the older man. 'I assume you haven't brought me here to talk about the weather.'

As before, the conversation between Cassidy and his companion was conducted in German.

Cassidy concentrated to arrange his thoughts. He was

feeling the cold more than usual because he was tired. He and the other members of his team, all hand-picked and loyal to him personally first and the Agency second, had been travelling for fourteen hours, having started off (in different aircraft to deter the curious) from Washington DC during the afternoon of the previous day. They had changed planes in London for Berlin's Tegel Airport, where they had met up and been forced to hang around for two hours until a courier arrived giving the time and place for the meeting.

'I'm waiting.'

'We've hit a couple of snags,' said Cassidy. 'Maybe nothing serious but snags nevertheless. There was no other way to explain what's happened except in person.'

'Go on.' The older man's voice betrayed no emotion. He had lived many years and witnessed all sorts of snags during the majority of them. None was insurmountable.

'I told you when we last met that the computer had thrown up an interesting variation,' went on Cassidy. 'Since then things have gone a little wrong.' He did not mention Nick Tasker's death; the name would have meant nothing to the other man. 'We may have to put the whole idea on the front burner.'

This did not translate well; Cassidy was asked to be more specific.

'Bring matters forward, move faster,' he rephrased the idiom.

'Impossible!' The word came out like a whiplash. 'You know that's impossible. In any event, last time we met you advised that there might be a delay. Now you're telling me that the reverse could be the case.'

'I know, I know. The trouble is, no operation works out exactly as it's planned on paper or in a computer. We try to foresee the imponderables, but we never get them all. My problem is that the man around whom everything hinges is moving much quicker than I anticipated or thought possible. He enlisted the aid of a local gangster in Bangkok and found out in no time flat that what he was looking for was not there. He's now in Hong Kong. He's . . .'

'You're telling me more than I need or find it desirable to know,' said the older man. 'I don't care about the present whereabouts of this man, but I do know where I want him in the not-too-distant future. Note that well, my friend. The not-too-distant future. Not tomorrow or the next day or the day after that. If he's running ahead of the schedule you and' – with a note of contempt in his voice – 'your computer have calculated, find a way to slow him down. Except in the case of the direst emergency, my plans cannot be altered one jot. We are both playing for very high stakes, Herr Cassidy. The higher the stake, the greater the loss in the event of failure. Stop him, Herr Cassidy. Keep to the timetable.'

The older man peered at the dial of his wristwatch.

'Is that *all* you had to say to me?'

'I would hardly call a possible change of timetable *all*,' retorted Cassidy, stung by the implied rebuke but determined not to be intimidated. Christ, he and his team had travelled thousands of miles to get here.

'Nonetheless, there can be no changes. And if that *is* all, you're keeping an old man needlessly from his bed. It would be ironic, would it not, if I died of pneumonia because of this meeting? Come, let's walk back to the cars.'

Several dozen pairs of eyes saw them reverse their steps. From a street corner Frank Stone sincerely hoped that that was it for the night. What he needed was a hot bath, a stiff drink and a woman. The two on the team were both good lookers. Maybe he'd get lucky tonight and not have to pay for it.

LONDON

Six hundred air miles due west of Berlin, in his office at Century House, London, SE1, Calderwood was also preparing for a long night. His personal secretary, a very attractive widow in her middle to late forties (who, surprisingly incorrectly considering the organization which employed them both, rumour had down as Calderwood's mistress) had also volunteered to stay behind; to make coffee, keep an eye on the Telex machine, operate the computer terminal or simply act as a sounding board if Calderwood wanted to throw out a few ideas. Her late husband had been killed on active service many years before, in Aden, while her two boys were mere infants. Apart from her pension there was a little money in the family but only a little. She had therefore taken a secretarial job, the only skill, at that time, for which she had qualifications, and had managed at considerable sacrifice to herself to put her boys through a minor public school. When they went on to university she decided to do the same thing herself, and enrolled as a mature student. Remarkably she found she had an untapped gift for languages, and had graduated in German Literature. She also spoke French fluently and had a good working knowledge of Russian. Several years ago, during one of his periodic visits to GCHQ Cheltenham, Calderwood had struck up a casual conversation with her (something he rarely did) in the canteen, discovered that she was being driven out of her mind by the dullness of her job, assessed her qualities instantly and wangled her transfer to him the minute he ascertained her security classification was high enough. Her name was Brionie Ainsworth, though everyone called her Bunty.

Century House never closed, of course, and there were many people, male and female, upon whom Calderwood could call for assistance at any time of the day or night. But Bunty was his right hand, especially when he had a seemingly logical problem that would not resolve itself.

Open in front of Calderwood was a cable from Alex Dunbar, sent in clear to a 'front' address the Firm used for routine traffic. It was datelined Hong Kong late the previous day.

BANGKOK PROSPECTS COLD STOP FIRST
INDICATIONS ARE THAT HONG KONG WILL
PRODUCE NO CUSTOM EITHER STOP HAMILTON
STILL IN BANGKOK STOP DO I WAIT FOR HIM
HERE OR PRESS ON TO TOKYO ALONE QUERY

Calderwood had already dictated a one-word reply.

HOLD

Taking into account the time difference between London and Hong Kong, Dunbar would probably be reading that over his breakfast on his second day in the Crown colony.

Instructing Dunbar to sit tight was not much of an answer, thought Calderwood, sipping his coffee. On the other hand, what else could he tell the man until he, the man's chief, had come up with a more sensible solution than simply an instruction to press on, leaving Hamilton a couple of flights and a country or two behind, like Little Bo Peep's sheep? True, Coughlin and Garfield might well be in Tokyo and findable there. Bangkok and Hong Kong could have been red herrings all along. But with Japan the most Americanized of the three countries involved, surely that was the last place Coughlin and Garfield would be. Every third American in Tokyo worked for one government agency or another, in some capacity. Coughlin and Garfield would be unearthed in no time, no matter where they were hiding out. Yet they hadn't been unearthed, taken or killed by the Company; reports coming in from various sources confirmed that the hunt was still on, wherein lay the seemingly logical problem that would not be resolved. Just where the devil were they?

He could not help feeling that he was approaching, and had approached all along, the matter of their disappearance from the wrong angle, taken too much on trust. Which was why he was staying up this night, surrounded by files, notebooks and God knows what else. He had to crack it before he went to sleep or he suspected he never would. Similarly, as he knew from past experience, when the mind had absorbed vast quantities of data and become overtired, exhausted, into an hallucinatory state almost, then – sometimes – up popped the answer like a slice of perfectly made toast.

He started by pushing every file he had requested to one side: those on the CIA, particularly Berlin personnel past and present; those on the various KGB directorates and Soviet military intentions; those on Berlin in general and the intelligence networks there in particular; those on neo-Nazis, German or otherwise. Many others.

In these days of high technology, most of the information he needed now or would ever need was stored on computer and available at the touch of a few keys. But Calderwood knew himself to be of the old-fashioned school, was proud of it, in fact. He did not scorn magnetic tapes, technology, computers; far from it. Nevertheless, he liked the reassuring nearness of a file or two – or thirty as he seemed to have here. In every file, some of which went back to the war years, a man or a woman had written something out by hand or signed something that had been typed. Files were 'human'. They gave one continuity and also a better 'feel' for the subject. Certainly a computer could find in a fraction of a second what would take him or Bunty a couple of hours of cursing and getting in each other's way, but one could not develop an instinct with a computer. For that matter, if computers were so bloody clever, why the hell couldn't the Century House electronic genius-in-residence find Coughlin and Garfield? It had been asked; Bunty had suggested that to start with. It had come up with a blank, no data, nothing; nothing, that is, which antedated Coughlin and Garfield's initial entries several weeks before. Who, it had more or less asked, are Coughlin and Garfield?

A damned good question, thought Calderwood.

He headed a blank sheet of paper COUGAR. After a moment or two he underlined the word in red ink. Then he sat staring at it mesmerized until Bunty reappeared.

'That coffee looks absolutely disgusting,' she said, whisking away the cup and saucer. 'I'll bring you a fresh cup.'

The timbre of her voice was soft and, somehow, redolent of woodsmoke to Calderwood's mind, though he had never really worked out what he meant by that and had eventually dismissed the simile as sentimental and nonsensical poppycock. Nevertheless, her gentle, unflappable tones seemed to suit the night hours, and there were those in the Firm who swore that her inflection would alter not one iota whether she was told that the Russians had just carried out a pre-emptive strike in Europe or whether she had a run in her stockings. Some of the junior officers had a sweepstake going, entry fee one pound, should either event occur. The object was to write down what would be Bunty's first words. The most popular entry so far was, 'Damn.' This was closely followed by 'How inconvenient.'

The officer who had asked, in all innocence, how anyone could be sure that Bunty wore stockings as opposed to tights was ostracized for three days. Of course Bunty would wear stockings. She would consider tights to be a product of the same age that had produced an over-abundance of Italian restaurants; young men with strange-coloured hair who plucked at guitars and wailed about the wickedness of the world (as if they knew); extra television channels, totally unnecessary; spelling mistakes in the London *Times*. She would no more contemplate wearing tights than she would dream of addressing Her Majesty as ma'am with a soft 'a' – *marm* – instead of a hard 'a' – *mam*; or of discussing her work with *anyone* outside the office; or of placing scented soap in the guest's bathroom.

'You might put something in it,' said Calderwood watching Bunty pour.

'How much something?'

'A thimbleful. It's going to be a long night.'

The fresh coffee, black, smelling faintly of whisky, and naturally in a completely clean cup and saucer, Bunty placed at Calderwood's right elbow. 'Stuck?' she asked.

'Barren.'

Bunty leaned over and saw the word COUGAR on the otherwise empty sheet of paper. 'May I make a suggestion?'

'I should be delighted.'

'I was thinking about it when I was downstairs a moment or two ago, that we may be approaching the problem from the wrong angle.' Bunty pulled up her own chair and sat next to Calderwood. 'We've asked the computer about Cougar. It's told us only what we've fed in ourselves recently. The same goes for Coughlin and Garfield. Why, therefore, don't we ask it about something it can tell us – about Alex Dunbar? It seems to me that Alex is the key. He was out of the Firm for two years and a liability for two years before that. Yet within weeks of us learning of Cougar, Alex's brother is murdered in mysterious circumstances and we receive a report that Coughlin and Garfield killed Melanie Dunbar. That report, you will remember, came through an irregular channel. Do you have the account Alex wrote in your flat about his experiences in America?'

Calderwood did, in his left-hand desk drawer and still in the original OHMS envelope. He brought it out.

'It's long,' he warned Bunty.

'Yes, I've read it. There was a piece somewhere that bothered me at the time. I didn't mention it because it didn't seem that important and I had a hundred other matters to attend to on the same day.'

She sorted through the handwritten pages until she found what she was looking for.

'Here it is. It was when Alex was in Arlington, talking to George Andrus, their first meeting, I think, in Amelia's. Now Andrus was the Company's deputy head of station in Berlin during part of the time Alex was there, and kicked back home when Langley sent in Cassidy. If I remember correctly, though this is on another page, Andrus told Alex he would give a lot to have Cassidy's private parts as trophies. Let me see. Yes, this is the line I wanted. Alex asked Andrus about Coughlin and Garfield, adding that they were in the field in Berlin during Andrus' residency. Andrus answers: *During my time? I don't think so.*'

'Therefore?'

'Well, don't you see?' said Bunty triumphantly. 'How could it possibly be that the deputy chief of station doesn't know the names of two of his field agents. The report we received on Melanie Dunbar's murder definitely states that they were field agents, not casuals flown in for a one-off assignment. Didn't you have that file on CIA Berlin personnel past and present out? I saw it on your desk.'

Calderwood disinterred it from the heap he had pushed to one side. The names of every known Company agent who had served in the Berlin station since the CIA was formed from the remnants of the OSS were listed in the folder. Alongside each name was a series of letters and numbers, which would direct the researcher to a more detailed breakdown of each operative's career. Coughlin and Garfield did not appear anywhere.

Calderwood would have been the first to admit that the register did not claim to be exhaustive. Some agents would be 'blown' or dead within twenty-four hours of arrival; others would not mix with the general intelligence community because their assignments demanded anonymity; yet others could have been omitted from the file due to human error. Nevertheless, he had a sneaking suspicion that neither Coughlin nor Garfield fell into any of those categories.

'There might be a more in-depth breakdown on the computer,' he said, realizing that that was a non-starter even as the words were uttered. They had already asked the computer to search its memory banks for *any* reference to Coughlin and Garfield, without success. 'Perhaps they once operated under different names,' he offered tentatively.

'Or perhaps,' said Bunty, giving voice to what was going through both their minds, 'they don't exist at all and never have.'

They allowed that startling notion to lie fallow for several minutes, while Bunty poured herself a cup of coffee and Calderwood drank his own.

'And if they never existed,' said Bunty eventually,

resuming her seat, 'they could not have killed Melanie Dunbar.'

'But we both saw the report,' protested Calderwood, dismayed to think that Alex Dunbar and Duncan Hamilton were on the far side of the world, on a wild-goose chase.

'Which was signed by Cassidy.'

'A plant?' said Calderwood incredulously. 'Are you seriously suggesting that we have been duped, that the document we received, and which I allowed Alex to read, reopening an old wound, was a work of fiction?'

'It's beginning to look that way.'

'But why?' demanded Calderwood, crashing the coffee cup into the saucer with such force that Bunty jumped. 'Why in God's name would the CIA in general and Cassidy in particular want us – by which I mean me – to resurrect a retired agent and send him haring from continent to continent in the belief that he is tracking down the men who murdered his wife? Why are they using Alex Dunbar for whatever they're up to? I mean, why Dunbar *especially*?'

'Perhaps it didn't have to be Alex *necessarily*,' conjectured Bunty. 'Perhaps his name just came out of the hat.'

'An agent retired in disgrace, a man who was close to becoming an alcoholic? I can't accept that Alex Dunbar was chosen at random.'

'Perhaps you're right,' said Bunty. 'In any event, only Cassidy can answer that question for certain.'

'Yes, Cassidy,' intoned Calderwood in an odd voice. 'Well there, perhaps for the first time, we might have the edge on Mr Cassidy, because I have someone with him. I know where he was a dozen hours ago, four hours ago, and two hours ago. And I might know a great deal more before the night's out. He's in West Berlin,' he said to Bunty, from whom he had few professional secrets.

'My God.' Bunty put a hand to her mouth. 'Are you expecting something from Berlin tonight?'

'Or tomorrow. Why?'

'Because that's why I disappeared fifteen minutes ago, after my extension rang. Down to the cipher room. A coded telex arrived for you around two forty-five. It wasn't marked priority or Eyes Only and they wanted to know how urgent it was. They're very busy down there and they asked me if I'd bring it up for you to decode personally. When I saw how long it was and realizing how preoccupied you were, I told the cipher chief to let his own section handle it but treat it as routine.'

'Get it,' said Calderwood fiercely, using a tone he rarely adopted with Bunty. 'I don't give a damn about the length of the message, go down there and stand over them until it's deciphered. Tell them to drop everything else and have that decode on my desk in fifteen minutes.'

BERLIN

In the hotel room he was sharing with Frank Stone, Cassidy paced the floor nervously, an unlighted cigarette between his fingers. Short of abducting Dunbar and keeping him locked up for several weeks, which presented all kinds of problems, he had no idea of how to stop the Englishman being out of Hong Kong *and* Tokyo within a couple of days. Sooner or later Dunbar would realize that the fictitious Coughlin and Garfield were not to be found in the Far East. His next port of call would then be Berlin, which he knew well from the past and where Calderwood would almost certainly work out soon that Cougar would reach its climax. All the clues had been carefully designed to get Dunbar to Berlin. But not yet. The old man was right. They had to keep to the timetable.

The bastard of it was, Cassidy thought viciously, he had to be back in Washington the day after tomorrow at the latest. A man in his position could not simply vanish without someone asking questions. However, if Dunbar *did* materialize unexpectedly, he, Cassidy, really should be on the spot to supervise matters personally, organize another cat-and-mouse game with the Englishman until his unknowing part in the affair could be concluded. Was Stone capable of doing that? He would have to be. He and the others would have to remain in the city. In fact, it was probably better they did so anyway. They would not be missed; he could cover for them.

Damn Dunbar. How the hell could they slow him down?

It was Stone who came up with the answer. While his chief wore out the carpet, he was sitting in an armchair, drinking a bourbon and branch, and flicking through the English editions of the day's newspapers. He was feeling thoroughly pissed off. Everyone else would be tucked up in bed by now, two of the men doubtless with the two women on the team. Getting laid was out of the question for him this night, not with Cassidy on edge.

Then he saw the captioned photograph and the short news item beneath it. The newspaper was the English *Daily Express*.

He showed the photograph to Cassidy, who barely glanced at it.

'Recognize her?'

'No,' said Cassidy irritably.

Being an agency photograph Stone would not have recognized her either – except that he had stood within a few feet of her three weeks earlier.

'Then let me read you the caption and the news item,' he said. '"World famous model Alison Cameron and magazine publisher Vincent Kaplan shown here against a picturesque background of Chinese junks on the Kowloon waterfront. Miss Cameron is on an extended modelling tour of the Far East. After Hong Kong her travels will take her to Tokyo." They're doing a feature on Hong Kong,' concluded Stone.

Nothing registered with Cassidy, whose thoughts were elsewhere.

'Don't you remember who Alison Cameron is?' asked Stone. 'Let me refresh your memory. This beautiful young lady is the late Nick Tasker's girl, who, if you recall, Dunbar picked up at his brother's funeral. Am I getting through? Alison Cameron's in Hong Kong. Dunbar's in Hong Kong. Now does that suggest anything to you?'

Cassidy snatched at the newspaper.

'This picture could be way out of date. It doesn't say anywhere that she's still in Hong Kong. She could have moved on to Tokyo or even be back home by now.'

Stone barely succeeded in concealing his contempt. Cassidy was cracking up.

'It says she's on an *extended* tour of the Far East. Tasker's funeral was only what, twelve days ago. Even if she left the following morning I'd hardly call eleven days extended. If she's not still in Hong Kong she'll be in Tokyo, and either would work for us. Anyway, a couple of phone calls will give us the answer on her whereabouts.'

'She was Tasker's girl, not Dunbar's,' Cassidy pointed out. 'Dunbar hardly knew her. What makes you think we've got anything here that will work for us?'

Stone answered that question with one of his own.

'Have you ever come across the theory that women tend to fall in love with men who in some respects resemble their own father?' Cassidy said he had. 'Well let me tell you for nothing that the same applies to brothers. Neither Miss Cameron nor Dunbar may know it yet, but they're attracted to one another. It only needs a little shove to see it develop.'

'Possible,' said Cassidy.

'Probable,' retorted Stone. 'And do you know what the sex manuals say is the best, the most potent aphrodisiac of all?'

'Of course not.'

'Propinquity,' said Stone.

LONDON

Calderwood read through the decode several times while Bunty prepared more coffee.

The entire Cassidy party waited at Tegel Airport for two hours. Cassidy made two telephone calls from a public booth, the first on arrival, the second twenty minutes later. Approximately thirty minutes after that, in response, it appeared, to an announcement over the airport's public address system, he took a message on one of the courtesy phones. I regret I did not hear the name the p.a. gave, although I am sure it was not Cassidy. Throughout the entire wait Cassidy spoke to no one other than Stone.

When the party moved off they rendezvoused in a Moabit side street with several other cars. Guards were present from both factions, apparently to prevent the private conversation which took place between Cassidy and his contact being overheard or otherwise interrupted.

Contact was a man in his middle sixties. Taller than Cassidy he was also thinner; not, my guess would be, due to ill-health but to regular diet and exercise. I caught one reasonably good look at his face when he bent his head under a street lamp to examine his wristwatch. It is my considered opinion that Cassidy's contact was Marshal Nikolei Nikitchenko. This however must repeat must be verified via some other source. My degree of certitude, however, is point eight. Contact of course was in civilian clothes. Nevertheless, the face was definitely Russian and the security surrounding him suggested a Russian of considerable rank. Instructions please. Ends.

'Jesus Christ!' profaned Calderwood finally. From the percolator Bunty looked up in alarm. She rarely heard him blaspheme; it was quite out of character. Nor did she know the reason. She had not read the decode. It was standard procedure that all messages from the cipher room were sent to the named recipient in a sealed envelope, a ridiculous display of bureaucracy considering that the cryptanalyst knew what was in the message, as did the senior officer on duty who had to check the flimsy for possible errors in transcription. Two copies were also on their way via channels to other parts of the building for filing and recording.

'Another trip down to the cipher room, if you don't mind, Bunty,' said Calderwood, scribbling on a message blank. He wondered briefly what he should tell his Berlin agent before concluding that it was wiser, as always, to stick to the original plan.

'To be encoded and sent immediately,' he said, handing the form to Bunty. 'And apologize for me, would you, for making so many peremptory demands of the cipher room duty officer. And while I'm about it, include yourself in that apology. I'm sorry I snarled at you earlier.'

'I didn't notice a snarl,' said Bunty, smiling. 'Perhaps a tiny growl, but no more.'

Calderwood almost managed a smile himself. 'And hurry back,' he said. 'We've got a lot of work to do and I'm going to need your help to operate that infernal gadget.' He indicated the computer console. 'You're not tired, I hope?'

'Not in the least.'

When she returned he handed her his copy of the decode. She scanned it quickly.

'Cassidy again,' she said, half to herself 'And having clandestine meetings with Soviet ranking officers.'

'Not just a Soviet ranking officer,' Calderwood corrected her, though fully aware that Bunty knew precisely who Marshal Nikitchenko was. 'The Soviet ranking officer – defence minister and chief of the Red Army which in Russia includes the navy and air force as well. More importantly, he's a member of the Politburo, one of a dozen men who make *all* the decisions in the USSR, standing as they do at the apex of the Central Committee. With the exception of Andropov and the head of the KGB, General Chebrikov, Nikitchenko is doubtless the most powerful man in the Soviet Union. The Red Army is his; they are the puppets and he is the puppeteer. Yet here we see him having secret meetings with a high-ranking CIA officer. The implications are earth-moving, my dear Bunty, earth-moving.'

'Defection?' suggested Bunty, regretting the words the moment they were uttered. It was an absurd notion.

'Out of the question.'

Calderwood picked up the sheet of paper which he had previously headed COUGAR. He had added several other letters in Bunty's absence, but for the moment he kept his hand over what he had written.

'This is becoming very confusing, Bunty. We have assumed all along that Cougar was a CIA operation *against* the Soviets, somehow involving spurious film. Now we find Cassidy meeting secretly not just with anyone but with Marshal Nikolei Nikitchenko, the top Russian soldier and one of the most important policy makers in the Soviet Union. I don't believe that Cougar is an operation against the Soviets at all. Quite the reverse, in fact.'

He took his hand from the sheet of paper formerly headed COUGAR and showed Bunty what he had added – the letters O.V.I.T.C.H. The heading on the otherwise blank sheet now read:

COUGAROVITCH

'Cassidy,' said Calderwood deliberately, 'is not working against the Russians. He's working for them or with them.'

'You mean he's a mole?' said Bunty incredulously.

Calderwood grunted. 'Now that would be a happy thought, would it not? If the Firm could unearth a high-ranking traitor operating out of Langley? After our own scandals of recent years and the manner in which, as a result, the Americans have begun treating us as not-too-bright children, that would be sweet revenge indeed.' His eyes glittered at the prospect. 'Unfortunately,' he said, returning to reality, 'I do not believe Cassidy to be a mole of any description. That would not fit in with what I know of the man. But he's up to something very devious and I doubt his masters know about it. If it were official we'd have received a hint. Not because the Agency trusts us or would let us in on the game, but they would surely have let us know that a game was in progress in case one of our people in West Berlin happened to see Nikitchenko. The man took a fearful risk having a meeting in the west, though there are ways and means of crossing the Wall with impunity if one knows them. No, I firmly believe that Cassidy and perhaps a few trusted henchmen are in this alone. Which, with someone like Nikitchenko sitting, as it were, on the other side of the chessboard, makes the game very dangerous indeed. For all of us.'

'We could inform Langley,' said Bunty. 'Not directly, of course. Circumspectly.'

'Not yet, I think,' said Calderwood, his mind considering the possibilities. 'Not just yet.'

'You should at least tell the Director,' cautioned Bunty.

'At this hour of the morning? Sir Nigel would not thank me for disturbing his beauty sleep with wild hypothesis.'

'I would hardly call the CIA meeting a leading member of the Politburo, the defence minister, to boot, wild hypothesis.'

'Nevertheless, Bunty, let us allow him to sleep a few hours longer. While he dreams we shall endeavour to discover a little more about said member of the Politburo. So if you will kindly refer to your book of instructions and punch in the correct requests, we shall see what our electronic brain has to say on the subject of Marshal Nikitchenko.'

Very little, it transpired after an hour. The usual information was held in the memory bank and duly appeared on the console. Where Nikitchenko was born; his war career against the might of the Wehrmacht (impressive); his various decorations for valour and his rise through the ranks; his wife and children; his membership of the Party and his rapid advancement there too; his known vices (none); his public utterances on all subjects from the inevitable victory of world communism to NATO. He had received the ultimate accolade of being made head of the Red Army three years earlier and simultaneously been elected to that inner sanctum of sanctums, the Politburo.

It could have been the curriculum vitae of any successful man in any country in the world. He appeared to have made few enemies in the Soviet Union and had never quarrelled with, or interfered in the workings of, the KGB. He had ability, of that there was little doubt, and he kept his nose clean. In short, Nikitchenko was almost unbelievably dull. And unusually, for someone who exercised absolute control over the largest army on earth, he was classified by the computer as a 'dove', unlike many other members of the Politburo and indeed some of Nikitchenko's army commanders, who were categorized as 'hawks'. Certainly the defence minister had made belligerent speeches from time to time, but the Kremlin-watchers in the Firm, whose opinions were also filed in the computer's memory bank, judged these diatribes to be no more than the Soviet equivalent of jingoism. But if he was a dove, he was one with teeth.

'Punch up his recent history,' said Calderwood wearily. 'It can only be the last few months we're really concerned with. Let's see if anything has happened since, say, last October.'

Something had. Nikitchenko had become less of a dove. His speeches in the analysts' assessments, now sounded more threatening; no longer were they the idle and predictable mouthings of a man anxious to stay on good terms with his colleagues. When he warned against western interference, economically or militarily, in 'domestic' matters such as Poland or Afghanistan, he sounded (so the analysts opined) as if he meant it. When he accused the Americans of escalating the arms race and paying only lip service to SALT, he was not merely trying to impress the members of the Central Committee. And when he berated the United Kingdom Government for allowing its islands to be turned into a front-line missile base for the United States, he followed up with a vicious attack on the Prime Minister, calling her a warmonger and using phrases about her character which, had Nikitchenko been British and published his words, would have involved him in a massive libel suit he would not have won.

Calderwood was not an experienced Kremlin-watcher. He did, however, respect those who were, who studied each and every utterance made by Soviet leaders, who could spot a tiny nuance and make a large deduction. And the analysts were now saying without ifs or buts, that Nikitchenko had accomplished a remarkable volte-face. Far from being the dove of earlier years, the defence minister was now looked upon as being among the foremost ranks of the hawks.

Suddenly Calderwood saw it – the answer, or something that must surely approximate to the answer. The trick with his brain had worked. His subconscious had absorbed the data hour after hour, section after section, until now, when he was desperately tired – and with his mind 'clean' in a manner of speaking – he had the solution.

He examined it for flaws. He could find few. Certainly there remained vast areas of ignorance, but they were incidental. The outline of the jigsaw was complete; only some of the pieces needed to be found places.

Bunty noticed the change in him immediately.

'You've thought of something?'

'Perhaps,' answered Calderwood warily. 'Only perhaps.' He glanced at the office clock; it was five thirty a.m. although what the day was he could not for the life of him remember. 'I think we should arouse Sir Nigel from his slumbers. Do it for me, would you, Bunty, while I wash and run a razor over my face. Ask if I can see him right away. After that get a duty driver and car to the side entrance. One for yourself too. I don't want you looking for taxis at this ungodly hour.'

'Am I going home?' Bunty was rather hurt. It was unlike her chief not to confide in her.

'You are. And I don't want to see you tomorrow, either. Take the day off.' He saw the disappointment in her eyes. 'Don't worry, you'll know everything before long. But I must talk it through with Sir Nigel before anyone else.'

Bunty understood.

'What about Alex Dunbar?' she said.

'What about him?'

'Well, if we're agreed that Coughlin and Garfield do not exist and could not therefore have killed Melanie, shouldn't he be told?'

'I'll have to think about that,' said Calderwood. 'There's much else we don't know about Coughlin and Garfield.'

'I like Alex Dunbar,' said Bunty stubbornly. 'I've never met him but I've read his dossier and I like him. He's been through a lot and the least you can do is tell him that Coughlin and Garfield could not have killed his wife.'

'No,' said Calderwood, 'for two reasons. Number one is that we don't know how our fictitious Americans and Alex fit into the scheme of things as yet. And number two,' he added sagaciously, 'it would remove hope. He has something to live for now – a cause, hate, revenge. Call it what you will. Are you suggesting I destroy him?'

'Of course not. But you might replace that hope by telling him who did rape and murder Melanie Dunbar.'

'We'll never know that. The West Berlin police made a thorough investigation at the time, as did our own people out there. It is as it originally seemed, non-sinister. She was killed by a person or persons unknown, a freak tragedy.'

'Then you should tell him that.'

'It doesn't work that way, Bunty, not in this organization. I need Alex for a reason I'm not really sure of yet. That's his job, his choice. Now enough of this. Talk to Sir Nigel, please.'

Two hours later, in the rambling former abbey that was the MI6 Director's home, Calderwood finished speaking. Although it was still only seven thirty and the remainder of the household was not yet awake, the two men were drinking brandy in the Director's book-lined study. Sir Nigel had offered to make coffee as an accompaniment. Calderwood had declined. At that moment he didn't give a damn if he never saw another cup of coffee again in his life.

Sir Nigel McCracken knew most of the background to Cougar, including Alex Dunbar's findings in the United States, from the regular summaries Calderwood sent him. But Calderwood's theory regarding the object of the whole exercise was, of course, completely new. Nevertheless, his relationship with Calderwood went back to the war years. He trusted his subordinate's judgement, however outlandish it would appear to others.

Sir Nigel had risen through the Firm on ability alone, and without political or family connections had become its chief. A short and somewhat tubby man, he was now virtually bald and, to many, gave the impression of being vague. On numerous occasions he had been mistaken for a country clergyman or a school-master. Yet he possessed the keenest mind that Calderwood (who considered his own first-class) had ever come across. His opposite number in MI5 was a dunderhead by comparison.

'Would you stake your life on all you've told me?' he asked when Calderwood indicated that he had no more to add.

'An arm and a leg,' said Calderwood. 'Not my life.'

'And we leave Dunbar and Hamilton chasing their tails for the present?'

'Until I can rearrange Cassidy's timetable to suit our own purposes.'

'Bring it forward?'

'If I can.'

'Without knowing, I mean *really* knowing what Cassidy and Nikitchenko are playing at?'

'Yes.'

'There's no personal animus in this, is there?' asked Sir Nigel shrewdly.

'A little,' admitted Calderwood, knowing better than to be less than candid. 'Cassidy is a poisonous individual who caused me a great a deal of trouble several years ago. Nonetheless, if this all works out *precisely* as has been planned and the Service comes out ahead, what does it matter?'

'Not at all, I suppose. I might have some explaining to do to the Joint Intelligence Committee, but it wouldn't be the first time. Help yourself to the brandy.'

Calderwood did so. He was so tired now that he could have polished off the entire decanter without feeling the least drunk.

'I'm not sure about leaving Dunbar in the dark about

Coughlin and Garfield,' said Sir Nigel, rejecting a further brandy for himself.

'Neither was Bunty. On the other hand, he must do everything Cassidy expects him to do, otherwise we upset the applecart completely.'

'Trouble is, we're not really quite sure *what* Cassidy expects of him.'

'I've told you what I think.'

'Yes, you have. And I'm inclined to agree. Let's just hope that Cassidy does not have something up his sleeve about which you do not have a theory.'

Somewhere above their heads Calderwood heard the sound of a child's squeals and running footsteps.

'My granddaughter,' explained Sir Nigel. 'Aged nine. She and her mother are staying with me for a few days. Fortunately at her present age she rises at a reasonable hour. Four years ago she insisted upon treating my chest as a punchbag at six a.m. every morning.'

Calderwood took the hint, emptied his brandy goblet, and rose to his feet. Sir Nigel led the way to the porch, which overlooked an acre or so of lawn. Behind the house were several more acres and a tennis court. Now a widower, Sir Nigel's late wife had been born to money and a title in her own right. Neither money nor title had affected the Director in the least. The loss of his wife five years earlier had, although he had never allowed his bereavement to impair his efficiency.

He walked Calderwood to the duty car, whose driver already had the door open. Out of earshot, Sir Nigel placed a hand on Calderwood's arm.

'You know,' he said, 'I was hosting lunch at my club the other day for people who know full well how I earn my corn. The conversation came round, in general terms, to the Firm. The consensus was that we were finished. By we I don't just mean you, me, the old school, or even the somewhat younger school such as Dunbar. I mean all of us. All finished. A rather senior Member of Parliament conjectured that with advanced technology, what he was pleased to call spy-in-the-sky satellites, computers and so forth, intelligence-gathering by individuals would soon be a thing of the past. If

213

a satellite can show clearly something as tiny as a man's thumbnail and relay the picture within seconds to its control, what need for people? What satellites can do with a man's thumbnail, they can do equally with armies, navies, silos. The computers which receive, assimilate and analyse this information can give a nation's leaders options, tell them that the movement of army A means situation B or C. I almost laughed in his face. Would you like to know why?'

'Naturally,' said Calderwood politely.

'Because while a satellite can show one what is happening and a computer can predict, within limits, the consequences of those happenings, it's all after the event. No piece of electronic wizardry, however sophisticated, can tell what will happen *before* it happens. For that you need one man to read another's mind, which you seem to have done here.'

'Thank you,' said Calderwood. 'I appreciate that.'

'Another of my guests had a further point,' said Sir Nigel as childish shrieks of 'Grandpa' were heard from behind. 'When I had caused quiet hilarity by proposing man's superiority over machine, this guest remarked – and philosophic it may be – Ah, but a machine can sleep easily at night. What I'm trying to say is, Bunty may have a point. About Dunbar. Man is a fragile creature, Calderwood. Treat him gently, otherwise we become what the other side is. Please keep me posted.'

KOWLOON (i)

Although known throughout the world by the collective name of Hong Kong, this British Administered Territory (still called the Crown Colony by the old sweats) actually comprises Hong Kong Island – plus two hundred other islands – Kowloon, and the New Territories, the latter districts being on the Chinese mainland and separated from Hong Kong Island by Victoria Harbour, across which runs the Star Ferry and below which a motor tunnel, neither journey taking more than a few minutes. The two main centres for commerce and residence are the Island and Kowloon. The former was acquired in perpetuity from the Chinese by the Treaty of Nanking in 1842. Kowloon came under the British flag eighteen years later. The New Territories are on lease from big brother to the north until 1997, at which time he could want them back, together with, treaties or no treaties, the remainder of Hong Kong.

1997 was far from Alex Dunbar's mind that afternoon. Seven thirty in the morning in the UK, the hour a bleary-eyed Calderwood was climbing into his car, was three thirty p.m. in Hong Kong. From the window of his hotel, situated at the foot of the Kowloon peninsula and overlooking Victoria Harbour, he could see the ferry ploughing towards the Island terminal. In the distance, Victoria Peak bathed majestically in the afternoon sun, which in Hong Kong was far less enervating than Bangkok. The outside temperature at this time of the year was in the middle sixties, ideal for someone born and raised in northern latitudes.

Open on Alex's bed was a copy of the previous day's *Daily Express*, the photograph of Alison Cameron and Vincent

Kaplan prominent. He had not ordered the newspaper. After a refreshing Pimms and a pleasantly light lunch, he had taken the elevator to his room, intending to lie down for an hour and consider his next move. Before he could kick off his shoes, there had come a timid knock at his door. A room boy (they were all known thus even though this one wouldn't see thirty again) with a wicked-looking knife scar on his right cheek had held out the *Daily Express*. When Alex tried to tell him he had the wrong bedroom, the 'boy' simply nodded and smiled and pressed the newspaper into Alex's hands. He did not seem to speak any English at all, which seemed, to Alex, unusual for a Hong Kong Chinese.

Having nothing better to do he glanced through the paper, and there was Alison's photograph. Challenging the legendary efficiency of the Chinese, Alex rang the desk and asked if they could trace Miss Cameron. It took the receptionist next to no time. Miss Cameron was staying at the Peninsula Hotel on Salisbury Road, five minutes away.

Alex thought about it before ringing her. After New York he had never expected to see her again. He had quite forgotten Kaplan telling him he had arranged a Far East modelling tour for her. Nor did he recall Kaplan saying that he would be making the trip also. Meeting her again could cause all manner of complications.

On the other hand, he argued with himself, why not call her? She was very easy on the eye – and what else was he supposed to do with his time? Calderwood's one-word cable lay open on the dressing-table: HOLD. For Hamilton, presumably, with whom Alex had spoken in Bangkok that morning. The young SIS officer had confessed that he was getting nowhere in his search for Coughlin and Garfield, who had still not turned up. He was therefore planning to take the first flight out the following day. After thanking Alex for the 'gift' he and Herrick had provided, Hamilton had enquired if Hong Kong was proving more fruitful than Bangkok. Alex had had to admit it was not. The senior SIS resident – because of its proximity to mainland China Hong Kong was regarded as foreign territory for intelligence purposes, thus allowing the Firm, Five and Special Branch equal rights – had looked at Alex in astonishment on hearing that his query concerned *two* Americans.

'There are five million people packed into this few hundred square miles of real estate, old boy, most of them in Kowloon and on the Island. I'll have a word with Special Branch and see if they've heard any whispers, but I wouldn't hold my breath if I were you. Americans fly in and out of here in droves daily, and I take it the two you're after will not be travelling on their own passports.'

Alex had said it was unlikely, adding that he did not even have descriptions.

'Christ, London's really handed you one. Am I to understand you can't contact Company representatives on this?'

'You are. In fact, you could say the Company would like to get to them before I do.'

'One of those, eh.'

'One of those. How thick on the ground is the Company in this part of the world?'

'Not very. They're here, of course, but providing they don't get under our feet, we leave them alone.'

'No sign of recent increased activity?'

'None that I've noticed. Still, I'll make a few enquiries and let you know. In the meantime, I suggest you put your feet up.'

With that advice in mind as well as Calderwood's direct orders not to move, Alex called the Peninsula and asked for Miss Cameron's room.

'Suite,' the telephonist corrected him politely.

A man's voice answered, an American, though it was not Kaplan.

'May I speak to Miss Cameron, please.'

The response came back at machine-gun speed. 'No, you can't. She's being made up between shots. Who the hell wants her anyway?'

Alex swallowed hard. 'Someone who's going to involve you in two thousand dollars' worth of dentistry if we ever meet up.'

'Oh, heavens, the macho type. Don't push too hard, *hombre*, or I might take you up on that offer and consider I've got a bargain. Now, I repeat, who the hell wants her?'

217

Alex found himself smiling in spite of himself.

'Tell her it's Alex Dunbar.'

She was on the line within seconds. 'Alex . . . ? I mean, Mr Dunbar? Where are you calling from?'

'Round the corner, the Hong Kong. I saw your photograph in one of yesterday's London papers.'

'You're here, in Kowloon?'

'That's right. Who was that I just spoke to?'

'My manager. He's a little aggressive, I agree, but he's worth his weight in gold, even if he does wear too much of it around his neck.' Alex heard a raspberry blown from a distance. 'What are you doing in Kowloon? Have you discovered who killed Nick?'

She said his brother's name without hesitation or awkwardness, as though she had come to terms with his death.

'Not exactly,' hedged Alex. 'Anyway, I thought we might discuss it in person. I'm not very keen on phones.'

'Me neither. When I was a freckled thirteen-year-old I was told over the phone by the most important man in my life – he was fifteen – that he couldn't see me any more because he'd fallen for someone else. She had freckles too, I later discovered, but her family also had its own pool. I've had a phobia about phones ever since.'

Someone shouted from the background of her suite that time was passing and would she please move her ass. He heard her reply that if she moved it the way she *knew*, there'd be riots between here and Peking.

'Yes, I'd love to discuss it in person,' she said, coming back to Alex, 'except it will have to be much later. When they've got this wreck of a face of mine back to something near normal, I have another hour and a half's session with a fag of a photographer who just happens to be a genius. After that, I have to permit the security guards who accompany me everywhere to take back the two million dollars' worth of rocks I'm currently wearing on a couple of wrists, three fingers and a neck. I use the word permit advisedly because I may put up a fight. I've grown rather attached to a quarter-million dollar ring. However, no doubt the security rough-necks will emerge victorious, after which, allowing time for a shower and a change of clothes, I'm free. Around seven?'

'Fine. Where?'

'You choose – but not the Peninsula Hotel. It's wonderful, marvellous and luxurious, and they treat me like the Queen of England, but I've seen enough of it for the time being. What are the eateries in your hovel like?'

Alex had dined in one of the Hong Kong Hotel's several restaurants the previous evening, the Spice Market, which overlooked the harbour. Although it specialized in spicy Eastern cuisine, there had been all kinds of sea food on the menu as well.

'How do large prawns or lobsters cooked with what could well be a dash of curry sound to you?'

'Exquisite. I am a well-known pig for things fishy and hot, in spite of this world-famous body which is insured for roughly twice the amount that hangs from my delicate wrists. Said body can also quaff with the best of them.'

'I'll pick you up around seven, then?'

'I wouldn't dream of it. I am now fully familiar with the geography of Kowloon, and I do believe that even my meagre intelligence can direct me a few hundred yards.' He heard her giggle. 'To hell with it. I'll flash my teeth and take a taxi. The thing is,' she added more seriously, 'this marathon photo session, which seems to have been going on since Texas joined the Union, may overrun. It really would be easier if I came to you.'

Alex suggested the hotel's Brewery Bar, which, in spite of its name and pseudo-Swiss styling, had served him a delicious Pimms several hours earlier.

'The Brewery it is,' confirmed Alison, 'as soon as I can shake these little rats who point the lenses. Forgive me if I'm late.'

'Of course,' said Alex. 'Will you be coming alone? I mean, Kaplan's obviously here with you.'

'Not with me, near me, and that only occasionally. He spends most of his evenings in the gambling hell across the water, Macao, trying to crack the system. I went with him once but didn't like it, mainly because I didn't win a nickel. But yes, Vincent's here, as you saw from that agency photograph which made me look like Zsa Zsa Gabor's great aunt. He may join us for a drink before he heads for sin city. So doubtless will this gilded lily of a manager of mine. You'd better watch yourself there. While hitherto said manager has concentrated on finding the prettiest Chinese boys in the seediest quarters, he may take a shine to you. As I recall, your shoulders are broad.'

'My hair's also greying.'

'Talk not to me of grey hairs,' Alison pleaded. 'I found one a couple of mornings ago and reached for the Nembutal. Grey and chestnut do not go well together – unless of course you're a horse or a two-tone Rolls. Will it be all right if Vincent and this wretched pimp of mine join us? We generally all unwind together until around eight after a session, discuss the grisly events of the day and the grislier ones that await us. I can assure you both will be long gone before even a morsel of prawn appears, pimp to pimpdom and Vincent to the ritzy friend who ferries him across to Macao each evening in a private launch, returning him in the small hours a poorer if wiser man. Well, infinitely poorer, anyways. He swears every morning he's taking the next flight out, back home. Seems he never gets the gambling bug in the States.'

'He's not here on business, then? I seem to recall him saying that the photographs being taken will appear in one of his magazines.'

'So they will, though business he is not on; whatever his tax return says. I doubt he'll accompany us to the Land of the Rising Sun when we move on there in a few days.' Her manner became less flippant. 'I suppose he really came to look after me. In the purest sense. I'm a mite geriatric compared to his usual playmates.'

'You don't sound as though you need much looking after,' said Alex, biting his tongue a moment later. 'I mean . . .'

'I know precisely what you mean, dear Mr Dunbar,' interrupted Alison. 'Until seven, then. My crimper and public await.'

The trio were ten minutes late. Alex had his head bent towards the straw of his second Pimms when he became aware that a sudden hush had descended over the bar. Glancing up, he soon established why. Alison Cameron looked sensational. Her evening dress was knee-length and loose, swishing as she walked. It was an off-one-shoulder creation that shrieked of exclusivity, mostly white but with a subtle shade of green woven into the design that complemented her mop of chestnut hair perfectly. She had acquired a light tan since he last saw her, the kind most redheads never get. Apart from several rings and a bracelet, she wore no other jewellery, not even a wristwatch. With her natural height of five feet seven accentuated by three-inch heels, it was small wonder that people had stopped talking the moment she entered.

On her right, Kaplan was wearing a white tuxedo and a thoughtful expression. On her left, dwarfed by Alison, her manager wore chino pants, loafers, and a pale-blue silk shirt open to the navel to show off his chest. Alex saw what Alison had meant about gold, for around her manager's neck were two heavy box-link chains; a third, matching, was on his left wrist. A gold Rolex adorned the other wrist. He was roughly Alex's age, dark-haired and slim. In spite of his attitude on the phone earlier, Alex took an immediate liking to him. Alison introduce him as Nathan Tauber. 'He's Jewish,' she added, 'which explains the gold. He doesn't trust any bank he doesn't own.'

'Take no notice of her, Alex,' said Tauber, putting the whole company on a first-name basis instantly and effortlessly. Until then, Alex reflected, it had been Mr Dunbar and Mr Kaplan and Miss Cameron. 'I have to put up with her racial slurs and gutter humour because she pays the rent. You, however, have my full permission to bop her if she gives you any lip. On second thoughts, wait until the photographer's finished with her. And I did say bop, not boff. A pregnant Alison my ulcers could not stand.'

'Alison wouldn't be mad keen on the idea either,' said Alison. 'I am the sleek, ocean-going racer type of model, not the cuddly, voluptuous variety.'

'She writes most of her own copy too,' said Tauber. 'What are we drinking, folks?'

Although the Brewery had tables and booths, most customers preferred to sit at one of the two circular bars, where the service was faster. Alex found himself between

221

Tauber and Alison, with Kaplan on Alison's other side.

The fifty minutes until eight o'clock passed very quickly, with Tauber and Alison doing most of the talking, keeping up the kind of crosstalk vaudeville act they had perfected over the years. There was only one awkward moment, when Kaplan asked Alex what he was doing in Hong Kong.

There were standard replies to cover questions such as that, and Alex used the first that came into his head: that the minor government department for which he worked occasionally needed items delivering in a hurry to foreign parts. Unwilling to trust the vagaries of the world's postal services, the department had introduced a courier system. The assignments were allocated on a rota basis. Sometimes the duty courier got no further than Brussels; other times more exotic destinations were involved. Alex had struck lucky. He would remain in Hong Kong for another day or two, pick up anything that was needed in the UK equally urgently, then fly home.

Kaplan didn't press him further, though Alex got the distinct impression that the publisher would have been able to make a shrewd guess at the department concerned.

Nick's name didn't crop up once. It seemed to Alex that the other three had made an agreement not to discuss his dead brother during drinks. If there was any news, Alex would no doubt give it to Alison later.

At two minutes past eight Kaplan got off his stool.

'His carriage awaits,' Alison explained. 'Down on the waterfront. Play my age, twenty-six, and the numbers on either side,' she advised Kaplan.

'Combined they might make your age,' grunted Tauber.

Alison punched him playfully. 'Rat. On reflection, though, I *do* tell lies about my age. The hell with it, play whatever takes your fancy. You're going to come back losing, anyway.'

'Not tonight. Tonight I feel lucky.'

Alison groaned theatrically. 'For a man who's made untold millions in the magazine business,' she said to Alex, 'Vincent has a touching belief in luck and no grasp at all of basic arithmetic. There are thirty-seven slots on that roulette wheel into which the bouncing ball can fall. Even if he wins,

222

the house only pays him thirty-five to one. Now where's the sense in that?'

'I didn't claim it made sense,' said Kaplan, heading for the exit. 'Living in Manhattan doesn't make sense when there are islands like Tahiti in the world. Working twenty-five hours a day, fifty-three weeks of the year doesn't make sense. Owning a Rembrandt that has to stay locked up in a vault doesn't make sense. Who the hell cares what makes sense? For a few days I'm not making sense, and *that* makes sense. Nice to see you again, Alex.'

'Time for me to be heading for the fleshpots also,' announced Tauber, finishing his drink. 'Unless,' he added wickedly, with a sidelong glance at Alex, 'you two would like my company for dinner.'

'No way,' declared Alison. 'Alex and I are going to devour prawns and lobsters and lots of other high-calorie goodies. I don't want you leaning over my shoulder telling me that every mouthful is going to make me fat.'

'It had better not,' joshed Tauber, 'or it's back to stealing hubcaps for yours truly. And get her to bed early, Alex,' he concluded on his way to the door. 'If you understand my meaning. She's got another heavy day tomorrow, big close-ups. Any dark rings under her eyes and I sue.'

'I hope you get mugged,' called Alison.

'Me too.'

'Another drink?' asked Alex.

'Not for this girl.' Alison had stuck rigidly to her customary white wine. 'I could eat a horse, though.'

Alex had booked a table overlooking Victoria Harbour. On seeing Alison, the maître d' directed them to it personally, seating them opposite one another in a quiet corner. Several storeys below a gang of Chinese stevedores were moving stores to a nearby warehouse, along the wharf. As far as the eye could see the whole of Hong Kong was alive with millions of lights in dozens of different colours.

'It just needs Humphrey Bogart to emerge from the shadows and light a cigarette, and I'll die content,' said Alison happily.

Dinner was perfect. Alex examined the menu briefly before tossing it to one side and beckoning the maître d',

223

who was at their table in a flash. Alex kept it simple, two courses only, at Alison's request: giant prawns to start followed by cold lobster. Dry white wine, Chablis, throughout.

'Sorry about the white wine bit,' apologized Alison, 'and with being less than adventurous with the menu. But I really do have to watch the avoirdupois. Now, where shall we begin?'

They began with Nick because that was the obvious place to start. Alex lied to her, saying that South Dakota had turned out to be a dead end, after which he had flown home. They would probably never discover who had killed Nick, or why.

Not unexpectedly, Alison steered the conversation in other directions once she learned that Alex had no more to add to what she already knew. Alex understood her motives from the recollection of the way he had reacted once the initial shock, anger and sadness had passed when Melanie was killed. He was nonetheless surprised to find himself talking about his dead wife, though he did not relate the full circumstances of her death. She had been killed while on holiday in Berlin four years earlier. Her murderers were never found.

'How horrible for you,' said Alison finally.

After that, they changed the subject completely, with Alex gently encouraging Alison to do most of the talking because he could tell her nothing of his own life. He found it very easy to listen to her vastly amusing stories of what it was like being a highly-paid, world-famous model, and he was astonished, when next glancing at his wristwatch, to see that the time was a few minutes after eleven. Three hours had flown by, and Alex was fully aware that he could become very, very attached to Alison Cameron unless he was careful. That she had been Nick's girl did not concern him; Nick had been almost a stranger. But men who worked in the twilight world of intelligence should not form close personal relationships with women. Melanie had been different; she had grown up an army brat and married into the army.

It was true that Calderwood had promised the Cougar assignment to be a one-off shot, and after it Alex would be free to rejoin the Firm or go his own way. In the beginning, he had been determined to exercise the latter option; now he was not so sure. The last few weeks had made him a different man, more the one he used to be. He felt fitter, more alert. If he turned down Calderwood's offer of re-engagement, what were the alternatives? Another tedious clerical job with another builder's merchant? He would be back on the bottle within a week.

'Already?' said Alison, when he suggested it was time to leave.

'I'm afraid so. You heard what Nathan made me promise.'

'He's a son of a bitch.' Alison feigned petulance. 'He can enjoy himself until the small hours but I can't. Just as I was too.' She placed a hand on one of Alex's. 'I've had a marvellous time,' she said. 'Thank you. I'm not sure the second bottle of wine was such a good idea, but if I'm puffy-eyed in the morning, the hell with them. I'll tell Nathan straight that in future I model nothing but footwear and hose. At least you can't get bloodshot ankles.'

Alex walked her back to her hotel, Alison's arm linked through his. The evening air was mild, the noises and smells from all quarters invigorating, heady; a mixture of spices, fish, the sea, a ship's siren, late-night tradesmen plying their wares. A mile due south the lights from the Wanchai district of Hong Kong Island beckoned.

'Susie Wong country,' said Alison knowledgeably. 'I'll bet they're having fun over there.'

In the large forecourt of the Peninsula Hotel, beyond the fountain and near one of a pair of Chinese lions which, according to legend, protected the building, Alison suddenly stopped and, on impulse, kissed Alex full on the mouth. It was much more than a polite thank-you-for-dinner gesture: a long kiss that sent shivers down his spine. He was responding spontaneously when she pulled away.

'Sorry,' she said, 'that was wrong of me.'

'Because of Nick?'

'Yes.'

'People aren't machines,' said Alex. 'You can't carry around your grief for ever or feel guilty if you're attracted to someone else. When does that become acceptable? After a week, three months, a year? There aren't any rules.'

'You're the expert. When did it happen for you? How long did it take?'

'Over four years. In other words, not until some time during the last three hours.'

'I thought so,' said Alison softly. 'I thought it was mutual. I was also wrong in New York. I said you and Nick weren't very much alike. You are. Not physically – well, not very much – but there's something about you that reminds me of him. And please don't misunderstand me. I thought about it frequently while I was chatting away over dinner. Nick and I were friends, good friends, intimate friends. But I wouldn't be trying to relive my months of Nick through you.'

Alex said nothing. It would be foolish to become involved with Alison while working for Calderwood, and if he stopped working for Calderwood what else could he do?

She misinterpreted his silence, deduced it to be a reluctance to make an emotional commitment.

'Still,' she said lightly, reverting to her customary way of speaking, 'we must make no impulsive decisions here and now. I wouldn't want you to think that the only thing on my mind is to get you out of your pants and into mine. Let's talk about it again tomorrow and put tonight down to the booze and the wonderful dinner and Hong Kong.'

'Perhaps that would be better,' said Alex.

Alison's green eyes flashed, part hurt, part anger.

'You're a cautious son of a bitch, aren't you, Alex Dunbar? A girl throws herself at you and you turn your back, leaving her spread-eagled with more than a little egg foo yong on her face. I'd be calling you a fag if I hadn't felt the way you kissed me just now. Right, I'd better go in and take a cold shower before I do or say anything else I might regret in the morning.'

On this occasion the kiss was on the cheek and no more than a friendly peck. Alex watched her disappear into the hotel lobby.

'Damn it,' he muttered, so preoccupied with his own thoughts that he failed to notice the two men in the shadows, two men who had evidently overheard every word.

KOWLOON (ii)

Alex's room extension rang the following morning while he was still deeply asleep. He peered at his watch; it was only six forty-five and he'd asked the desk not to call him until seven thirty.

Kaplan was on the line, phoning from the Peninsula.

'Is Alison with you?'

'What? No, of course she's not damned well with me,' snapped Alex. 'What the hell are you talking about?'

'She has an eight a.m. photocall and she's not in her suite. Nathan got the floor manager to use his pass key fifteen minutes ago. Her bed's not been slept in. Nathan woke me up and naturally I thought . . .'

'You were wrong,' interrupted Alex. 'I left her at the main entrance around eleven thirty.'

'And there was no trouble between you? Look, Alex,' said Kaplan, adopting a more friendly tone, 'I'm sorry to be asking you all these questions but we've a host of talent costing fifteen thousand bucks a day lined up in one of the banqueting rooms, all waiting for Alison to shower, grab a glass of juice and get herself made up. I'm just trying to establish if you had a fight or anything.'

'We didn't.' What they'd had was a minor disagreement, and the subject matter had nothing to do with Kaplan.

Alex was wide awake now, sitting on the edge of the bed, the bedside lamp switched on. Out of the corner of his eye he saw something white lying by the door, under which it had been pushed while he was asleep.

'Hold on a minute.'

The envelope contained a single sheet of paper and a short

227

message.

If you want to see her alive again, lay off Coughlin and Garfield but do not leave Hong Kong. We'll require proof you're not continuing the pursuit elsewhere. You will be watched. You will also be contacted again in a few days. Do not inform the police.

Alex read it through twice before returning to the phone.

'We'd better meet. Just the two of us. Let's say on the Kowloon Pier opposite the clock tower in half an hour.'

'What's the matter?' Kaplan had heard the gravity in Alex's voice.

'I can't talk about it over the phone.'

'Is it Alison?'

'Later.'

'If something's happened to her I want to know about it,' insisted Kaplan. 'Maybe this is something the police should be handling.'

'No police,' said Alex. 'Don't do anything until I've had a chance to talk to you.'

There was a lengthy pause before Kaplan agreed. 'All right, but I have to give Nathan and the rest a reason for cancelling the photocall. I take it Alison will not be putting in an appearance.'

'She won't. Blame me or make any other excuse you like, but don't allow anyone, especially Nathan, to call the police.'

Alex was five minutes early at the rendezvous. Even so, Kaplan was already there, staring out across the bay. He looked terrible. He was unshaven, and beneath his tan his face was ashen. Alex recalled he'd been on Macao the previous night. He had probably not returned until the small hours.

'What's going on?' Kaplan asked grimly. There was murder in his eyes. Alison's disappearance was somehow connected with Alex Dunbar, and Vincent Kaplan wanted answers.

Since putting down the phone Alex had debated how much to tell Kaplan, concluding that it would have to be most, if not all, if he was to convince the publisher that going to the police would probably write the signature on Alison's death warrant. Besides, Alex recalled Kaplan saying in New York that he had offered a reward for information leading to Nick's killers 'among certain people'; the publisher had also mentioned he had 'connections in a few odd places'. Alex hoped to God he had not misunderstood the implications of either phrase and that Kaplan's connections would not turn out to be Members of Congress or minor political figures.

Showing Kaplan the message, Alex was aware as he passed over the envelope without comment, was a terrible breach of security. Calderwood would rightly pillory him if he ever found out. Nonetheless, Alison had been abducted because she was seen with him. If anything happened to her he would never forgive himself. The day Melanie died was one when the pressure had really been on in Berlin, when it had been essential that he debrief an agent and get him back across the Wall before nightfall. He had been too busy to accompany Melanie sightseeing. 'I'll meet you for a drink around six,' he had told her.

'Just who the hell are Coughlin and Garfield?' demanded Kaplan, handing back the envelope.

Alex told him as much as he dared: that they were CIA field agents who had killed Melanie in Berlin; that certain British sources believed them and/or the CIA to be mounting a dangerous anti-Soviet operation centred on Berlin; that neo-Nazi groups were involved.

'And who are you?' asked Kaplan. 'Who are these certain British sources? MI6? Some other spook outfit?'

'Near enough.'

'Which makes all that malarkey about working as a pen-pusher and an occasional courier for a minor government department garbage?'

'Yes.'

'You thoughtless bastard. Why for the love of Christ did you allow Alison to become involved?'

Alex had no answer to that. Last night had begun as nothing more than a friendly dinner. If he'd considered for a moment that someone would use Alison to get at him, he would never have called her.

'Come on,' said Kaplan, 'let's take a stroll and think this thing through. If I stand here much longer I'm going to be tempted to take a swing at you.'

They walked north along Canton Road, towards Kowloon Park, in silence. Wisely, Alex allowed Kaplan's anger to subside.

'So the CIA have her and are holding her to keep you away from Coughlin and Garfield, is that how you read it?' said Kaplan eventually.

'I'd stake my life on it.'

'I'm glad to hear it,' said the publisher without humour. They turned into the park. 'I'm also inclined to agree with you. There's something you don't know.'

'Go on.'

'Nathan was going out of his mind when I hung up on you earlier. He's a funny little man with some bizarre tastes, but he loves Alison like a brother. Worships her. He'd roused the night manager and half the night staff before I'd finished talking to you. Someone must have seen her leave the hotel, was his argument. Someone had. One of the desk clerks confirmed that two men had asked for Alison shortly after midnight. The clerk remembered them clearly because he'd handed Alison her key only twenty minutes before. The men didn't go up to her suite; she came down to the lobby. The desk clerk overheard one of them tell Alison that Nathan had been mixed up in a brawl across in Wanchai. He wasn't badly hurt but he was in police custody. They claimed to be plainclothes cops themselves and showed Alison some ID. They wanted her to go with them and bail Nathan out. According to the clerk, the two men were definitely American.'

'What was Nathan's reaction?'

'To call the police himself. He hadn't been anywhere near a brawl or in custody. His first thought was that Alison had been kidnapped, which turns out to be close to the truth. I told him I was meeting you, that you had some information, that it would be stupid and embarrassing to bring in the police if you had the answer. That kind of publicity Alison doesn't need. He said some very uncomplimentary things about you, incidentally, but he'll lay off the police angle until he hears from me. Which he expects to do soon. I left a very worried man behind. He'll stay worried until he sees Alison again.'

Kaplan shook his head in despair.

'Christ, this kind of thing just doesn't happen! This is a British possession, for God's sake. The whole world knows that the CIA gets up to some funny business in the banana republics, but here we're standing on land that's as British as Buckingham Palace. They can't be serious. They wouldn't harm her. She's not just some little punk they can drop from a chopper. This is Alison Cameron we're talking about. She's a household name.'

'So was Marilyn Monroe. Believe me, they mean every word. Back off, no police. And in case you've half a mind to get on the phone to the States, call in a few favours, don't forget there's nothing in that message that says she was abducted by the CIA. Two Americans walked out of her hotel with her. That's all we know.'

'What about your own people out here?' asked Kaplan. 'And don't act dumb. That's Red China over there. Hong Kong must be crawling with British spooks.'

Who could be of no possible help. While dressing, Alex had considered contacting the senior SIS resident before rejecting the idea as unviable. Bringing in the Firm or Special Branch to look for one missing model would raise a few eyebrows. The manpower needed would inevitably make it official. There would be a report on Calderwood's desk within twelve hours, after which Calderwood would take the only course of action open to him. If Alex could not or would not press on with his assignment for fear of endangering a girl's life, then Alex would be pulled out and replaced. And Alison would die.

He explained as much to Kaplan.

'Jesus,' said the American in disgust, 'you're a pleasant bunch of bastards.'

'You pay us,' snapped Alex, a little sick and tired of being on the receiving end. 'You meaning the sanctimonious multitude – which included my brother, I might add – who want your sort of world kept safe from the Soviets and the Chinese and the Cubans and the urban revolutionaries, or anyone else who wants to take away your East River penthouses, expense-account lunches, Rolls-Royces. You and the politicians you control can call it all off tomorrow and take your chances. Just say the word. In the meantime, shut up and try to be constructive, otherwise the punch you were going to land on my jaw back there will be accepted willingly and returned doubled and redoubled.'

'Well, well,' said Kaplan shrewdly, 'maybe I misread you. Could be that Alison means more to you than I thought. That must have been some dinner you two had last night. Come on, let's turn round. Nathan'll be jumping out of his socks by now. Whatever else we decide between here and the hotel, we've got to figure out what to do about him. He won't buy not informing the police. He's one of the sharpest business-men I've ever met, but he has a touching faith in law and order. You get robbed, you call the cops. If you're planning to tell him all you've told me – and I don't see how you can avoid it – he'll be on the phone to the nearest precinct before you can spit.'

'Which won't get Alison back. Believe me, if I thought it would I'd go along with it. I know these people.' There was no guarantee that Alison was still alive, though Alex refused to dwell on that prospect or mention it to Kaplan.

'I asked you to be constructive a minute ago,' he said. 'Here's how. You told me once you have some friends in odd places. I took that to mean underworld connections. I don't know whether that assumption was correct or, if correct, you just meant in the States. But you have business interests in Hong Kong, I understand. If those interests involve the underworld, I might have a suggestion to make.'

Kaplan hesitated. 'I'm not into the Triad, if that's what you're hinting at. That's heavy stuff, drugs mainly. But you're right, I do some publishing out here and occasionally have trouble with characters whose sympathies lie north.' He jerked his head in the direction of Red China. 'Once every eighteen months or so they try to unionize me. Then I've been known to play rough. Yes, I have some links with what passes for mob activity out here. What of it?'

'I can get you some names and addresses,' said Alex. 'CIA names. There shouldn't be too many and I think I can get them without making it official. In fact, to be on the safe side I won't involve myself personally. I'll get a colleague who's flying in from Bangkok this morning to do it for me. The regular addresses should be easy enough. I may have a problem with the safe houses, and they could have Alison anywhere. However, if you can supply the manpower and the money, neither of which I can do, we may get Alison back in one piece.'

Kaplan thought about it.

'Are the men I employ – assuming I can reach them and they agree – to do anything about Alison themselves?'

'No. Absolutely not. That's something my colleague and I will take care of. If a bunch of Hong Kong gangsters go wading in with machetes, somebody will start shooting and Alison could get hurt. The address where she's being held is all I want.'

'I'll do what I can,' promised Kaplan. 'In the meantime, there's Nathan to be considered.'

They were level with the crowds waiting to board the Star Ferry for Hong Kong Island. The travellers were mainly Chinese. Of the few Caucasians, males outnumbered females considerably, and something about one of the women attracted Alex's attention; he'd seen her before, an ash-blonde in her thirties, slim, around five-four. He and Kaplan were well past the terminal before he remembered Karen Deuntzer! The woman who had pulled him from the path of the oncoming traffic in Arlington and who had kept him talking while the loop of film was stolen.

Leaving Kaplan staring after him in astonishment, Alex raced back. The ferry had already left the quay. Anxiously he scanned the decks, upper and lower. He saw no ash-blonde.

There was a policeman standing a few yards away. Alex's immediate impulse was to tell him to contact the Island terminal and instruct whoever he spoke to to hold all female Caucasian passengers with blonde hair. But that was out of the question, of course. The note had specifically forbidden any contact with the police. If Karen Deuntzer was around she would not be alone; she would have friends observing him whose faces he did not know.

He caught up with Kaplan. From her position in the crowds awaiting the next ferry, Karen Deuntzer, who had not taken the earlier one and who had quickly covered her hair with a headscarf, watched him go.

'What the hell was all that about?' asked Kaplan.

'Nothing.' There would be little point in informing Kaplan that they were under CIA surveillance. 'Someone I thought I recognized. I was wrong. Now, what were you saying about Nathan, because I've got a couple of ideas on the subject.'

In Alison's suite, where they found her manager drinking straight vodka and surrounded by the camera crew, all anxious to learn if they would be working that day, Alex pulled no punches. Asking Kaplan to clear the room, Alex spelled it out, telling Tauber everything.

'You schmuck,' said Tauber, finally. 'Big as you are, I'd like to wipe the floor with you – if I didn't think it would dirty the floor.'

At a gesture from Alex, Kaplan led Tauber from the sitting room to the bedroom and closed the communicating door. Ten minutes later the publisher re-emerged.

'Okay, he'll play ball, though I don't know for how long. The official version for the crew and the hotel management will be that Alison's temporarily flipped her lid due to overwork. I'll also tell them, as we agreed, that we've tracked her down and that she's under sedation in a private clinic on the Island. Everyone will be on full pay until she's fit to resume shooting.'

'Thank you.'

'Don't thank me. Money I've got; time we're all short of. Didn't you say you had a partner to meet?'

'He knows where to reach me.'

'Which is not here. No offence, but I'd like to make my phone calls in private.'

'I'm on my way,' said Alex, 'after one more item.'

'Name it.'

'I don't know how all this is going to work out. We may pull it off, we may not. Whatever happens, I'll be doing things that are not strictly according to the book, and London will not be viewing me as its favourite son. I carry a diplomatic passport, which London could revoke at the stroke of a pen, making it awkward if I have to get out in a hurry. I'm going to need a second passport, for which I can't use channels. Once Alison's safe, I don't really give a damn. However, I'm no different from anyone else. I'd like to survive. Can one of those calls you're going to make get me a new passport in a new name, just in case? I can pay.'

Alex still had the larger part of Calderwood's dollars in his pocket, and Calderwood would certainly not bail him out if things went wrong.

'Nothing easier,' said Kaplan, 'not in this part of the world. Canadian's best. Canada has few enemies and it's easy to get into the States with Canadian papers. Apart from that, I happen to know there are quite a number of blank passports around. All you have to provide is a photograph. There's an instant machine in the lobby. Put the print in an envelope and ask the desk clerk to drop it in my mail slot.'

'Make sure the issuing date is not too recent,' advised Alex, 'and that it has a Hong Kong entry stamp. A visa or two and a few other stamps would make it look more authentic.'

'Please,' said Kaplan, 'these guys are pros. Don't forget to choose a name you can answer easy to in a crowd, though I guess that's teaching my grandmother to suck eggs.'

Kaplan declined any offer of payment.

'This one's on the house. I had you figured all wrong, Alex. I thought your interest in Alison was strictly basic. That was a mistake. Whether you know it or not, you're hooked. And my bet would be that Alison feels the same. You're a lucky man.'

'You can tell me that again when we've located her. And when that happens I'll need a couple of handguns, one each for my partner and myself. I can't use channels for those either, which would involve signatures and maybe explanations. I'm most familiar with the 9mm Browning, but anything that packs a punch will do.'

'Leave it to me. Now get the hell out of here and let me do some work. I'll be in touch.

235

KOWLOON (iii)

To save time, Alex met Hamilton at the airport. Later, in his hotel room, Alex apologized for involving Hamilton.

'For me this is now a personal matter. Our brief is to find Coughlin and Garfield. As far as I'm concerned yours still is. All I ask is that you obtain some addresses for me from the local resident-in-chief, then go down with 'flu for a few days, not make waves. Naturally I could use your help, but if things go wrong and any of this leaks back to Calderwood, you'll be putting your head on the block. Calderwood will be right behind you with an axe.'

'Don't be idiotic,' said Hamilton. 'Of course I'll help.'

Alex nodded his thanks. 'Okay, here's what I want you to do. The resident's a nice enough bloke but this is his territory. He might not care for outsiders poking around. He's had his instructions from London to co-operate, though the parameters of his co-operation will have been carefully defined. I don't want him to know we're exceeding our brief or telexing Calderwood.'

Hamilton was back by five o'clock.

'Easy,' he said, handing Alex a sheet of paper on which were typed around a dozen names and addresses. 'He was most helpful. He even expressed his regrets that he hadn't learned anything of value from Special Branch. Nor had he checked out Company addresses because he recalled you saying that Langley wanted Coughlin and Garfield more than we did. He didn't question my suggestion – your suggestion – that they could have Company friends out here who were keeping them under cover, and positively jumped at the idea that we do our own leg work.'

'He had nothing from London for us?'

'Nothing. That's not like Calderwood, is it? A one-word cable – HOLD – with no follow-up.'

'It's certainly not like him,' agreed Alex. 'Still, let sleeping dogs lie.'

Alex called Kaplan's suite at the Peninsula. The receiver was picked up at the second ring. Alex recognized Kaplan's voice.

'I've got some names and addresses for you,' said Alex. 'I'd better give them to you in person. Same place as this morning, the clock tower?'

'I'll be there in fifteen minutes.'

Kaplan looked better than he had earlier. He had shaved and changed his clothes, though he obviously hadn't slept. Alex introduced Hamilton and handed over the list.

'How did you make out with your phone calls?'

'Fine.' Kaplan grunted cynically. 'The power of the dollar. They'll play all right, and they can really go to work now they have this.'

'And they understand the conditions?' queried Alex anxiously. 'All they do is find out where Alison is being held. They take no action themselves.'

'They understand. They were puzzled, however. If we have names and addresses, I was asked, why don't we check them out ourselves?'

'Because they know Hong Kong better than we do. Because they're Chinese and we're not. Because if Alison's at any of those addresses they'll have posted lookouts. A Caucasian nosing around could start trouble we can't handle.'

Alex did not add: And because Company field men were doubtless keeping them under constant surveillance. Some things Kaplan did not have to know.

'They're to check out each occupant too,' said Alex. 'Follow him whenever he leaves his apartment, see where he goes. Anywhere. To shops, offices, even if he goes to the cinema. I can't guarantee that the list contains every address the Company uses. There may be one or two missing, which we'll only find out by putting a tail on each operative.'

'I'll get on to it right away. Christ knows how long it's all going to take, but stick close to your phone. That other item you ordered, will be in your hotel mail drop first thing tomorrow morning, in a sealed envelope.'

Hamilton was far too well trained to enquire about 'the other item'.

'What do we do now?' he asked.

'Wait.'

They ate in Alex's room. Kaplan came through at nine o'clock. He had nothing to report. He rang again at eleven p.m. and one a.m. Still nothing.

'It's not going to be easy,' he said wearily. 'Of the seven addresses covered so far, five have had people in residence, all Caucasian Americans. My contacts can't just go barging in like gangbusters to see if there's a tall redhead tied up in one of the rooms.'

'Careful,' warned Alex, reminding Kaplan that he was speaking on an open line.

'Yeah. Sorry. Lack of sleep's getting to me. Anyway, the two addresses that were unoccupied have been gone over. No sign of anything we're looking for. The first five are under surveillance, with my people waiting to see if the occupants plan to go out, which is doubtful at this hour. The last five I haven't had reports on yet. It's going to take time, Alex, maybe several days.'

'I don't mind it slow as long as it's safe.' Alex saw Hamilton trying to attract his attention. 'Hold it a minute, Vincent.'

'Did you get a good look at that list before you handed it over?' asked Hamilton.

'Not a good look, no. I just glanced down it. Why?'

'Because I had a chance to study it on my way back here. Several of the names were pretty obviously husbands and wives. Okay, wives generally know what their husbands do for a living in this business, but is it likely the Agency would risk keeping Miss Cameron in an apartment where another woman lives? Wouldn't that create unnecessary problems?'

Alex agreed that the point was valid. He explained Hamilton's reasoning to Kaplan. 'Where does that leave us? I gave the only copy to you.'

'Leaves us with nine, all unexplored. Taking into account

238

the two where nothing was found, seven. But it's still going to take time, Alex. I'd advise you to get some sleep, which is what I'm going to do. We're not going to be much use if we can't think straight.'

'How's Nathan holding up?'

'Reasonably. I've got him in my suite. Right now he's out for the count on a bottle of vodka.'

For the next thirty-six hours Alex slept fitfully and ate irregularly. He wanted to be out there, doing something, except he knew there was nothing constructive to be achieved by walking the streets.

Periodically he spoke to Kaplan on the telephone. Slowly each address on the list was eliminated by Kaplan's underworld associates. Until there was none.

On Thursday morning Kaplan came through with the final negative. All the apartments had been broken into during their occupant's absence, including, to cover every eventuality, those where women were usually in residence. Only one address, the normal home of two sharing Agency bachelors, had not been lived in recently. Kaplan's theory was that they were on furlough in the States. Alison had been missing for almost sixty hours, and they were no nearer finding her.

'We'd better meet,' said Alex.

'Let me come to you,' suggested Kaplan. 'This place is driving me nuts.'

'What about Nathan?'

'He's sober, if four bottles of vodka in half as many days can be called sober, and he's back in his own suite. He now realizes how serious all this is, and he's promised to behave. Are you sure about the cops, Alex?'

'I'm sure. But we might have to start leaning on a few people.' To hell with telephone security, thought Alex. 'We have a list of addresses and can identify the occupants. The Company has someone we want back. Maybe it's time your friends snatched one of theirs, to give us some leverage. Do an exchange.'

'We'll talk about it.'

'The bar where we first met up, the Brewery.'

'Right. Have you seen a newspaper recently?'

'Not for days.'

'I'll bring one over. I remember our first conversation by the clock tower. Maybe it helps us, maybe it doesn't, but it seems things are happening in Berlin.'

Alex broke the connection and rang Hamilton's room. A sleepy voice answered.

'Get up, get dressed, go down to the lobby and buy me a newspaper,' said Alex. 'The latest from the UK. Then meet me in the Brewery.'

Kaplan was there before Hamilton. He joined Alex in a beer and showed him a copy of the previous day's London *Daily Telegraph*.

'Front page, third column.'

The story was datelined Berlin. Summarized, it read that during the past twenty-four hours there had been outbreaks of street violence on the West Berlin streets between left-wingers and neo-Nazis. Rumours had been circulating within the city that films would shortly be produced which would largely exculpate Hitler and the other leaders of the Third Reich insofar as Jewish deaths in extermination camps were concerned. A spokesman for the neo-Nazis had gone on record as saying that he and his supporters had known for forty years that the majority of the atrocities historically attributed to Hitler were lies, Allied propaganda at best and a Soviet cover-up at worst. The victors had written the history books, though soon the neo-Nazis would have proof that the victims of Nuremberg, the Nazi leaders who had been executed, were innocent. They would be acquitted, albeit too late. If six million Jews had died, their deaths were not the result of the Third Reich's policies. The Soviets were the killers, not the Germans. Remember Katyn, and look how the Russians treated the Jews in the Soviet Union today.

The article went on to say that street violence had also broken out in Bonn, Frankfurt, Munich, Hamburg, and many other West German cities. It added that the Soviet Foreign minister had voiced his contempt for the rumours. 'If this is an attempt by the new Federal leadership, either unilaterally or in concert with other NATO powers, particularly the clandestine security services of those

240

powers, to rewrite history and foment sedition within the German Democratic Republic as a prelude to talks on reunification – or for any more sinister reason – it will fail. A greater Germany does not exist today and will not exist in the future. The Soviet Union views with grave concern the imputation that its military and political leaders during the Great Patriotic War were in any manner responsible for all or any part of the Holocaust, and demands that the Federal Government dissociate itself immediately from those who are promulgating these foul lies, and arrest the ringleaders. The West Berlin city parliament and the Mayor are similarly warned. The people and government of the German Democratic Republic – in whose territory, let it be added, Berlin stands – will not tolerate a new age of Nazism, nor men whose hatred of the Soviet Union and the GDR is well-documented. The Soviet Union cannot and will not permit another gang of Hitlers to arise.'

Alex finished reading as Hamilton walked into the bar, a copy of the *Daily Express* under his arm. 'Someone's trigger finger will be getting itchy in another seventy-two hours at this rate.'

Alex scanned the *Express* story. Its style aside – the writing being more dramatic – the facts were essentially the same as the *Telegraph*'s.

'So what's going on?' asked Hamilton. 'Are Coughlin and Garfield already in Berlin, or what? Or have they made some other deal?'

'Be quiet and order yourself a drink,' said Alex. 'I'm thinking.'

But no answers were emerging. If Coughlin and Garfield were already in Berlin, why had the Company gone to the lengths it had and abducted Alison, threatened her life? More importantly, why hadn't Calderwood been in touch? That was a mystery. Germany could be a battleground in a few days, and under normal circumstances Alex would have expected Calderwood to be shouting down the other end of a phone or overworking the resident's telex machine. But nothing.

Alex stared at the front page of the *Daily Express* without really seeing it. Something about the newspaper bothered him, though he was damned if he knew what it was. He closed his eyes and concentrated, trying to remember. It was the *Express* and . . . And it had something to do with Kaplan. What was it Kaplan had said to him on the telephone thirty minutes ago, in response to his suggestion that they use Kaplan's connections to abduct a Company operative, maybe a wife or a girl friend? Do an exchange. Kaplan had said: *We'll talk about it.* And then something else. That's right. *Have you seen a newspaper recently?* And he had answered: *No, not for days.*

He had not seen one, in fact, since his second day in Hong Kong, when the Chinese room boy with the scar had delivered . . . a *Daily Express* that hadn't been ordered. The room boy had not – strangely, Alex recalled thinking – appeared to understand English. He had just nodded and smiled, and handed over the newspaper. And there, in the Hong Kong feature, had been a photograph of Alison and Vincent Kaplan.

It took a moment for it to register, before Alex understood. At the back of his mind it had bothered him from the beginning that the Company would go to the lengths of kidnapping Alison and use her survival to put pressure on him. How could they possibly have known that he'd agree to the conditions? He'd only met her once before Hong Kong, something the men who'd abducted her were surely aware of.

The answer was that they had not known. They'd got one of their lackeys to give him the newspaper and had made the assumption that he'd call her, meet her. After that they'd relied upon chemistry. If it hadn't worked they'd have tried something else. For some reason they wanted him temporarily *hors de combat* but not dead, which would have been easier. They wanted him trapped in Hong Kong while other events were taking place in Germany. Or did they? Were they still controlling events in Germany? Had they ever controlled events in Germany? Who *was* controlling events?

More questions, fewer answers. The questions did not tell him where Alison was or even if she was still alive, though one answer told him where to look – if the room boy was a member of the hotel staff. It was logical that he was, and not just because of the uniform he had been wearing. All intelligence outfits either recruited and paid retainers to one or two people in various large hotels, to keep tabs on the movements of important guests, or infiltrated their own men. Usually the former method was adopted because the employees were then in situ and ethnic. The room boy hadn't opened his mouth since that would have revealed he spoke excellent English, in which case Alex could have told him to take the *Daily Express* to the right room.

Would he recognize the 'boy' again, he asked himself? Of course he would; the knife scar. What he could not do was hunt through the staff sections of a hotel that probably had five hundred employees. But Kaplan's underworld associates could. They would have connections in all kinds of places, and should be able to trace a room boy with a scar and frighten him to death in no time flat. Then the interrogation could begin. All they needed was somewhere to carry it out.

They found that in a second-floor back room of an hotel that doubled as a brothel. When Alex and Hamilton arrived on the premises, having been collected by a silent Chinese in a Mercedes at Wanchai Pier, the scarred room boy, although physically unmarked, was rigid with fear. His name was Michael Ling. Three men (Alex established later), not one of them taller or heavier than a bantamweight, had picked him up from his home during the afternoon, after making enquiries at the hotel. In front of his wife and small child they had threatened to cut off his testicles and feed them to the infant unless he accompanied them and agreed to answer a few questions. Unsurprisingly he had raised no objections, though he informed his captors he could tell them nothing because he had nothing to tell.

Which was the same situation fifteen minutes after Alex and Hamilton entered the room. Ling was unbound, sitting on the bed. Only one other Chinese was present, a middle-aged man wearing a smart fawn business suit, who introduced himself as Tai Sing. He spoke excellent English with only the slightest trace of an accent, as did Ling, in whom Tai Sing had apparently instilled absolute terror.

To no avail. Ling admitted he worked for people who professed to represent a US Government department, as did others in the hotel. He had not known they were CIA, although he had suspected as much. He was a poor man, his hotel salary minimal. The Americans subsidized it, paying him a small monthly wage to report to them anything he saw that he considered unusual. He never contacted them; they always got in touch with him, sometimes once a week, sometimes more. Occasionally he was asked to do a favour, for which he was given a bonus. Such a favour had been delivering the *Express* to Alex's room and leaving without saying a word. He had been given the task in the lobby by the two Americans he always dealt with. They also had an arrangement with one of the hall porters, whose function it was to locate any employee the Americans wanted to talk to. He, Ling, did not know the Americans' names. He knew nothing of a missing woman or where she might be. He had no addresses whatsoever.

Although disappointed, Alex was inclined to believe him. Ling, however, was his one link with Alison. He was not going to free him in a hurry. Nor, as had been obliquely suggested by Tai Sing, was he going to permit physical torture, which he would have countenanced had he supposed Ling to be lying.

'They must have said something else,' repeated Alex for what seemed the fiftieth time. 'They must have said more than deliver the newspaper and leave without opening your mouth. Even if it was only "good morning" or "we're relying on you" or "we'll pay you in the usual manner". They must have said something else.'

Alex was conversant with the theory of selective memory, of a man only recalling what he chose to or what he considered would please his interrogators.

'They didn't,' said Ling fearfully, wondering what would eventually happen to him. 'I was to deliver the newspaper and leave. If you said anything I was to pretend I didn't understand English.' He hesitated.

'Go on,' encouraged Alex.

'It's nothing,' said Ling. 'I simply asked what I was to do if you refused the newspaper, if you gave it back to me. How would I be able to tell them I had been unsuccessful? They told me they would be somewhere in the hotel lobby but that I was not to be seen talking to them again. They would wait ten minutes. If I hadn't been successful I was to pick up a house phone and ask for one of them to be paged. If they hadn't heard the name in ten minutes they would assume I had delivered the newspaper.'

'You said you didn't know either of their names,' Alex

accused.

'I don't,' whimpered Ling. 'At least, I'd never heard a name mentioned before. And this didn't sound like a name, not a real one, not an American one. I had to ask for it to be repeated. It was "Mr Ismail" or something like that. The one who gave me my instructions turned to his companion and laughed. He said, "Yes, you can call me Mr Ismail." They both seemed to think it was very funny. I didn't have to page them, however, which is why I forgot that part of the conversation. You accepted the newspaper.'

Hamilton pricked up his ears. He had taken no part in the interrogation until that moment. He had been standing by the window, which overlooked a narrow, fetid passage, watching an old man struggle to load a chest of drawers on to a hand cart.

'What was that name again?' he asked sharply.

Ling turned to him. 'Mr Ismail. Something like that. I don't remember exactly.'

'No, go back a moment, to what the American said when he laughed. What were his exact words?'

'I just told you,' wailed Ling. 'He said, "You can call me Mr Ismail."'

'Are you sure he didn't say *Ishmael*? And are you sure he prefixed it with *Mr*? Didn't he just say "Call me Ishmael"?'

'I don't know. He might have done. Yes, I think those were his words.'

'What is it, Duncan?' asked Alex impatiently.

Hamilton raised a clenched fist in triumph.

'What,' he asked Alex, 'has Hong Kong got almost as many of as it has high-rise buildings and people? *Boats, that's what!* Tens of thousands of the bastards! Small boats, large boats, yachts, junks, sampans, cabin cruisers, launches! We've been looking in the wrong bloody places! All known addresses have been searched. No Alison. All the addresses were normally occupied – except one: the apartment of two sharing bachelors who haven't been seen around for a few days. I know where they are. I know where they've got Alison and I can even tell you the name of the cabin cruiser or yacht or whatever. They slipped up. They got too clever when they were giving Ling a name to page. The name of the ship is the *Pequod*, Captain Ahab's whaling vessel. You had a lousy education, Alex. *Call me Ishmael* are the opening words to Melville's *Moby Dick*. All we've got to do is contact the local maritime authorities and find out where the *Pequod* is moored.'

Alex was unimpressed. 'And that's *all* we have to do? Hong Kong is a couple of big islands, a slice of mainland, and around *two hundred* smaller islands. You have a vessel's name. You think. But you just said it yourself: there are tens of thousands of junks, sampans and such like scattered all over the place. We're looking for one that you think is called the *Pequod*. I doubt the maritime authorities and the Royal Yacht Club combined know where a fraction of the ships are moored or to be located most of the time.'

Hamilton glanced at Tai Sing who, while listening to the entire conversation with undisguised interest, had pulled a thin sheaf of papers from his inside jacket pocket.

'Can I have a word with you outside for a second?'

Alex followed Hamilton into the corridor, where a pretty Eurasian girl was guiding a drunken white tourist into the room opposite.

'Sorry if I'm being melodramatic,' said Hamilton, 'but I'm not sure how much our Chinese friend is supposed to know about us.'

'He probably knows more than we do ourselves. However, we're out here now, so carry on.'

'When you sent me out for that list of names and addresses the other day,' said Hamilton, 'you didn't mention boats because we hadn't thought about them. Therefore I didn't ask the question. But if the Company does have a boat, do you think it's likely that the Firm or Special Branch don't know where it is? Even if it moved, they'd keep tabs on it as a matter of routine. A phone call is all it would take.'

'It's a thought,' said Alex.

But not a good one, he decided a moment later. With trouble breaking out in Berlin, he wanted to keep well away from the senior resident for fear Calderwood was trying to reach him. A recall cable to the hotel he could ignore. It wouldn't be so easy to say he hadn't received a direct order from the resident. If Hamilton was right and Alison was being held captive on a boat called the *Pequod*, it wouldn't matter what direct orders he was getting from Calderwood. He'd stall for as long as it took to free Alison. But if Hamilton's hunch was wrong, contacting the Firm was too risky.

'Sorry,' he said. 'It can't be done.' He explained his reasons.

Hamilton gave a resigned shrug. 'So where does that leave us?'

It left them with Tai Sing, who was waiting patiently for their return.

'May I ask you to spell the name of the vessel you were talking about?' he asked politely.

Hamilton did so. 'P-E-Q-U-O-D.'

The Chinese referred to his sheaf of papers. 'Then I believe I am able to help you. When Mr Kaplan originally gave me the list of names and addresses, his instructions were to inspect each apartment and follow each occupant, to see if anyone visited an address that was not on the list. Which my men did. Mostly the occupants went to restaurants or shops or to the cinema. One, however, took the ferry from Central District to Cheung Chau, which is a small island south-west of here, about an hour by ship. His eventual destination was a thirty-foot cabin cruiser moored in a bay on the south side of Cheung Chau. My man could not get close to the cruiser, as the American, on making a signal from the shore, was met by a dinghy and rowed out. He stayed for thirty minutes before returning to the island and taking the next ferry back. All this happened only today, and I regret that I did not receive the report until this afternoon, since when we have been otherwise occupied. You will understand that Mr Kaplan would have been given the information this evening. The name of the cabin cruiser is, of course, the *Pequod*.'

'For the love of God,' swore Hamilton. Alex shut him up by nudging him hard. They could not afford to upset Tai Sing; they were going to need his assistance more than ever now.

'Can you get us back to Mr Kaplan at his hotel fast?' asked Alex. 'You as well. I'll explain what I need on the way.'

248

'Of course.' Tai Sing nodded. 'My car is outside. What about this miserable specimen?'

Ling looked at Alex anxiously.

'Keep him here for forty eight hours, then let him go.'

'That would be most unwise.'

'Nevertheless, it's what I want.' Alex addressed Ling, who was close to tears now that he realized he was to be released and returned to his wife and child. 'You'll be home in two days. My friend here will ensure you do not survive a further two if you ever breathe a word of what you heard in this room.'

In the Mercedes Alex gave Tai Sing a summary of his requirements. First, that he get a good fast launch or cabin cruiser, something capable, anyway, of making the trip to Cheung Chau in the dark, and crewed by Tai Sing's own people. Second, that Tai Sing accompany the raiding party to ensure, by his authority, that the crew executed all orders without hesitation. Third, that the man who had followed the American to Cheung Chau and who could thus pinpoint the *Pequod*'s mooring be among the crew. Fourth, handguns and ammunition for everyone aboard.

Tai Sing cleared his throat delicately.

'You realize that this will all cost a great deal of money. Especially if my men are to be used in freeing Miss Cameron.'

'I hope they won't be,' said Alex. 'I hope we'll be able to do that ourselves, without help. By the looks of things there are only two Americans on board, the two missing from their apartment. But I can't be sure. As for money, Kaplan will pay whatever it costs.'

'I accept your word on that.'

'Two more items,' Alex went on. 'I need all this fast – two hours, three at the outside. We have to leave by seven at the latest. You said the crossing took an hour. Allowing for other difficulties, we may not be in position before nine or ten, and I don't want those aboard the *Pequod* becoming curious regarding why a big boat is manoeuvring in the bay later than that.'

'I may have misled you there,' said Tai Sing. 'The ferry takes an hour. The cabin cruiser I have in mind will take less.

Still, as it's dark . . . Yes, we'll be ready to leave by seven.' He muttered something in Cantonese to the driver, who increased speed in spite of the restrictions in the road tunnel separating the Island from Kowloon. 'He will drop me at the railway station before taking you to the Peninsula. I'll call Mr Kaplan there and inform him where to meet the cruiser. You said there were two other items. The urgency is only one.'

Alex gave him the other, a list of chemicals purchasable openly at any druggist's. When combined in the right proportions, the result would be a small explosive device, a handmade grenade. A makeshift detonator could be fashioned from a bullet.*

Tai Sing raised his thin eyebrows in surprise, recognizing what the list added up to. Hamilton recalled the combination from his days at Fort Monkton.

'We may need a diversion,' Alex explained. 'I'll make sure we get one. I'd do the buying myself except I think you can probably accomplish it easier.'

The greatest difficulty Alex encountered at the Peninsula was trying to dissuade Kaplan and Nathan Tauber from accompanying the raiding party. While Hamilton was dispatched to their own hotel to pick up a change of clothing for both of them – dark sweaters and trousers, rope-soled yachting shoes, buying what they didn't own – Alex argued fiercely with the two Americans. It could be dangerous. Amateurs would get in the way. This was Alison's life they were discussing, not some boy scout expedition to win a merit badge.

Neither Kaplan nor Tauber was impressed.

'As I understand it,' said the publisher, 'I'm financing all this. Knowing Tai Sing it's not going to come cheap. I'd like to see where my money's going.'

Tauber was equally adamant, stone-cold sober for the first time in three days and also less antagonistic now that he finally understood Alex's concern.

'Anything happens to Alison, I, personally, weighing all

* Author's note: On the advice of a former member of the intelligence community who read this book in typescript, it was decided, with regret, not to list the precise combination of these materials.

of one hundred and thirty pounds including gold chains, am going to kill the guys who hurt her. Besides,' he added deadpan, 'I've got a stake in this too – a big percentage of a lot of annual folding paper.'.

Alex gave in. They could come, providing they did as they were told and kept their heads down if someone started shooting.

'And take off the gold, Nathan. If they put a spotlight on us, you'll shine like a Hallowe'en mask.'

Hamilton was back within three-quarters of an hour, carrying an airline bag containing the required clothing. While they changed in Kaplan's bedroom, he gave Alex the cable he had in his pocket. Alex read:

TROUT TEGEL AT ONCE CABLE ARRIVALS
ETA CALDERWOOD.

Alex showed Hamilton the text.

'Trout?'

'Before your time,' said Alex. 'Before mine too, for that matter. One of Calderwood's little jokes. Trout was the RAF's wartime Bomber Command code word for Berlin.'

'Some joke,' grunted Hamilton. 'If Calderwood's conjoining "wartime" and "Bomber Command", I'm not sure I care for the implications. Maybe we should stay in Hong Kong.'

'We've got a date, remember.'

CHEUNG CHAU

Tai Sing came through at ten minutes to seven, with precise instructions regarding where to meet the cabin cruiser, a beautiful forty-footer whose paintwork gleamed. If he was surprised to see Kaplan and Tauber, both well wrapped up in dark windcheaters, he made no comment. In fact, for much of the crossing he and Kaplan remained deep in conversation in the wheelhouse – no doubt, thought Alex, himself busy in the six-berth lower-deck cabin with the chemicals Tai Sing had provided, talking money.

Alex finally held up for Hamilton's inspection two objects each the rough size and shape of a kitchen matchbox. Strips of plasticine held the contents of each contraption in place.

'What hits what, what goes bang, and how big is the bang?' asked Hamilton, who had followed every move but had not understood, as he freely admitted to himself, the intricacies of the operation. After all, this was Alex Dunbar, who had once wired up the Fort Monkton officers' mess so that he could see a girl.

Alex pointed to the neck of a small corked bottle which was adjacent to the snub nose of a 9mm bullet. 'You hit that.'

'*I* do. Thank you very much. My mother's not going to be very happy with you – at the funeral. With what do I hit it?'

'Anything. I usually use the muzzle of a gun or the blade of a knife. But do remember that *you* hit the *bottle*. You do *not* tap the neck of the bottle against the nearest solid object. That could upset the balance inside and start things a-popping before you're out of the way. Hit and throw. Immediately.'

'I don't like the sound of that. How long have I got?'

'Two or three seconds. Once the bottle's shattered, the acid will burn through the cotton wool and the plastic capsule holding the phosphorous. The heat generated by the phosphorous will detonate the cartridge, which sets off the chain reaction. The bang won't be very big.'

'Grenades would have been simpler.' Hamilton studied each bomb suspiciously. 'Tai Sing's probably got a warehouse full of them.'

'Would you recognize the sound of a grenade going off?'

'Of course.'

'So will the people on board. If they think they're under attack, somebody's going to get hurt. They'll be below deck at this time of night. I want them to hear a couple of explosions from above and think that something's gone wrong in the wheelhouse. This is just a diversionary tactic, not the end of the world. You'll be in one of the dinghies on one side of the *Pequod*. Break each bottle and throw. Make sure both bombs land on your side of the cruiser. In other words, don't throw too hard. When whoever's below comes up on deck and maybe decides to look over the rails, I want them looking in your direction.'

'Where I'll be sitting in the dinghy. This is one hell of a diversion.'

'Where you'll now be in and under the water. If there are only two of them, I won't be needing your help.'

Hamilton picked up one of the bombs gingerly. He shook his head. 'Why don't we do it commando style? I'm more used to that. Why all the noise?'

'Because it's virtually impossible to board a smallish boat without the occupants feeling the change of list when someone climbs over the side.'

Hamilton accepted the logic of that. 'And what will you be doing while I'm busily winning a posthumous Victoria Cross?'

'I'll be in the other dinghy on the other side of the *Pequod* or at the stern, depending upon where the ladder is – not getting too close until I hear the first explosion. After that, I'll be freeing Alison and doing some small damage to the men who abducted her, not necessarily in that order. With any luck it'll all be over in a couple of minutes.'

253

'And this is just the two of us?'

As well as the helmsman and the Chinese who knew where the *Pequod* was moored, Tai Sing had brought along four other well-armed henchmen. Including Kaplan and Tauber, that made nine who would be nothing more than observers.

'That's how I'd like it,' admitted Alex, 'though it depends what we see when we get closer. If there's no one patrolling the deck, that will undoubtedly mean there are only two of them.'

'Two of them, one of you. That doesn't sound like good odds.'

'I can handle two of anything that doesn't know I'm coming,' said Alex sharply.

'I meant the odds were stacked against them,' said Hamilton drily. 'I just caught the look in your eye when you mentioned Alison.'

Alex grunted. 'Let's get topsides, dig up a piece of oilskin to wrap that Browning of yours in. If I do happen to need you and it, I don't want you with a wet magazine.'

In answer to Alex's question, Tai Sing said that they were in the West Lamma Channel, west of Lamma Island and approaching Cheung Chau from the east. 'We should be in the bay in ten minutes.'

'Fine. When we're close enough to see the *Pequod* heave to and cut engines. I'd like to scan the deck with the glasses before we lower the dinghies.'

'Will you be needing any of my men, to row or for any other reason?'

'I'll tell you later.'

Kaplan and Tauber were sitting aft. Alex walked across to them while Hamilton waterproofed his automatic.

Tauber pulled a long face when Alex explained what he and Hamilton proposed doing. 'And we don't get a look in? I can swim like a fish if there's any swimming to be done. No kidding, I mean it.'

'I hope only Hamilton will be doing any swimming.'

Alex saw the look of bleak disappointment on Tauber's face and guessed that for someone who had always been small and scrawny, life must have been tough in the early years, tougher still for a homosexual. He'd clawed his way to the top of his own profession on guts alone, but there must have been times, when he was younger, when he'd wished he was six feet tall and weighed one-eighty.

'Still, I do have a job for you, if you can swim as well as you claim. When we've gone, keep the glasses on the *Pequod*. I should be able to handle any trouble that crops up, but if you see anyone resembling a tall redhead go over the side, get in the water.'

Tauber smiled his appreciation. 'Gotcha. Thanks.'

A little later, at a signal from Tai Sing, the helmsman cut the motors. Another crew member dropped the sea anchor.

Tai Sing handed Alex the night glasses, although there was enough illumination coming from the shore and other vessels to have used ordinary binoculars. The *Pequod* was moored a hundred yards away, its bows facing west. The wheelhouse was lit up and there were lights shining from the lower-deck cabin. The boarding ladder was astern. No one appeared to be on deck.

While crewmen lowered the dinghies, Alex gave Hamilton his final instructions.

'You'll go in from the far side, starboard. Take the long way round, give her a wide berth in case someone comes topsides for a breath of fresh air.'

Alex peered at his wristwatch; it was eight thirty. All things considered they had made excellent time.

'I'll give you a ten-minute start because I've got the short, direct route. I'll be laying-to astern at exactly eight forty-five, which is when you start making a noise. The hatch from the cabin is in the wheelhouse, facing aft, so pitch the bombs for'ard. Anything goes wrong, we improvise.'

'Right. I'll be seeing you in about twenty minutes, then.'

'Something like that.'

They did not shake hands or wish each other good luck; that would have been bad luck. Taking their cue, neither Kaplan or Tauber said anything when Alex slipped over the side.

He was thirty yards from the *Pequod*, astern and slightly to port, with two minutes to go. He could not see Hamilton and resisted the temptation to row any closer for the next, agonizingly long ninety seconds. Only when the sweep hand of his wristwatch showed eight forty-five and thirty seconds did he pick up the oars again.

He was still twenty yards astern when the first of the bombs went off. He didn't see the flash because his back was to the *Pequod*, but he heard the bomb clatter against the wheelhouse a fraction of a second before it exploded with a much louder roar than he had anticipated. Then the second bomb landed and detonated. He'd overdone the charge, he thought incidentally. That was the trouble with these rush jobs. A moment later the dinghy bumped the *Pequod*'s stern and he heard the sound of running feet and startled male voices.

Deliberately he counted to ten and kept his head down before hoisting himself aboard, the Browning, cocked, in his right fist. There were two of them, for'ard and starboard. Snatches of conversation floated back.

'. . . dinghy . . .'

'. . . some bastard swimming . . . see . . . something in the water . . .'

'. . . don't shoot, for Chrissake . . . whole bloody harbour down on us . . .'

But one of them was shooting and the target could only be Duncan Hamilton. Alex was to wonder afterwards whether he would have killed either man if Hamilton's life had not been at risk. He concluded he would have had no alternative.

'*Hold it!*' He raced forward at the crouch, using the wheelhouse as cover.

The two men spun round together, one of them already firing, when Alex shot them, the automatic kicking in his fist. Three bullets for the man with the gun, two for his companion, all five shots aimed at the broadest part of the target, the chest, all five hitting the mark.

When they were still Alex went for'ard to confirm that they were dead. He recognized neither of them. Afterwards, he turned and ran back towards the wheelhouse and the cabin hatch – where he found Alison coming up the companionway to meet him, wearing the same outfit in which he had last seen her. Unfortunately she was not alone. Christ, there had been three of them!

The man using her as a shield also had a gun to her temple. 'Back off, Dunbar, or I cancel her ticket. And lose the pistol. Toss it overboard.'

There were standard formulae for dealing with such predicaments. Rule one was never to allow your adversary to gain the initiative. If he was going to kill you anyway, you stood a better chance by reacting instantly. Rule two was never to permit a threat against someone else's life to jeopardize your own. Alex disobeyed both. He backed off and threw the Browning into the bay, over the starboard side where he prayed Hamilton was still alive.

'All you all right?' he asked Alison.

'Yes,' she managed. 'Yes.'

The Agency field man was short and balding, mid-thirties. He was also plainly scared and confused. Pushing Alison in front of him while Alex continued to retreat, he emerged from the wheelhouse on to the deck, looking over his shoulder for his partners.

'They're dead,' Alex informed him, raising his voice, hoping Hamilton would hear. 'As you're going to be shortly unless you show a little sense. How do you think I got here, on water-skis? There are a dozen more of us out there.' He jerked his head seawards. 'If I haven't returned with Miss Cameron in fifteen minutes, they'll be across. And you'll be dead.'

'Not while I've got the girl.'

If Hamilton had not been hit when he was shot at, thought Alex, he would have to get aboard using the stern ladder. Thus it was essential to reverse the positions he and the American were now in. The American had to be standing with his back to the stern.

Still on the retreat, Alex casually changed direction and leaned against the port rail. The American stood opposite him, with Alison as protection.

'Suit yourself,' said Alex. 'You can only use Miss Cameron once, however. Once you kill her, that's your ace gone. I hope you can drive one of these things single-handed because you're going to have to drive like hell.'

To his right, beyond the stern, Alex heard something in the water. *Not yet, Duncan,* he pleaded silently. The noise, however, drew closer. Then the *Pequod* rocked as someone grabbed one of the ladder rungs. A split second later a head appeared over the stern. The American saw it too and loosed off three shots at the boarder. To do so he had to take his gun off Alison. Alex seized his opportunity and catapulted across the deck, bulldozing into the American and Alison, knocking them both into a sprawling heap. In the melee, the American lost grip of his gun.

Without ceremony, Alex hurled Alison out of harm's way. He took hold of the American by the throat and slammed his head against the deck – four, five, six, a dozen times, venting his rage towards all of them on the one he had. When he finished, the man was scarcely breathing.

Shaking with anger, Alex scrambled to his feet and went over to Alison. He was helping her to her feet when Hamilton appeared from behind the wheel house, from for'ard. *For'ard?* Alex could not take it in.

'Are you okay?' he asked Alison.

She nodded. Her dress was torn and there was a nasty swelling on her right cheekbone. Otherwise she appeared unharmed.

'But I think tomorrow's shampoo commercial is out,' she said, before fainting clean away.

Alex caught her as she fell and lay her on one of the after-deck's banquettes. 'What kept you?' he asked Hamilton. Then he noticed the bloodstained sweater.

'It's nothing,' said Hamilton. 'Just a graze. The bombs worked a treat but I was a little slow getting out of the dinghy. I was swimming away when somebody started shooting. I felt a nick on the shoulder and then I guess I passed out. When I came to I was full fathom five down and swallowing water. On the surface I could hear your voice aft so I shinned up the for'ard anchor chain. Then you were banging this one's head.'

'Wait a minute, wait a minute,' said Alex. '*For'ard?* You came up *for'ard*? Then who the hell was that aft?'

'Nathan went in like a dolphin at the first explosion,' Kaplan was saying later, as the cruiser made the return journey up the West Lamma Channel. 'One boom and he'd gone.'

'You think I was going to let Alex and Duncan have all the fun?' demanded Tauber. He had one arm around Alison. 'As John Wayne would have said, the hell I was. Besides, anything happened to Alison, who's going to pay the rent?'

They were in the cabin – Alison, Kaplan, Tauber, Alex and Hamilton. They'd also raided the fridge, which was well stocked with beer and hard liquor. On deck, delighted that he had been paid for a night's work without losing or risking a man, Tai Sing was navigating them back to Kowloon. He had announced a few minutes earlier that they would be docking in three-quarters of an hour. Anonymously, at Alex's request, he had informed the Cheung Chau police via ship-to-shore that there had been an incident on the *Pequod* and that there was an injured man aboard. 'As if they didn't know there'd been an "incident",' said Hamilton. 'The whole of Hong Kong must have heard those explosions. Are you sure you've got the ingredients right, Alex?'

'Anyway,' went on Tauber, 'I swam across in time to hear most of what was going on. I didn't know what the hell to do. Nobody'd given *me* a gun. So I poked my head up. Then that bastard bloody near shot it off. After that I stayed in the water until I knew it was safe.' He hugged Alison.

Alison kissed him. 'Bless you, Nathan.'

She was looking and sounding much better now. Her customary white wine had been abandoned in favour of whisky and Perrier. Her Far East work schedule had also been shelved. There was no way she could be photographed with her cheek as it was, make-up artists notwithstanding. Kaplan said he would handle the rearrangements. He, Tauber and Alison would fly back to the States in a day or two.

'How long did the Chinese gentleman say it would take to reach Kowloon?' she asked.

'About forty-five minutes five minutes ago.'

'In that case I'd like a few quiet words with Alex.' She smiled across the cabin at him.

'Say no more, sweetheart,' said Nathan. 'We're all long gone.'

Alison held out her glass. Alex refilled it and sat beside her.

'Remember the calories.'

'To hell with the calories,' she said. 'I may never count another one as long as I live.' She faced him, her expression sombre. 'I've heard a little about the lengths you went to. From Vincent, Nathan and Duncan. I also heard from Duncan that you'll be flying out soon.'

'True.'

'To more knight errantry?'

'No. A piece of cake, the next destination.'

'Berlin, I hear with my great granny ears.'

'Yes.'

Alison took hold of his hand. 'I don't know why I was abducted and, quite frankly, I don't want to. You can tell me another day. I *do* think I know a little more about the business you're in and why, in some respects, you were reluctant to take up my offer of a few nights ago.'

'It's a business like any other,' said Alex. 'In any case, it's all I know.' He attempted to change the subject. 'They didn't hurt you, did they?'

'Not half as much as you hurt them. If you mean did they molest me, they didn't. I think the idea was in one or two minds, but nothing came of it. They were frightened of the avenging angel, namely you.'

'Don't forget Duncan and Nathan – and Vincent, who bankrolled the whole thing. Don't forget Tai Sing, either. Without him it couldn't have been done.'

'Without *you* it couldn't have been done,' insisted Alison. 'I was scared windless when you faced that little thug who had my arms pinned up my back. But I thought, no, it'll work out.'

'Nathan played his part in that. If he hadn't swum across we could all now be extremely dead.'

'Don't be modest.' She was silent for a moment. 'What happens after Berlin? Are you planning a trip to New York?'

'That could be. I'd hate to let it go like this.'

'It's not about to. And don't bother to lock the door. Upstairs, or whatever they call it on a boat, they know how *I* feel.'

BERLIN

Bunty Ainsworth collected them at Tegel. Hamilton had met her before; Alex had not but took to her at once.

'You both look tired,' she said, navigating her way expertly through the West Berlin traffic.

The time was ten o'clock at night in Germany, dawn the following morning in Hong Kong. Alex and Hamilton had taken the best connections they could get: Hong Kong to Tokyo then over the Pole, via Anchorage, Alaska, to Amsterdam, from where they had caught a British Airways flight to Tegel. All in all, they had been in the air or sitting around departure lounges for twenty-four hours, thirty-odd using Hong Kong time.

'I once flew with my husband from London to New Zealand,' said Bunty. 'When we landed I felt three years older. I told him before we took off that after New Zealand one fell off the end of the world, into the abyss, that the earth was flat, not round as the scientists would have us believe, that we were flying to our doom. He wouldn't accept it until we set down in Auckland. Then he took a look at my face. "My God," he said, "you were right. You look as if you died a week ago." I never forgave him for that.'

Alex noticed the tense. 'Forgave?'

'He was killed in Aden.'

'I'm sorry.'

'You weren't to know.'

Cunning old Calderwood, thought Alex, sending a widow to meet a man whose wife had been murdered in Berlin and who had not revisited the city since. It didn't hurt, being back, he realized, which disconcerted him.

261

'We read in the newspapers about civil disturbance in the streets,' he said. 'I don't see any signs of it.'

'It's not exactly the apocalypse,' Bunty smiled across at him, 'but it does occur from time to time, mostly near the Wall. The authorities have it largely under control. Besides, since the promised films haven't yet materialized, some of the sting has been taken out of the neo-Nazis. Even the Russians haven't made any further belligerent statements during the last twenty-four hours. It's all still there, though, sub-surface. One can occasionally feel the tension in the streets. Everyone is simply waiting now. Either the films will appear soon, or never. Mr Calderwood is inclined to believe the former.'

'Which means he also believes Coughlin and Garfield are here.'

If it was a question Bunty chose to evade it. 'That's something you'd better discuss with him.'

'I don't want to worry anyone,' said Hamilton from the back seat, 'but I think we're being followed. Black Opel, two men in it.'

Bunty had spotted it five minutes earlier, not because she was a field-trained operative, which she wasn't, but because she had been expecting a tail. In a manner of speaking, she had arranged it, by paging Alex Dunbar and Duncan Hamilton to meet Mrs Ainsworth at the British Airways desk if she missed them in the arrivals lounge. Neither man would have heard the announcement, of course, as they were still on board. That wasn't the object of the exercise. Calderwood had told her that all he wanted was to let interested parties, namely the Company, know that Alex was in Berlin. They would have someone watching the airport as a matter of routine; he wanted to make it easier for them. She had asked him why.

'Because, my dear Bunty, nothing is happening, no one is making a move. We've agreed that, somehow, Alex is the key to all this. Let's see what they do when they know he's here.'

Bunty had obeyed her instructions to the letter, without enthusiasm. She wasn't sure she liked Calderwood in his present frame of mind. Since his visit to Sir Nigel he had become uncharacteristically secretive, not confiding in her as he used to.

'They'll probably follow you for a couple of miles before turning off. They know we're here and where we are. That was something we couldn't avoid. They'll just want to make sure you're bringing Alex to me.'

'No, I was wrong,' said Hamilton, peering out of the rear window. 'The Opel's gone. Sorry.'

'No back-up car?'

'Not one I can pick out.'

'Keep looking. Where are we going?' Alex asked Bunty.

'Wilmersdorf. Düsseldorferstrasse. We have a fifth-floor apartment there.' Alex knew the street, south of the Kurfürstendamm, but not the apartment. 'It's vast. No wonder the department's budget is never discussed in public.'

She parked the car in the underground garage, from where they took the lift to the fifth floor. Calderwood was in the sitting-room, drinking whisky and water. He appeared unusually on edge. Curiously too, Alex was to think later, he did not ask about Hong Kong – as though he knew it all already.

He poured Alex and Hamilton a drink. Bunty declined, leaving the room. She had, she said, some calls to return.

'A short chat and then you can go to bed,' said Calderwood. 'You must be exhausted.'

Alex nodded towards the window. 'It all seems pretty quiet out there. The reports we saw led us to believe the place was falling apart. Bunty says the Russians aren't making as much noise either.'

'Bunty is wrong,' said Calderwood. 'We're sitting on a powder keg. I heard less than an hour ago some disturbing news regarding Soviet troop dispositions. Two tank divisions of the 2nd Guards Army based at Neustrelitz and Perleberg have been placed on secondary alert. Neustrelitz is approximately one hundred and thirty miles east of Hamburg. In Bernau, Döberitz and Jüterbog three divisions of the 20th Guards are also on secondary alert. The commander of the Third Shock Army at Magdeburg, which is a mere twenty-five miles from the West German border, has, I understand, been summoned by the Commander in Chief GSFG (Group of Soviet Forces Germany) to his headquarters in Zossen, which is fifteen miles south of where we are now sitting. Satellite pictures have shown abnormal activity around the missile sites at Tashevo, Kozelsk, Derazhnya and Pervomaysk. I could go on. Needless to say, our own people are taking counter-measures. No, Alex, it's far from quiet, far from it.'

Alex and Hamilton exchanged glances. Calderwood was saying that Europe was but a step or two away from war.

'It's incredible,' said Alex. 'All this because of unsubstantiated rumours concerning a few feet of fake film.'

'What film, Alex?' asked Calderwood. 'Where is this film? Perhaps no one intends producing film. The plot could be even deeper than we imagined, don't you see? Look how the situation has degenerated on mere hearsay. You and Hamilton are ex-military men. You both know the logistics involved in moving vast numbers of men and quantities of *matériel*. There comes a point when the only option is to go forward.

'Imagine two boxers in a ring. Does one boxer allow the other to hit him before he retaliates? Of course not. He defends himself and tries to strike first. Besides, how do we know that the Soviets themselves are not delighted at the turn of events? While crying "foul" they are secretly rubbing their hands with glee.'

Calderwood passed a hand over his eyes. He hadn't had much rest in the last four days and his night was far from over yet.

'Look, it's too late now to continue this discussion. We'll carry on in the morning, with fresh minds.' He raised his voice and called for Bunty. 'Sleep as long as you like. I doubt the position will degenerate much in the next twenty-four hours. If I'm not here when you awake and you decide to go out, please be careful.'

Bunty appeared in the doorway to show them to their rooms. When she returned Calderwood said, 'Did you hear all that?'

'Yes. I took it down verbatim, as you asked.' Her tone contained an element of disapproval.

'We have to have records, Bunty, for the files. What we don't have to do is let others know we're keeping records. Transcribe your notes and let me have them. While you're doing that I shall take a bath and change my clothes. Then I have to go out. I may not be back for some hours, perhaps not until tomorrow evening. Oh, and ring the number I gave you earlier. You know what to say.'

'But not why.'

'All in good time, Bunty, all in good time.'

'You're a very devious man, do you know that?'

Calderwood did not reply. Indeed, he appeared not to have heard.

Several miles north-west of Düsseldorferstrasse, in Charlottenburg, Cassidy replaced the telephone and shook a cigarette from his fourth pack of the day. He had been chain-smoking for forty-eight hours, since he had flown in from the States to take charge personally of a situation that was rapidly getting out of hand. He had told no one at Langley where he was going, though doubtless someone from the Berlin station had witnessed his arrival and had already filed a routine report. Not that it mattered. In another day or so his position would either be impregnable, or he would be fertilizer.

'Nothing,' he said to Stone. 'Absolutely nothing. Every line of communication responding negatively. Nikitchenko can't or won't get in touch. What the hell is he up to?'

Frank Stone didn't know. What he did know was that he might soon have to start putting some distance between himself and Cassidy. If the scenario worked, fine. Cassidy would float to the top like a bubble. If it did not work, the execution squads would be looking for them.

'Dunbar,' he said. 'We know he's here with that sidekick of his, and we know where they are. You've got to call the final play.'

'It's too soon, damn it,' snarled Cassidy. 'None of this was supposed to happen for three weeks. And how the hell can I call the final play when I can't reach Nikitchenko?'

'Have it your way,' shrugged Stone, 'but we're being outmanoeuvred and I don't like it or understand it. We baited two traps and somebody's sprung one of them.'

'Calderwood? That bastard owes me one from years ago.'

'How could it be Calderwood? Forget Calderwood. Concentrate on Dunbar.'

'Maybe you're right,' said Cassidy thoughtfully, 'maybe you're right. But let's go over the whole thing once more, to make sure we're missing nothing. Then I'll try for Nikitchenko again. Dunbar can wait. He's not going anywhere.'

Which was true enough until late the following afternoon, when Calderwood had still not returned to the apartment.

'He said he might not be back until this evening,' Bunty informed Alex and Hamilton.

They both felt considerably better after sleeping the clock round. Both had also been kicking their heels since midday, waiting for Calderwood. They had seen the newspapers, listened to the radio and watched the television news, Alex translating as necessary for Hamilton, whose command of spoken German was limited though he could read it well enough. There had been no mention of Soviet troop movements, naturally enough. Such information would be classified.

At five thirty Alex announced that they were going out.

'Where?' asked Bunty. 'In case he comes back.'

'I'm not sure,' said Alex. 'Bars; restaurants, districts. Places that were regular Agency haunts in the old days. We're not achieving anything here.'

As they were about to leave the telephone rang. Bunty answered it. 'It's for you,' she told Alex.

'Calderwood?'

'No, a Miss Deuntzer, Karen Deuntzer.'

Alex crossed the room in three strides and snatched at the receiver. 'Yes?'

'Karen Deuntzer, Alex. I understand you're looking for some film and maybe the people who're carrying it. Perhaps I can help you.'

'Why would you do that?'

'My own reasons. Are you interested, or not?'

'Of course I'm interested. Go on.'

'No, not over the phone. I'm taking a big chance. We'll have to meet.'

'Where and when?'

'Do you know Lehrterstrasse?'

'Yes. It runs past the Post-Stadion and the Fritz-Schloss Park.'

'There, then. North-east of the park, at the junction of Lehrterstrasse and Kruppstrasse. Nine thirty. Come alone.' She hung up.

'Well, well,' said Alex.

'Who is Karen Deuntzer?' asked Bunty.

'An American lady, Agency. She kept me occupied in Arlington while other members of her team ransacked my hotel room. She also turned up in Hong Kong, but I lost her. She wants to meet me.'

'You're not going, surely to God,' said Hamilton. 'It's a trap.'

'Of course it's a trap,' agreed Alex. 'She's the only lead we have, however. If she wants to meet me, I'll be there.'

Hamilton grimaced in disgust. 'Make sense, Alex. What's the bait – the films, Coughlin and Garfield? She's Company, who've been trying to keep you away from both up to now. Besides, you're in debt to them for Cheung Chau.'

'What's Cheung Chau?' asked Bunty.

'Another story,' said Hamilton. 'They'll have a dozen people there,' he went on, 'maybe two dozen. Go anywhere near her and you're a dead man.'

'Not necessarily,' contradicted Alex. 'Bunty, we're going to need your help on this. Did Calderwood tell you to hang fire here until he returned?'

'No. What sort of help?'

Alex explained where Karen Deuntzer would be at nine thirty. 'We'll take the car, you driving, Bunty. I'll be in the passenger seat and Duncan will be in the back. If she's alone on the corner, you'll cruise up to her, Bunty, and stop. I'll hop out and bundle her into the back, where by this time, Duncan, you'll have your door open. If we can get our hands on Karen Deuntzer we may crack this thing.'

'They'll be ready for every move,' protested Hamilton. 'They know you'll try something like that.'

'Then we'll just have to work fast. Game, Bunty?'

'I suppose so. I can handle a car, but my knowledge of Berlin is limited to the major roads.'

'We'll worry about that when they start chasing us. Duncan?'

'You're the boss, though it all sounds a bit iffy. However, there's another problem. It's now five forty. The rendezvous is four hours off. What if Calderwood comes back between then and now? He'll order us not to take the risk, and that will be that.'

'If he comes back we won't be here. We're leaving. Now. I'll buy you both an early dinner. Alex contemplated the window for a moment. 'Would you suppose the Company has this building under surveillance?'

'It would be as well to believe so,' said Hamilton. 'If Karen Deuntzer knows the telephone number, you can bet your life they know the address.'

'That sounds logical. How many men, two?'

'Four, I'd say. And a car. One man at least on the garage exit or hovering in the vicinity, in case we try the old one of hiding under rugs.'

'Would they follow Bunty if she were obviously alone?'

Alex was thinking aloud. Hamilton answered anyway.

'I doubt it. They'll have just one car, two at the outside. They won't waste one on Bunty for fear we leave in separate cabs.'

That gave Alex an idea. 'Can you still shake a tail, Duncan?'

'Under normal circumstances, yes. Bit difficult not knowing the city, though, the buses and the subway system.'

'Yes, that is a problem, but not insoluble. Bunty, you'll take the car. Duncan's probably right. You won't be followed if they see you're alone. Keep your eyes peeled, nevertheless. Can you find the Opera House in Bismarckstrasse? It's due north of here and west of the Tiergarten. If you can't find it, ask. Anyone will be able to give you directions.'

'I know Bismarckstrasse. I'll find the Opera House.'

'Fine. Park the car somewhere and wait in front of the main entrance. I've no idea how long we'll be, but it

268

shouldn't be more than an hour and a half. Do you have a hat?'

'I have a headscarf.'

'Wear it if you think you've been followed. If you're bareheaded we'll assume you haven't been.

'Duncan, you and I will leave together and take separate cabs. We'll go a few minutes before Bunty in order to commit their cars. My destination doesn't matter. You're going to Tegel Airport. Take a suitcase containing one or two items because the weight will have to register on the scales. Don't pack anything you're too fond of, however, because you're going to lose the bag. Make like you're in a hell of a hurry when you reach Tegel and book yourself on any flight boarding in less than fifteen minutes. Nothing on the other side of the world, though, as you're going to lose your fare also. Copenhagen, Stockholm, somewhere like that.'

'Check in your bag and go through the whole emigration procedure, passport control, security, the lot. Then wait in the departure lounge until the flight has taken off. Whoever's tailing you won't have the authority or the need to catch the same flight. Fifteen minutes after take-off time, go back through passport control and security, complaining that you didn't hear the flight called. They'll make a bit of a song and dance, so wave your diplomatic credentials at them. By now your tail will have disappeared to report in. Grab another cab and meet up with Bunty outside the Opera House. Watch for the headscarf.'

'What are you going to do?' asked Hamilton.

Alex smiled. 'Well, I know this city, or I used to. I'm going to have a bit of fun losing whoever's on me.'

As they were going through the front door the phone rang again. 'Don't answer it,' said Alex.

Alex and Hamilton left the elevator at the ground floor, while Bunty continued on to the underground car park. Outside, Alex let Hamilton take the first cruising cab. He flagged the one behind.

'Neu-Westend U-Bahn, bitte.'

When the cab had covered half a mile, Alex checked the rear window. There was a black Opel two vehicles behind. Black Opel? Hamilton had thought they were being followed from the airport by a black Opel, which had eventually turned off. Still.

At the subway station he paid off the first cab and immediately signalled another. *'Ernst-Reuterplatz U-Bahn.'*

Neu-Westend was north-west of Düsseldorferstrasse; Ernst-Reuterplatz due east of Neu-Westend. Now Alex was sure; the same black Opel was following the second cab.

At Ernst-Reuterplatz Alex settled the fare and dived into the subway, where he caught the first train to come along, leaving it at the Zoo and returning to street level. From there he walked south and then west along Wilmersdorferstrasse. He had his tail spotted now; two men, nationality undetermined. He had also succeeded in his first objective; they had been forced to abandon their transport. All that was left was to lose them.

He found what he was looking for fifteen minutes later, in one of the streets off the Ku-damm; half a dozen or more strolling hookers hunting early-evening custom. As this was the fashionable part of central West Berlin, they were all reasonably young, pretty and very well-dressed. Doubtless their prices matched the territory.

Alex remembered that Berlin prostitutes operated in one of three ways. Some had apartments nearby; some would accompany you to your own apartment or hotel room. He needed a girl in the third category.

He allowed himself to be accosted and asked his question. He received three negatives before he got the answer he wanted.

'How much?' he asked.

'You're not German, are you?' The petite brunette had a beautiful smile, full of promises. 'You're very fluent but I don't think you're German.'

'American,' said Alex, knowing from past experience that few German whores like the British, who were reputedly mean, always wanting to bargain. Americans, on the other hand, were generous and sometimes paid in dollars. 'And you still haven't said how much.'

'That depends on what you require. I don't . . .' She flicked her tongue rapidly over her lips. 'You understand?'

'Yes. The usual then.'

'Two hundred marks.'

About fifty pounds or a hundred and twenty dollars, thought Alex. Christ.

'It would, of course, be slightly less if you had a room or an apartment close by.' She knew she was on safe ground there; he had just confessed that he hadn't.

'One hundred American dollars,' he offered.

'One hundred and ten.'

'Agreed. Where's your car?'

'Round the corner.'

The third category of whore did not have apartments in the area, lived further out and drove in to ply their trade. Their fees were high because while they were driving a customer home and, afterwards, returning to their beat, they were not doing any business.

'Money first,' said the girl, opening her hand.

Alex counted it out, wanting his tail to see the transaction. By now they would be puzzled, asking themselves: had Dunbar just been looking for a woman?

'Which is yours?' asked Alex, standing on the corner in full view of his pursuers, who were each fifty yards behind on either side of the street.

'The green Mercedes.'

'Get in and drive up to me. Once I'm beside you, off you go.'

The girl frowned at him. 'Hey, you're not a weirdo, are you?'

Alex gave her a reassuring smile. 'Of course not. I'm in Berlin with my wife and her brother. I've got a feeling my wife doesn't trust me out alone and that her brother's back there, seeing what I'm up to.'

'Then he'll have seen you hand me one hundred and ten dollars. What will you say I was, a collector for the dog's home?'

'I'll explain that somehow, say I was asking you for directions, that he was mistaken about the money. What I wouldn't be able to explain is why I was getting into a young lady's car.'

'Jesus, you must want to get laid awful bad.'

The Mercedes was parked a hundred yards up the side

271

street, facing Alex. He remained where he was until the car was within twenty yards of the corner. Then he ran towards it, yanked open the door, and sank into the passenger seat.

'Put your foot down.'

The girl did so. Alex turned and waved to his two stranded pursuers.

'My name's Kitty,' said the hooker. 'I live over in Spandau. It will take some time in this traffic, so if you'd like to go to the Grünewald or find a dark alley, we can save half an hour.'

'Forget alleys, the Grünewald and Spandau, Kitty,' said Alex. 'Hang a right here. You can drop me off at the Opera House.' It was seven twenty. Bunty would have been there for ages. Hamilton too should have arrived by now.

Kitty shot a startled glance across at him. '*The Opera House!* Here, what is this? I knew there was something funny about you!'

'There isn't. I was in a hurry and couldn't find a taxi. And don't worry about a refund. You can add the money I gave you to the next payment on the Merc.'

Bunty was waiting by the entrance. Next to her was Hamilton. Bunty was bareheaded.

'Any problems?' asked Alex. Two negatives. 'Then let's eat.'

'That's her,' said Alex, almost two hours later. 'The blonde in the trouser-suit.'

Karen Deuntzer was standing where she had said she would be, on the corner of Krupp and Lehrter. She appeared to be alone, but Alex knew that to be an illusion.

'Drive past at normal speed, Bunty. Once around the block. Keep your eyes open, Duncan, see if you can spot where the opposition is.'

Hamilton saw nothing out of the ordinary. Nor did Alex. Then they were driving along Lehrterstrasse again. The Kruppstrasse intersection was a hundred yards away. Karen Deuntzer was still there, still apparently alone.

'As we planned it, Bunty,' said Alex calmly, feeling the tension in the woman at the wheel. 'Drop down a couple of gears when we're fifty yards off. No more than a crawl when you're almost level with her. Ready with the door, Duncan?'

'Ready.'

Everything happened in quick, nightmarish succession after that. Alex had his own door partly open. As the car drew closer to Karen Deuntzer, she bent her head and peered through the windscreen – suspiciously before, apparently sensing danger and panicking, turning on her heel and running down Kruppstrasse. She was wearing flat shoes and could move. Alex was on the pavement in an instant, racing after her. Behind him he heard the sudden squeal of brakes, of skidding tyres on tarmac; raised voices, breaking glass, Hamilton's shout of alarm.

Alex threw a glance over his shoulder. A dark-coloured sedan had pulled in front of Bunty. Two men were smashing her windscreen with hammers while a third stabbed at the front offside tyre with something sharp. Hamilton was struggling with a fourth.

That should have warned Alex. It didn't. All he could think of was catching up with Karen Deuntzer.

He was within reach of her and level with a fawn Volkswagen when the driver of the VW flung open the door, slamming it into Alex, hurling him to the ground. Dazed and winded, he heard more voices, other vehicles. Then he was hit on the head very hard. His senses reeling, he felt someone grab him under the arms. Someone else took his feet. He was being lifted. More voices. He couldn't understand what they were saying. Then he blacked out.

At the junction Hamilton picked himself up. He had been winning the battle against his assailant when another had struck him with one of the hammers that had smashed the windscreen. His attackers had now disappeared. As had Alex. As had Karen Deuntzer. It had all taken only seconds.

Bunty was holding her head behind the wheel. Hamilton pushed his way through the gathering bystanders. He couldn't hear what she was saying to begin with.

'What is it, Bunty? Are you all right?'

He had to ask her to repeat it. Stunned, he heard her say: 'They weren't Americans at all. They were calling to each other in *Russian*.'

EAST

When Alex regained consciousness he found himself lying on a mattressless bunk in a narrow cell. A single light bulb burned in the middle of the high ceiling, the only illumination. Nor was there any ventilation, no outside grille. His watch had stopped at 9.34. He had no idea whether it was day or night, or how long he had been unconscious. Judging by the stubble on his chin, he would say no more than twelve hours.

He sat up gingerly. His head ached, as did his ribs. So, for some unaccountable reason, did his inner right arm. He took off his jacket and rolled up his sleeve. A speck of blood and a bruise showed where the hypodermic needle had punctured the skin. That explained why he had been comatose for so long.

In one corner of the cell was a chemical lavatory, which he made use of immediately. After that he pounded on the heavy cell door. He had a terrible thirst, doubtless a symptom of the injection, and nothing with which to quench it.

Several minutes passed before an eye-level panel was pulled aside. Alex caught a quick glimpse of a youngish male face before the panel was slammed shut.

'Water!' he shouted. '*Wasser!*'

While he was still hammering on the door, a second panel opened, this time at his feet. A steel tray was pushed into the cell and the panel closed. The tray held a mug of milkless and sugarless coffee, a plate of what looked like stew, and a chunk of black bread. Alex drank the coffee greedily, scalding though it was. He left the stew but forced himself to eat the bread, masticating each mouthful to activate his saliva glands. When he had finished he lay back on his bunk, using his coat as a pillow, and slept. He made little attempt to reconstruct the events that had brought him here or why, or ask himself where 'here' was. That would have been a futile exercise. The voices he had heard before he blacked out had been talking in Russian. Karen Deuntzer had set him up. She wasn't CIA after all but KGB. Someone would explain it all to him sooner or later, and then he would know.

He was awakened some hours later by the cell door being flung open. He struggled to sit up, blinking at the sudden fierce light from the corridor beyond. A man in his late thirties entered the cell. He was an inch or two shorter than Alex and had light-brown hair, cropped military fashion. He was thin to the point of emaciation. He was also wearing the uniform of a KGB lieutenant-colonel.

'Get up, put on your jacket, and come with me,' he commanded in excellent German.

Alex followed him into the corridor and along it. No guard accompanied them, though the lieutenant-colonel was unarmed.

'Where am I, the Lubyanka?' asked Alex, also speaking in German.

'Do you think you're that important?'

'I haven't the faintest idea what to think. I know the KGB don't operate in full uniform in the west, therefore I must be in the east.'

The Russian led the way up a flight of stairs and into a sparsely furnished office. The window was barred but unshuttered, and overlooked a courtyard. Daylight shone through. Other than the time, however, the view afforded no clues.

The Russian took the seat on the far side of the desk, his back to the window. He motioned Alex to sit opposite him, and opened a folder.

'Alexander Dunbar,' he read aloud. 'A good Russian name if a trifle imperial. Age forty. Formerly with British Intelligence in Berlin. Believed to have been compulsorily retired in disgrace.' He closed the folder. 'Apparently not.'

Alex shrugged non-committally.

'What, no protests?' said the colonel. 'No pleas that you have diplomatic status and that you should not be here?'

'Would it do any good?'

'Absolutely not. Nevertheless, I believe we would try to come up with some mitigating story.'

'We?'

'We.' The Russian extracted a cigarette from a packet on the desk, an English brand, Player's. He did not offer Alex one. 'We,' he repeated. 'But I haven't introduced myself, have I? My name is Colonel Sadirov. For your trial, I am your defence counsel.'

Alex stared at him in astonishment.

'Trial? With what am I charged?'

Sadirov referred to a typewritten sheet pinned to the outside of Alex's dossier.

'Crimes against the Soviet Union; crimes against the German Democratic Republic; espionage.'

Alex resisted the urge to laugh.

'That's madness. You know the rules. Your people picked me up in West Berlin, where I was legitimately permitted to be. Now that *is* a crime. Espionage? I've never set foot on Soviet soil in my life.'

'East Berlin can be considered Soviet soil, as can East Germany. I doubt you'll be found guiltless on the first charge when it's presented properly. Even if you are, the second will hold. As will the third.'

'Absurd,' said Alex. He did not understand this at all. 'Nor have I set foot in East Germany or entered East Berlin for over four years. Whatever else you're up to, I'm certain it has nothing to do with events that occurred that long ago. When is this trial to take place?'

'Soon, very soon. Within the hour if the principals have arrived.'

Sadirov puffed at his cigarette and thought for a moment.

'Perhaps I use the word trial inadvisedly. There is to be, at least to begin with, an informal hearing, that is all. An investigation into the part you have played in Cougar. Oh yes, we know all about Cougar – or mostly all. You will provide the details.'

'You're going to be one hell of a defence counsel, I can see that,' sneered Alex. 'And I can't tell you what I don't know.'

'But you can tell us what you *do* know. And then I shall use whatever advocatory skills I possess to minimize your sentence.'

'Don't bother. It'll be thirty years or a firing squad, depending upon which side the judge got out of bed. Or perhaps you'll attempt to exchange me in a couple of years for one of yours that we've got. That won't work, Sadirov. They'll spit in your face.'

The telephone on the desk rang. Sadirov picked up the receiver, listened for a few seconds, then spoke a few sentences in Russian to the caller before hanging up. He pressed a buzzer on the desk top.

'The guard outside the door will return you to your cell now. Apparently the principals are here. We shall be ready to begin in forty-five minutes. Please try to answer any question I put to you as openly as you feel able to. That same injunction applies to questions that may be put to you by others. Do not be arrogant, Dunbar. It will serve you ill.'

Alex stood up. 'Am I to be allowed to shave and wash before I appear?'

'You are not.'

'So that I'll be seen as a scruffy, decadent capitalist spy for the cameras, presumably?'

'There will be no cameras.'

'I think I should tell you before we start that your KGB snatch squad got the wrong man,' said Alex from the door. 'It wasn't me you wanted.'

Back in his cell, Alex attempted to figure it all out. He failed. This wasn't standard operating procedure for the KGB at all. No softening-up process, beatings, periods of solitary confinement and sleeplessness to disorientate him. They must be in a hell of a hurry or, as he had suggested, they'd realized overnight that they had abducted the wrong person, made the kind of mistake that they wanted to shovel under the carpet as quickly as possible. That had to be it, and he would take great pleasure in telling them as much. He had nothing to lose. They were going to lock him up for the remainder of his life anyway, or worse. They could not be so naïve as to believe that Calderwood or anyone else would agree to an exchange for someone now incarcerated in a top-security British gaol. SIS field officers disappeared all the time, usually for ever. Their names never made the newspapers because they were not sufficiently important, anonymous bodies inhabiting a twilight world where success was generally measured not in major coups but in how long they stayed alive.

When the cell door next opened two KGB guards stood behind Sadirov. 'Come,' said the Russian.

With a guard at either elbow, Alex followed Sadirov along the corridor, up the same flight of stairs as before and then another flight to the floor above. Occasionally the quartet passed open doors where various uniformed figures, male and female, were working at desks or making telephone calls, but Alex still had no idea what sort of building they were in, whether it was a prison or court or barracks. For that matter, he had no idea what city he was in.

The room Sadirov eventually led the way into offered no clues either. All the windows were shuttered, the lights on. If it was a court, it was certainly unlike any Alex had ever seen. It reminded him more of a small lecture hall. At one end was a dais, on which there stood a long table, seating for three, with notepads, pencils, carafes of water and glasses already in position. In front of the dais and some distance from it were eight or ten rows of chairs, eight chairs to a row. Only one, at the back of the room, was occupied – by an elderly man wearing a double-breasted dark-grey suit. He had one hand to his mouth. Alex vaguely recognized him, though he could not put a name to the face.

Sadirov indicated that Alex should sit on the second chair in, front row right. Close by was a lectern. The guards were dismissed.

'Are you quite certain I won't try to make a run for it?'

Sadirov ignored the sarcasm. 'Let me explain the procedure to you,' he said. 'In a few moments three men will come through that door. One will be an army general, one a KGB general, one a high-ranking civilian. You will not know them, I am sure, and neither do their names concern you. Let me assure you, however, that they are very powerful men indeed. None of them speaks English and only one has German. They will therefore be accompanied by an interpreter. As I am your defence counsel, it would be improper for me to interpret. Also with them will be a shorthand stenographer who will take down every word that is said. You will stand up when they enter. You will remain standing until I instruct you otherwise.

'I shall address them from the lectern. They know who you are, but I'll make it formal, for the record. They will ask you questions. I shall translate the questions into German. Your answers will be relayed to them through the interpreter, who is there to ensure that I translate accurately. What you British call fair play.'

'Aren't we missing someone?' asked Alex. 'If this is a trial or an investigation or whatever you choose to call it, where's the prosecution?'

'The men on the dais will be your prosecutors. And your judges. On your feet now!'

Knowing that the only satisfaction he would get was in seeing their faces when he revealed that he could tell them little or nothing about Cougar, Alex stood up, willing to play their rules, go along with the charade. The civilian took the middle chair on the dais, with the army general on his right, the KGB general on his left. All three men were in or approaching their seventies, all would have been infants at the time of the October Revolution. Not one seemed to have a spark of compassion remaining. Hardly surprising, thought Alex. Though it was tough to gain the summit of the political or military professions in the western world, at least there the penalty for failure was not a blindfold and a firing squad on a cold morning.

Unexpectedly, the interpreter turned out to be a young woman, not bad looking as Russian women went, the stenographer a man. The latter took a seat in front of the dais, facing Sadirov. The woman stood a deferential distance behind the civilian judge.

Sadirov spoke for fifteen minutes in Russian, not bothering to translate his words for Alex who nevertheless heard his name mentioned on several occasions. The judges said nothing until Sadirov indicated that he had concluded his opening remarks. Then the civilian held a whispered consultation with his colleagues before asking the first question. Sadirov relayed it to Alex.

'The prisoner will tell the court of his involvement in the anti-Soviet operation known as Cougar.'

Alex did so in one word. 'None.'

Sadirov glared at him. The woman appeared flustered. Although the monosyllable scarcely needed translating, she did so. The civilian tried again.

'The prisoner will explain that remark,' said Sadirov.

'It's perfectly simple,' said Alex. 'Whatever I say about Cougar will be conjectural. Cougar was a CIA-mounted operation. British Intelligence was never informed of its existence or purpose.' Alex sought the civilian judge's eyes and held them with his own. 'As I explained to Colonel Sadirov earlier, you've got the wrong man. You should have someone from the CIA standing here, not me.'

'British Intelligence has been involved from the start,' intoned Sadirov sternly, interpreting for the KGB general. 'In the United States, Bangkok and Hong Kong.'

No need to guess how they knew that, thought Alex. Karen Deuntzer.

'British Intelligence,' he riposted, 'has *not* been involved from the start, or at all. We were as anxious as anyone else to establish the motive behind Cougar, which, in case you're unaware of the fact, is an acronym of the first three letters of two CIA agents' names, Coughlin and Garfield. We knew they were the key which would unlock Cougar. I was in the Far East hunting them.'

'Only because they were the key? Not because they also killed your wife?' Sadirov for the army general.

Now how the devil did they know that, wondered Alex?

'That was why I was selected for the assignment as opposed to anyone else, doubtless.'

'Brought out of retirement.' Sadirov for the KGB general. 'You have been inactive for several years.'

'Yes.'

The civilian consulted with his colleagues before asking a lengthy question, one that seemed to contain many subheadings. Sadirov summarized it in a few sentences.

'The court is not of a mind to accept that the operation was the exclusive brainchild of the CIA. The CIA is known to work closely with MI6. The prisoner will elaborate his previous remark regarding conjecture. What does the prisoner mean by that? How did the prisoner become involved in the first instance if British Intelligence is not, in this matter, collaborating with the CIA?'

'MI6 doesn't work closely with the CIA, and hasn't done for years,' said Alex. 'The Americans don't trust us. They think KGB-run moles have penetrated our security too deeply, that, although we've caught some, there are others still active.' He managed a feeble joke. 'But of course you'll know more about that than I do.'

The civilian growled a short and sharp sentence. Sadirov nodded. 'The prisoner is warned not to treat his hearing lightly.' Sadirov addressed Alex directly. 'You will now answer the question already put. How did you become involved?'

Alex began at the beginning, impatient to see their expressions when they finally realized that everything he was telling them was hypothesis. After a while, watching their faces, he found he was enjoying himself. He started using complicated German compounds to confuse the interpreter, who'd already had trouble with 'acronym' and who, as Alex spoke, had to ask for frequent repetitions.

He related to the court how his brother had been writing a series of articles on the rise of neo-Nazism, how Nick was killed pursuing a line of enquiry, probably in South Dakota by the CIA, his body dumped in Denver. Next came the film and camera lens found in the valley, both items purporting to show that the Soviet Union had administered extermination camps for Jews during the war, on a massive scale. He told the three judges about George Andrus, now also dead. He summed up by saying that he and other elements of the British Intelligence believed that the CIA had planned, possibly still planned, to release the South Dakota films in Berlin, West Germany and elsewhere; that the CIA wanted to stir up the neo-Nazis by apparently vindicating many of the crimes allegedly sanctioned by the leaders of the Third Reich, especially Hitler. Then the Russians would react precisely as they had done, belligerently, fearing a potential right-wing West German government. Hawks in the CIA wished to bring about a limited war in Europe, with the Soviet Union appearing the aggressor in the eyes of world opinion.

'That's what Cougar is all about.'

The three judges put their heads together. Alex could sense that they believed him. He had the nerve to wink at Sadirov: I told you so. If you want the fine print, old chap, go catch yourself Coughlin and Garfield.

Finally the civilian made a lengthy speech, directing his remarks not at Alex or Sadirov but over their heads, towards the man in the dark-grey suit. When Alex attempted to take a curious peek over his shoulder, Sadirov snapped his fingers and told him to face the front.

The civilian went on for a good twenty minutes, his tone deferential. The moment he finished he stood up abruptly and, the army and KGB generals following, descended the dais and left the room. At attention, Sadirov held the door open for the trio.

'Is that it?' asked Alex, while the woman interpreter tidied the long table and the stenographer collected his notebooks.

'For now.'

'Am I guilty or acquitted?'

'That has not been decided here. There may be a more formal hearing at a later date, during which I shall again represent you. On that occasion you shall have your cameras. You may even get your acquittal.'

'And my freedom?'

'That's a different matter. You're a confessed member of British Intelligence. You've admitted operating in East Germany and East Berlin in the past. No, your freedom I cannot guarantee.'

'Then you're taking a lot for granted. I may not choose to repeat in open court what I said here.'

'Why ever not?' Sadirov was genuinely surprised. 'In the last hour you have probably prevented a major European conflict. Come on.'

'Where to now?'

'Back to your cell. After that, we'll have to see. You may be moved. It's not my decision.'

At the door, a movement towards the rear of the room caused Alex to glance in that direction. The man in the dark-grey suit had risen to his feet. There was a look of extreme satisfaction on his face. Alex recognized him now. Marshal Nikolei Nikitchenko, the Soviet defence minister.

Alex lay on his bunk, his hands clasped behind his head, staring at the naked light bulb in the ceiling. He had asked Sadirov to obtain for him a plate of something more substantial than stew. That had arrived an hour ago, a dish of meat, vegetables and dumplings covered with a lumpy liquid that passed for gravy. Ravenous, he had eaten every morsel. The guard had also brought a mattress and several blankets, though a request for a razor and a chance to brush his teeth had been rejected by Sadirov. 'Perhaps tomorrow.'

He would have to get used to that phrase – 'perhaps tomorrow'. The KGB was a notoriously capricious animal, capable of changing its mind at will. Although for the moment, now that he had given his testimony, they were treating him with a little more consideration, it only needed someone in Dzerzhinsky Square to decide that a show trial would not be in Moscow's best interests, and that would be the end of him. He would finish up in a camp or against a wall. Offered a choice, he would take the wall.

By now Calderwood would have learned from Hamilton that he, Alex, had been abducted by the KGB. Regrettably, Calderwood wasn't in a position to do much about it. Golden rule number one in the Firm was to deny that anyone actually worked for it. If Calderwood was feeling benevolent he might arrange to pull in a few known KGB operatives, raise a little hell in West Berlin. On the other hand, he could conclude that such a move would be provocative, counter-productive; the KGB would respond in kind and round up twice the number of the Firm's East Berlin agents. Though it would doubtless seem a paradox to outsiders, opposing intelligence services only existed in each other's territories by mutual consent. Known small fry were generally left alone, providing they remained small fry; otherwise the game couldn't continue. Each side would give the other's agents their marching or termination orders, and that would be that. Nothing except genuine diplomats in every embassy.

Much later Alex drifted off into an uneasy sleep. When he awoke it was in response to a key rattling in the cell door. The door opened to reveal a guard he had not seen before. The guard gestured impatiently for Alex to get to his feet. The rifle in his hands left no room for argument.

They turned right outside the cell, heading in the opposite direction from the court and Sadirov's office, the guard urging Alex forward with the rifle muzzle.

'Where are we going?' Alex asked the question in German, repeating it in French and English. The guard did not reply.

An unlocked door at the end of the corridor lead into an empty room. A second door brought them into a partly-lit courtyard, fresh air, and the night.

They were going to shoot him, thought Alex. Then he saw Marshal Nikitchenko standing next to an ancient Volkswagen. The engine was running. Behind the wheel sat Karen Deuntzer.

BERLIN

'I thought we should meet,' said Calderwood, showing
Cassidy and Stone into the Düsseldorferstrasse apartment's
sitting-room, where Hamilton, a dressing on his forehead,
and Bunty were waiting. Calderwood introduced the quartet
to one another. There were no handshakes, as there had been
none between Calderwood, Cassidy and Stone when
Calderwood had greeted the two Americans in the
underground garage a few minutes earlier. 'Pool resources,
exchange views and up-to-date intelligence, don't you
know. We seem to be pulling in opposite directions to the
detriment of us all.'

'So you said on the phone,' grunted Cassidy, settling
himself in an armchair and immediately lighting a cigarette.
'You also said we'd be having a private meeting.'

'And so we shall if that's what you wish. Of course, I
should have to insist upon Stone leaving the room also.'

'Nothing doing,' Cassidy didn't fancy not having a
witness of his own to whatever Calderwood had in mind.
Nor, for that mater, did he feel completely at ease meeting
the MI6 officer on this far from neutral ground, even though
he had one back-up team in the garage and another out front.
He would have insisted on an alternative rendezvous had
things not, as far as he was concerned, reached crisis point.
'Stone stays.'

'I'm glad you're taking a reasonable attitude.' Calderwood
smiled thinly. 'In the matter of Cougar I have no secrets from
Mrs Ainsworth and Hamilton.'

Which was far from the truth, thought Hamilton. When
he and Bunty had returned in a panic to the apartment the

previous evening, Calderwood had been waiting for them, apparently unconcerned that the KGB had Alex. 'Everything will be resolved within the next twenty-four hours,' he had said. 'Until then, we sit tight. No questions, please.'

Bunty brought a drinks tray to the low table in the middle of the room. Cassidy stretched forward and poured himself a generous glass of brandy. 'Cougar?'

'Come, come,' said Calderwood amiably. 'We'll get nowhere unless we all put our cards on the table. I know we've had our differences in the past, Cassidy, but today we should bury the hatchet, preferably not in each other's skulls. I've lost a man over there. I'd rather like him back. You're going to need my assistance or your masters will be hunting your head. Stone's too, and the other members of your little coterie.'

'Over where have you lost a man?' asked Cassidy, suddenly alert. 'East?'

'Yes. He was taken by the KGB last evening.'

'Dunbar?'

'I didn't say that.'

Cassidy and Stone exchanged glances. Could Dunbar be in the hands of the KGB? Was it possible that Cougar would work out as planned after all?

Cassidy suppressed a surge of elation. These were early days, and Calderwood as slippery as an eel. 'What makes you think Stone and I are in trouble with anyone? Even if we were, how can you help? More to the point, why would you?'

'One question at a time. In the first place, I know you're in trouble because Cougar has failed.'

'Not from where I'm sitting.'

'Please,' frowned Calderwood, 'allow me to finish. I made some enquiries – very discreetly, you'll be happy to hear. Cougar had no official sanction. It was a maverick operation, conceived by yourself at Nikitchenko's request. Had you pulled it off, I have no doubt your next appointment would have been Deputy Director of Planning. But you did not pull it off. Ergo, far from being DDP you will be extremely lucky to survive the next seventy-two hours. As for how I can help and why I should bother, that will come later, when I know we can trust each other. You would have done better to have used living agents, not the non-existent Coughlin and Garfield. Other than that, it was a brilliant conception, absolutely brilliant. Tell me, did Nikitchenko approach you directly or through a middleman?'

Cassidy hesitated. Either by accident or inspiration Calderwood seemed to know most of it. 'Through one of his own men in their Washington embassy to begin with. He knew of me from my days as station chief here in Berlin.'

'Be careful,' cautioned Stone. 'I'd bet money he's guessing a lot of this. You don't have to tell him anything. If the KGB have got Dunbar we're home and dry.'

Calderwood looked scornfully down his nose at Stone. He would not employ this sort of individual to empty the garbage cans. Cassidy had a certain amount of style and, self-evidently, a keen brain. The Stones of the world were ten a penny.

'Guessing?' said Calderwood. 'Guessing? I don't guess, Stone. Much though it may surprise you people in Langley, we too have files and computers. Besides, you're jumping to conclusions. The KGB may not have Dunbar – yet.'

'You mentioned Nikitchenko,' said Cassidy.

'Indeed I did.' Calderwood steepled his fingers. 'Let me see how the scenario might have developed.

'Nikitchenko is a well-known dove despite being a member of the Politburo and holding the office of defence minister. Some time ago, let us say during the last six months for the sake of argument, he found his position threatened because other senior ministers as well as junior officers within his own department considered him too soft in his dealings with the West. What could he do? The pressures were building, the hawkish factions growing stronger daily. Within a few months he would be dismissed, possibly executed. Certainly exiled. He had served as a tank officer during World War Two, had witnessed at first hand the horrors of a war which, no matter how cruel, would be the equivalent of a schoolboy brawl compared with the next one. If he went, whoever replaced him would adopt a tougher attitude towards the West, thus bringing the world closer to annihilation. He needed to consolidate his power base, place himself beyond criticism, demonstrate to his colleagues that he was not the propitiator they considered him to be. But how to do it?

'He could alter the tenor of his public speeches, of course, make them more belligerent. But the Politburo, the Central Committee and his junior officers would see that ploy for what it was: a pathetic attempt by an elderly man to find favour with his peers. He needed more. He needed to become more hawkish than the hawks. Not only by his speeches *but by his actions* he had to push the Soviet Union to the brink of war, threaten the West – *while all the time knowing there would be no war*. Which is when he decided to approach you. I expect he did his research very thoroughly. He wanted someone near the top of the Langley tree, someone with ambition, foresight and daring. Someone who would risk Armageddon for a far greater prize, that of having a proven dove in an immovable position of power in the Kremlin.'

'Go on,' said Cassidy, not in the least flattered by Calderwood's honeyed words.

'He wanted a war situation without the war, a set of circumstances whereby it would *appear* that the Soviet Union was under threat and in which he could advocate intransigence. He would counsel force with force to remove the threat, knowing full well that, at the eleventh hour, so to speak, something would happen to make force unnecessary. That something was Alex Dunbar.'

Out of the corner of his eye Calderwood saw the bewildered expressions on Hamilton's and Bunty's faces.

'Dunbar was the catalyst,' he continued. 'How you selected him no doubt you'll tell us shortly. But he was fundamental to the scenario. Purporting Coughlin and Garfield to be Melanie Dunbar's killers was a stroke of genius, though I'm sure we're both aware that poor Melanie was murdered by a person or persons unknown. However, Alex believed them culpable, and he would travel anywhere to get his hands on them. Bangkok, Hong Kong, Berlin. You needed to keep him on the wild-goose chase, out of Berlin, until ten days or so before Russian spring manoeuvres, three weeks hence, when the entire Soviet war machine would be geared up to roll – westward across the North German Plain if it came down to it, though you had no intention of allowing matters to deteriorate that far. Nonetheless, within the inner sanctums, Nikitchenko would be urging it, realizing that it's that particular time of year that NATO commanders view with the greatest unease.

'Then Dunbar would have been directed towards Berlin, believing Coughlin and Garfield to be in the city. Once here, the KGB were to snatch him. Across the Wall he would reveal to the Soviets, under interrogation, what he understood to be the truth: that the CIA were actively backing a neo-Nazi resurgence in order to provoke the Soviets into attacking the West. They would find Dunbar a highly credible witness. No drug or maltreatment would be able to shake him. After all, he's seen a strip of film.'

'You could be right,' said Cassidy non-committally, realizing that he had seriously underestimated Calderwood's powers of deduction. Not that it was relevant.

'I'm glad you think so.'

Calderwood motioned Bunty to pour him a drink. Glass in hand, he went on.

'The remainder of the scenario would take but a few hours. Moscow would get on the hot line to Washington, who'd be perplexed until you stepped in and explained. Your Director might have rapped your knuckles for taking such a wild, unauthorized gamble, though I doubt it. Success is the one criterion in our business, and you'd have succeeded. You could tell him that you and Nikitchenko had conspired from the beginning and that now Nikitchenko's position was unassailable. You and you alone would have been responsible for keeping a sincere dove near the head of the Kremlin's counsel tables, for who within the Politburo could now accuse Nikitchenko of being an appeaser? You'd have achieved a massive coup. No films or documents would see the light of day. The crisis would be over, the neo-Nazis back in the woodwork.

'But Dunbar arrived in Berlin a few weeks too soon, regardless of your attempts to detain him in Hong Kong. Rumours of the films were disseminated too early also.'

'You?' queried Cassidy.

'My dear chap,' lied Calderwood, 'you give me too much credit. Besides, what could I possibly gain?'

'I don't know.' Cassidy refilled his brandy glass. 'Anyway, now or in three weeks' time, the end product is identical – if the KGB have Dunbar.'

'Yes,' said Calderwood, 'always assuming that. Tell me, were neither you nor Nikitchenko ever concerned that the KGB might insist on subjecting Dunbar to a public trail, to blacken the CIA?'

'No.'

Calderwood nodded his head sagely. 'Dunbar was not to survive, was that it? Once he'd served his purpose by rehabilitating Nikitchenko, he would have been quietly removed, shot by the Marshal's men – while trying to escape or something like that?'

'Something like that,' agreed Cassidy.

Hamilton swore savagely under his breath. Calderwood turned on him. 'Enough of that. If you don't know how to behave properly, you can leave.'

Hamilton bit his lip. He glanced at Bunty, who shook her head. She too, her expression revealed, did not understand Calderwood in this mood.

'Yes, positively brilliant,' said Calderwood after a moment. 'Still I'd like to know why Dunbar was selected as opposed to anyone else.'

'Tell him nothing,' said Stone. 'This whole friggin' conversation will be going down on tape.'

'Untrue,' Calderwood corrected him, 'though would it matter if it was? Think about it, Cassidy. Everything I've said up to now is conjecture, I admit, though I'm sure it's an accurate summary of Cougar. I've already submitted a report, which is now a matter of record. I'm interested in the details, of course, to satisfy my own curiosity. Besides, as I mentioned earlier, you may need my help. If the KGB have Dunbar, regardless of what he tells them, one telephone call from me to a contact in the East would result in Nikitchenko facing a firing squad before midnight. If they do not have Dunbar, I might be able to tell them where they can find him.'

'For God's sake,' said Hamilton.

'Out,' ordered Calderwood. 'Go with him, Bunty. Take him into your office and pour him a stiff drink.'

Bunty understood. In her office, at the flick of a switch, she and Hamilton would be able to overhear everything.

When the door had closed, Cassidy said, 'Why would you allow the KGB to get their hands on Dunbar, now I've told you of his probable fate?'

Calderwood feigned world-weariness.

'Because unlike young Hamilton, I've been in this business for many years. During the course of those years I've learned that the end always justifies the means. Small sacrifices for large gains. I too would like to see Nikitchenko in a position of unassailability. So indulge me with the details. For example, where does Nick Tasker fit into the scheme of things?'

Cassidy put a match to another cigarette and blew a stream of smoke towards the ceiling.

'It started with Tasker,' he said. 'No, I suppose it started with Nikitchenko himself. When he approached me six or seven months ago, he informed me that his days were numbered. The neo-Nazis revival was his idea; the mechanics of the operation mine. I checked him out carefully, of course, because it's not every day the number three man in the Politburo asks the CIA to help him retain power. I discovered he was genuine, as much as those bastards can ever be.'

'This is crazy,' protested Stone.

'Button it, Frank,' said Cassidy mildly. 'Calderwood's a pragmatist. So am I. You're a hatchet-man, as you proved when you unnecessarily shot Tasker. It became more complicated after that.'

'Jesus Christ,' muttered Stone, appalled by Cassidy's admission.

'Since Nikitchenko had mentioned neo-Nazis,' Cassidy explained to Calderwood, 'I fed that into the computer. I had to start somewhere. Among the thousands of names that were spewed out was Tasker's. It meant nothing to me at the time, but during an in-depth search I discovered that Tasker's real name, that on his immigration documents, was Dunbar, and that he was English. Dunbar rang a bell from

291

my days here as station chief. I did another search and turned up Alex Dunbar. A couple of phone calls established that Dunbar and Tasker were brothers, a few more that Dunbar had been canned by MI6 for drunkenness and was on the skids in London. It seemed too good an opportunity to miss. Tasker, researching neo-Nazism, lived in New York. His brother was ex-MI6. There had to be a way of tying those two factors together.'

Cassidy contemplated the glowing end of his cigarette for a moment before stubbing it out.

'The phoney camp in South Dakota came about by accident, in the same way that the discovery of penicillin can be termed an accident. In other words, hard work and a little luck. During yet another computer search I landed on the wartime OSS stratagem, which happened exactly as George Andrus, on my instructions, told Dunbar it did. A fake camp, watchtowers, barbed-wire fences, searchlights, dogs, mock executions. I couldn't use prisoners as the OSS did, so instead I set up a dummy film-production company and pretended I was shooting a pilot for a proposed TV series. Money was no problem. You know how it is. Budgets are flexible, accounts can be falsified. What should go in one column goes in another. Nor did I have any trouble winding up the corporation once it had served my purpose. The unit was told that shooting exteriors on location was proving too costly. We'd all get together again once we'd found some studio space.

'I hired regular actors and actresses. No children, though. Like the OSS I used small women to play the kids. I even hired a second-unit director and a camera crew. The camp buildings were constructed out of hardboard. They were just shells. The technicians became so expert that they could erect the camp and dismantle it in a couple of hours. We put a stopwatch on them. They had to be fast because I'd only need the camp for one night, the night Tasker was due to put in an appearance. Next day the camp was gone, the crew paid off. I couldn't afford to have it up for too long in case we attracted too much attention, though the local sheriff and the county administrators had been told we were making a film.

'We shot a lot of footage but it was all destroyed except for the strip Dunbar found. I didn't want the rest falling into the wrong hands and somehow winding up on television, where the actors would have recognized themselves. More than a strip wasn't necessary. I only needed rumours of a complete film and for Dunbar to believe absolutely in the conclusions we'd led him to. The night Tasker was killed the whole crew and most of the actors had gone home, since I didn't want Tasker to see cameras. The actors who remained were told they were rehearsing a sequence to be shot the following day.'

Cassidy got to his feet and paced the room, glass in one hand, lighted cigarette in the other. Periodically he returned to the table to tap ash in the ashtray.

'Tasker was not supposed to die. He was meant to see what was happening in the camp, especially the guard in the uniform of a wartime Red Army soldier. After that, Stone and Tyson were going to knock him cold and transport him to an institution the Company owns in Virginia.'

'A mental institution?' queried Calderwood.

'Yes.' Cassidy didn't bother to sidestep the question. After all, MI6 had their own versions of the same thing. 'There he would have been incarcerated for a month to fit in with my timetable. Under the influence of hallucinogenic drugs he would have been fed the names of Coughlin and Garfield and brainwashed into thinking they were up to their necks in some kind of CIA plot connected with the camp he'd seen. London had already heard of Cougar. I'd made sure of that.

'Nearer the time Russian spring manoeuvres were due to start, I planned to inform your Foreign Office that a Nick Tasker a.k.a. Dunbar was being held in a mental institution in the States. He was not a citizen and what were we to do with him? He was out of his mind, his particular form of insanity consisting of ravings about concentration camps run by the Russians and two men named Coughlin and Garfield. I was relying on the FO unearthing the fact that Tasker was the brother of a former intelligence officer and contacting MI6. If that didn't happen in a few days, I'd have found some other means of telling you that Tasker was Dunbar's brother.'

'After which,' said Calderwood thoughtfully, 'I would have brought Alex temporarily out of retirement and sent him to the States, with instructions to make a full report to me.'

'You would.' Cassidy's face was flushed, part brandy, part a sense of achievement. 'Especially as I'd already leaked supposedly stolen documents to you incriminating Coughlin and Garfield in Melanie Dunbar's murder. I doubted London would be able to resist the coincidences: Cougar – Coughlin and Garfield – Melanie Dunbar – Tasker – Alex Dunbar. I assumed you'd send Dunbar to Berlin, his old stamping ground, to find out precisely what was going on. I also assumed, should he be reluctant, that the carrot of tracking down his wife's killers would be incentive enough. What I didn't bargain for was Tasker being killed, which brought everything forward by a month. While keeping London intrigued, I also had to keep Dunbar out of Berlin until I needed him. Without Tasker, I had to improvise. Hence the strip of film. Hence Tasker's body turning up in Denver. Hence George Andrus' tale of Coughlin and Garfield being on the run in the Far East.'

'And hence the rather cruel artifice of abducting Alison Cameron,' said Calderwood.

'A necessary evil. Regrettably, Dunbar is much more resourceful than I gave him credit for, for a man so long out of the field.'

Cassidy placed his empty glass on the table. Calderwood pushed the brandy towards him. Cassidy shook his head.

'Check the garage and out front,' he ordered Stone. 'Stay with your own car. This shouldn't take much longer.'

'You're sure?'

'I'm sure. Beat it.'

Stone nodded curtly and left the room.

'Are you expecting trouble?' enquired Calderwood.

'I hope not.'

'I can assure you that none of my people have instructions to interfere with any of yours, if that's what's worrying you.'

'It isn't. I asked Stone to check outside for another reason. Tasker was a British citizen. Stone shot him. It occurs to me that you might want to even the score.'

'You're offering me Stone?'

'Not exactly. I'll see he pays the penalty for murder, though.'

'In other words, you don't need him any longer.'

'I've been watching him recently. He's about ready to cut and run if this doesn't work out, leaving me holding the bag.'

'And in return for what will Stone pay the penalty?'

'Dunbar. Either the KGB have him now, in which case my worries are over, or you'll ensure they get him shortly. That was the arrangement, wasn't it? Stone's just the icing on the cake. You said it yourself: Nikitchenko remaining in power will be of great value to the West. We've bought ourselves a few years. He may even become top man if anything happens to Andropov, a not unlikely eventuality.' Cassidy managed a glimmer of a smile. 'The CIA has a poor image with the general public, who associate us with El Salvador, Vietnam, Nicaragua. But it's not all like that. This time the Company's earning its funding.'

'Not the Company,' Calderwood corrected him. 'You, Stone, a handful of others.'

'Okay, me then.'

'And at an enormous risk.'

'Would you have handled it any other way?'

'I don't know. You never made me the offer.'

'For some obvious and some not so obvious reasons. Your intelligence services are full of holes, Calderwood. Look at Cheltenham. I tell you, there are people at Langley who break out in a cold sweat whenever they open a British newspaper.'

'You did not inform your Director either,' Calderwood reminded Cassidy. 'I doubt you would have received his imprimatur.'

'Probably not, which is why I didn't tell him. He would have played it safe, and while he was doing that Nikitchenko would have been shot. I saw an opportunity, calculated the odds, and placed my bet.'

'Oh, I'm not denying it was brilliant. There again, a meteor's brilliant, the brightest object in the heavens.

Ephemerally. I'll walk with you to the lift.'

Cassidy was surprised. 'What about Dunbar?'

'Let me think about that, how it should be handled. You'll know the position in a couple of hours.'

At the door Cassidy said, 'It was you who started the rumours of the films, wasn't it? I've been thinking about it. It could only have been you.'

'Correct. I realized what Cougar was all about a week ago. As a matter of interest I re-entitled the operation Cougarovitch.'

'Neat. But you should have come to me instead of letting the hare loose early. We could have worked something out between us.'

'I very much doubt that,' said Calderwood, 'judging from our previous dealings with one another. No, it was better this way. Here's the lift.'

Cassidy stepped inside. 'You'll be in touch shortly?'

'Perhaps not in person, but someone will.'

Calderwood returned to the sitting-room. Hamilton and Bunty were already there.

'You're letting him walk out of here,' accused Hamilton.

'Naturally. He represents a friendly intelligence agency. What else can I do?'

'Friendly!' Hamilton was incensed. 'Karen Deuntzer, one of his people, had Alex abducted last evening. And you call that friendly!'

'Bunty,' said Calderwood calmly, 'kindly give this young hothead a drink. One for yourself and one for me also.'

'I don't think *I'll* bother,' said Bunty.

'As you wish. Do I detect a note of disapproval in your tone? Dear me, Bunty, I thought you knew me better than that.'

'I thought I did too.'

Lounging back in his armchair, legs crossed, Calderwood addressed Hamilton.

'Has it not occurred to you, if Karen Deuntzer is working for Cassidy, that he is extraordinarily ill-informed regarding last night's events? He doesn't know where Alex is. Why doesn't he?'

Hamilton looked at Bunty. *That* had not occurred to

296

either of them.

'I don't know,' admitted Hamilton.

'Then it's high time you did.'

EAST

'Get in,' snapped Nikitchenko in German.

Alex was too stunned to do other than mumble something incomprehensible, and comply. Once he was inside the Volkswagen, Karen Deuntzer let out the clutch. In response to a command from Nikitchenko, the huge gates were opened. Seconds later the VW was through them.

'What the hell's going on?' Alex managed.

'We are,' answered Karen. 'On and out.'

'You're driving from Moscow?' Alex's head was spinning.

'Don't be an idiot. You're not in Moscow, you're in East Berlin. About three miles from Checkpoint Charlie if you want the geography. We have to stop off at an address this side of the Wall for maybe an hour, until I receive word we can proceed. Then it's through Charlie and home.'

'East Berlin passes expire at midnight,' said Alex, knowing he was being absurd. For someone with the power to release him from captivity, crossing Checkpoint Charlie would be child's play.

'Not for us they don't.'

Alex couldn't take it in.

'Why is the KGB freeing me?'

'The KGB isn't. Nikitchenko is. With a little help from me if I don't run this heap of scrap iron off the road. Jesus, you'd think they'd have given us a decent car. The KGB isn't in on this. Not yet.'

'But you're KGB,' protested Alex. The world had gone mad. Nothing made sense.

'Me?' Karen laughed. It was the most attractive sound Alex had heard in ages. 'Because of that business last night in

Kruppstrasse? No, not me. Christ, Alex, you're dim. I'm your *backstop*. Don't you remember Calderwood asking you over the phone when you were in South Dakota if you wanted your back covered? You told him no. He went ahead anyway. Just as well. You nearly had a nasty accident in Arlington thanks to one of the Company boys having a little fun. I only just got you from under the wheels of that traffic. Not that they wanted you dead, naturally. That wasn't part of the scenario. Made my job a lot harder though, once you'd seen my face. I've been ducking and diving ever since, trying to keep an eye on you without you seeing me. I succeeded too most of the time, though I've gone through more different coloured wigs than a bald lady. I was unlucky in Hong Kong, at the ferry. And the answer to your next question is that I have no young son.'

That would not have been Alex's next question. His mind was reeling. He didn't understand any of it. Not only was Karen Deuntzer not KGB, she wasn't Company either. She was working for Calderwood.

'Sure,' she said when he put it to her. 'Mr Calderwood and I go back four or five years. I've done the Fort Monkton bit too. Heard a lot of nice things about you down there. Saw a few of them put into action in Hong Kong. You had me worried there. I had no way of following you when you went off to liberate the beautiful Miss Cameron. Christ, was I relieved when you got back in one piece. Calderwood would have had my hide if I'd lost you, though, to be fair, he left you uncovered in Bangkok because he needed me in Berlin to see who Cassidy was meeting.'

'Calderwood,' said Alex. 'You're an American and you work for Calderwood.'

'So I'm American. Tai Sing was Chinese and he worked for you. Michael Ling was Chinese. He worked for the Agency. My mother was English, not that that has anything to do with it. Nor do I work both sides of the street, Agency and Six. The Firm pays my salary exclusively, once a month into Chase Manhattan. I'll tell you another day how I got into this racket – if you can spare me some time from Alison Cameron, of course,' she added mischievously.

'I don't believe it,' said Alex, although he did. 'Then last night's snatch was Calderwood's idea.'

'Bull's-eye. He got you in, now he's getting you out. As I said, we've got an hour before we cross. I'll explain it all while we're waiting, patiently and gently since you're sounding shellshocked. Just pray that Calderwood's doing his part while you're listening to me, or we could be here for ever. You're the star, Alex, but Calderwood's the producer. Right about now he should be lowering the curtain on the final act.'

BERLIN

'Once I reached Nikitchenko and he realized full well that I knew what was going on,' Calderwood was saying later, 'the good Marshal was quick to see the advantage of liaising with me rather than Cassidy. After all, I could execute him with a phone call. And what had he to lose? He was still saving his own neck. I meant every word I said to Cassidy. About his scheme being brilliant. I simply moulded it to my own specifications.'

Hamilton and Bunty had listened in almost total silence for the better part of half an hour. Calderwood had witnessed their demeanour change from open hostility through incredulity to admiration, and found himself experiencing a greater glow than was proper. He would really have to be careful. Overweening pride was followed by nemesis.

'Since Alex's abduction was part of Cassidy's plan, there was nothing I could do about that if Nikitchenko was to survive. But allow Cassidy and, by implication, the Company to take the credit? Dear me no. They've looked upon us as poor relations for far too long. What were Cassidy's words, that our intelligence services are full of holes? Perhaps so. All the more reason for wanting success to compensate for things that have gone wrong recently. And I had a personal score to settle with Cassidy.'

The telephone rang.

'No,' said Calderwood, rising. 'This will be for me, Bunty. I'll take it in your office.'

When he returned he said, 'Alex is in good condition and the exchange is under way. It shouldn't be long before he and Miss Deuntzer are back on this side of the Wall.'

301

'Who have you given them?' asked Hamilton, realizing as he spoke what Calderwood's answer would be.

'Why, Cassidy and Stone, of course. Although they had several back-up teams with them, unfortunately our Russian friends had many more men. That was the arrangement I made with Nikitchenko. Alex would do what he was programmed by Cassidy to do, but why hold on to him when the Soviets could hear, so to speak, everything from the horse's mouth? I didn't lie when I said that none of my own people was downstairs. I did omit to tell Cassidy that there were several dozen Russians awaiting the pleasure of his company.'

Calderwood rubbed his eyes. When Alex and Karen were safely in the West, he would take a pill and sleep for twenty-four hours. No, he wouldn't. He still had to talk to Sir Nigel. In person.

'Regrettably,' he went on, 'that was one of the few entire truths to pass my lips for quite some time. Needless to say, there were no satellite pictures showing abnormal activity around Soviet missile sites. Nor were the 2nd Guards Army or any other Soviet detachments placed on alert. Nikitchenko was making a lot of noise, as he had to, but we were a long way from war.'

'They'll put Cassidy and Stone on public trial,' argued Hamilton. 'They won't miss a propaganda coup such as that.'

'There will be no trial,' pronounced Calderwood. 'No formal trial, at least. Cassidy and Stone will go through what I imagine Alex went through. And then.' He drew the blade of his hand across his throat. 'After all, Nikitchenko will scarcely want to keep them alive for too long, in case they reveal his part in the conspiracy. He will brief them on what to say, which will be no more than Alex has said. He'll make them promises, agree to free them if they behave. Then he'll have them shot one dark morning.'

'You're a very wicked, unfeeling man,' said Bunty, not entirely without humour.

'Yes, I'm rather afraid I am. Nonetheless, nowhere in Cassidy's scenario did it say that Alex would not have suffered an identical fate.'

'Talking of Alex,' Hamilton interjected, 'he's unlikely to be too happy with you.'

'Alex is a realist,' countered Calderwood. 'When you've been with us as long as he has and if you ever become a fraction as good, you'll understand. We're symbiotic creatures, he and I. We don't especially like each other, but we are mutually dependent. I needed him to do a job and he, whether he'll admit it or not, needed me and the Firm. For four years he was a zombie, a drunk wallowing in self-pity. In just a few weeks he's become alive again.

'We all have our destinies, Hamilton. God forbid that I should turn to philosophy in my dotage. Alex has found his. He'll arrive boiling, threatening to have my head. Then he'll reflect. Cassidy would have allowed him to die. I've freed him. He'll get drunk, hopefully with you, Hamilton, because Bunty must return with me to London. After that, he'll take the first plane to New York and reacquaint himself with Miss Cameron. That could be a good match from what I've heard of the lady in question. He'll use the dollars he thinks I've forgotten about to finance his trip. As a matter of fact, I will forget about them. In a few weeks I'll contact him, offer him another assignment. Perhaps you'll be included, Hamilton. You can be the legs and Alex, with all due respect to you, will be the brains. I'll put him partly behind a desk, partly in the field. He'll jump at the opportunity.'

'He may jump down your throat.' Hamilton grinned openly at the prospect. 'Dollars that will buy him a ticket to New York will also buy him a ticket to London.'

'Not without this.' Calderwood produced Alex's diplomatic passport with a flourish. 'And in case he thinks I have become totally senile, without this either.' Calderwood showed Hamilton the Hong Kong-obtained passport in the name of Alec Duncannon. 'The UK immigration authorities have the name and number. Alex will not be permitted to land until I say so. There's a note inside the passport. Don't read it. Give the entire package to Alex tomorrow. Come along, Bunty. Pack our suitcases.'

The telephone rang again while Bunty was within reach. She looked at Calderwood questioningly. He nodded.

Bunty picked up the receiver and listened.

'That was Miss Deuntzer. She and Alex crossed Checkpoint Charlie five minutes ago.'

EPILOGUE

'I think we can improve on that,' said Calderwood.

He and Sir Nigel were sitting in the latter's garden, drinking gins and tonic. It was a beautiful spring afternoon, the sort, thought Calderwood, only to be found in England.

'Subtly, through channels,' he went on, 'we'll let Langley know that Cassidy and Stone have defected. That should keep them quiet for a while. I, for one, have had more than enough of terse little memoranda stating that our security is as leaky as a sieve, even though much of the blame for that lies at the doorstep of our snooty colleagues in Five.'

'I'm not sure I approve of that,' frowned Sir Nigel. 'The CIA are, after all, our friends, and we have precious few left in this world.'

'Agreed.' Calderwood sipped his drink. A pheasant rose from a distant copse, chortling, knowing the shooting season was past. 'On the other hand, Cassidy and Stone were not acting officially.'

'Nonetheless, there will be a major panic in Langley if it is believed that a ranking officer and his immediate subordinate have gone over. They could both be invaluable to the Soviets if the KGB elect to interrogate them in depth.'

'Nikitchenko will not permit that. My vote says let Langley sweat.'

'I would never have thought you capable of malevolence, Calderwood.'

'We all have our foibles, Sir Nigel.'

'*You* have foibles?' Sir Nigel McCracken smiled indulgently.

'Even I.'

'What are your plans for Dunbar?'

'Nebulous. He will decide the substance.'

Alex finished his beer. Hamilton was drinking whisky. And had been, thought Alex, for the last three hours.

'Do I get my passport now?'

'Only when you promise that you won't try to slip through immigration, that it's New York you're going to, not London, there to beat upon Calderwood's patrician head.'

'You're drunk.'

'You're absolutely right. I deserve to be drunk. Calderwood didn't tell us you were getting out until the last minute.'

'Calderwood is a very devious man.'

The flight was announced, change planes at Amsterdam.

'Passport,' said Alex.

Hamilton produced it after a search of his pockets.

'There's a note inside.'

'I imagined there would be.'

'What does it say? I didn't look.'

Alex read aloud: '*Im übrigen ist es zuletzt die grösste Kunst, sich zu beschränken und zu isolieren.*'

'And what the devil does that mean?'

'It's a quotation. Goethe, I think. Calderwood probably looked it up. I quote: For the rest of it, the last and greatest art is to limit and isolate oneself.'

Hamilton peered at Alex through bloodshot eyes. 'I don't understand.'

'It's Calderwood's way of saying that Alison and the business we're in can't coexist, that I'd be better off on my own.'

On the plane, Alex realized that he was wrong, that Calderwood had meant nothing of the kind. Far from it and quite the reverse. The cunning old fox was saying that it was never a question of either/or, that it all depended on the individual. Much though it would irk him to pay, Alex decided he owed Calderwood a bottle of decent claret.

THE END